THE CATASTROPHE TEST

A KENNEDY LOGAN THRILLER

NJ BARKER

For Claire and James,
and Mum and Dad x

TUESDAY

1

3:30PM

Kennedy Logan's mother had always told her that 'actions speak louder than words,' so she said nothing, and smiled.

Three men were sitting on the far side of a large Perspex desk, but it wasn't them that put her on edge; she was relaxed with odds of three to one. Nor was it the lack of any attempt they'd made to greet her. She understood some people's need for social convention, but she wasn't some people. The rectangular room had dull grey walls and no pictures or furniture beyond the table and chairs. A solitary strip light on the ceiling buzzed quietly. All normal enough.

When she'd walked into the room she'd heard a click from behind her. It was subtle but it was enough to suggest that she wouldn't be leaving the same way that she'd entered. Behind the three seated gentlemen were three other doors. And it was those doors that were throwing her off.

A hand-sized screen was fixed on the wall, one beside each door. All the screens were blank, as if they had been deactivated.

Perhaps it was nothing and all three doors led to the exit. But that seemed unlikely.

She wouldn't have been concerned if this was a normal meeting. The type of meeting when you're told who else is attending, and what you're going to discuss. The kind of meeting that you get to decide whether you want to attend or not.

But this meeting was nothing like that.

The men were staring at her. She knew first impressions counted but she would wager that this was far from a first impression. If she was right, these men would've spent several months vetting her; they'd know everything about her. *Almost* everything. They'd probably built a model of her. Not a physical model, but a representation of her emotional response and her moral code. They'd have tried to mirror her soul. Well, good luck with that.

All of which might explain why none of them had felt the need to say anything to her since she'd entered the room. They were used to her because they'd been living with her for months.

She walked towards them. There was a solitary chair on her side of the table. They probably thought they weren't giving her any choice on that one. She stopped next to the chair but stayed standing. After all, *everything* was a choice. Like what to wear. She'd chosen Converse trainers, cut-off jeans and a t-shirt. Not standard dress for an interview, but then again this wasn't a standard interview.

The man on her left was the oldest, in his late forties. Grey hair, glasses, and a squint. She'd never seen him before, but although he was the oldest, she'd lay good money on the fact that he wasn't in charge. That would be the guy on the right. The youngster. Early twenties, pale blue eyes and his hair shaved close. Unlike the t-shirt preferred by the older man, he was wearing a suit and a white, open necked shirt with faint grey vertical stripes. He didn't break eye contact. Didn't smile. Didn't speak. She'd met plenty of men like him before.

The man who sat in the middle had aged more than she'd expected. Nathaniel Gissing wouldn't have been able to hide his reaction if he'd recognised her, and he hadn't so much as flinched. Good. One thing that would nudge things in her favour. Their file on her was clearly missing a section, or two. None of them would suspect that she was aware of what they had planned for her that day.

Pale Blue Eyes opened up his laptop. She waited whilst he tapped on the keyboard. He didn't so much as glance at her. She didn't want to look as though she was seeking their permission to do anything so, after a while, she walked around the table and stopped in front of the door on the right.

Kennedy frowned. An anchor was etched on it, invisible until she'd caught it in the right light. The adjacent screen flickered into life and the word OPEN appeared on it.

She edged along to the middle door and saw an etched cross by which time she knew what symbol would complete the set.

A heart. The three theological virtues: hope, faith, and charity.

A little too contrived for her tastes, but she'd known it would be. That was how they rolled.

This was her first test. She had a flashback to an old computer game where you started in a room with a single door. Only that door was locked and you had to find the key. This was different. They would all open. But the test wasn't even for her to choose the correct door. No, the initial test was whether she'd go through any door at all.

And only if she did would the challenges truly begin.

She wasn't superstitious but she didn't like to be played. This wasn't Monty Hall, the Three Prisoners problem, or Bertrand's box paradox. And this was no game show. But it was, very definitely, a test.

The three men still hadn't uttered a word. But Kennedy had made up her mind. She placed her palm on the screen next to the anchor. The door slid open.

2

3:33PM

For the second time in the space of a few minutes, Kennedy Logan heard a door close behind her. She blinked at the bright light dazzling her eyes.

She was in a lift. It started to drop but there was no display revealing her destination. Her meeting had been on the 64th floor of the skyscraper but, from her recollection of the walk to the interview room, this lift shaft had to be at the opposite side of the building from the reception lift. It could be an access lift although it felt too sterile. Kennedy closed her eyes and concentrated on her breathing.

After a couple of exhales she felt the subtle shift in the speed of the lift, and a few seconds later, it stopped moving. But the door stayed closed. And then a voice started speaking. She glanced up and saw the speaker in the ceiling.

'Ten seconds after the end of this message, the lift will start to fill with water.' Kennedy swallowed, her mind kicking into gear. Was she underground? Could she open the lift doors? 'It will take less than a minute for the chamber to fill.' Christ. Had she miscalculated? Had they brought her here simply to kill her? It didn't make sense unless they did, after all, know *everything* about her. 'You will be able to operate the lift at precisely the same time as the water enters the lift. You can move up or down a floor. Or open the doors.' Kennedy blinked. It couldn't be that simple. 'If you open the doors, the water will drain away. You are free to exit at any floor, including this one.'

So, she could open the doors as soon as the water started pouring in. That would be the obvious thing to do. There had to be a catch. Something that would counter the overwhelming desire to get out as soon as the chamber started to fill. A portion of the steel lift wall slid back to reveal a screen. She was going to be shown something. Something that would make her not want to get out.

At the foot of the screen were three buttons. Up. Down. And open,

The voice had stopped. How long ago was that? Five seconds? Kennedy reached out and her finger hovered above the button to open the lift. The screen shimmered and there was a hiss. A jet of water shot out from each side of the lift. Jesus. She flicked her eyes at the screen. Some text had appeared.

YOUR SISTER WILL DIE TODAY.

PROBABILITY: 30%

Kennedy's stomach knotted. Sandra, her younger sister, was pregnant and her due date was later that week. She balled her hands. Sandra was not dying. Not if Kennedy had anything to do with it. The water was seeping through her converse boots and was moving up her calves. She couldn't make any sense of what was going on. She hit the up button and the lift moved smoothly. The text disappeared and as the lift slowed for the next floor, a new message appeared.

A BOMB WILL EXPLODE AT OXFORD CIRCUS TUBE STATION.

PROBABILITY: 40%

This time she didn't even think, but she jabbed her finger on the up button. The water tickled around the bottom of her cut-off jeans. At this rate she'd have a choice of maybe five floors before she couldn't breathe. She stared at the screen.

CYANIDE WILL BE RELEASED INTO THE PARIS WATER SUPPLY.

PROBABILTY: 50%

Her brain was trying to process what was happening. On one level she couldn't believe that any of it was true. Would those three men do any of those things? Did they have that capability?

But there was something else. A pattern. The likely death toll was rising and the odds were increasing. Which meant she had to go down. She felt the blood pumping in her ears as she hammered the down button. She knew what she'd see on the floor below.

A BOMB WILL EXPLODE AT OXFORD CIRCUS TUBE STATION.

PROBABILITY: 50%.

What? The catastrophe was the same but the odds had shortened since her first visit to that floor. The water was now lapping around her waist and rising rapidly up her chest. The screen itself was disappearing below the rising water line. She ducked under the water, blinking hard to read the text.

YOUR SISTER WILL DIE TODAY.

PROBABILITY: 40%.

Shit. She jabbed the down button, again.

Then she stood up to her full height and sucked in air. Her shoulders were under water. Two more chances. Maybe three if she could hold her breath for that long. She stretched on her tiptoes and tipped her neck backwards. The water crept up to her chin. She took a gulp of air and ducked back under. She blinked several times to clear her vision sufficiently to read the next message.

YOU WILL MURDER SOMEONE.

PROBABILITY: 60%.

Kennedy stared at the message. How could that be possible, let alone likely to happen? She didn't have the first clue but she didn't have time to process it now. The lift wasn't full of water. Not yet. She had enough time to push up and suck in one last mouthful of air. She could hit down. Or open. Or up.

They were her only choices. She was out of time to go any further. She tried to get her brain to function but her chest was tight and pressure was building in her lungs. Somewhere she was fighting to bring order to the chaos. Time slowed. And her mind cleared. The lower she went the more personal the risk became. Paris. London. Her sister. Her. What would the next rung down be? Still her. But not her killing someone else. It would be *her* death. And the prediction would be around an 80% likelihood. Well, everyone has to die someday.

She pushed her hand against the down button and let her feet float off the floor as the lift dropped. Her fingers touched the metal at the top of the lift. There was the smallest of gaps, not enough for her to tilt her head and breathe. She closed her eyes and tried to ignore the crush on her chest. She needed to breathe. Now. The lift juddered to a stop and she reached down to press the open button. She didn't even read the message. It didn't matter what it said. She only knew the choices that she'd rejected.

The release was instantaneous. A rectangular grid appeared around the edge of the lift floor and the water gushed out, leaving Kennedy sitting on the floor. She sucked in a mouthful of water and air. She coughed, spluttering out the water. Her chest heaved as she took a deep, clear breath. The air released in a series of jagged gasps as she tried to regulate her breathing. How long had it been? What had the voice said? Less than a minute to fill the chamber. Sixty seconds that had been like no other in her life. The lift was empty and now she could feel a hot blast on her skin. The doors hadn't opened but the lift had become an impromptu sauna. Her clothes clung tightly to her body. It was going to take more than a full-body dryer to reverse that effect.

She pushed herself upright and prodded at the open-door button once more. The metallic voice kicked in.

The doors will open in five minutes.

It was only then that Kennedy focused on the screen.

CONGRATULATIONS. YOU'VE SUCCEEDED IN THE FIRST CHALLENGE.

3

3:36PM

Kennedy leant against the wall of the lift. Remarkably the air dryer was starting to deal with the worst of the water that had soaked her clothes. She peeled the t-shirt away from her skin and fanned the material to allow the hot air to blow underneath it.

The message was still displayed on the screen. She thought of the three men, sitting silently in the room. They would be watching her; she was sure of that. What would they be thinking? Would they be surprised that she'd survived?

But she was always going to survive, wasn't she. She might have opened the door on one of the other levels and the water would have emptied out. Perhaps it didn't matter which floor one chose, you just had to choose. But what would've happened if she hadn't hit open? There was no way that she'd have been left to die. Sure, she'd signed some liability waivers at reception, but they couldn't just kill people, as part of some selection exercise. No one could do that. Not even these guys. No. They would've been watching her and they would have released the water as soon as she had looked as though she was in real trouble. She was sure that that was right. It *had* to be correct.

She thought about the last few seconds when she'd been fighting to hold her breath, waiting for the lift to stop moving and the open-door button to illuminate. How would that have looked? Were they about to hit the kill switch? Or the save switch, in this case.

More importantly, what did she think of working for a group that operated in such a way? She shook her head. She was getting ahead of herself. She'd only passed the initial test. Her guess was that there was more to come.

There was nothing that she could do until the doors opened. She didn't have a watch and she'd had to leave her phone at the front desk. The security to get in to the place was reminiscent of entering a foreign embassy. She'd gone along with it because, because what? Because she wanted to be selected? No. Not necessarily. Although maybe, in the end, it came down to that. But to be more precise, she wanted to prove that she could pass their tests. Whatever they chose to throw at her. And if they made her an offer, she could still refuse. After all, it's not as if they were the mafia. She shivered.

A flash caught her eye and she looked towards the screen. The text had disappeared and been replaced with a count-down. She had just over one minute to wait. Then the doors would open. And the next test would begin.

4

3:37PM

Kennedy waited. Her clothes were surprisingly dry but she could still feel the moisture when she ran her fingers through her hair. She could vaguely make out her orange coloured, asymmetric bob in the shimmer of the lift wall. Just as well she hadn't bothered to blow dry it before the interview. She pushed herself forward and then took a step to stand at the rear of the lift. She had no idea what to expect but she felt safer with a little distance between her and the doors. Only a few seconds, now.

The timer hit zero and the light went out. She heard the doors slide open but couldn't see anything. She paused, peering into the darkness, and straining to hear anything that might tell her what was waiting for her. She counted silently to ten, and then, with her hands held out in front of her, she stepped out of the lift. The floor was solid and as she felt to the sides, her hands pressed against cold brick. She couldn't immediately place the smell but she had the sense she was in a corridor and it had the feel of an older building than the smart chrome and LCD's she had come across in the rest of the building. She moved her hand lower on the wall and felt the mortar between the bricks. There was a clunk behind her as the lift doors closed. Her eyes were adjusting slowly to the darkness but she couldn't see any control panel outside the lift doors. There was no way back. She turned and faced away from the lift. She only had one choice to make. Wait. Or move.

Kennedy began walking, her fingers skimming the wall on her right as she went. She tried to keep her breathing even and focused on her senses, desperate for any information. Moments later her fingers lost touch with the wall. She froze. Then she reached out to the left side. No wall there either. Wait. She nudged her hand back a fraction and felt a corner. The same on the other side. Taking a half step forward she felt a wall directly opposite her. She was at a T-junction. She kept her touch light but rubbed her hands across the facing wall, trying to find a sign. Just as she was about to give up her hand snagged on something. She worked her fingers around it. It was a rectangle, perhaps three times as wide as it was high. The blackness was impenetrable. There was no way that she could read whatever the sign might say. Unless ...

She rubbed her hands together, trying to get them as dry as possible and then she touched her finger onto the sign. She allowed it to glide over the surface. Yes. There it was. A slight bump. The paint of the letters. She smiled to herself. This was going to take a while but she'd be able to read the sign. With painstaking precision Kennedy traced the outline of the paint, spelling out the partial words as she uncovered each letter.

GRE

GREE

GREEN

Her fingers dotted around the word, trying to find something else, an arrow, maybe, but there was nothing. Green.

What the hell did that mean? Her guess was that it was the name of an area rather than a direction. But beyond that, she had nothing. Sighing, she chose to turn left and continued along the corridor, feeling her way as before. After less than a minute she came to another T-junction. This time she went straight to the opposite wall and felt for the sign. Sure enough, there was a similar rectangle. She let out a deep breath as the slight bump confirmed that this too, was a painted sign.

The first letter was a capital B. It had to be 'blue' and her fingers confirmed that she was right. So, she'd walked from Green to Blue. What next? She couldn't stay there, there had to be a way out. And the answer seemed to be some sort of colour code. She chose left again. Stick with what you know. Arms out beside her, she walked forward, correctly guessing that after approximately forty steps she would reach another junction. But this one was different. Only her right-hand lost contact with the wall. This was a straight on or a right turn. It took her a while to locate the zone sign but once she'd found it she didn't hesitate to finger-read the letters.

INDIGO.

Indigo. Not purple. The mnemonic ran through her head. Richard Of York Gave Battle In Vain. The colours of the rainbow. Instinctively Kennedy knew she had to find the end of the rainbow. To discover the pot of gold. She opted to take the right fork and worked her way along the wall. She felt the pitch of the wall change, the corridor was curving round. She double checked to make sure that there weren't any passages turning off, and satisfied that they weren't, she pushed on. The wall curved again. It was hard to have any sense of direction in the dark but she felt that she was turning back on herself. After a few minutes she came to another junction. Straight on or left. Again she found the sign.

BLUE.

She was back at the previous zone. Further away from the end of the rainbow. Did that make sense? She tried to plan out the route in her head. If Indigo was due south of Blue, could the curving corridor have swept all the way around to re-join Blue coming in from the north? Yes, that was certainly possible. Which meant that had she chosen to turn right she would have ended up at Indigo via the curved path.

This maze was designed to make sure you ended up at the end of the rainbow. She headed straight on, knowing this time that she would arrive back at Indigo. Only this time she would keep going straight on.

She slowed, sensing she would be hitting the end of the corridor. She stretched her hand out in front and felt a smooth wooden panel. Kennedy found the sign on the door. She already knew what it would say but felt a small jolt of satisfaction when she traced out the letters for Violet. She'd reached the end. Somewhat surprisingly this door had a conventional metal handle. She reached forward, twisted down and yanked the door open.

5

3:49PM

Light flooded Kennedy's face and she scrunched her eyes shut for a moment before blinking them open. Some of the tension drained from her body. She scanned the room she was in. It was pure white and it was empty with the exception of three large monitors hanging on the far wall. A green sinewave oscillated across screen one. The same wave, but displayed in red, was playing on the middle screen. Kennedy looked more closely. The phasing of the middle wave was slightly out of synch with the first one. The third screen displayed a curve appearing from the bottom of the screen, travelling upwards before hitting an inflection point and then heading off the top of the screen. They must have known that Kennedy would recognise them. The sine, cosine, and tangent functions. But why the hell were graphs of trigonometric functions being displayed? These guys needed to get out more.

Kennedy shuffled on the spot, taking a closer look at the room to ensure she wasn't missing anything. She thought about the first two tasks. In a sense they could've been fool proof. With the rainbow maze she'd have ended up here regardless. She was willing to bet that if she'd turned right at the very first junction she would have come to Yellow. And then a similar pattern would've eventually taken her to Red. She frowned. There was only one door into this room. Which meant there was likely another room, like this, at the other end of the rainbow path.

Which prompted the question, was she even in the correct room?

She stared again at the displays. All three had changed. Three different graphs were tracing across the screens. Kennedy tapped her fingers against her lips as she studied them. She nodded. The new displays were the inverse of the original functions.

She made her decision, walked over to the door, and pulled it open. She hesitated at the thought of plunging back into a world without light but she was sure it was the right thing to do. She reached out with her right hand to touch the wall. She started moving, knowing she'd go past Indigo and turn right at Blue. If she was correct then she'd travel straight past Green and reach a junction. She didn't bother to check that the junction was the Yellow zone, instead she turned right. She kept going until she reached the end of the corridor. She could feel a door in front of her. Exactly as she'd suspected. She found the label and traced out the letters.

RED.

Bingo. She sucked in a breath, closed her eyes, and opened the door. She opened her eyes slowly to allow them to adjust to the light. The set-up of this room was the same as the other one. Three screens, with a single word on each.

Left.

Dust.

Oversight.

A virtual keyboard appeared underneath each word, a blinking cursor waiting for Kennedy to type.

But type what? The graphs from the Indigo room had to be the key. Which meant she needed the inverse words, their opposites. The first one, left, was simple but something made her hold back from typing the answer.

Dust. She frowned. What was the opposite of dust? Which meaning was it even taking here? Dusting a cake with icing, or dusting furniture. One was adding dust, the other was removing it. The same verb, to dust, had two different meanings. Which one was it? She looked at the third word. Oversight. Same issue. Not seeing something. *It was an oversight.* Or the act of keeping an eye on something. *We need some oversight.* Kennedy went back to the first word. Left. As in left behind. *She'd been left behind.* Or, as in someone departing. *She left.* And then it clicked.

She walked towards the first screen. Each word had two different meanings and the two meanings were opposites. The opposite of *left*, in this case, wasn't *right*. Holding her breath she typed in the word *left* and hit the enter button.

The text disappeared and then the screen turned black. She moved to the second keyboard and typed in *dust.* The same thing happened. She bit down on her bottom lip. She was sure that she was right. She typed the final answer. *Oversight.* The final word also resulted in the black screen.

Just as she was beginning to think that she had, after all, not chosen the right answers, the screens burst back into life.

SECOND CHALLENGE COMPLETED.

6

3:56PM

Kennedy hid her smile as she read the message. The second task had been nowhere near as demanding as the first although, on reflection, perhaps there'd actually been something to solve whereas challenge one, she was almost certain, was more a test of staying calm than anything else.

She briefly considered opening the door and leaving the room. Whether or not it was the memory of the total darkness that made her hesitate, or something else, she wasn't sure. But she didn't move. She had a feeling that if she waited, something would happen. She lowered herself onto the floor and crossed her legs. She leant back against the wall and closed her eyes.

It took her a few seconds to make sense of what was happening. She was moving, but she was still sitting on the floor. The wall, or a section of it, was rotating. She tried to keep her heart rate under control. This was merely the mechanism for getting her to the start of challenge three. She wasn't in any hurry. She'd just roll with the punches, and if she didn't get knocked out, she'd make it through to the end.

She thought about the men in the interview room. Nathaniel Gissing had been employed by TUBE for well over a decade. She had no idea what he'd done before that. Her only knowledge of him was from fourteen years ago. Kennedy had been in a relationship with a man called Glen Farthing. Well, maybe relationship was overstating it. She'd been on a couple of dates with the guy. And then he'd ghosted her. Before ghosting was even a thing. He'd simply disappeared. Kennedy hadn't been that fussed about the premature end of their relationship but there'd been nothing in his actions, in what he'd said, or in how he'd acted, that suggested he was going to disappear. And he hadn't just disappeared from her life. He'd vanished off the face of the earth.

Kennedy had undertaken an investigation of her own. Nothing formal. In fact, it'd been highly informal. No names given; no records kept. She'd tapped a few sources, people who owed her a favour or two. And she'd hung out in the darker chat rooms of the internet. And that's where she'd come across TUBE. And, more precisely, Nathaniel Gissing. But she'd been careful. Very careful. The last thing she needed was to leave a trace, any trace. No. She wanted to learn *everything* about TUBE, before they learnt *anything* about her.

Having found them, she wondered whether they'd come looking for her. She certainly seemed like their type. After a while, she dropped a few breadcrumbs to give them a helping hand. But for an organisation that prided themselves on being smarter than everyone else, it had taken them a long time.

Funny, to consider they thought that she knew nothing. That she'd be totally bewildered right now. They'd think of her like any of their other recruits. Which was exactly how she wanted it. And precisely why she was the perfect hire.

7

4PM

Kennedy had expected to find herself where she was. Back in the room she had started in. Two of the men, including Nathaniel Gissing, were no longer there. The leader, Pale Blue Eyes, was standing in the corner of the room, and he was looking directly at her.

'Hello, Miss Logan.' His accent was American. Perhaps not a surprise. Although it was subtle. 'Welcome back.'

'It's Kennedy.' She stared at him. No blinking. How long have you got?

There was a slight nod of his head. 'My name is Noah.'

'Okay. What's next?' she asked.

His brow furrowed. 'That's your question? After what you've just been through.'

'Sure.' She smiled. 'What's next?'

He looked at her for a few seconds, saying nothing. Kennedy was sure he wasn't thinking about what to say, he would know *exactly* what he was going to say. He just wanted her to think that he was weighing her up. His lips narrowed. 'Do you know why you're here, Kennedy?'

She considered setting it all out, everything she knew

about them. She'd have enjoyed watching his reaction. But now wasn't the right time. Should she perhaps make a reference to TUBE? There hadn't been any mention of its name in the very limited correspondence that she'd received. The initial teaser email, and the subsequent offer of a meeting. She returned his stare before replying. 'I'm here because I choose to be.'

'Fair enough.' Noah nodded. He walked over to the Perspex desk and picked up a thin blue folder. Kennedy didn't know exactly what was in it, but she knew enough. He held it out towards her. 'This is your first assignment. You have one hour to study this file. If you wish to accept the assignment, place the folder on the desk when you leave, and report back here tomorrow at midday.'

Kennedy took the folder, a shiver of excitement running down her back. Noah walked across the room and out through the door, closing it behind him, leaving her alone.

She lowered herself into one of the chairs and positioned the file in front of her. There'd be a camera on her, for sure. *Actions speak louder than words.* But Kennedy was happier moving through the world in the warmth of the shadows. She let her hair fall over her face, and allowed herself a smile.

She was in.

8

4:07PM

Kennedy opened the file. In the centre of the first page was a picture of a man with a few facts printed beneath it. He had a square jaw, brown hair peppered with grey streaks, rectangular framed glasses with a vivid red tint on the inside of the arms. Grey-blue eyes. He was tanned, and looked confident.

She scanned the details. Such as they were.

Client name: Marcus Bell

Age:51

Kennedy frowned as she looked at the Client Category. There was no key to explain the categorisation. Seven circles, a filled-in circle, followed by another circle. She scratched her nose. Nine circles. Dante's inferno. And this was circle eight. Which, if she remembered correctly, was fraud.

Was that how TUBE allocated its cases? Each client was walking in one of the nine circles and poor Marcus was taking a stroll in a hellscape of fraudsters and charlatans. Kennedy's job would be to extract him.

She chewed her lip as she turned the page. The next

section covered the client's personal life. Married, two children. Home in Sevenoaks, Kent.

The work history was more interesting. A patchwork of manual jobs; landscaping, construction, security. But it was the next move which made Kennedy sit up. Marcus had trained as a doctor. He'd started late, ten years after most graduates, but he'd clearly made the grade. He'd just been promoted to consultant, which meant that, in the medical world, he'd made it.

There was nothing in the work history to explain why he'd made the change. But perhaps that was the wrong way of looking at it. Why hadn't he gone into medicine at eighteen?

Parents, maybe. Money? Kennedy felt a tickle at the base of her neck. She knew the signal by now. Her intuition wasn't always right but she'd learnt not to ignore it. There was something in Marcus's past, something that blocked the path he'd wanted to take. It might be something. Or it might be nothing. Kennedy tucked the thought away and moved to the next section of the file. The final few pages were a transcript of a conversation between Marcus and someone reported simply as Employee 011 (E11).

TRANSCRIPT OF INTERVIEW WITH MB

Monday 24 April 23

E11: Please could you explain why you're asking for our help?

MB: A friend told me about you guys. I'd never heard ... Well, I never imagined there'd be something like this ... something like you. My friend said-

E11: We don't need to talk about your friend. Just tell me why you need help.

MB: I'm being blackmailed.

EII: Go on.

MB: Well, it's delicate. I ... I'm a doctor. But I have a history. Something happened. Some time ago.

EII: And someone is blackmailing you now, because of what happened then?

MB: Yes. Exactly, yes.

EII: What are the terms of the blackmail?

MB: The terms? Oh, right. Well. They want money.

EII: How much, when and in what form?

MB: Fifty thousand pounds. By the end of this week. And they want it in Bitcoin.

EII: And what have you said so far?

MB: I told them I didn't have that sort of money. I said I could get them five thousand. Max.

EII: And have they accepted your offer?

MB: No. They said, actually, *she* said. It's a woman, but I don't know who she is. Not yet. Not for sure. She said if I don't give her the fifty thousand by Sunday 7th May, she'll take the story to a newspaper.

EII: Okay. That's all we need to know.

MB: Really?

EII: And you understand how we operate?

MB: Well, I thought you guys, you fix stuff like this.

EII: In a manner of speaking, yes. We fix stuff like this.

MB: Okay, then. Well, I'd like you to fix this for me.

EII: We won't fix it *for you*. We just fix it.

MB: I don't understand.

EII: Think of us as a kind of moral authority. We collect the evidence and then we make our ruling.

MB: And then what?

EII: And then, we enforce it.

MB: Well, I ... err. Okay, blackmail is wrong, yeah? So,

once you get the evidence that this woman's blackmailing me, you'll stop her.

EII: Perhaps. Perhaps not. It depends on the evidence. All the evidence.

MB: Yeah, sure. I guess. That makes sense.

EII: You don't have to move ahead Mr Bell. We can end this process right now if you're not totally comfortable.

MB: No. I'm sure. Yeah. I want to do this. What do I do next?

EII: Next? Nothing. Your part in this is over. From this moment on, it's all in our hands.

MB: Right. Okay. That sounds ...Well, okay then. Let's do it.

END OF TRANSCRIPT

The final page contained one sentence.

The name of the woman blackmailing Marcus Bell is Dr Carolyn Manning.

Kennedy closed the folder. Marcus Bell had no idea what he'd done. And she was pretty sure that the friend that had recommended that Marcus seek out TUBE was no friend at all. She tapped her fingers on the table. She'd memorised the details about Marcus, and the name of the woman who was blackmailing him.

The transcript was dated last Monday. She'd report for duty at midday tomorrow, Wednesday. Which would give her four days to complete the assignment. She stood up and walked towards the door. She'd get an early night, because she wouldn't be getting much sleep over the next few days.

She stepped into the lift and noticed the tension in her shoulders. Given what had happened to her only an hour or so ago, she could live with that being the extent of her PTSD. No messages flashed up, no odds, no warnings of impending catastrophes. The doors slid open and she walked across the foyer and through the revolving door, enjoying the cool breeze against her skin.

A burst of energy radiated from her chest. She'd made the right decision to come for the interview. She'd been bored for far too long.

WEDNESDAY

9

2:30PM

Kennedy stood inside the office and waited until she had the attention of the woman wearing the white coat. The doctor was at her desk. She stopped typing, pushed up her glasses, and turned to face Kennedy.

'I'm sorry, I'm not ready for-' The doctor frowned as she watched Kennedy lock the door. 'What are you doing?'

'Dr Manning, I need a few minutes of your time.'

'Who are you?' The doctor wasn't panicking. Not yet. She studied her visitor, no doubt trying to assess the reason that someone would lock themselves in a consultation room with a doctor.

'I'm here to talk about Marcus Bell.' The words had the desired impact. A pinch across the top of her nose, and a slight flush of her cheeks.

'Are you his wife?' The doctor was standing now.

'No,' Kennedy said.

'A friend?' A smile played over the doctor's face.

'Nope.' A pause. 'But it doesn't matter who I am. It matters why I'm here.' Kennedy was impressed. She'd expected the woman to lose her composure, to threaten to call security or at least to become agitated. The confidence of her response was ... interesting.

'Police?' This time she raised her eyebrows.

'No. Not police.'

'Shame,' Dr Manning said. She sat back down and glanced at her computer screen. 'I can only give you a few minutes. But you're lucky. Most people have to wait months for that.' She indicated for Kennedy to take a seat. 'So, I'm intrigued. What do you know, or what do you want to know, about Mr Marcus Bell, consultant surgeon, walks-on-water, butter wouldn't melt?'

Which was an interesting description of her colleague. Kennedy considered her options and then decided to take the seat. 'I'm wondering why a successful doctor would blackmail a fellow doctor for the sum of fifty thousand pounds.'

Dr Manning tapped her fingers against her chin. 'Hypothetically speaking?'

'Hypothetically speaking,' Kennedy confirmed. 'Fifty thousand pounds is a lot of money. But also,' she focused on the woman opposite her, paused to take in the Armani glasses, the expensive looking haircut and the faint scent of what Kennedy was fairly sure was White Amber by Creed, 'not a *lot* of money.'

'It's not about the money. Well, that's not quite true.' She shuffled forward on her chair. 'It needs to be enough money so that he won't actually want to pay it.' She smiled. 'Hypothetically.'

Kennedy processed what she'd heard. Dr Carolyn Manning didn't want or need the money. What she wanted was for Marcus Bell to have to live with the fact that she knew his secret. And, when she released his secret, he'd have to struggle with the knowledge that, although he could've paid her off, he'd chosen not to. Because he was the type of man who thought he could have everything.

'Will you tell me what he did?' Kennedy asked. The doctor tilted her head, her dark brown hair momentarily covering her face. 'Or do I also have to wait until Sunday?'

Dr Manning looked down at her wrist. 'Oops. I think time's up. Thank you so much for popping in.'

'The pleasure was all mine,' Kennedy said, almost on autopilot. But she'd enjoyed the few minutes she'd spent talking with Dr Carolyn Manning. Her hand was already on the door handle when Dr Manning spoke again.

'I should be finished around 6pm. I'll be in the wine bar opposite the hospital.'

Kennedy nodded. That sounded a hell of a lot better than waiting until Sunday.

10

6:12PM

Kennedy sipped her water.

'You're seriously not going to tell me anything about you?' Dr Manning was sitting on a bar stool, her hand wrapped around a wine glass. 'You are quite the enigma.'

'Enigma as in mystery or as in the machine?'

'Oh. Well, now you say it, you're sort of a hybrid of both.' She grinned. 'A mystery machine.'

Kennedy had been called worse. She said nothing for a moment. Music started playing in the background. She recognised the guitar riff. Her ex-boyfriend had been a fan of The Smiths. The opening lyric of *What difference does it make* floated across the room. Secrets. Everyone had secrets. Not just men. Even Kennedy. Especially Kennedy.

Part of her wanted to confide in Dr Manning. There was something appealing about the woman. Her confidence. Her charm. Kennedy wasn't quite sure. She didn't ordinarily do friends. And her new role at TUBE wouldn't exactly make that any easier. No, she couldn't tell Carolyn Manning anything. But she could enjoy a drink, and ask her about Dr Marcus Bell.

'The Mystery Machine is thinking ...' Dr Manning said.

'Whatever it is that will be revealed on Sunday, I'm assuming that you think it's important that it's widely known.'

Dr Manning chewed on her lip. 'Not widely, necessarily. But certain people should know.' She nodded. 'People who should've known for a long time.'

Kennedy did the maths. Marcus Bell was 51 years old. If her suspicion was right then the relevant incident would have been over three decades ago. 'For say more than thirty years?' she asked.

Dr Manning frowned. 'Not that long. I've only known him since he moved to the hospital.' She tilted her head. 'Nearly ten years though.' She raised her glass in the air. 'It's been a long time coming.'

'Have you told him? Marcus Bell. Have you told him what it is that you know.'

Dr Manning lowered her glass and placed it on the bar. 'I said to him,' she leant over towards Kennedy and whispered in her ear; her breath sending a tingle down Kennedy's back, 'I'm going to tell the GMC about what you did.'

Kennedy let the words sink in. She'd been wrong about it being something that had happened when Bell was a teenager. The General Medical Council was the professional standards authority for the medical profession. *What you did.* Dr Manning's words were clear enough. And she was going to report him.

'But it's complicated.' The doctor cleared her throat, closed her eyes for a few seconds and pushed out a breath. 'I've not always been the confident, self-assured woman you see in front of you.' She raised her eyebrows. 'My life was a mess. My husband left me. I've been in therapy for years.'

'I'm sorry,' Kennedy bowed her head.

'But the main complication is that the incident happened eight years ago.' She grimaced. 'And that's beyond the GMC's five-year time limit.'

Kennedy nodded. Maybe there were exceptions to the rule, but she feared what a tribunal would see. The question as to why Dr Manning didn't come forward earlier, would be judged by looking at Dr Manning today. A seemingly strong, confident woman, at the top of her profession. And yet, if they were able to ask the question of Dr Manning eight years ago, or even three years ago, perhaps they would've been confronted with a very different reality. Someone who was broken, who was in no state to confront her attacker. Was five years a long time? No, five years was the blink of an eye.

'What about a criminal case?' she asked.

Dr Manning didn't speak but she shook her head. Was that because it wasn't a crime, Kennedy wondered? Or because the doctor didn't want to go down that route? 'What do you think will happen? When you tell the GMC what he did?'

Dr Manning sniffed, and pulled herself upright. 'They'll say they can't do anything about it. But they'll know. And, more importantly, he'll know they know.'

'And?' Kennedy said it softly.

The doctor shrugged. But it wasn't resignation, there was a strength there that Kennedy found strangely moving. She stretched her neck, tilting her head back and then to either side before she fixed Kennedy with a stare. 'Hopefully, he'll never do it again.'

Something fused inside Kennedy at hearing the word 'again.' What if it wasn't a one-time offence? What if Bell was a repeat offender. An idea began to take shape in her mind, an idea born in the past.

11

8:49PM

Kennedy was sitting on a wall. It was dark and even the traffic on the main road was sparse. She'd spent the last hour keeping watch on Bell's house. He lived in a well-maintained town house, a short walk from Sevenoaks station, everything you'd expect for a successful surgeon.

There were two cars parked in the driveway. Kennedy wasn't interested in cars but she'd had plenty of time to work out that the vehicles were a Porsche Cayenne and a Tesla Model Y. Just then the front door swung open and someone came out. The outside light flicked on. Bell was wearing what looked like a leather jacket, jeans, and trainers. He continued past the car and turned left onto the road. Kennedy waited a few seconds and then followed him. She kept her distance, and a few minutes later they were in the centre of Sevenoaks. He made his way into a pub. Kennedy watched through the window as Bell greeted a friend and settled down with a pint of beer.

She scanned the outside of the building. There was a back entrance but it led into a small carpark which could only be accessed from the main road. When Bell left he'd be visible. But did she have time to wait for him to finish his drink and then what, walk home? She'd be none the wiser. She needed to take more direct action.

The door chimed as she pushed it open. She approached the bar and ordered a lime and soda, took the drink and moved to a table in Bell's eyeline. He was chatting with his mate, but Kennedy was hyper aware that he'd tracked her as she carried her drink over. His eyes lingered, as if they weren't even connected to the same part of his brain that was processing his conversation with his friend. Kennedy pulled out her phone, and tried to recapture the feeling she used to have when she'd text with her ex. Before he was her ex. She typed and smiled, occasionally covering her pretend smile.

Bell and his friend had finished their pints and were saying their goodbyes. The friend gave a hearty wave and walked out of the pub. Bell, however, slid into a chair opposite Kennedy.

'Can I buy you a drink?'

Kennedy blinked. His confidence would have been overwhelming if it hadn't been so utterly predictable. She glanced at her phone. 'I'm fine, thanks. I'm just waiting for a friend to join me.'

'You don't want company until they arrive?'

'I don't know you.'

'Well here's your chance to get to know me.' He grinned what he no doubt thought was a winning smile. 'I'm a nice guy. I'm a surgeon, too, but don't let that put you off.'

And Kennedy could see how it could work. He was trim, not bad looking, and, as it happened, he was actually a surgeon. Although he'd simply forgotten the more relevant details. Such as being married with two kids. She blinked. 'Really?'

He laughed. 'Yeah, really. Well, have a good evening, ...?' He looked at her and raised his eyebrows.

'Jenny,' Kennedy said.

'Good to meet you, Jenny. I'm Mark. Hopefully I'll see you again.' He stood up. Good guy Mark. Surgeon Mark. The doppelganger of Marcus Bell.

'You can give me your number if you want?' she said.

He leant on the table, leaning in close to her. 'I only give my number to people who might need me in an emergency.'

Kennedy forced herself to keep eye contact. 'You never know, I might need to call you later tonight.' The way his pupils dilated as good as shouted out the thought running through his imagination. She held up her phone, her finger poised. Bell's voice cracked slightly as he told her his number. 'Okay. Got it. See you around, Mark.'

He slowly pushed himself up. 'I hope so, Jenny. I really hope so.'

THURSDAY

12

1:50PM

Kennedy left it until the early afternoon of the following day before sending Marcus Bell a message.

I'm going to report you. You can't get away with what you did to me.

She waited for the reply. It didn't take long.

Who is this? I don't know what you're talking about.

Then she typed her reply but didn't send it. She picked up a second phone and called him, hitting send on the message the moment he answered.

You know exactly what I'm talking about.

'Hi Mark, it's Jenny.' The silence that followed was enough to confirm that Jenny from the pub was far away from Marcus Bell's current thoughts. 'From the pub, last night.'

'Oh, Jenny. Yeah, hello.' He forced a laugh down the line. 'Sorry, you caught me on the hop.'

'I'm sorry. I shouldn't have called. It was an impulse thing, I-'

'No, I'm glad you called.' Kennedy typed out the next text and hit send. She heard the chime as it arrived on Bell's phone. 'I'm glad ... I ... Sorry. Just a minute.' She could hear his breathing quicken as he read the message.

I know that I'm not the only one you've done this to.

He swore under his breath.

'I think this may have been a mistake, Mark. I'm going to hang up.'

'Jenny, wait. Look, I'm just caught up in something. Can I call you back on this number? We can arrange to meet up.'

'Okay, I guess so,' Kennedy said, making sure that she sounded uncertain. 'Speak to you later.'

She ended the call and stared at the second phone screen, waiting for his reply. Just then it started to ring. Kennedy clicked the button to answer the call and Bell's voice exploded in her ear.

'Is that you, Bonnie?' His voice was ragged. 'Bonnie? We've talked about this. I've said I'm sorry. It was a misunderstanding. But you're not going to blackmail me. Bonnie? Say something.' All Kennedy could hear was his breathing. 'Bonnie? You bloody nurses, you're all the same. Everything has to be on your terms. Jesus Christ. You'll regret this.' The line went dead.

She typed another message.

I'm not Bonnie.

She tapped her fingers on the table. Where was she? She wasn't certain that Carolyn Manning had been assaulted. Her story was slightly off. But she was involved with Marcus Bell, somehow.

She needed to find Bonnie, the nurse. She would almost certainly be in the same hospital as Bell. Kennedy checked the time. She could be at the hospital in just under an hour.

13

3:15PM

Kennedy stood close to the desk, her red scarf draping on the wooden surface.

'Can I help you madam?' The receptionist didn't look up but Kennedy noticed he twisted slightly as if to indicate that he was giving her his full attention.

'Thank you. I'm looking for one of the nurses, Bonnie.'

The receptionist peered at Kennedy. 'Do you have an appointment?'

'No.' It'd been easy to find Marcus Bell, Consultant Thoracic Surgeon at Guy's hospital. And from there it'd been easy to find Bonnie Pike, Thoracic Nurse Practitioner. LinkedIn had given up everything Kennedy needed, without so much as having to leave a cookie. She caught the glimmer of recognition in his eyes. 'But I have a message for her. An important message.'

The man folded his arms. 'I'm not a personal WhatsApp delivery service.'

Kennedy smiled and took a step back. 'Yes, of course. I'll wait.'

His expression hardened slightly and he glanced up at the clock on the wall. 'It's a free country.'

Kennedy lowered herself onto one of the moulded plastic chairs in the waiting area. She'd always planned on waiting it out. She knew what Bonnie looked like. But if she was lucky, the protective receptionist might just accelerate everything. She'd heard him pick up the phone even as she was walking away. If he was warning the nurse that there was someone waiting to see her, Bonnie herself might well make an appearance.

The floor was open plan. From her vantage point Kennedy could see the reception desk, the front door, the small café, and the large double doors than led into the heart of the hospital. It was a sure thing that Bonnie would have to come through those doors. How would the receptionist have described her visitor? Kennedy smiled as she removed her red scarf and folded it into the small bag that she was carrying. Then she tucked the bag under the chair.

It was twelve minutes before Bonnie arrived. Kennedy saw her peer through the glass doors before opening them. The nurse scanned the crowd before a wave of irritation crossed her face. Kennedy was moving before Bonnie had started towards the reception desk. The receptionist was busy dealing with a patient. As seemed to be his way, he wasn't looking up.

Kennedy touched Bonnie on the arm. The nurse flinched and spun round. 'I'm a friend, Bonnie. I'm here to help.' Kennedy kept her voice low. 'I know what Marcus Bell did to you. I'm on your side.'

Bonnie went rigid, and her face paled. She chewed her lip, leaving a smear of lipstick on her tooth. Her eyes darted around and then settled back on Kennedy.

'Not here,' she said and strode towards the exit.

. . .

THE PARK BENCH WAS PUBLIC, but it felt safer than being in a coffee shop or a bar. There was no one sitting with them and they could see precisely who was near enough that they might be overheard.

'Why should I trust you?' Bonnie's eyes were bloodshot, her voice unsteady.

'I can't give you a good answer to that,' Kennedy said. 'My role is to make sure that people like Marcus Bell pay the price for their behaviour.'

Bonnie glanced around. Her hands were shaking in her lap. She linked her fingers, as if to stop the tremors. 'He said he'd destroy me.' Her voice was soft, but the words caught in her throat. A chill ran down Kennedy's spine as Bonnie swallowed before carrying on. 'If I speak to anyone. He told me no one would believe me.'

'Listen to me, Bonnie.' Kennedy twisted on the bench so that she was facing the nurse. She took the nurse's hands in hers. They were cold and she resisted the urge to rub some warmth into them. 'I need to know exactly what happened. And I need to know what else you know. If you trust me, I will help you. And I promise you, Marcus Bell won't even be able to look at you again.'

'Who are you?' Bonnie asked.

'I'm the person who is going to make things right.'

Bonnie blinked. Then she sniffed. 'I'm scared. He's powerful.' She paused, sucking in some breaths. 'And he's right. No one will believe me.'

'I believe you.' Kennedy paused. Bonnie was chewing her lip again, but her hands had stopped shaking. 'I know he's done this before, to other women. And we both know that, if he isn't stopped, he'll keep on doing this.'

Bonnie's shoulders jerked. She screwed her eyes tightly closed and started to rock on the bench. 'Okay,' she said.

'Okay.' A deep breath, and then she opened her eyes. 'I'll tell you everything.'

Kennedy listened silently whilst Bonnie told her about the abuse she'd suffered from Marcus Bell. And the details were, unfortunately, almost precisely what Kennedy had expected to hear. Comments, suggestions, touching. All inappropriate. And then the power play. Coercion and threats. Kennedy felt a knot tighten in her stomach.

Bonnie wiped the tears from her cheeks. 'I know of three others.'

'They've experienced the same as you?'

Bonnie sniffed. 'More or less, yes. Two of them have shared the details. The third ...' She shrugged. 'She hasn't said, but I know. I see how she is when they're in theatre together.'

Which was more than enough for Kennedy. There were at least four nurses amongst his victims, and possibly also Dr Carolyn Manning, although Kennedy had a very particular theory about her. Whatever the truth about Dr Manning, it was clear that Marcus Bell was a repeat offender.

But there was a missing piece of the jigsaw. Kennedy was sure of it. She needed to dig into Marcus Bell's teenage years. And she knew exactly how she was going to do it.

FRIDAY

14

11:27AM

As a rule, Kennedy hated social media. But she had to admit that it was remarkable.

In the space of two hours she'd identified Marcus Bell's secondary school. She'd built a list of twenty people who were in his year at school. And she was in email contact with four of them.

A couple of replies suggested that the senders were still in touch with Bell. She hadn't replied to those, focusing instead on the four fifty-year-old men, marvelling at how many years had passed since they'd been in touch.

Kennedy had been sparse with her own updates, after all, she didn't know that much about Marcus Bell. She just had to hope that none of them knew more than she did. But she'd duly updated them on married life, the joys of parenthood and, of course the life of a surgeon. She tapped her fingers on the table. She had no idea how quickly they would reply.

The alert signalled a new email. This was from someone who hadn't replied already. She started to read.

From: Tmackin1971@hotmail.com

Re: Blast from the past

Message: I've spent two hours trying to decide whether to simply delete your message. But I can't. I can't let this go. I can't allow you to think that it's okay.

Kennedy felt a tingling in her neck. She'd hit pay dirt.

Even after all these years, I didn't think you'd ever dare to get in touch.

And your message? As if nothing had happened.

You think I want to hear about your life? ... your wife and kids?

And not even a reference to Emily?

Are you even more crazy than you were all those years ago? Jesus. My parents should have buried you back then. God only knows why they didn't.

But I'm warning you, if you try and have any contact with me, or my family, I will bury you myself, so help me God.

Kennedy read the message twice. She pursed her lips as she acknowledged the twinge of guilt she felt at upsetting Trevor Macklin. She shook her head and then googled Emily Macklin, narrowing the search down by including the region of Bell's school. After a couple of minutes scrolling through links, Kennedy found a newspaper article. Her mouth went dry as she started to read.

Body of woman, 29, found at base of cliffs.

Emergency services were called to the cliffs at 1.20pm on Saturday, June 25th where Police say the body of a 29-year-old woman was found. The woman has been identified as Emily Macklin, who lived locally her entire life.

Kennedy scanned the report, including the Samaritans hotline included at the end of the article. She didn't know exactly what Marcus Bell had done to Emily Macklin, but she could guess. One man had destroyed so many lives. And, left unchecked, he wasn't done yet. Kennedy paused. She thought about his wife, his kids. And then she thought about Emily Macklin. And Bonnie Pike. And the two other nurses. And the third nurse. And the possibility of nameless others.

She picked up the phone that she'd used to message Bell, and clipped the voice distorter over the microphone. He answered on the third ring, but he didn't speak.

She started to speak. 'Marcus Bell, listen to me very carefully.'

'Who is this?' Bell was practically hissing.

'You will report to your local police station by six o'clock this evening. You will confess to all of the assaults you have committed. Starting with Bonnie Pike.'

'What? You're crazy. I don't know what you're talking about.'

'I know everything.' A beat, before she dropped the bombshell. 'I know what you did to Emily Macklin.' She paused to listen to his breath rasping down the phone line, before continuing. 'And unlike Trevor, and Emily's parents, I have no reason to bury the truth.' Silence echoed down the line. Kennedy waited.

'Trevor? Is that you?' His voice was shaky now. He stuttered before pushing on. 'I can speak to Emily. I can explain-'

Kennedy briefly closed her eyes. He didn't even know. 'Emily's dead, Marcus. She took her own life. Twenty years ago.'

'I ... I ...' Marcus Bell, finally lost for words.

'Six o'clock.' Kennedy ended the call.

SATURDAY

15

11AM

Kennedy opened the door. She knew she was meeting Noah but there was someone else waiting for her, too. The woman smiled.

'Hello Mystery Machine, how nice to see you again.' Dr Manning didn't get up. She was dressed more casually than the last time they'd met. The hoodie and hairband suited her.

'I told you you'd be fine,' Kennedy said.

'You knew I worked for TUBE?' Dr Manning asked.

It was Kennedy's turn to smile. 'You made it a little too easy for me.'

'Duly noted.' Carolyn's eyes narrowed as she studied Kennedy, which Kennedy didn't mind one bit.

'Please, have a seat, Kennedy.' Noah waved towards the empty chair.

'I prefer to stand,' Kennedy replied.

'Very well. Carolyn was already working the case; we thought you might need the head start.' Kennedy didn't say anything. It'd always struck her as odd that the file contained Carolyn Manning's name and yet Marcus Bell hadn't said who was blackmailing him. Which meant that TUBE had known about Bell before Bell knew about TUBE. He thought he'd come to them. But he'd been wrong because they'd already found him.

Noah slid the red folder that was on the desk in front of him over towards her.

Kennedy picked it up but didn't open it immediately. 'Assignment two?' she asked.

'No.' He straightened his tie. 'It's your performance review.'

Kennedy nodded and then dropped the file unopened onto the table. 'I crushed it.' She saw Carolyn hide a smile.

Noah stared at her, as if he was unsure what to do. Then he pulled open the desk drawer next to him and produced two more files. He very deliberately placed them in front of her. 'Assignment two. Your choice.'

One file was green, the other yellow.

Kennedy cocked her head and stared at Noah. 'In my interview, my sister was mentioned. I want your assurance that TUBE would never do anything to put her in danger.'

Noah frowned and blinked. 'How many sisters do you have?'

'One. Sandra.'

Noah nodded. 'Very well. You have my word.'

'Thank you.' Kennedy pointed at the two files. 'Which category are they?'

Noah flicked a glance at Carolyn and cleared his throat. 'This one,' he tapped the green folder, 'is a two. The yellow folder is a seven.' He paused. 'The number doesn't, of itself, signify the level of risk or complexity.'

But Kennedy had already done the translation.

Green was Lust.

And Yellow was Violence.
Spoilt for choice. What's a girl to do?
She smiled and picked up the yellow folder.

THE END

COMING SOON

THE HONESTY INDEX

The Honesty Index is a game, but it's *you* who's being played.

When Trent Ryder and his old school friends are simultaneously invited to play a mysterious online game called the Honesty Index they think it's intriguing, fun even. But they soon realise that the game knows everything about them and if they refuse to play, or if they lie, their secrets will be ruthlessly exposed to the world.

Can the Honesty Index possibly know the truth behind the fire that ripped through Trent's family home when he was a teenager? He must investigate who is behind the game before it's time for his round or he too will face five allegations and be granted five pleas.

If time runs out, his only hope will be to tell the truth. Which might just break him.

Ready to play?

TURN THE PAGE TO READ THE PROLOGUE

THE HONESTY INDEX

NJ BARKER

'I'm sorry,' Kennedy bowed her head.

'But the main complication is that the incident happened eight years ago.' She grimaced. 'And that's beyond the GMC's five-year time limit.'

Kennedy nodded. Maybe there were exceptions to the rule, but she feared what a tribunal would see. The question as to why Dr Manning didn't come forward earlier, would be judged by looking at Dr Manning today. A seemingly strong, confident woman, at the top of her profession. And yet, if they were able to ask the question of Dr Manning eight years ago, or even three years ago, perhaps they would've been confronted with a very different reality. Someone who was broken, who was in no state to confront her attacker. Was five years a long time? No, five years was the blink of an eye.

'What about a criminal case?' she asked.

Dr Manning didn't speak but she shook her head. Was that because it wasn't a crime, Kennedy wondered? Or because the doctor didn't want to go down that route? 'What do you think will happen? When you tell the GMC what he did?'

Dr Manning sniffed, and pulled herself upright. 'They'll say they can't do anything about it. But they'll know. And, more importantly, he'll know they know.'

'And?' Kennedy said it softly.

The doctor shrugged. But it wasn't resignation, there was a strength there that Kennedy found strangely moving. She stretched her neck, tilting her head back and then to either side before she fixed Kennedy with a stare. 'Hopefully, he'll never do it again.'

Something fused inside Kennedy at hearing the word 'again.' What if it wasn't a one-time offence? What if Bell was a repeat offender. An idea began to take shape in her mind, an idea born in the past.

'The Mystery Machine is thinking,' the doctor said resting her hand on Kennedy's arm. She was looking over the top of her glasses. 'Should I be worried?' The doctor's phone buzzed on the bar. She picked it up, read the message and raised her eyebrows. 'Duty calls.' She slipped off the bar stool and pulled on her green lightweight coat. 'I get the feeling I won't see you again, which is a shame. I don't have many friends.'

'I'm sorry.' Kennedy hadn't expected to make a connection on her first assignment. Hadn't counted on there being anything except hard, cold truth. She swallowed. 'I can't.'

Dr Manning nodded. 'I suspected as much. Well,' she said as she pulled Kennedy into a warm embrace, 'it was lovely to meet you, Mystery Machine.' She released Kennedy and turned to walk away.

'Carolyn?' The doctor looked back over her shoulder. 'Don't be worried. You're going to be fine.'

Dr Manning nodded, but there was a question in her eyes.

Kennedy watched her walk towards the exit, and if it hadn't been clear before, it was then. Marcus Bell was the client. And all clients had to pay. The only questions were, how much and what for?

PROLOGUE

Suburban London, April 2009

The seven teenagers were sitting on logs that formed a circle around the fire. A glitterball moon spun in the night sky to the ambient lo-fi techno soundtrack of the nightingale song. Around them, silhouettes of trees lurked in the shadows.

Trent Ryder shoved his hands deep into his donkey jacket pockets and flexed his fingers to warm them. The party was winding down and the fire had dulled to an amber glow. He looked at the packet of cigarettes Paddy was holding out. With sandy brown hair and freckles and eyes to match, Paddy was the kind of kid that parents found easy to like but hard to trust.

Trent didn't really like cigarettes but he accepted the offer because he had an audience. He blew out the smoke, turned and locked eyes with Lila Jain: Bollywood princess meets home counties girl-next-door. Flawless skin, radiant smile and not even a blush of make-up. Her crimson down jacket was zipped up to the neck; her breath hung in frosty clouds, her eyes reflecting the firelight.

He held her gaze for a fraction too long. He would have carried on forever but she turned away – which was a bad sign. But she was smiling. Which was a good sign.

Trent had suggested to her earlier that they do some exploring, but she'd just laughed. First at him, because he was being suggestive. And then she'd laughed with him, because he was funny. *Good-looking, with a great sense of humour. Keen explorer. Contact Trent if you're looking for love.*

Trent sighed and watched the smoke spiral up to greet the stars as he sat flanked by Nicholas Samson and Lila. Between the devil and heaven on earth. How many more minutes of this bonfire to Samson's vanity could he take?

The six of them had known each other for years but they'd agreed to give the new kid a chance. It was Samson's birthday, after all. But the evening hadn't been easy. Samson was academically precocious, already a school year ahead of his age, which maybe didn't help. Copper, sitting on the other side of Samson, had tried to engage him in conversation but after each question the silences had lengthened. Trent imagined Mrs Samson insisting on the birthday party to help her son to make some friends. *They just need to get to know you, Nicky darling. The real you. The completely freaky, wide-eyed nutjob that Mummy loves so dearly.* Well, maybe not those precise words. But Nicholas Samson had cornered them all in the lunch queue two fateful weeks ago. Once Copper had said yes, no one had the heart to decline. Although the idea of leaving Copper to fly solo at Samson's birthday party had been almost funny enough to swing the balance.

They still had an hour before Paddy's father was due to pick them up in his battered old Volvo Estate. Trent could think of plenty of ways he'd like to pass the time with Lila but none of them involved smoking. He was about to stub the cigarette out when he caught her glancing at him. He took another puff – cool, nonchalant – and gave her a wink. She shook her head gently in response, her dark bobbed hair swaying in front of her smile.Samson had led the group of friends to the clearing by torchlight, then left the light switched off by his feet. Trent was peering into the shadows trying to count the shades of grey, when a shaft of torchlight illuminated Nicholas Samson's face, making his skin look pale and unworldly. The fire spat out a bright orange spark which sizzled on the dry ground.

'It's time,' Nicholas said. His voice was pure gargled gravel, like he thought he was auditioning for a voice-over in a horror film trailer.

Lila covered her mouth with her hand, shoulders twitching. Dub, on the other side of the fire, caught Trent's eye. Maybe Samson thought edgy was the way to go. Boy, had he read that wrong. But he could still recover it with a joke.

'Everyone has to reveal a secret,' Samson continued. 'And we all swear to keep it. Forever.' His words would have been a good effort, if only Samson hadn't been deadly serious.

'Jesus, Samson,' laughed Paddy, 'this isn't the Blair Witch Project.' His voice was louder than normal. He'd rolled off his log and was lying back on the grass, propped up on his elbows. His round face was glowing, his eyes unfocused. The six pack of lager he'd smuggled into the party was now safely hidden in his bloodstream, the empty cans kicked under a hedge at the end of the garden.

Secret. Trent folded his arms. Despite the warmth of his coat across his shoulders, there was a knot gathering in his stomach.

'I think it sounds like fun,' said Oli. You could tell she

meant it. Fun was her personal stamp of endorsement. *He's so much fun. They're all really fun.* When she was sure everyone was looking at her, she flicked her blonde hair and slowly tilted her head until she caught the perfect angle for the freeze frame.

'You go first, then, Olivia.' Samson was still shining the torch up at his own face because, he was so, you know, fun, fun, fun.

Oli took a moment to arrange herself as if she were on the cover of a magazine and started to talk. 'Well, my favourite sixteenth birthday present last year ... was the sex.'

Trent tuned her out. Not in an 'I'm so bored, I'm too cool to follow the rule' sort of way. But because his mind had flashed back to the fire. Memories clawed for his attention. He blinked and shuffled forward. Before he knew it, Oli had finished and Paddy was sitting up and talking, clearly having warmed to the idea of sharing secrets.

Trent chewed on his thumb, his teeth biting into the fleshy pad until he could feel the resistance of the bone underneath. Samson's secrets game was just that. A game. And the others already knew about the fire a year ago. Even Samson would know, although Trent had never told him directly. He didn't have to. Trent could rely on others to do that. *He doesn't like to talk about it but I should tell you, so you don't, you know, say something by accident.* So they all knew about the fire, about how his parents and younger brother had died and that only he and his sister had survived. But that was all they knew.

Trent shook his head. Just because Samson said they were going to reveal a secret didn't mean he *had* to say anything. He could just keep quiet, even if that looked odd, as though he had something to hide.

He could hear the birdsong. More insistent than before.

Everyone was laughing, Paddy the loudest. Paddy dialled everything up to eleven. A few of the group clapped as he finished his confession, although Trent had heard the story of Paddy's father interrupting his son's 'private bedroom activity' several times before.

And then Dub was talking. Dub was so thin, as if he only ate one square meal a day, but as tall as if he ate four. His expression matched his tone. Serious.

'... and I didn't know what to do. Whoever it was, they were face down on the grass next to the river. I was sure they were dead.'

The laughter froze and died. Anxious glances shot around the circle and Lila blew out air from her cheeks. A ripple of wind pulsed the fire, which glowed a deep red; its dying breath.

'Jesus, Dub. What did you do?' asked Oli, her eyes movie star wide.

'I ran home and told my dad. I reckon we were back to the riverbank within ten minutes.' Dub was staring at the floor, shaking his head. The others leant in. 'But there was no one there. I checked all the local news sites for weeks. I was sure there'd be a report of a body being found somewhere, but nothing.'

Paddy slapped Dub on the back. 'Maybe it was a ghost. I remember reading about a girl who was murdered down by the river, forty years ago. She's come back to haunt you.' He raised his hands over his head and rolled his eyes back. 'I'm coming for you, Andrew Dubnyk.' His voice was a high-pitched wail. 'I'm watching you.' Paddy's laugh triggered the others. Even Dub managed a grin.

Copper was next up. Copper by name and copper by hair colour, although the hair came first. Trent couldn't imagine *she* would have any earth-shattering secrets. The only rule-books she hadn't read were the ones she'd written. Fifteen years old but already middle-aged.

'I discovered my father's stash of porn mags at the bottom of his cupboard,' she said with the confidence of a teacher setting lines. Write it out one hundred times.

'Copper.' Paddy's mouth was wide open. 'No way. I don't believe it. Does he know?' He was clutching his stomach.

'Of course not. I'm hardly going to tell him, am I? So, that's my secret.' A flicker of a smile. 'Well, my dad's secret.' She turned to Samson, who was next in the circle.

Trent needed to decide on what he was going to say. Paddy and Copper had opted for humour. Samson was still talking and Trent forced himself to tune in.

'... and it was all over Facebook. So my mum decided I had to move school. And that's why you are now lucky enough to have me in your lives.'

He flicked the torch off and back on again, his expression blank. There was something weirdly staged about the whole thing. Samson had suggested the game and it had sounded spontaneous but he could easily have planned it just to be the centre of attention.

Trent scanned his friends' faces, looking for a clue as to what Samson had just said. Lila wore a Mona-Lisa smile, Copper was frowning, and he caught Dub raising an eyebrow at Paddy. Trent frowned. His desire to know the secret wrestled against his reluctance to admit he hadn't been paying attention. He cleared his throat. 'Sorry. I didn't catch the beginning of that. What was all over Facebook?'

Samson flipped the torch down until it was shining directly into Trent's eyes.

Trent blinked and turned away. 'Jesus. What was that for?'

'You must be punished for not listening to the secrets.' Samson's voice was hollow.

Trent shook his head. He could only take so much, and Samson's capacity for playing the oddball appeared endless. Although it was possible that he wasn't acting at all.

Lila leant towards Trent. 'His dad was accused of election fraud and a group of vigilantes targeted him. A mob turned up at the family home.'

'Blimey.' Trent said. Everyone was staring at him. Why were they expecting him to provide a more detailed reaction? It took a few further seconds of silence before he realised they were waiting to hear his secret. A few seconds in which he locked away his emotions. He couldn't share those, because if he started he wouldn't be able to stop. He glanced at Lila, whose turn followed his.

He started to speak. 'You all know about the fire.' *The* fire. That was enough. The others looked as if they had turned to stone.

Lila rested her hand on his arm. 'You don't have to talk about that night, Trent,' she said. 'This whole thing is just a bit of fun.'

Trent cleared his throat and continued. 'Which is why,' he smiled, 'I'm not going to talk about that.' Lila punched his arm and he saw Paddy's shoulders drop. 'My secret is,' he looked at each of them in turn, 'I have no secrets.'

'Boo.' Paddy's foghorn of derision was magnified by his hands cupped around his mouth.

'I think I'd better take my turn.' Lila was looking at Trent. He shrugged at her and felt the spotlight swing away from him and towards Lila. The natural order of things restored.

Trent sunk back into the moonlight shadows. It was only a game. Not just that. It was Nicholas Samson's game. There was no reason to share anything of consequence. No reason at all.

Lila leant forward, looked around the circle of friends,

and smiled. She spoke in a conspiratorial whisper. 'Okay, guys. Here's my secret.' She shot Trent one quick, intense glance, then looked back at the others. What had that meant?

Trent's brain scrambled to make some sense of how he was feeling. And then he heard her words.

'I have a massive crush on someone.' Her hair fell across her face so he could no longer see her expression. Did she mean *him*? Was she going to announce it here? Lila brushed her hair back again. All eyes were on her – especially his.

'I love it. A real secret,' Paddy shouted. He pointed at Oli. 'Countdown please, Olivia.'

'Five, four, ...'

Lila laughed. Paddy began clapping in time with Oli's chanting. Trent held his breath.

'Three, two, one.'

'I'm not going to tell you his name,' Lila said, grinning. Trent let out a slow breath. Lila tucked a strand of hair behind her ear. 'But I will say that he's older than me.'

Trent's world tilted. He was younger than Lila. He scratched his nose. Were the others looking at him? He forced himself to grin and prayed that someone else would say something.

'No, no, no,' Samson said, raking his fingers through his hair. He rocked backwards and forwards. 'That's not ...' Trent didn't understand why Samson was upset. But now their host was on his feet, his pointing hand sweeping round the circle of friends. '*None* of you are taking this seriously. I don't *care* about your superficial lives. Give me something *real*.'

Trent glanced at Paddy just in time to catch the eye roll.

Copper stood up and rested her hand on Samson's shoulder. 'We were just having fun, Nicholas.'

He shrugged her off. 'I don't care about fun.'

Oli was blinking, no doubt trying to digest a worldview so

opposed to her own. Trent was caught between laughing and processing Lila's announcement when Samson leant back and screamed into the night sky.

They all stared at him. It must have lasted ten seconds. When he finally lowered his face Trent could see tears in Samson's eyes. What the hell?

'You're supposed to be my friends.' Samson's voice cracked as he wiped his face. 'And friends trust each other with secrets.' He turned away from them and started walking back towards the house.

Trent risked a glance at Lila. He'd thought that the two of them had something special. But it seemed he'd been wrong. His thoughts were interrupted by Samson screaming again.

'What did he say?' Trent asked.

Lila was frowning. 'He said, *you should've trusted me.*'

NJ BARKER READERS' CLUB - SIGN UP

If you enjoyed the prologue of *The Honesty Index,* you can sign up to my readers' club for details of publication. I send newsletters with details on new releases and special offers. That also means that you will be the first to hear about future Kennedy Logan stories.

You can sign up by typing the link below into your browser and you'll receive a free download of my flash fiction, *I couldn't find you.* I ended up incorporating an adapted version of this scene in my second full-length thriller, *The Genius Club,* which I plan to publish later in 2023 or early 2024.

https://BookHip.com/WRVALAQ

Thanks again for reading. I'm very grateful for you taking the time.

ENJOYED THIS NOVELLA?

YOU CAN MAKE A BIG DIFFERENCE

I hope you enjoyed reading *The Catastrophe Test*; it was certainly fun to write.

Reviews are very helpful in raising the profile of my books. Honest reviews increase the chances of other readers discovering my stories and, hopefully, buying them.

If you enjoyed *The Catastrophe Test* I would be very grateful if you could spend just a couple of minutes leaving a review (it can be as short as you like) on the book's Amazon page.

Thank you very much.

ABOUT NJ BARKER

NJ Barker first started writing books when he was eight, but he took his time before completing his first thriller some forty years later. He studied Pure Mathematics (truly a branch of the arts) at Warwick University and law at The College of Law before building a career in personal tax.

In 2019 he retired to focus on his passion. As it turned out, this wasn't maths (surprised?) or tax (shocked?) but writing fiction. He is a graduate of the Faber Academy and is drawn to stories where people are forced to follow someone else's rules or face the consequences.

The opening of his debut thriller, *The Honesty Index*, was long-listed by Jericho Writers in their Friday Night Live competition.

As well as finalising *The Honesty Index* for publication, NJ Barker is editing books two and three, writing three more stand alone thrillers, and developing a series for Kennedy Logan, the star of *The Catastrophe Test*.

He lives in Kent together with his wife, teenage son and their cocker spaniel.

www.njbarker.com

Printed in Great Britain
by Amazon

25358568R00047

Night Fishing

Night Fishing

GORDON WOOD

THE BOYDELL PRESS

First published 1992 by The Boydell Press, Woodbridge

The Boydell Press is an imprint of Boydell & Brewer Ltd
PO Box 9, Woodbridge, Suffolk IP12 3DF

ISBN 0 85115 287 2

British Library Cataloguing-in-Publication Data
Wood, Gordon
Night Fishing.
I. Title
799.1
ISBN 0–85115–287–2

This publication is printed on acid-free paper

Printed in Great Britain by
Dotesios Ltd, Trowbridge, Wiltshire

Contents

This book is dedicated to the memory of my old night fishing pal Bernard Alfrey – or So-Big, as he was fondly known to his friends for the manner in which he always described the ones that got away. Sadly, Bernard is no longer with us, but recollections of nights spent together – of living, sleeping and fishing for entire weeks at a time in a not so dried up creek bed that gave us access to a certain River Thames weirpool, will never cease to linger. My thanks Bernard for sharing so many of those early nights with me. I only wish to God that you still could.

Gordon Wood
London
12 December 1990

Night fishing: A time for talking in lowered tones about the ones that got away. A time for thinking – about the thunder and the lightning and the rain. About the bats, with designs on your head as a landing strip. About Dracula. About werewolves and the like. About whatever the hell is crashing through the bushes behind you. That's what night fishing is all about – things that go bump in the dark.

Introduction

There is something to be said for being abroad at night, when those of fainter heart are loath to leave the security of their own fireplaces. Take for instance the joy of treading a rainswept pavement in the dark – deserted, now, and not a sound to be heard save for your own footsteps; the reflected images of bright neon signs at your feet being all there is to ward off a sensation of evil; of total isolation; of being forlornly alone in the dark. Driving a car through the rain at night promotes a similar sensation; the swishing sound of the wipers instilling in one a sense of not just seclusion but soothing security as well; for there's a token presence of the latter in being alone at moments like this, when the rest of the world (so you think) is safely tucked up in bed – and missing out on one of life's little pleasures. To me, these fleeting moments are very personal, most private, and I'm loath to share them with a single soul.

Therein probably lies one of my main reasons for fishing at night. I enjoy the solitude it affords me, the opportunity to do my thing without the interference of others. Add to that the greatly increased chances of coming face to face with the fish of a lifetime at night and you'll appreciate even more profoundly why fishing in the dark appeals to me so. And yet you're still examining the mere tip of the iceberg.

I'm a nocturnal kind of creature – I must be, to derive such pleasure from being on the banks of a water on my own in the dark, for I often take off for a week at a time to fish an eerie type of water that even the bailiffs are hesitant to check for most of the time. Although it is within a stone's throw of the City of London, scarcely a soul do I see throughout the entire week. The Bomb could go off, and not a thing would I know about it while enveloped in a cocoon of my own making, for such is the tranquillity I seek, find and sink myself in to a depth of happy oblivion.

I'm not entirely on my own, however, for other nocturnal

creatures pay me a visit, be they rats, voles, bats, foxes or whatever; there's always some disturbance in the bushes behind me or at my feet. For the night really does have a thousand eyes, I've learned, and they're not all twinkling in the heavens above – far from it. One cheeky little vole that I have come to know quite well is in the habit of helping itself from my sweetcorn tray then coming back for more. And why not, I ask, when it entertains me so? Unlike other anglers I've known, who to their shame put down poison to rid the pitch of all manner of furry interlopers (although in reality we, not they, are interlopers), I experience no fear whatsoever of waterside dwellers (in this country at least) and offer them no malice, only a welcome to my swim. They are a delight to watch as they go about their business blissfully, comically, to my mind, so why then should I resent them?

And then there are the noises of the night – sounds so insignificant during the hours of daylight as to become almost indiscernible – but not so at night, I fear, as each is carried on the wind to convey a message of sorts – a warning perhaps to the uninitiated. The chimes emitted from a distant clock tower; the hammering of a forge, to remind the nightstalker that others too are active at this ghostly hour, working on some far off factory floor. Then there are the whispers of the night – like voices, reaching out from the water at your very feet. This is what night fishing is all about, and much, much more.

The weather at times represents the real threat, indeed, the only threat: it isn't always as you'd like it even in June, and while you can perhaps wrap up against the cold and even the rain, there's no sure way that I know of for sitting safely and soundly through a ferocious thunder storm, and believe me, I've tried! I once fished the old Ham Pits by the side of the Thames at Twickenham, London, for eels at night below a malevolent ceiling that was literally ripped apart by the inclement weather. Teeming rain, wind, lurid streaks of lightning and deafening thunder claps finally forced me to seek shelter in the only possible refuge, that happened to be beneath an ancient tree. I was worried then all right, I can tell you, but marooned on an island as I was, with no chance of a ferry back across the Thames till the following morning, I had no alternative but to stand my ground and get on with my eeling. (I never could understand what I was doing there in the first place, the eels being of the bootlace variety.)

One does learn, however, and since I was first taken night fishing by my father and grandfather, long before I could even crawl, let alone walk, I have had time to learn – fifty-odd years in all, and yet

There's something to be said for being alone in the dark. This angler enjoys a read, while waiting for nightfall.

still I continue to learn. Indeed, only in more recent years have I owned up to needing a bit more comfort when at the waterside at night; until then I did not possess even a brolly. Why, I can't rightly say, other than that I neither thought nor bothered about such things, getting soaked through, dried out and then soaked through yet again. Perhaps it was as a penance for daring to be out there in the first place, some might have thought, but I've seen the light now, of that you can be sure.

It is perhaps because I have suffered so in the past that I am writing this book, to save others suffering in a like manner when fishing at night. For he who dares, there are many hurdles to be surmounted in the dark, obstacles to be negotiated, and traps waiting to be sprung. The newcomer to night fishing could fall victim to any one of these before he has taken the first step, and even after all these years I continue to find new snares. Doing your thing in the dark is not to be taken lightly, if I can be excused a pun – it never can be. To learn from the mistakes of others can lighten the way considerably, often effortlessly, which is exactly what I have endeavoured to do for you in this book. I hope I have succeeded in my task.

Fisheries and the Rule Book

So where then can the angler wet a line at night? That would have been a valid question in the sixties, when access to still waters after dark appeared to be largely reserved for those in the know, and applied only slightly less so to many rivers and streams. Today however that same question barely warrants an answer, for look where you will and there will be night fishing available to you. It doesn't all have to be paid for by purchasing a permit either, although most do in fact require as much. This may vary from as little as a few pounds per night on some waters, to the colossal sums demanded in order to join very exclusive syndicates – when you can talk your way in – making it a typical case of you get what you pay for.

Rivers can lend themselves most favourably to night fishing, where it's allowed, and offer more of a mixed variety of species to catch. Sadly, on the more highly rated rivers, such as the Hampshire Avon and the Dorset Stour, the opportunity to fish at night is very restricted, while other rivers, of admittedly less appeal, do offer a better chance of presenting a bait to the fish after dark. If in doubt about this, you only have to ask your local tackle dealer or, failing that, the relevant branch of the National Water Authority.

One stretch of river to be wary of is where the incoming tide from the sea leaves its mark. You mightn't realise it's tidal until you suddenly notice you're nearer to the edge of the water than was at first intended. This might be brought home to you by the sight of your bait-box floating away – or even your rod, if you've been stealing a bit of shut-eye. Do make sure beforehand then that the venue you intend to fish is not influenced by the tide. If it is, then be extra vigilant throughout the night. Don't just drop off in your chair if tiredness stakes its claim on you. Instead, reel in your baits and shift your gear to a safer place that's well away from the water; you will then sleep much better and find that your tackle is still safely beside you in the morning.

By far your best bet, though, is to take out a seasonal permit on one of the professionally run fisheries that have sprung up all over the country during the last decade or so. You will find them advertised in the angling press. These offer good value for money, and while rules and regulations pertaining to them do tend to vary somewhat, they are there for the good of the water, and indirectly therefore the angler also. He mightn't appreciate this much at first, in which case he'd be well advised to try elsewhere.

Most waters, whether still or moving, do of course require a rod licence, if not a permit to fish them, and each is linked (however loosely at times) to the rules that most of us know only too well. One general rule is no fires (well, would you like the trees on your property decimated for firewood?), yet still I see them often enough to wonder about the reading ability of some anglers, never mind their capacity for reasoning, and if you're one who believes that rules are made to be broken then please go and break 'em elsewhere.

The 'no litter' sign is another we come across irrespective of where we might fish. It is also the most wantonly disregarded, judging by the disgusting amount of litter that continues to be seen wherever an impression of an angler's boot is left at the water's edge. 'But it's not all anglers' litter,' I hear some bitterly cry. Well, I've got news for you, buddy: on most of the waters I fish you'll find nothing but anglers! You'll also discover by the pile of junk left behind them the exact spot where most were fishing and, 'If they can carry cartons and cans to the waterside when full, then surely they can take them away again when empty.' Now that's a well known saying connected with litter, with which I wholeheartedly agree. But the vast majority of anglers, by all accounts, fail to see the logic in the message. Why, I have no idea, because it stands to reason that sooner or later this litter problem is going to result in more waters closing their gates to us, and who in all honesty can blame the management for that?

Rods are usually restricted in number, by the local river authority if not by those managing the water, and again not without good reason. This rule is levelled, not at the thinking angler, who finds two or at most three rods as many as he can efficiently handle, but rather at those who never seem to think about the mayhem they could cause below the surface of the water as well as above it by using a battery of rods. They have no consideration at all for hooked fish left lying on the bottom awaiting attention, or of other anglers in futile search of a pitch.

Obviously then we do need rules, without which access to most

The penalty for misbehaviour. Signs like this were once commonplace, thanks to litter-bugs and the more rowdy element in our sport. Thinking anglers learn to play the game, but unfortunately many others don't.

waters would have been denied us long ago, and if they do appear to have escalated somewhat since the days when you were merely asked to shut the gate behind you lest the cattle stray, we have only ourselves to blame for that.

A ban on radios may at first appear to be almost laughable. Have one blaring in your ear all night, though, and you suddenly appreciate the ban, because some aren't happy unless they're entertaining everyone else on the water with their music as well as themselves, a fact well registered on a certain Thames island I used to night fish in the sixties. Such was the bedlam it culminated in the end with police raids to flush out drug-pushers and so forth, at which point I decided to try elsewhere for my sport. This was just as well under the circumstances prevailing at the time because night fishing became banned at the venue; and this happened, remember, during a period when waters to fish at night were very scarce indeed! A few seasons ago the ban was finally lifted, but how long will it take, I wonder, for the previous chaos to return? Not long at all, if some have their way, but hopefully others will have learned a lesson and prevent this nonsense from recurring.

So the evasion of one level of consideration for others can lead to those of a far more serious nature. When we leave tackle unattended, for example, we should expect to be called upon by the management to account for our ways, especially if we have left baited hooks in the water for a fish to swallow: there really can't be any excuse for that. And it just won't do to take up more or less permanent residence in a chosen swim either, which actually happens on some waters. This is achieved by leaving the bivvy in place while the occupier has returned to his home for a meal, bath, a good night's sleep or whatever, so denying the pitch to others who have also paid to fish.

Indeed, entire sections of a water can be hogged on a rota system (so to speak) whereby one party of anglers will hand them over to another and reclaim them again in a day or two so the other team can take a breather. In this way the pitches concerned virtually become the sole property of those involved in the manoeuvre, which can only be viewed as selfish and damned unsporting. Fortunately for the remainder of us this business is being rapidly stamped out, so be thankful that the rules are there.

One rule I would like to see enforced more than all others concerns the treatment of fish. Happily, as time goes by, the need for such a rule continues to diminish. Fish are rarely if ever taken home for the cat these days; not that they often were, in my opinion, poor

The battle is over, the pictures taken. Now's the time to give this pike the respect it deserves by returning it to the water without further delay.

old pussy having been for centuries a lame excuse for taking good fish home to show off to the neighbours. It's enlightening to see that most fisheries now stipulate that all fish must be returned to the water unless damaged. Damaged? Well, you can't have everything I suppose, but every fish hooked could be termed as being damaged, which leaves a great big loophole for the less desirable element in our midst to jump through. They are in this case few in number, but, having said that, the general handling of caught fish still leaves a lot to be desired. This is mainly down to ignorance rather than any deliberate attempt to harm them; there is hope yet, I trust, that we may all learn in time to afford our beaten quarry the respect it so richly deserves.

Fish that Feed at Night

What can we expect to catch at night? There are numerous species of fish which bite well in the dark and yet are very disinclined to entertain us during the day; this is mainly due to bankside traffic and that of the boating fraternity.

On the lower Thames, for example, the angler would be hard pressed to find even a few chub much before dark, never mind a bream or barbel, and it's all down to the continued disturbance the grand old river has to endure during the day. Indeed, so scarce can such fish become by day that you might be forgiven for thinking they don't exist in parts. Try those same regions at night, however, and what a different story you will have to tell, as each of the species mentioned above will begin to make their presence felt in no uncertain manner. And what a mixed bag you may encounter!

Almost anything can turn up at night, always assuming it's in the water to begin with of course. One of the more reliable is *Anguilla anguilla*, the eel. There is probably no fish which is more widespread and, pound for pound, it would be difficult to find one which could offer more resistance at the end of the line. The first eel I ever caught resembled a slimy entangled mess on the hook that was hell-bent on becoming more so and succeeded beyond comprehension.

Roach can bite well at night, even if they are very rarely sought then, being thought more of a daylight species. Yet I've made good catches of roach at night that far exceeded in size those I was accustomed to catching during the day. To be fair, it should be mentioned that my baits were invariably larger after dark, which undoubtedly had some bearing on results.

Bream of course are synonymous with night fishing, a time when the best catches of all are inevitably made. Indeed, some bream anglers will not fish at any other time, and normally I would agree with them, although there's always the exception which makes one think again. You'd be surprised at some of the freezing conditions in which I've found them prepared to feed, conditions which would have put even the chub down and out.

Carp were at one time considered to be largely a species of the night, but now seem to be taken just as regularly throughout the day. Nonetheless, most serious carp-fishers make their bid at night, at a time when the atmosphere is more befitting their own particular scene. For most, no other time will suffice, and who can condemn them for that? Carp fishing used to be an unenviable task – an impossible one, to some minds. Success was only to be had at night, if at all, but improvements in baits as well as in their presentation has reduced the 'uncatchable' status of the so-called wily carp.

Tench will respond to a bait very well in the dark and most of my better fish have come to net at the dead of night. Any time between midnight and four in the morning appears to be the peak period on my water, although that mightn't apply to your own. Contacting odd fish rather than a shoal is the norm for me, but I don't generally expect to encounter an actual shoal of good fish in any case, no matter what the species. Tench fishing holds for me much of the appeal of carp fishing and, occasionally, I hit into what I believe to be a very big tench and am informed in no time flat that it's a carp on the end of the line instead.

Pike are more active at night than most anglers would suppose, but what a daunting proposition they represent then. Most are more than a handful to deal with during the light of day, but the fact remains that I did catch my very first pike at night. It was only a small one and fell to a pellet of cheese paste meant for a chub, which I expect it grabbed while being wound in. Nevertheless some very big pike have been captured at night, in much the same way as they're taken during the day. I would suggest, however, that before venturing forth on a pike expedition during the hours of darkness, one becomes fully conversant with tackling them in daylight first. The battle is often fought more on the bank, to get the hooks out, than in the water, and if you have difficulty with this by day, then imagine how well you would cope in the dark. This is best left until you're able to manage better, for the benefit of the catch as well as yourself.

Chub appear to be happy to feed at almost any time, provided they're not spooked, which can be done all too easily. Personally, I think that chubbing on streams in particular calls for a lot more stealth than that required for many other species because, whether by day or night, the angler needs to approach them with infinite care. If he fails in that, he will lessen his chances considerably of

Chub like this trio mightn't be suspected of inhabiting a water, until tried for at night. What a different tale you'll have to tell then!

experiencing a delightfully taut line. Yet, however appreciative of the delicate approach, chub are sometimes not in the least bit shy when it comes to taking the bait – just like a barbel might, when in the mood, pull the rod-top right round and the rod also, if allowed to. I have found them so often in this mood I've almost come to accept it as second nature to them.

But what of the barbel at night? Dick Walker once said that in his experience barbel tended to feed well as dusk approached, then eased off noticeably at nightfall. He also suggested that this could simply mean that the fish had moved on, rather than stopped feeding, or that eels and chub had moved into the feeding area to get at the bait first. Whatever the case, it cannot be disputed that barbel feed well at night, on rivers that permit fishing then. Those that don't must have a question mark against them, for the simple reason that we have no way of knowing exactly how they would perform after dark. We can merely conjecture about such things, about the quality of the water and all we have learned about the species concerned. For instance, although we are sure that barbel feed at night, we also know perfectly well they'll feed just as well during the day, given the chance, so who's to say they wouldn't in fact prefer to feed then? As things stand I guess it all depends upon the water you're fishing and the rules that apply to the same. A more pertinent look at each species in turn will come later.

The Night Angler's Armoury

With respect to tackle, one might be expected to be more precise in its use at night, although that same rod and reel which has served you faithfully throughout any number of daytime sorties, shouldn't necessarily require replacing at night, unless of course there is a very good reason for this. One that comes rudely to mind concerns the situation in which I have found myself often (and to my discredit still do) and that's when I am trying to put a bait out to some distance with inadequate casting weight when fishing beneath the branches of a tree.

An overhead cast might offer my one chance of succeeding – especially with a totally lead-free line, which can be handled well enough in the light of day. Attempt the same manoeuvre in the dark, and you'll be surprised at how often the branches of that damned tree grow to get in your way. With all the experience in the world, this can continue to happen and the only satisfactory way I personally have managed to get the better of those tangled masses of foliage above my head is either to get on my knees to cast (not recommended in wet weather) or turn to a shorter rod, that permits me to cast overhead with mere inches to spare from that entangling, encroaching green umbrella. Think Green? That's about the only time I could describe it in unprintable terms!

So there are occasions when, for one very specific reason or another, a different rod might be advisable for night fishing. An increase in the size of baits used might be a case in point, for while some rods are quite capable of setting a small hook carrying a couple of maggots into a fish, those same rods may be left sadly wanting to achieve as much with a larger hook loaded with lobworms.

This much I was reminded of when visiting a weirpool at night. My intention was to fish while my friends had a drink in a nearby riverside pub. Thinking they'd be at most an hour or two, I took along a very light chub rod. This soon took on an agreeable curve, as

Take time to mull over your options. What are the possibilities on offer? What is the layout of the land? This angler has arrived at the water in plenty of time to do just that.

one small chub after another found its way to the net. Then the chub stopped feeding, as they tended to here quite early, just after dark in fact, and there was I willing the odd one to keep me busy while equally willing the return of my 'lost' friends, neither of which succumbed to my wishes.

Desperate to kill time while waiting, in weather that had now turned decidedly chilly, I tied on a larger hook to take one of the few big lobworms I had with me and was soon striking at a mighty pull. Barbel, most likely, I thought, which are rarely if ever seen on this stretch of water during the day but make their presence felt regularly at night. My strike had been spot on, and yet I didn't feel a thing. The same must be said of the next strike and the next. Indeed, this frustrating business was to continue until I was right out of bait. Not a fish did I feel on the end for more than a second or two, by which time I had concluded that the rod used simply lacked the power in the tip to set the larger hook firmly into the fish. In other words, my tackle was now inadequately balanced; for once in my life I was glad to leave the water behind me the moment my friends did at last materialise, albeit the worse for drink.

In circumstances such as that above, we have no option but to try and muddle through as best as we can, but it's not to be recommended. Normally I try to be prepared for whatever might confront me. There isn't likely to be much in the way of the unexpected on the waters I know well and fish regularly at night, but when venturing forth into the completely unknown, I am (I hope) ready for any eventuality. Should that fail to be the case, then I make doubly sure that I am ready with a vengeance the second time around, although by that time something else might have developed to stop me in my tracks. But eventually I anticipate reaching my goal, by one path or another, and if I don't, I can at least console myself in the knowledge that nobody at all is capable of winning them all, so why should I be any different? It saves me from going insane at least . . .

On the question of line, I'm bound to say that I rarely change its strength from day to night, although some have mixed feelings about this, being undecided about whether or not they ought to select a stronger line at night, seeing as how the fish are less likely to detect it then. I'm of the opinion that unless the angler is competent as well as confident with the line he regularly fishes with during the day, then he really should consider stepping it up in strength a little at night. There are several reasons for this, one being that bigger fish do tend to put in an appearance after dark, and therefore have to be catered for.

Another is that bringing a fish to net in the dark can present quite a problem initially, especially if that fish just happens to be a big'un. Any escape route on offer will then be sought by the catch on the end of the line, hell-bent on gaining whatever sanctuary it can to mock one's so-called expertise. It'll succeed, too, unless handled with extreme care. Side strain is brought into play when the need arises, to turn the fish away from any danger zones present, and that calls for sound tackle and line, as well as a clear precise mind, without which the fish will attain its goal and break you, to be left with a hook in its jaw and perhaps trailing behind it many metres of line. This is turn could entangle debris on the bottom to cause the demise of a mighty fish. Far better to be a bit on the heavy side than a fraction too light; at least you'll have a clear conscience. Most brands of line with a familiar label can be relied upon. If not, they'd have gone out of business long ago. Experienced anglers also use a finer and more supple hook link, these days, which they swear induces the fish to bite in a more positive manner, as well as lessening the chances of a bite-off. This does occur at times when tying the hook directly to the monofilament reel line. But moving on to 'soft' hook links can be pretty advanced stuff, until you're familiar with those available. It is better left, perhaps, until more important issues have been satisfactorily dealt with, such as tackling a hooked fish in the dark in the first place. The time for a more refined approach must necessarily come later.

Tactics by Moonlight

As we've just seen, our gear need not necessarily vary in the least at night from that which we habitually use during the day. The same can be said of techniques, dispelling at a single stroke, I hope, any notion entertained to the contrary. Angling methods and techniques can become very personal – almost sacrificial to some, myself included. Only rarely have I been swayed away from the ledger since adopting the method more than half a century ago, although I have during that time varied my terminal tackle often to keep abreast of any new developments taking place. I still do, when changes are called for, because as much as I prefer to fish with no lead at all on the line, it is a means to a very limited end, being ideally suited for the better part to perfectly still, or at most, very sluggish water, a situation which doesn't usually demand the weight of a sinker to take the bait to the bottom and hold it there fast.

As it happens, we don't always want the bait to remain stationary on the river bed, irrespective of how rapid the flow, and when conditions allow for it I'll attempt to free-line a bait even in the wrath of a weirpool. But it would need to be a very shallow one for the unweighted bait to touch bottom before being swept away, so that it can start to trickle attractively along the bottom to tempt any fish within the immediate vicinity.

There, then, is how I prefer to fish a weir during the day or night, and it's surprising just how often I can manage to do so without seriously impeding the outcome of the session. It must be stressed, nevertheless, that the more conversant an angler is with the many different tactics on call, so the more successful he must inevitably become, because the technique that is exactly right for all manner of angling situations has yet to evolve!

It is indeed perplexing that so many anglers appear to think otherwise, and do not vary their approach in the least in the face of widely different conditions. Perhaps they know something I don't, although

I sincerely doubt that. The more factual answer is likely to be that they're so accustomed to fishing in one familiar style that the idea of changing never enters their heads. They are in a rut, to put it bluntly, incapable of thinking beyond their link-ledger, paternoster or whatever; but that is their loss. Hopefully, they will come to realise in time that while their chosen technique may indeed be ideal in some circumstances, it can never ever meet the demands of them all. This is why we must be well versed in all manner of ledgering techniques and, what's more, be versatile in their use.

Having gone to some length in an effort to register that vital point, I can now confirm that usually whatever techniques work well enough during the day on a given water will probably work just as well, if not better, at night. This is true provided conditions remain the same. Should they change, as they're apt to after dark, if only by the force of the wind, which is generally more accommodating at night, then alterations to the terminal end of the gear may have to be made.

The tail leading to the hook may have to be varied in length, or, failing that, a smaller or larger lead used. A hitherto stationary bait might now be better rolled, or even paternostered, to lift it just a fraction off the river bed. Any one of a multitude of minor changes to the rig can transform what was initially destined to be a dull and unexciting non-event into a memorable action-packed encounter with the fish instead.

Therefore, don't be too hasty to wet a line that may well remain limp right through the night, without further thought to its business end. Take time out to mull over your options, the possibilities on offer, and the layout of the land. Then, and only then, should you proceed to tackle up, having acquired more idea of the manner of bait presentation that will succeed, be it a rolling ledger or a straight, stationary one; a link-ledger or paternoster, a feeder, or indeed a totally free line approach – the decision is yours alone to make.

There was a time when the aim of most thinking anglers was to fish their bottom rigs as light as was feasibly possible, in an attempt to reduce drag, which is how leadless line fishing came into being. It would seem now, however, that a new school of thought has pretty much abandoned that idea, insisting instead upon the adoption of unusually heavy leads. The thinking behind this suggests that while a taking fish may well shift a lighter sinker, and in so doing detect its drag, a more firmly anchored lead would stay put as the fish stole line through it without theoretically feeling a thing. Personally, I much prefer to fish with as little lead on the line (safe-lead, naturally) as I can reasonably get away with, disliking intensely an over-burdened business end, which in turn calls for a heavier approach all round. But each to his own, I suppose.

What I particularly like about free line fishing is the total absence of any resistance a fish just might feel, a very important plus, as far as I'm concerned, that's not to be overlooked. Bites, when they come to a lead-free presentation, are almost invariably registered without hesitation and appear to be greater in number. Hooked fish also tend to give a better account of themselves when no lead is on the line to dull proceedings, all of which encourages me to adopt these tactics whenever I can. But they are not, as I have already stated, suitable for all conditions – no rig is.

It is not my intention to describe the various ledger rigs in detail here, having taken the liberty of assuming that my audience will have already acquired as much, if not perhaps the inclination to ring the changes with them. I can only hope to inspire those still lagging behind to mend their ways, after which they'll learn in no time at all that having the ability to adapt when fishing can go a long, long way in terms of keeping the rod bent, the line tight and the landing net agreeably wet.

Baits and their Presentation

While tactics and gear may be similar, the night fisher's actual approach will vary from that of the daytime angler in many respects. Much will of course depend on the kind of water to be fished, the conditions encountered and the species sought. Bait presentation is also a deciding factor, because there's scant progress to be made by attempting to put out a couple of maggots on an unweighted line, for instance. It would have the angler concerned pulling his hair out in wicked frustration. You don't believe me? Why then do so many anglers go prematurely bald?

Happily, for those who enjoy freelining to the extent that I do, baits at night do tend to be larger, to allow them to be cast farther without sinkers. But that's quite incidental. Of greater interest is the keen sense of smell that a fish will have to depend upon, now that any visual contact with the bait on the bottom must be seriously impaired. So don't shy away from having a lobworm or two on the hook at night; a bigger helping than normal of breadpaste or flake; four grains of sweetcorn or a piece of luncheon meat big enough to require a size 4 hook to keep it firmly in place.

Such ample offerings may be avoided by the fish with the greatest of care during the cold light of day; but fish will often take them without a care in the world at night. That, seemingly, is down to the fish growing more secure and dropping their guard as darkness approaches, encouraging them to venture forth in search of a meal. Consequently they will feed in earnest, and take a bait with enough confidence to convince the angler that he was wise to be here at this time, in order to take full advantage of the transformation taking place beneath the surface of the water at his feet. Indeed, once accustomed to it, he'll lean more and more heavily on night fishing.

He shouldn't be fooled into thinking that his approach need be anything but discreet, now that the fish he seeks appear to be more obliging. The same rules apply equally at night as they do during the day in respect to putting the fish at their ease; indeed, taking into account the fact that often they will be nearer the bank at night and therefore in a better position to detect the angler's presence, even though they are less likely to spot him, they sure as hell will feel any vibrations he creates on the bank, a point to keep constantly in mind.

Remember also to keep your baits out of harm's way, where they won't be trodden underfoot as you go about your fishing, for this can easily happen in the dark. Bear in mind also, that that same bait can become just as easily tainted with undesirable scents at night, so be sure to wash your hands after messing about with insect spray and the like. Otherwise you'll contaminate your baits, and go throughout the night without a touch, making you turn your back on the very idea of angling in the dark for evermore.

The actual choice of baits will, as mentioned earlier, be dictated largely by the species sought, although the conditions fished will to a lesser degree add their influence also. There would be little sense in trying to keep a soft bait on the hook in a raging weirpool when it would be more at home on a placid duck pond, for instance; but so obvious are conclusions like this, they scarcely warrant a mention, being better left to the angler to arrive at himself. Generally speaking, however, the baits that work during the day will also work at night – with far better results.

A few observations I have made over the years may be helpful. When fishing with corn, I always empty the contents of the entire can into my Drennan mixing bowl, then drain off some of the liquid, leaving the remainder to keep the corn moist and fresh while adding the surplus to the groundbait or using it as a dip for the hook-bait. By the time I've catapulted the free feed in there's just enough corn left for hook baits to see me through the night, but it makes good sense to work up a swim in this fashion, as opposed to the antics of some I know, who seem to be rather reticent when it comes to free-feeding and yet dump by far the biggest bulk of their corn into the water at the *end* of the session, when it can do their sport the least good.

It is far better to introduce more feed at the very beginning of the session. The exact amount will vary a great deal, from a mere can on some waters, to several on others, making bulk buying a wise move. Catering-sized cans of corn are what some anglers use, while others can never unearth them. Bags of frozen pre-cooked corn tend to work out cheaper than tins. You might suppose that they could be used straight from the packet without further preparation, but I prefer to bring the contents to the boil as the instructions suggest, since I believe this enhances the taste and – more important – the smell.

How much to bait the swim with is anybody's guess on a strange water. Fish it a few times, and results will speak for themselves. On the waters where I fish for tench, a couple of normal-sized cans of corn are usually sufficient – perhaps even one – but this is a decision the angler will have to come to himself by trial and error, having fished the water a few times, the deciding factors involved being influenced by many individual things, some of which are so peculiar to a particular water that they're known only to those familiar with it.

On a more basic level, a single can of corn introduced to a well stocked carp lake would be but a drop in the ocean reaching only a few of the inhabitants; the vast majority would obtain not so much as a sniff of it. The same applies whatever the attractor may be, even one which is feeder proffered.

Feeder fishing mightn't be advisable for those out on the water for the first time at night, because to work proficiently, accurate casting is consistently called for to deposit the contents of the feeder into a very confined space. This is an unenviable task, for anyone inexperienced in meeting such stringent demands in the dark. But should the angler feel at home with this method, and have the kind of confidence required to use it efficiently at night, then he ought to be encouraged to try.

There's nothing I can add further to the subject of feeding the swim or groundbaiting here, other than that in my experience it usually pays dividends to put in more rather than less at night, if for no other reason than that more fish are likely to feed then and will need enticing to continue to keep their heads down.

Don't forget that they'll be accustomed to eating whatever the night brings them. Large slimy slugs, for example, are relished in common with the worm by all manner of fish (with the notable exception of perch, I find, which aren't truly nocturnal in any case). I also found when first attempting to fish with slugs that the main problem wasn't getting them on the hooks, but keeping them long enough to put there, for like Harry Houdini they would flee the coop, until I discovered that if some grass was put in the can with them they no longer felt a need to slither free. Not that I often use slugs now; I am tempted, repeatedly, but suspect I'm going soft in my old age, because try as I may I can no longer terminate a slug's midnight saunter at the water's edge by putting it on a hook.

Preparing for the Scene of Battle

Safety and comfort – those are the two main objectives to be strived for by those about to cast a line in anger for the very first time at night. While the latter may have to be forsaken at times, the angler should never ever put himself at bodily risk. Currents and the depth of water can be very deceptive at night, as can the firmness of banks. All of these should be checked out when first arriving at the projected scene of the exercise.

It is imperative to reach the water long before darkness descends, not only to familiarise yourself with your surroundings but also to get organised and be actually fishing while it's still light. Indeed, you could do far worse than centre your first attempt at this game on a water you already know well, and even a pitch you know well. This will alleviate much of the uncertainty of functioning in the dark, although it must be said that even familiar ground will seem strange at night. But at least you'll know from your previous daylight visits to the water how deep it is, how fast, and where the bulk of the snags lie.

It is also advisable to share the experience of an initial nocturnal stint with others of a like mind. For is there not safety in numbers? There is, and blessed reassurance as well, particularly if just one of that number has been this way before. He'll know what to expect, what to look out for and, more important to you of course, what time the fish are likely to come on the feed. However, alone or not, be there in plenty of time to set the scene.

This much I always insist upon, although in reality things don't always go as planned. I'm then faced with the dubious task of not only having to tackle up in the dark, which is bad enough, even for an old hand like me, but also having to guess, rather than know positively, the speed and course of the flow on rivers, or the whereabouts of floating weed and the like on lakes. These details are essential if I'm to be in with a good chance of catching – or bagging up, as those with less soul would put it.

Remember also that the last hour or so of twilight can be very productive, which gives us another reason for setting up our stall early, with baits out in anticipation of what may well turn out to be the most action-packed period of the entire overnight session. And, since it is to be overnight, you'll be in a position to take full advantage of the twilight hours, while the day-trippers will have been long gone. Add to that the fact that your baits will be out in the water at first light also, which on some still waters is a most desirable time to fish, and you will then perhaps begin to understand why I and so many like me are drawn to the water's edge when the majority of anglers are deep in slumber. But that's to their disadvantage, for what more could an angler possibly wish for than to be at his post for the duration of his quarry's feeding time, whether at twilight, throughout the night or at the crack of dawn? There's nothing I can think of other than more of the same.

All being well, then, you've arrived in plenty of time, so take stock of your surroundings before you do anything else. Check that depth and those waterside banks and, if you've any misgivings about either then move on to another swim. If you're groundbaiting or loose feeding then get the bulk of that in now, providing there's no smallfry present to mop it all up before night falls. In this case you'd be better advised to wait until then, topping up occasionally perhaps as the session gets underway. In the meantime the entire situation can be assessed and acted on, with the gear made ready while there is still plenty of light to see by. The keepnet (if you must use one) is pegged out in a position where it won't create problems during the night; there is nothing worse than losing a good fish because it fell foul of the net. Choose a spot that has a good depth and some shelter away from where you are actually fishing. This will prevent any fish held captive from becoming alarmed by your continued presence.

Ideally, everything should have a place and be in its place long before nightfall. Torches, for instance should be put within easy reach, as should all the other paraphernalia required, and if you thought you were overburdened on day trips then don't you believe it! Items other than tackle and bait are required at night, and if you're that fussed about being weighed down unduly by gear then I suggest you restrict your chosen swim to within a minimal walking distance from the car. Don't expect to catch too much then, however; swims within the vicinity of car parks are notorious for blanks.

Rod supports are set firmly into the ground – under the weight of a mallet, if necessary, despite the disturbance and the contrary feelings of others about such things. A bit of commotion now may well save you a lot of aggravation later, when the rod rests start to wobble and finally fall just as a good fish takes. I use Clip Base rod rests now, put out by Clip Products. These are especially good when regular rod rests can't be put into the ground, when fishing concrete aprons and such like. A mat of some kind is placed beneath the rods to ensure that nothing will tangle the bobbins or lines, and naturally, the landing net is made ready for use and laid in a handy position where it won't become entangled in the undergrowth. At this point I'm inclined to make a brew.

It's as well to get the brolly or bivvy up first though, just in case it rains; you'll then have at least a bit of dry ground to sit on, or dare I say lie on? Being warm and cosy when the fish aren't biting is a necessary part of the entire operation, as far as I'm concerned, however long it took me to come to such a happy conclusion. Simply to lie listening to the drum-beat of the rain on the roof of the bivvy is reward enough for having taken it along, for what a wonderful sense of well-being that brings me. Words cannot describe it adequately.

If he is wise, our would-be nightstalker will by now have also had the foresight to prevent himself being eaten alive by insects during the night, because it is most unpleasant to discover at dawn that you're covered in bites from the wretched mites, as I have learned to my cost. So take steps to prevent this by applying to yourself some kind of insect repellent (especially to your wrists, ankles and neck) to ensure that all the bites you do get actually come from the fish.

Having done all this, get the unhooking mat ready, and the weighing bag and the scales. Make sure the food is suitably protected from insects, and do whatever else is remaining to make your overnight stay a successful and memorable one. You can now take time out to gather your thoughts; take in the atmosphere about you. Hopefully, also, you've chosen well weatherwise.

A clear, star-studded sky is the kind that songs are written about, and young lovers rave about. In reality it often heralds a cold night, however attractive to the eye. A bright moonlit night doesn't help much either; in my experience it tends to encourage the fish to forsake baits on the bottom in favour of tasty morsels on the top, because they will be silhouetted for easy picking by the light of the moon.

A so-called leaden sky is better by far for our purpose and more inclined to induce the fish to feed. In such conditions I have often sat in shirtsleeves, and I have not been in the least cold, but we can't always have it like that. Snowflakes rather than delightful snowdrops have been at my feet before now when fishing at night. Only a brave man or fool would venture forth with too much dependence on the weather, and not a thing in his bag to combat it should it turn bad.

Lights at Night

Apart from warm clothing, which will be discussed later, it is most desirable to have some kind of light when fishing at night, even though it has been said that if you are truly dedicated to following your sport in the dark then you should do it completely without lights. What is to be gained by this owl-like existence I fail to see. Neither would I attempt such a feat myself because frankly, I see absolutely no point in it, despite the fact that it has been argued that lights at night ruin the entire concept of what angling in the dark is meant to be about. I agree, within reason – when the angler surrounds himself with excessive illumination for example. I do speak from experience here, having through various stages of my angling career progressed from a candle in a jar to a pressure lamp and back again to a nightlight in a jar and finally to a betalight on the line in front of the reel or at the tip of the rod.

Recently, when night fishing a particular stretch of the lower Thames for the first time in twenty-five years, I had cause enough to ponder the issue of lights again – for here, I was appalled to learn, time had stood still. To say I was dismayed at the number of pressure lamps burning brightly at the water's edge would be an understatement. I was horrified! I had in my innocence assumed that the means of detecting bites at night here had progressed to the more acceptable level that it had elsewhere, yet this wasn't the case. But why not, I wondered, when one could simply attach at least a Starlite to one's tip? It made no sense at all to me, especially since I learned that Starlites were in use – and lamps by which to see them better!

Thirty years must have elapsed since I last used a pressure lamp, when after winter barbel on the Thames. The drill then was to sit in the car supping coffee while waiting for the rod top to power over, a movement which was easy to spot in the glare of the lamp, then more commonly known as a Tilly. Sadly, the entire surrounding countryside was illuminated by that same glare, which did have something of a disturbing effect upon not only myself but my companions. They later – quite unfairly, I thought – christened me with the nickname of 'Tilly' Wood. I then rather reluctantly came to the conclusion that my trusty Tilly must go.

Betalights being still in their infancy, a twist of tin-foil around the rod tip to be spotted with a penlight replaced the Tilly very successfully. Even now, when taken short, so to speak, I am not above using this means of detecting bites at night. Indeed, against a clear or moonlit sky it can be seen quite adequately without any kind of artificial illumination whatsoever and certainly beats being blinded by a Tilly.

We do need to know when a fish takes in the dark, however; there's no question about that, and while some are content enough to rely entirely on their electronic buzzers to tell them as much, I am not – but more about that later. We require some kind of light to bait-up with, to tie on hooks with, untangle knots with, and that's to mention just a few of the more obvious reasons. Imagine trying to net a big eel in the dark without the aid of a light. The very idea leaves me speechless. So, disregarding the need to see bites, there's reason enough to take along a fairly powerful torch when you're fishing on the night shift, and to be on the safe side I'm in the habit of putting more than one in my bag.

I guess the tiny clip-on torch that takes a couple of 5V batteries is the one I use most, because the light it throws out is just enough for most of my needs without stealing from me my vital night vision, which comes into effect shortly after dark. I use the clip-on torch for baiting up and such things. For netting fish I now use a headlamp, leaving my hands free to deal with more important issues, like holding the rod steady with one while the other brings the landing net into play. I also have a powerful flashlight, which fortunately rarely leaves my bag. It's reassuring to know it's there however, charged and ready to deal with any emergency that might occur.

All my batteries are of the rechargeable kind and I wouldn't be without them, irrespective of how costly to purchase in the first place. They pay for themselves in just a few sessions; they can be recharged a thousand times, as the promotional literature describing them claims, are completely reliable and have never yet failed me. Contrary to popular belief, rechargeable batteries do retain their power for a considerable time when not in use. Indeed, I've known them to travel by container ship from Australia and still be functioning to some degree on their arrival in the UK, and that's a journey of several months.

They do tend to die without as much warning as ordinary batteries (known as primaries, by the way, while rechargeables are called secondaries), but not before they can be changed, and to offset this slight disadvantage they produce a uniform power throughout, unlike the other kind which begin to lose their sparkle in no time and thenceforth grow steadily dimmer. My only fear with rechargeables is that one day I'll forget to put them on the charger, a catastrophe that hasn't happened yet.

Rechargeable torches are not to be sniffed at, either, and although I don't actually own one I do have access to several, and have therefore put them thoroughly to test. While one must be prudent in their use – unfortunately some don't last long if kept constantly burning – the power they produce is strong and unwavering. Without batteries to contend with they're also very lightweight; you simply plug them into the mains to recharge them.

On the stillwater scene I have until recent years been quite content to fish with a nightlight in a jar, often I suspect to the amusement of my friends, and if that indeed be the case then so what? To fish efficiently matters more to me.

Nightlights are inexpensive yet very efficient, throwing out just enough illumination to highlight the angler's bobbins and I do not hesitate in the least to recommend these, especially to the uninitiated. They will discover that, however feeble in terms of brightness, the glow from a single nightlight will be enough to transform what may well seem a rather daunting situation into a most welcoming one. In a jar painted black, with a strip left clear for the light to escape, a nightlight cannot be faulted: it'll last throughout most of a short midsummer's night and will continue to do its job well even in bad weather, and so unobtrusive is its glimmer that nobody could in all honesty object to it.

The Disturbing Influence of Lights

There was a time when many heated arguments took place in the angling press about the use of lights at night – some for and others against, as was to be expected – and there was I caught up in the fray. This led to some in-depth thinking on my part about the implications involved and I eventually came to the conclusion that much depended upon the actual site on which a light was to be used.

It began to dawn on me that in a situation where lights were permanently stationed, such as on a bridge crossing a river, the disturbance created by yet another appearing within close proximity to them was most probably negligible. The same would also apply to an area where a footpath running alongside the water was illuminated at regular intervals by lamp-posts at night, for the fish would surely have come to accept them as a natural part of their surroundings, and were hardly likely to be thrown into a panic by another appearing in their midst.

Now imagine the effect a single light may have on a water that is normally as black as a photographer's darkroom at night (and aren't most stillwaters like that?). The effect might well be instantaneous, putting the fish therein on their guard immediately and right off the very idea of feeding. I say *might* because I'm not completely convinced that would be the case. We've still a great deal to learn about this subject and what I personally have learned is to treat it with caution. It's been an interesting lesson, nursed along over many years in the hope that one day the final answer would emerge. It hasn't, although I have come to understand the possibilities revolving around it better, to assess them more openly and to accept them in so far as one can without becoming fully committed to them.

For instance, I'm now absolutely certain that while some species may be alarmed by the sudden appearance of a shaft of light, others will not. This much has been proven to my own satisfaction when out on the banks with a powerful flashlight at night in an attempt to study its effect on the fish. Trout have remained quite unperturbed by the concentration of its piercing beam, whereas perch, dace and gudgeon appeared to be mesmerised by it. Of the bigger coarse species I have learned little; the opportunity to do so has seldom if ever presented itself on the waters I fish at night. No matter how apparently conclusive my findings as to the smaller fish, I'm loath to accept anything in connection with fishing as final, simply because the species in the spotlight may well react quite differently on another occasion.

With that possibility in mind, we should resist throwing caution to the winds, and should approach our sport prudently at all times. The thoughtless use of torches may not be detrimental to it, but while there's the slightest suggestion that it could be, we'd be wiser to take heed. So refrain from bringing a torch into play when netting fish until the last possible moment, and ensure that it is held steady so as not to alarm further the fish on the hook, never mind the one you hope to catch next.

If adopting the use of a torch to spot bites then I suggest you do so without moving it unnecessarily. Try also to prevent its beam from penetrating the water because, whether or not it matters, there's no point in taking a chance. Always be on the safe side, and you can't possibly lose. Indeed, if we're to take this issue to its logical conclusion, then we would even avoid getting grass in front of the torch, in case the light appeared to flicker, as it surely would in the least breath of wind.

A flickering sensation of this kind must, I feel, have a worse effect on the fish than an unwavering one, allowing for the likelihood of there really being any effect, to our disadvantage or otherwise. Lights have been known to actually attract fish, rather than deter them, and for this very reason isotopes attached to lures are in some quarters becoming increasingly common. But if your intention isn't to attract them, then why chance scaring them away with your light?

I have also pondered in the past on how the fish might react to the flickering flames of a waterside bonfire; from a merely hypothetical slant of course, seeing that fires are now supposed to be generally banned, but that shouldn't stop us from thinking about such things. Fish behaviour is a recognised science – a complex one at that – and we as laymen are doing well if we only begin to understand it. By accumulating knowledge as we go along we can perhaps add to our overall understanding of it, be that knowledge relevant at the time or not. It will one day fall into place to give us a more exact picture of the species concerned and in so doing afford us a better chance of outwitting it.

So no would-be fact-finding forage into the unknown world of the fish is too trivial for me to pursue. I have always tried to delve deeply into the domain of the scaly breed in an attempt to dredge from its chasm whatever I can to unravel, in the hope of throwing more light upon it, and should that light come from an artificial source then so be it. No knowledge is bad knowledge, in my book. Even if knowledge is hastily gathered and proved to be incorrect, it still has some merit: that of informing me how wrong I probably was in my assertions.

Having said that much, I must now confess to entertaining fixed ideas of all kinds – what experienced angler doesn't? But being committed to them in no way changes the fact that I could on occasion be quite wrong. It is the comforting realisation of being right on more occasions than wrong that matters most of all to me, not the dogmatic attitude that I couldn't possibly ever be wrong.

Bite Detection at Night

Spotting bites at night is no longer the chancy business it used to be, when a dough bobbin on the line presented us with the only visual means of a take, and a bell pegged to the rod top the only audible warning. Both of these went out of existence long ago, replaced by more modern gadgets.

The electronic buzzer has replaced the bell, and monkey-climbers have long been the *in* thing for visual detection, although not for everyone I'm relieved to say. We then have betalights of varying power and, last but by no means least, the Starlite, which as most anglers will know is a disposable betalight, in a sense, which is activated by bending between forefinger and thumb, after which it will continue to glow brightly (too brightly in the opinion of some, with whom I am bound to agree) for the duration of the entire night. Starlites are available from most tackle dealers, and now a mini form, which is said to last for approximately four hours and comes two to a packet, is becoming more widely available. They can be had for either ledger or float fishing, the former being attached to the tip of the rod by sticky tape and the latter to the float by a sleeve.

BETALIGHTS

Betalights – or isotopes, as they're sometimes referred to in more refined quarters – are slender tubes containing radioactive tritium gas which is said to have a life expectancy of twenty or even thirty years, during which time it will continue to glow, and therefore be of service throughout those years. It takes little imagination then to appreciate what a terrific buy betalights are, given that they're only several times the price of a Starlite, which is limited in use, remember, to a single solitary night. Multiply by thirty years what a Starlite every night would cost you and the figure would be astronomical, believe me, making it a better bet by far to begin with betalights in the first place. They'll be much cheaper than Starlites in the long run and you'll be quids in.

The power of these light sources varies, from very feeble to brilliant, and while the weaker versions do retain some credibility when used in conjunction with butt bobbins, I find they're of little use for attaching to the tip of the rod. Those with more power (500 microlamberts for example) fulfil this requirement admirably, although much will depend on their angle in relation to the user's eye and also on the density of the night. They're light in weight and can be taped to the tip in a jiffy, although I would suggest they're affixed to the rod before the line is run through the rings, otherwise you'll be frustrated to learn at this juncture that not only have you taped the betalight to the rod but the line also.

Of course, should your rod have a thread at the top to take a swingtip or such then a special fitting can be obtained to screw into this thread to which a betalight is attached via rubber tubing, allowing it to be placed more securely and in a better position on the rod altogether, which is at the extremity of its tip.

Having recently come by some extraordinarily powerful betalights (750s) I am saddened by the fact that because they're a mite thicker in the body than most, I haven't as yet managed to mate them successfully to the fitting mentioned above and am for the time being at least left with no alternative that I can see other than to tape them to my rod tips, but doubtless I'll stumble on a better way shortly.

The betalights in question reached me initially encased in a transparent bobbin with a heavy clip attached by which they were intended to hang from the line in the old Glow Bobbin fashion. Now as it happens, I'm most fastidiously fussy about such things, striving forever towards lighter bobbins, and these were of little use to me in their original form, being far too bulky and heavy in my view, so I retrieved the light source from inside and found they suited my needs better.

BOBBINS

Unlike the above mentioned rod-top isotopes, which are largely restricted to fishing running water at night, bobbins, be they monkey-climbers or whatever, are more generally at home on the stillwater scene, since the conditions in which bites are to be detected here are vastly different. Monkey-climbers, so called because of their ability to climb like a monkey up a stick when a fish takes (although in reality the stick is a metal needle), are very popular, and not without good reason, since on the surface at least they appear to be totally foolproof. In my opinion, however, they're anything but foolproof, being of an inflexible nature, to the point where their rigidity and restrictiveness could well offer a degree of resistance to a taking fish, unless it be a real whopper. Attempting to rid my approach of all resistance has been a hobby horse of mine for years.

Therefore I tend to shun monkey-climbers completely, in favour of ultra-light bobbins of my own design. These are fashioned from balsa, weigh about as much as a maggot and work wonderfully well in practice – just look at them go! Indeed, while others complain of tremors, twitches, or half-hearted knocks and pulls at the line, I can cross my heart and hope to die if I'm telling a fib when I say that only rarely if ever am I plagued by silly games like that from the fish. In fact, so light are my bobbins they're more inclined to react to a take by hitting the rod with a thud before I've time to respond, so perhaps they're a little over sensitive. Better that, however, than to sit through the night hoping, praying, and willing a bobbin to do more than just hang there on the line with little more than a flutter to get the old adrenalin pumping through the veins.

A short length of 12 amp fuse wire is passed through my bobbins; this is shaped into a hook at one end to hang on the line while the other end is twisted to form a ring to which a length of light thread is attached. The other end of the thread is secured to the back rod rest or by a drawing pin to a piece of heavy wood on the ground, placed beneath the natural drop of the bobbin just in front of the reel.

What happens then in effect is when a fish takes and I strike, the bobbin comes to the end of its tether, at which point the wire hook opens without effort, being so feeble, and the bobbin, still attached to the thread, falls out of harm's way to the ground, where it will remain secured until required again, while I in the meantime can let battle commence. Now, I ask you, what can be simpler than that?

Given a coat of brilliant white paint and then one of clear varnish to keep out the rain, these are easily seen in the faltering flame of a nightlight without the least strain on the eyes, although with a betalight attached even this means of illumination becomes redundant. And, being always on the lookout for ways to reduce the drag that a taking fish might detect, I now use the isotopes themselves as bobbins, encased in a short length of a Peter Drennan Crystal float of around 30mm (sorry for plundering your floats, Peter, but for this purpose there are none better!).

The fuse wire and thread used to tether the balsa bobbins are used here in much the same way, and should I need to add weight, which is very rarely the case, then a small split-shot or two can be pushed into the base of the Drennan casing. These 'mini' bobbins, as can be imagined, offer the very minimum of resistance to the fish, resulting in almost every take being a so-called flier, but care must be taken to ensure that nothing entangles the thread trailing from them to spook the fish on the take. It's as well also to make certain that the thread doesn't become waterlogged, to add to its weight, but a whisper of varnish will again take care of that.

ELECTRONIC BUZZERS

Where on earth would most anglers be without them! Night or day, on lake, river or stream we find buzzers, the only mystery to me being that some clown hasn't as yet adapted a buzzer for fly fishing or even spinning – but somebody, somewhere, is undoubtedly working on it! I have, incidentally, been accused of having a dislike of buzzers, which couldn't be further from the truth. What I do have an intense dislike of is automatic fishing, whereby the angler travels the same road irrespective of where he's going, or what for, and nothing these days appears to be more automatic than setting up the buzzers, whether they're needed or not.

A few seasons back I deliberately left my buzzers at home – and what a fantastically exhilarating experience I had, witnessing my bobbins springing into life without the least forewarning of a stuttering buzzer. No, I can't say it helped my fishing at all, modern buzzers being too advanced for that, but without them I did appreciate my fishing more. The air of expectancy was greater and more profound, while at the same time there was the uncertainty of whether I could react quickly enough to runs without the sound of the buzzer urging me into action. In a sense, then, I was forced to develop a keener edge to connect with those takes, which were seen rather than heard. The visual aspect of a take leaves any audible warning stone dead in its tracks, in terms of excitement, which is why I persevered without buzzers for a considerable length of time, returning to them again only when I'd proved to myself that I could if necessary manage well enough without them. Therein perhaps lies the reason why some anglers prefer to do their thing in total darkness: simply to prove as much.

'Big deal,' some might say. 'Where's the sense in making a difficult job even harder?' There's no sense at all, as far as I'm concerned, other than one of deep satisfaction, for it is indeed very satisfying to be trying something different and succeeding. It adds a bit of variety to the sport and prevents the thinking angler from becoming an automatic one. That's no excuse to prolong such indulgence, however. If lights or buzzers befit one better for angling at night – and they most assuredly do – then I'd be doing a disservice to my readers by suggesting otherwise.

Generally speaking buzzers are a great asset, provided we remain the master and not a slave to them. I never, for instance, use a buzzer on running water, preferring to either feel for bites in the touch ledger mode or watch the rod top for them, but on lakes, gravel pits and such like I'm as keen to use my buzzers as anyone else, normally, but do feel a need to give them a miss occasionally for the reasons outlined above.

While they're not exactly indispensable to the night fisher, the use of buzzers is definitely advised. They relieve him of much of the monotony involved in watching bobbins that at times never seem to move except in the imagination. We have all seen them in triplicate in the middle of the night, at which time we tend to think that enough is enough and promptly get our heads down.

Buzzers, like the train, take a good deal of the strain. They allow us to relax far more than we possibly could without them and the fish I've caught upon hearing them bleating while making a brew in the night are many indeed, some of which were bound to have been missed, as my attention was focused elsewhere. They also give us leave to enjoy our surroundings more, to drink in the atmosphere more, and slip into deep meditation as we sit alone in the dark with our thoughts, confident in the knowledge that should a fish decide to bite at this inopportune moment then our box of electronic wizardry will let us know as much. The rest is up to us, of course, and our ability to reach out for reality again in time to make a successful connection. The strike can then be fumbled and the fish lost, but that's the price paid when using a buzzer. Imagine the challenge of trying to cope without one: the price for many I fear would then be a sight higher.

Like most things, you get what you pay for and this is particularly true of buzzers, which come in many designs, the most popular, and arguably the best of them all, being the Optonic. When it comes to reliability they appear to be impossible to better.

THE AITONOLITE

The Aitonolite is a new invention awaiting the test of time to decide whether or not it is here to stay. It is different from the usual night bite detector in that the LED light is uncommonly bright, being seen from a distance of a quarter of a mile away, which gives ample warning of your presence to any approaching boats. Some anglers might consider this is far too bright, and the gadget perhaps a little heavy for the lighter rods, the balance of which it might disturb. It is an innovative creation however and deserves to do well. The Aitonolite, named after its inventor Mr J. Aiton, consists of an ABS plastic body containing two 1½V watch batteries (hence its brightness), and is screwed into the tip of the rod via a swingtip thread.

OTHER DETECTORS

A few additions to the more obvious bite indicators above should be mentioned because they are in their own right worthy of as much. The strip of tin-foil at the rod-tip referred to in a previous chapter, for instance, can also be fashioned into a tube and used as a bite indicator with great success, especially since it can be heard rustling through the grass when taken.

Another trick is to fold a short strip of tin-foil over the line just in front of the reel and anchor it lightly to the ground by a coin. When a run occurs, the indicator is whipped free of the coin to climb up to the first runner or ring. This device is a great boon in windy weather. If it is rested on an upturned Drennan mixing tray, it will make an easily discernible 'plop' in the quiet of the night as the coin is lifted by the line and then drops back on the tray again.

A light twig with tin-foil wrapped around at the tip and placed on the line in front of the reel will again let you know when a fish takes, because it will be thrown to one side. Obviously it's a good move to keep a little tin-foil permanently in your tackle box or bag. Space prevents me from mentioning other do-it-yourself detectors, with the exception of one I simply must include if only to show how desperate the night angler can get at times.

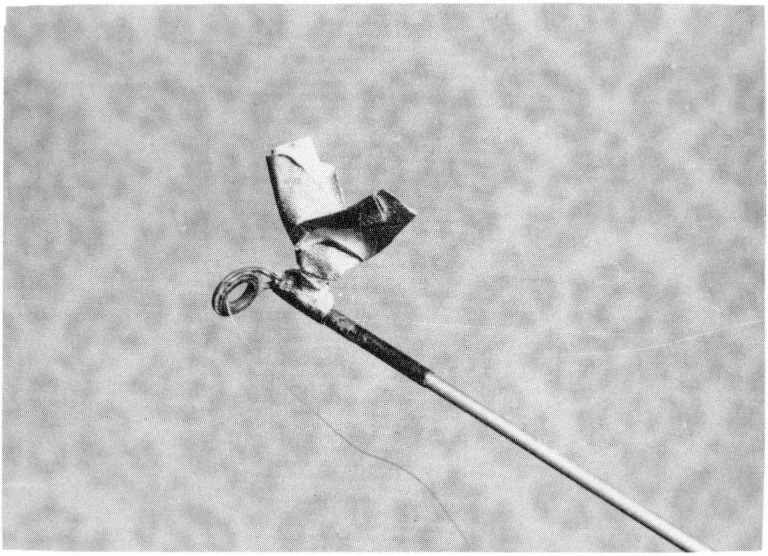

A twist of tin-foil around the rod top offers the nightstalker a very visible means of spotting a bite.

I was scarcely fifteen years of age when fishing a pond on a London common at night on my own and the target fish were tench; a species which, try as I might, had so far eluded me completely. Determined to put an end to this sad state of affairs at the earliest opportunity I had what was to me at the time the unique and brilliant idea of attaching a tea defuser to my line, which when laid several yards from the reel on the concrete path surrounding the pond, would rattle noisily over it if pulled by a fish. The trick worked a treat; the sad end to this sorry tale being that I was fast asleep when my bite came and too confused to react to it before my dubious detector came smack up against the rod to scare off whatever had taken the bait. I did think I deserved ten out of ten for effort, though.

Working a Float in the Dark

Fishing with a float at night was at one time practised far more widely than it is today. How exciting it was to see the float dither in the beam of the torch, then slide right out of its arc! It was a difficult task to spotlight the float in running water, for it would forever be creeping downstream into total blackness. Therefore, the method was more at home on a still or sluggish swim that allowed for a more relaxed float on the surface – and a fixed light that could pin-point it without the need for constant adjustment.

This was at a time prior to the invention of any worthwhile means of detecting bites at night, so the deployment of torch-light offered the one real hope for the float angler to continue fishing after dark. It was also during a period when float fishing was far more popular than ledgering, so it naturally followed that the former would be preferred at night. Since then, great strides have been taken in the development of bite detectors for ledgering in the dark while improvements for float fishing have been almost non-existent, save for attempts to equip a float with a bulb and batteries. But that (with hindsight) was bound to fail, as was the coating of the float tip with luminous paint. The latter did work after a fashion when conditions were perfect, yet even then had to be fished very close into the edge, to let you see the float's luminous tip. But what a strain it was on the eyes!

When in my teens, I went float crazy, making up at least several dozen with assorted tips. There were various light quills for snatching livebaits and bulkier cork-bodied floats for chub, although my pride and joy was the selection of long antenna floats I had designed specifically for night fishing. Okay, some were a bit top-heavy, but they were nice to look at in any case – a bit too nice, by all accounts, because shortly after I'd made them, somebody else took a fancy to them and walked off with the lot! I was absolutely devastated, believe me. A great deal of time and effort had gone into the making of those floats, and now I had nothing to show for it. Needless to say, I lost both heart and interest in the design and manufacture of floats after that little experience, and I have been unable to regain the interest.

Many years later (Eureka!) the betalight crawled upon the scene, with at least some semblance of success. And however lacking in terms of float fishing, it is obviously here to stay. Yet the very idea of watching for the betalight to disappear as the float goes under, is akin to waiting for the kettle to boil or pollution to subside; this kind of fishing leaves me quite cold. For whatever interest can there be in waiting for a light to go out as if motivated by a switch? None at all that I'm aware of. It's the action of the float before it disappears, that conjures up the magic, without which we may just as well use a spear.

In my mind's eye I can see the float now, caught in the cone of my torch: it leans to one side a little, pauses for a moment then returns to its former position, as straight and as proud as a sentry on duty at Buckingham Palace. Then, after leaning some more, out of the beam of light it would slide, to start the old adrenalin racing away in overdrive. Bream would more often than not be the culprit, it being a species that lends itself nicely to float fishing at night. This is mainly due to its liking for deep water close into the edge, where it can be reached and tempted with float gear. That same water will most likely have a placid flow, to allow for easy and accurate groundbaiting and the unhurried passage of the float.

From swims of this nature, I have taken numerous river bream over the years and, with the method, many still water bream and tench from local park lakes and common-ground ponds. Indeed, whenever fishing the Norfolk Broads and attendant waterways, I always found that float fishing by the light of a torch at night brought me by far the best action with the resident bream. They were present in greater numbers a few decades ago, and this was how great catches of bream were made during the decades prior to my own presence on the water. Alas, the shoals of those bream were somewhat depleted even then. And to think that old angling books describe those vast shoals as 'thick enough to walk on!' What a pitiful reminder we are left with today, of what was once considered to be the greatest big bream haunt of all time.

Fortunately, I arrived on the scene in time to have my share, even though the fish were by no means as big or as plentiful then. It was great, nevertheless, to see my float dance in the illuminated patch of water. Hitherto, it would have held me captive in a trance-like state of mild anticipation; expecting the tangible float or its reflected image on the calm surface to suddenly do an Irish jig, at which point I would be released from the spell in order to respond.

All things being equal, I harbour no qualms about spot-lighting a float with a torch at night. I'd rather not, as much as I enjoy it, but until a more realistic means than a betalight for seeing a float in the dark is invented, I'll either manage quite nicely with my torch or abandon float fishing altogether at night, in favour of ledgering. This is the method chosen by the vast majority of night anglers these days, and is that so surprising? I think not; especially when it's catered for so readily in terms of bite detection, in comparison to angling with a float at night. It would be nice, however, to be left with a choice.

Moving Water versus Still

As any experienced angler will tell you, river fishing, as opposed to the still water scene, is as different as chalk is from cheese. There are numerous reasons to account for this, all stemming from the fact that the former is moving, albeit ever so slowly at times. To counteract this we are obliged to change our thinking on many different levels when tackling the inhabitants of moving water, as opposed to the inhabitants of still water.

Both environments support much the same species with few exceptions, chub having now been introduced to some still waters, and even barbel. But there the similarities end, in some aspects, while in others, such as when it comes to the question of baits, they are welded together like Siamese twins. Other vital issues, like locating the fish, differ tremendously. Indeed, if I were asked to emphasise the widest gap between the two, it would have to rest with this business of fish location, without which of course we would catch nothing at all.

Finding fish on gravel pits and the like is largely a case of pinpointing the whereabouts of plateaux, shelves and drop-offs traversed by the fish. We have to trace the channels along which they travel to be intercepted, hopefully, by the angler's bait, and the floating weed and submerged weed beds, that in themselves represent to some species of fish a bountiful larder in terms of the insect life attached, while at the same time affording a degree of cover for others and a lair from which the predator may pounce.

On rivers we are called upon to read the flow, to study in some detail the direction and speed of the currents in an attempt to ascertain as best we can where anything of an edible nature is likely to come to rest on the bottom and so encourage the fish to congregate. Having done that after a fashion – we can never really be certain of how well we have done until results materialise – we next have to decide on how to present the bait.

Will it be rolled, paternostered or offered on a link ledger? Only by actually being there on the spot to digest all the relevant data can we hope to come up with an answer to that. In the end we might well choose a running ledger instead, or possibly even an unweighted bait, if the depth and flow of the water will allow it to reach the fish on the bottom and not whisk it away.

So the flow introduces many facets to be observed. It influences our mode of bite detection. Buzzers, for example, can play tricks with you in rapidly running water and I for one would rather dispense with them altogether, preferring to watch the rod top for takes, or failing that to feel for them in the touch-ledgering style, whereas on the still water scene buzzers do have a lot going for them. But more about that later, other than to say here and now that baits are generally seized with more gusto on rivers and streams – they have to be before the currents carry them away. And, once hooked, you can expect a more dramatic battle on the end of the line. This is again due to the flow, I reckon, which produces stronger fish, because they have to combat it throughout their lives. Yet quite apart from that you're now fighting a fish against the pull of the flow, and therefore, everything being equal, your gear is more likely to be tested to its limit on running water.

Other notable differences between river and lake fishing can be put down to the weather. The former I find have been more affected by the ludicrously warm and dry summers we've been having lately than are the lakes, although they too have in my experience suffered on this account but not quite so badly. It's a known fact also that as the weather deteriorates towards winter the lakes and pits produce fewer fish, except perhaps for pike, while the rivers for most species come into their own. That's how I see the situation in any case, and tend to turn more to the rivers as the season gets progressively nearer its closure.

Needless to say, then, it's a great advantage to be familiar with both lake and river fishing – and an even bigger advantage to feel at home on both at night. Indeed, while night fishing in winter, the lake will invariably take a turn for the worse, to compensate us for this is the irrefutable fact that the river or stream may well during the same period reach its very zenith in terms of the sport provided. It is usually reborn then, attaining more colour and flow, pushing on to journey's end with more purpose and motivating the fish therein to respond in the manner that we as anglers like best.

They will start to feed better, occasionally like there's to be no tomorrow. So what a sin it would be should we miss out because it'll be cold and might just rain, or the ground will be damp or . . . I could give you a dozen reasons for opting out of night fishing in winter, and each would be valid. Nevertheless I urge you to try. You will at least have the banks to yourself, being more hardy, more keen or just more stupid than most, depending on how you see yourself on a wet and windy night with a rod in your hand. Should that rod be well bent over, though, I imagine you'll see yourself in a very favourable light.

The River at Night

We have seen that the angler's approach to river fishing is far removed from that required upon the lakes. There is a much wider variety of conditions to be found on rivers, and each river – or stream – is blessed with characteristics of its own making, or, in other words each is different in nature, be this found in the quality of the water, the fish therein or merely in terms of depth and flow. Yet most have a great deal in common. The River Medway for instance is a dull, dawdling water for much of its length, and so as it happens are certain reaches of the River Thames. The Hampshire Avon is a chalk stream (although I'd hardly call it a stream), as is its close relative the Dorset Stour, and the similarities which link both with the delightful River Kennet can scarcely be missed – not just for the huge barbel that all three contain or for the dense growth of streamer weed associated with each in which the barbel love to hide. There's also the clarity of these waters to bind them together, in which fish spotting can often be done with comparative ease (not that you're likely to spot them at night). Discover their whereabouts during the day though and you will at least be in with a chance of finding them in the same spot at night, and that's a tremendous plus to begin with.

To accomplish as much on the Thames (especially the lower Thames) you'll probably need x-ray eyes, so dense is the water generally and too deep to see the bottom, let alone anything on it, which means in effect that here we have to fish blind. We have to rely much more on any instincts we have accumulated over the years or concentrate more fully on reading the flow. Other than this we can only depend on guesswork or past experience to determine where the fish just might be lurking, and that can vary from one swim to the next. What follows is based on my own observation of the rivers I have fished over the years and offers at least a starting point for those foundering in the completely unknown.

First of all I must stress once more how vital it is for you to arrive at the water in plenty of time to size it up, to study carefully the depths and flow, and to try to work out in your mind's eye where it is most likely to deposit tasty morsels on the bottom for the fish to find. And, if you suspect this business to contain an element of doubt then I'm bound to agree with you that it does. Nevertheless, in reality, should you take time out to prove as much to yourself, you will discover more often than not that the fidgety surface of the water holds enough clues to point you in the right direction. You'll find them in the darting currents that sheer off in one direction or another to carry all manner of edible matter to the point where they will pause momentarily to shed their goodly loads, and these in turn will be gleefully anticipated by the fish on the bottom that have come to expect them there.

Pay particular attention to where deep water in the edge is visited by the flow, for there all kinds of fish will have gathered. Indeed, at one venue from which I regularly take out winter pike the float has to be so close to the bank as to continuously caress it before I can hope to get a take, so never treat with just a mere cursory glance deep water close in that is serviced by the stream – it may well transpire to be the most rewarding spot of all. This reading of the water is great Sherlock Holmes stuff. It brings enormous satisfaction when it leads to a positive conclusion – and some decent fish, which might otherwise have been missed!

Imagine my elation then when once discovering a path in the flow of a very large but nevertheless fairly shallow weirpool that led not away from the weir apron, as one might suppose, but directly back to it. Chub water, this was, from which I had done well enough by casting a bait at the apron and allowing it to trundle downstream to my right. From past experience of weir fishing, however, I knew that most had a deep, almost dormant trench right under the sill, and so proceeded to work a bait back to it via the newly discovered path that I knew would allow me to achieve as much.

The rod had to be held high to avoid interference from the main flow closer in and I soon began to get good pulls. Some of these were missed, unfortunately, due to the longer line now fished, while those I did manage to connect with resulted in chub which were in no way superior to those already taken by fishing the stream proper. This was a bit disappointing, I must admit, since I had reasoned that I was now fishing virtually virgin water; as far as I knew it hadn't seen an angler's bait before, and I had hoped it might produce something special. Alas, that wasn't to be; but my detection of that wayward

Read the path of the currents like a book and they'll lead you to where the fish are holed up.

flow had borne at least some fruit, while at the same time presenting me with a few problems that I was unaccustomed to here: of casting farther out than usual to reach just the right spot; of diligently working the bait along the correct path in the currents to attain its projected goal; of attaching the correct amount of substitute lead to the line. If too heavy it would sabotage every endeavour to make my approach work, simply by plummeting straight to the bottom. A swan-shot did the trick in the end and so success was mine.

Out there in the playful currents, then, is all you need to make you succeed. There's a mighty volume of information open for inspection for all to see, read and digest. Do that much and I cannot see how you can possibly fail, although you will at times of course, because we all do. That's what angling is all about. It's a contrary business, filled with uncertainties and doubts, riddled with claims and counter claims – with facts and fallacies which when tested prove to be no such thing. But there we have the overall appeal of the sport – its very roots and foundations; its argumentative values; its impulsiveness, that drives us back and back again to the water's edge to become an intrinsic part of it. For me, that is never more so than when fishing at night on river or lake.

On the Weirs after Dark

Because it is such a complex subject, weir fishing at any time demands to be examined in its own right: indeed, such are the complexities involved, that it deserves a book of its very own to do it fair justice, while all I can hope to do here is to scratch the surface of it.

Most rivers have weirs to control the level of the water, be they waterfalls in miniature, cascading from a height of many feet, or tiny pathetic dribbles that join the surface of the main stream a few mere inches below; each, of whatever size, influences the flow of the river proper. Its speed will be drastically increased, by the pushing water tumbling down upon it and that in turn attracts all manner of fish – from pike to perch, from barbel to chub – assuming they inhabit the water, and the same effect on a smaller scale is applicable to even the smallest of weirs. But no matter; they will serve our purpose well.

Little or large, they each call for some special attention, and never more so than at the height of a warm, long drawn out summer, when oxygen levels may well have plummeted on the lower reaches of the river or stream but are continuously recharged in the vicinity of weirpools – provided they still flow, and the situation has to be really desperate for them not to. I have over the years fished many weirpools, in other parts of the world as well as in the UK, and must say here and now that there's no other kind of running water that appeals to me more.

Weirs offer a unique challenge in beating that flow, which can be mastered generally by the application of a little thought. Therefore, the first thing to take into consideration must be the flow, and how best to beat it or even make it work for you, so it's as well to remember, initially, that the flow presents a barrier to the fish we seek, in that whatever we offer them will come into contact with that barrier and be swept way downstream by it before the fish on the bottom have a chance to examine our bait.

To counteract this action by the driving force of the stream, those

Some so-called weirs are nothing but a splash of cascading water, like this one; but they do attract the fish.

game enough to throw down the gauntlet are inclined to resist it with the help of ludicrously heavy lead weights, which plummet straight to the bottom to become snagged. A few hefty heaves later and the line snaps, to be followed by a heavier one to avoid the same thing happening again. What does happen in effect is that this thicker line presents an even bigger area for the flow to bully, and that in turn calls for a heavier sinker than used in the first place to oppose this renewed energy affecting the line, and so it goes on.

If we were to reduce resistance to the flow by actually reducing rather than strengthening the power of our line, we would then find the line cutting through the rushing water to leave our terminal gear less affected by it. We could then of course dispense with all but a fraction of the lead we had been forced to use earlier when employing the heavier line because it has now become redundant. Having heavy lead on a light line serves no purpose at all other than to entice the currents to seize it again, in which case any advance made by the lighter line is now lost, a point I do hope I've made clear here, however difficult to set down in words. On this topic I can only suggest further that the angler thinks in terms of the lighter the line so the lighter the lead required in weirpool fishing; he'll then at least get nearer to solving its intricacies.

But what constitutes a light or heavy line? The answer to that can be different for different anglers. Mention a four-pound line as being light to the roach purist, for instance, and he'll probably laugh in your face, whereas the same line will be deemed as exceedingly light by the carp or pike angler, who rarely if ever drops that low in strength. The deciding factor rests quite obviously with the type of fish sought and the conditions pertaining to their eventual capture.

That much should be made clear to prevent the inexperienced angler from trying to tempt barbel from a weirpool, say, on totally inadequate line, strengthwise, rather than using one in the region of six-pounds test. Don't laugh, I've seen it happen: good barbel hooked and lost on one-pound-plus line that resulted in no contest at all for the beginner, and precious little more for the highly experienced.

Given the nature of most weirpool beds, which are strewn with rocks and other rubbish for a hooked fish to find, I tend to use a three or four pound line for chub, but will not hesitate in the least to up that by a pound or two if I suspect barbel are present and feeding. I don't reduce it a great deal even for roach, the quality of which may well be better here than accustomed to in the main river. Quality dace may also be had and, should you be a masochist, some very nice eels.

For bite detection I like to 'feel' for them, until, becoming too weary for that, I then watch either the tip of my rod or springtip, if the water powering past allows. I have never been known to use a buzzer or butt indicator on a weirpool; although in the good old days, when anything more sensitive than a dough bobbin on the line extending from the rod top seemed to be awaiting invention a thousand years hence, I had no option but to use just that for bite indication, so I am appreciative of some things that change.

The banks adjacent to weirs can be steep and treacherous, especially when negotiated in the dark, so select your swim with care before darkness falls. It's also advantageous to have a long landing net pole to make netting a fish a less hazardous adventure. But don't fret, the banks of some of the weirs I fish are much more agreeable, so much so that I can have my seat actually sitting in the water and fish quite comfortably from there. It affords me a position from which I can control proceedings better and net fish with little or no fuss at all. Therefore, should conditions offer you as much then jump at the opportunity of doing likewise yourself. Being in the water puts you nearer the biting fish, which can be dealt with more proficiently on the shorter line now in use. Keep the tip of the rod well above the flow and watch it carefully for takes. They'll be more positive in white water like this and so easier to connect with.

Just when to strike depends on many factors, not the least being the bait used. A large lobworm, for instance, will normally take seconds longer to be engulfed than a couple of maggots, but that's about all. The species concerned will also influence this business of striking; bream and the like being sometimes too finicky for words when taking a bait, while chub, and more so barbel, can have it off the hook before you could blink. In actual fact, it's anyone's guess as to when to strike. Personally, I like a good pull down of the rod-top (who doesn't?), for I'm then confident that the fish has taken the bait and is moving away with it. Other than that delightful possibility, timing the strike must rest with the angler's own instinct, his own accumulated knowledge of such things. His own keen sense of timing will tell him when to strike as he hovers over his rod in readiness to make his bid.

The bait used will largely depend upon the target fish and will be discussed later in relation to it. Here I will only say that in rapidly running water I'm inclined to keep it moving along the bottom, with a pause here and there to allow it to flutter enticingly in the flow. To permit this, leads should be kept to the absolute minimum in terms of weight, irrespective of the tactics being used. For me it is usually nothing more complicated than a swan shot or two pinched directly to the line about eighteen inches or so above the hook, the actual length being adjusted if necessary to produce better results.

At night especially, a weirpool has an added attraction for me. I have never found a weirpool to be in the grip of true darkness; there is always some redemption from the heavens above, just enough perhaps to highlight the specks of spray escaping the custody of the weir apron, or to pick out perhaps the crest of the white water, impatiently intent upon the termination of its long journey when it reaches the sea. It is however the refreshing smell of weir water that I enjoy most at night and the sound of it tumbling, murmuring, or even singing as it hurries past.

Whatever the description, it's a harmony of collated voices, that the angler comes to appreciate at night, and which lures him back often. It's not just for the angling, which can be out of this world at times, but also for the many other attributes of weir fishing at night, that combine to convince me that I really am out of this world, and quite determined to stay out, until the cold, materialistic demands of life bring me down to earth again with an almighty bump, after which I must await my next trip into happy oblivion.

The Darkened Lake

Lakes can be shrouded in mystery at night. Many are surrounded by the kind of silence that can only be described as haunting; for while there may be noises in the night on most rivers (albeit the mere murmurings of such) the quiet of still waters can be absolute, save for the scampering of the inhabitants of the water's edge. Indeed, such is the peace and tranquillity in which the angler has buried himself that it can become almost a drugged existence, whereas the uninitiated may well find himself seemingly threatened in an environment which he could be excused for thinking was a bit like being in outer space.

To convince him that he isn't, there are those mighty splashes on the otherwise silk-like surface of the water to contend with in the middle of the night. And they don't help much either; for whatever monster could possibly have caused those? If fishing Loch Ness, he would have no doubts whatsoever – but not on this water, surely? It is at moments like this when every relevant tale we've ever come up against is recalled. One I think of often concerns the Scottish (or was it Irish?) loch from which many anglers were taken from their boats at night. A gigantic eel with the head of a pike, would you believe it, was responsible for that. Yet another concerned an angler found dead in his seat with an equally dead carp in his lap. He had died from heart failure, brought on by the exhilarating encounter with his catch, a then very fanciful one hundred pounds, but not quite so very fanciful these days, I reckon. Who wrote these memorable pieces of fiction which I read so long ago I have no idea now, but they certainly fired the imagination. But my job here is to encourage the angler to fish at night, not to deter him with the tales of those who have in the past understood as well as anyone the innermost depths of the night stalker's mind, as much as I personally relish such tales. Enjoy them for the very essence of the subject matter they contain, the very soul of being out there on your own in the dark, conjuring up all manner of imaginative wanderings, which don't surprisingly send us insane – well, not often . . .

To move on to the practicalities of fishing still water at night, I find that in many ways it presents less of a problem than does moving water, yet more so in some. Groundbaiting can be accomplished with comparative ease for a start, now we've no flow to snatch it away, and the banks usually offer more level space, and if you think that's immaterial than you haven't tried night fishing yet.

Bite detection on still water affords us an entirely different ball game to that demanded by its moving counterpart, since so many options are open to us. At the very head of the list are Optonic buzzers and such like in association with monkey-climbers, although one can manage after a fashion with nothing but a twig on the line in front of the reel, which will be thrown to one side as a fish takes. I have already dealt extensively with bite detection elsewhere, so will simply add that here, there is nothing wanting as far as I'm concerned. I only wish as much could be said for running water, but in terms of bite detection this isn't the case. Since principles differ, we have a long way to go to bring bite detection on running water at night to the standard already enjoyed elsewhere, and because of the difficulties involved, due to the pull of the flow, I doubt if we ever will.

We can present a bait more delicately on still water, if only by virtue of the drastically reduced weighted line we can now get away with and that in turn puts more fish on the bank. I suppose it must also be said that those fish will generally be larger, what with carp of over fifty pounds having come out of still water and pike of well over forty, not to mention tremendous tench and bream. One has merely to check the record fish list to ascertain for oneself from which kind of water the real heavyweights come. And don't forget the solitude enjoyed on some still waters that most rivers couldn't aspire to in a million years.

So what then are the disadvantages to be found on the still water scene? Well, I've had to think profoundly about that one, since there aren't many. Lakes tend to be more isolated than rivers, which is a boon in the sense of getting away from it all, but a real drag if you need to go to the shops, remember, which mightn't seem a problem until you're suddenly out of cigarettes, or if your stay at the waterside is for several days or longer. You are then faced with the task of taking along with you enough supplies to last for the duration of your extended visit – so tin cans galore they'll be, on waters that permit them (and some don't). Also, because of this isolation, help following an

In just the right setting at just the right time, there's nowhere on earth I'd rather be than at the edge of a beautiful lake.

accident might be a long time in coming, and don't say it couldn't happen to you. None of us are spared that dreadful possibility, no matter how experienced. That's why I always carry a powerful flashlight in my bag, with which to summon help, hopefully, should the need ever arise. A whistle on a cord around your neck isn't a bad thing to have, either. But there I go again, dampening the would-be night-fisher's enthusiasm before he has taken the first step to becoming an accomplished one, but it's as well to know the score right from the very beginning and to keep any such eventualities in mind.

And, when continually falling foul of them, the trees surrounding a water can become a liability to some, while others cherish their very presence. For what kind of joy can a pool of water on barren land offer? None at all to me, irrespective of how good the fishing. It'd be too reminiscent of some of the London reservoirs I've met, great concrete-lined holes in the ground topped up with water, which I have never had the slightest wish to fish. But yes, there can be a tree too many for our purpose; yet rather too many than too few is my view, and never would I advocate the removal of even one, on my behalf, believing that nature should be permitted to take its course, wherever possible, without any unnecessary interference from us.

Where that has been allowed to happen is where you'll find me most. I appreciate the wilderness around me, the unknown quality of a water, being not in the least interested in chasing fish so familiar with the inside of a landing net as to be honoured with pet names. We've all heard of them – Raspberry of Redmire fame – Penny of Broadlands – Heather the Leather and so forth; all carp, I'll grant you, which are to be more readily recognised as old friends when they turn up again and again. Why identifiable big pike are not honoured thus, I have no idea, unless it be because they either don't come out as often or lack the atmospheric appeal of carp, arguably the most sought-after species of all.

Yes indeed, still water angling does have a lot going for it, in terms other than those referred to here. For each individual angler it embraces something different, something very special, so special in fact that many are pressed to define exactly what it is. For me personally it undoubtedly rests with the kind of atmosphere I love, soak in and become totally mesmerised by whenever feeling its tentacles reach out to me from the water's edge as twilight, dusk and then true darkness descend upon its surface, having first been washed in the soft, golden reflection of the sinking sun. At this precise moment there's no other place on earth I'd rather be.

Creatures Great and Small

Since we are in the ideal terrain at the best possible moment, we are bound to cross the paths of many nocturnal creatures. To me, this is part and parcel of night fishing. I look forward to these encounters with wild beasts with a great deal of delightful anticipation; and I've met a few in my time. As to be expected, they're not so easily alarmed in the dark. In fact, it's the angler who views them with suspicion, rather than the other way round, for he may shoulder a conviction, unfairly, that he ought to be there and not they. Such an attitude is very bad news for both parties – for the furry creatures because they're likely to be harmed by this human who fails to see that they too have rights and needs that are every bit as pressing as his own, if not more so – and for the angler who is convinced that he simply cannot share his surroundings with what he sees as obnoxious interlopers who might just present something of a threat to him, which simply isn't true. I have already mentioned previously how I personally enjoy the company of my furry friends. They help to while away the hours with their antics, and never ever would I harm a single hair of them.

Apart from the more commonly encountered rabbit, hare or fox, you'll meet with stoats, weasels and many other forms of wildlife which to my shame I cannot put a name to, but each will find a warm welcome in my camp, plus a bit of a feed. They evidently know as much has well, which is why they don't stand off in stark terror of me, with eyes bulging and whiskers quivering. Instead they try to stare me out, challenge me to make the first move, which I invariably do, to send them scurrying off into the undergrowth. They soon return though to go through the same ritual again and again, making a game of it, one could suppose. Eventually, however, obviously sensing that I mean them no harm, they gain more confidence and tend to linger longer in the hope of obtaining a free feed – or are they merely as curious about my presence as I am about theirs?

They also become more friendly, if such a word can be used in relation to wild animals, at which point they can become a pest. I've had rats running up my legs as I lie down before now and have even known them to invade sleeping bags, although I should add for the peace of mind of my reader, that this is no common occurrence. They will get into your food, though, and might well bite your fingers if you unwittingly thrust them into a bag containing rats as well as food, so be sure to check that food bags are safely secured and that nothing inside moves, before dipping your fingers in. Rats can transmit deadly diseases, as we all know, so it's better to keep them at a safe distance.

One memorable encounter with a fox, which I shall never forget, occurred on a very bitter winter's night. It was in January (just to show the kind of weather I regularly night fish in), and so cold that my drinking water was frozen solid, as was the line to the rings of my rods, and I knew that unless I sought the comparative warmth of the car without further delay I would undoubtedly suffer from the effects of hypothermia. But where was the car? Due to a heavy ground fog that shrouded my entire surroundings I wandered across this field and that, in search of the car, the whereabouts of which I didn't discover till dawn. What I did find in my tracks was a fox, and thought it was as daft as I was to be caught out in the open on a night such as this.

Its opinion of me couldn't have been any better, for that crafty old fox, which had glided before me as stealthily as the fog itself, acted in a most peculiar manner, I thought, expecting it to bolt for cover as any self-respecting fox would have done the moment it sensed my presence. This one approached me instead to sniff at my boots with the least pretence of being cautious and then quite unexpectedly circled me a few times before settling back on its haunches to study me some more. Flabbergasted by its strange behaviour I moved warily yet hastily back in the direction from whence I came – and I'm damned if that beast didn't follow me, like a dog on a leash!

It made odd noises, as if it had a cold, and I reckon it might have been lonely, and therefore overjoyed at my approach. I have since regretted not having spent more time with it, since I felt sure it yearned for my company. But was it normal, I wondered, for a fox to behave in such a way? From my own experience of them it wasn't; but who knows? Perhaps somebody out there can enlighten me on this matter.

I have of course met foxes before, but usually in the day, when they're more likely to be noticed, and I shall always remember the one I spotted on the far bank of Australia's Goulburn River, in the

State of Victoria. Indeed, such a bright shade of red was it that I at first took it to be a large ginger cat. Another that came out of the bush behind me at much the same spot, curled-up almost at my feet before detecting my presence, but was gone in a flash as soon as I reached for the camera.

Foxes do, however, appear to be creatures of the night or of the early morning – and I do mean early! At first light is the most favourable time to spot them, often haring after rabbits with a fleetness of foot which you wouldn't believe. It is at such times that you're more able to study them. At any other time they're bound to melt away before your very eyes. But what's all this to do with night fishing, you may ask, in which case I can only reply by saying that the wildlife featured is an inherited bonus, and in no way do I wish to see it diminish. It adds so much to our pleasure, what with the harmless fun it affords us.

That's why I am always loading my bag with discarded fishing line and empty cans whenever at the waterside – and you'd be surprised at the volume I shift. Sadly, it's a fact of life that I can never remove it all, as much as I try. The very thought, however, of some innocent creature becoming ensnared in it, and perhaps left to die, induces me to do whatever I can to prevent this happening. More's the pity that others cannot be equally concerned. They would then perhaps take away their own rubbish instead of donating it to people like me to deal with. Indeed, how they can sleep at night, knowing that some poor creature might well have been cut to ribbons by the corn or meat can they so mindlessly left behind them, I just don't know. To avoid such a possibility, some fisheries have wisely banned cans altogether.

THE AUSTRALIAN CONNECTION

Contrary perhaps to popular belief, the British aren't the only litter bugs around. Most Australian anglers, for instance, would rather forget their bait than their beer cans, of which at least several dozen are taken along in an insulated box known as an Esky. This will contain bags of ice as well as beer to keep the latter cool. Imagine, then, what happens to the cans when they're empty. Now Australia is also blessed abundantly with wildlife – and it's not all of a loveable disposition, either. Therefore, if you've been literally plagued with rats at night, as I have, (or even during the day, for that matter) then do spare a thought for those angling in the dark Down Under.

Creatures great and small they may be, but don't assume for a moment that they're all of the nice, cuddly kind, because you couldn't be further from the truth. Take the so-called cuddly koala bears, of which I have met many in the wild. You wouldn't believe they have claws to sink deeply into your skin, but that's a fact, and despite the endearing promotional pictures of models in bikinis cuddling them to their breasts, it's an exercise I would want no part of, unless I were playing the role of the bear. Koalas are, nevertheless, one of the more friendly creatures found Down Under.

The biggest headache comes from the ever-present threat of snakes. The majority of Australians appear never to have seen one, surprisingly, since the cat wasn't above waltzing into the house with them from the back garden – and I lived in a built-up area not more than a dozen or so miles from the City of Melbourne!

You can guess what a constant threat they represented when night fishing in the bush then. If I added that although Africa has more snakes, the percentage of poisonous ones is far smaller than that found in Australia, you will perhaps begin to understand the situation better and appreciate more fully the threat of these reptiles, especially since they're far more active at night. Be thankful then that you've not got their like to contend with here. Adders? I do something unmentionable to them.

Australia is credited with having the six deadliest snakes on earth. Blacks, browns, copperheads, tigers – they're just a few of nearly two hundred different species stumbled upon Down Under, of which an incredible 95% are known to be venomous; more than a few most deadly. A while ago I did some research on these and learned that some are more lethal than even the celebrated King Cobra of India, which is said to produce enough venom from a single bite to kill 31 sheep. Big deal – what's that to the Queensland taipan's ability to put 200 sheep to death – or the tiger snake's score of 118 – a gnat's bite? Some gnat!

Exactly why sheep should be used as a comparison is difficult to understand, until we learn that Down Under, where humans are out-numbered by sheep by a massive seven to one, these frolicking future–woolly–jumpers lend themselves more readily to the purpose. But, working on the generous assumption that two fully-grown sheep equal the weight of one fully-grown man, we're left with little cause to feel over elated about these figures, and the particular snake I encountered most was the tiger (with a score of 118, remember). Just how often these encounters took place I have no idea, having had no

A deadly tiger snake, with enough venom from a single bite to put 118 sheep to death. This one is a threat no longer.

wish to dally in order to make a tally. Suffice it to say it was very rare indeed to go fishing and not come across one.

Imagine what it was like when night fishing the place. During the day there was always the chance that you'd see them first, but at night there was next to no hope of spotting them lying in the deep grass at your elbow. You'd have more chance of putting your hand on one when fiddling about in the dark! Should that happen, you're advised to get medical help within two hours; the irony of this being that it would often take us that long to return to the car, never mind find a two-horse town with a resident doctor prepared to get out of his bed in the middle of the night. So, if you were unfortunate enough to sustain a snake bite you became, in a nutshell, a mere statistic – or history if you like. Don't believe what you've read about cutting out the poison, either. It's now been established that more people have died from heart failure due to this course of action being taken than have actually expired because a snake bit them.

There are a couple of amusing yet nevertheless true stories associated with those who were bitten. The first concerned a victim who left the hospital because he couldn't be bothered to wait; needless to say, he was never heard of again. Another entered a packed surgery with the snake that bit him still in his grasp, as this is advised to enhance the chance of finding an antidote in time. This poor fellow was at his wit's end (who wouldn't be?); he came over faint, dropped the snake on the ground and emptied the surgery before you could say 'Bloody Oath!'.

Writing about all this has recharged my recall of the Australian fishing scene, and of just how careful I always was to look before I leaped. And I haven't even touched on spiders, such as the redback – or the deadly funnelweb found in the regions of New South Wales and elsewhere. It was while researching a book entitled *Freshwater Fishing in Australia* for the publishers Reeds Pty Ltd, and which was published in 1982 and reissued in 1989, that I began to appreciate just how tame the State of Victoria, where I lived, was in comparison to most other parts of Australia. Elsewhere there were crocodiles – try to visualise catching one of those on a waggler and a couple of maggots! The very thought boggles the mind. Nonetheless, for that Fred J. Taylor can confirm all that is written here. He's up to his neck in it almost every other year. He probably wouldn't know about the sea fishing Down Under, however, which embraces still more dangers than found in freshwater, what with sharks and stingrays, cobblers and stone fish and the like, and the dainty but most decidedly deadly blue ringed octopus, with a bite for which no known antivenene exists even today. Indeed, I once wrote in a magazine out there that if what you caught from the sea didn't prick you, then it bit, stung or poisoned you, and I don't think I was exaggerating in the least. Oh, what joy then to return to the more friendly banks of Britain's rivers and lakes. Is it any wonder that I treat the beasts that roam them more like pets than pests?

Some Peculiar Catches made at Night

With so much livestock around we shouldn't be that taken aback if just occasionally we reel in something which has neither scales nor fins, to prompt the question of 'Whatever's that on the end of the line?' Australia has again, not surprisingly, supplied the bulk of these for me. So, how about a bundle of fur with a duck's bill at one end and flippers at the other? Such a creature was hooked by me one night when fishing on the bottom with a dead frog I'd found.

The bite when it came was the kind we dream of yet so rarely experience; the tip of the rod taking on a life of its own in such a way as to make me almost keel over and expire. Fortunately I didn't, and the ensuing battle wasn't exactly to be dismissed either, being fought more on the top than the bottom, and this alone convinced me that I had hooked into something mighty peculiar indeed. My netsman must have had similar thoughts, for down at my feet went the net and away went he to give me the benefit of his opinion from a fair distance away. 'It's a snake! Let it go,' was the extent of his advice and why he wasn't offended by my reply I shall never know.

Anyhow, there was I with the net in hand waiting to meet my antagonist alone, which on reflection might well have been a snake. I was relieved beyond comprehension then when this loudly protesting misshapen form of fur was by one means or another bullied to the net and then lifted onto the bank where, thankfully, it ejected the hook and took off for pastures new. It was, if you haven't already guessed, a duck-billed platypus, which isn't anywhere near as rare as some Aussies would have you believe. They do have lethal claws on the back of their poor excuse for feet, so I was happy to let this one wander at will. Never had I heard of a platypus taking an angler's bait, before this one decided to give it a try, and it left me with an experience I'd rather not repeat.

My second sighting of something very peculiar that oughtn't to have been on the end of a line also happened to be a sight more ferocious than it was given credit for. It had taken a dead fish bait intended for an eel, and was doubtless responsible, we decided later, for leaving just the head of the bait on the hook on numerous occasions. The friend mentioned in the platypus episode above and I had lain the blame for the dismembered baits we kept reeling in on the Murray cod that we knew frequented the water here in small numbers, rather than on eels, and were perhaps a bit concerned as well as disappointed when he finally brought to the net a writhing terrapin. It took just one glance at its cruel, mincing mouth to add weight to what we thought it had done to our baits – and would likely as not do to our fingers also, if given half-a-chance, which we made damned sure it didn't get.

A catch with fins but again without any scales that you'd notice, would turn up on occasion to delight me no end. This was the Australian native freshwater species known as the blackfish (*Gadopsis marmoratus*), or Old Slippery, if you prefer, due to its eel-like touch to the hand. It is found mainly in the upper reaches of the Murray-Darling system, but has also infiltrated parts of Victoria. It is dark brown on top and pale yellow underneath, with a dark blotch here and there on its back. In size, it is of little interest to the angler, attaining at best a mere 14 inches in length. It was the appearance of the fish that intrigued me so, looking as though it had already passed its sale by date in prehistoric times. You could, if you tried hard enough, liken it to a ling, but I found the blackfish more similar in shape to the turbot, now believed to be extinct in this country, so probably that's the nearest I shall ever get to one.

Although we've no shortage of oddball creatures at this end of the globe, we don't often find them attached to fishing line. One I did happen to witness looked like something out of a second-rate horror movie, but transpired to be nothing more alarming than a small bat, entangled in a young angler's line. But don't let that fool you. This thing appeared to be every bit as creepy as something that had just dropped in from outer space. It's a fact that although everyone present recognized this bat in the light of a torch for what it was, not one of us was game enough to try and free the poor creature, which in some way managed as much by itself in the end and left us all to wallow in our shame.

But what about those monsters on the end that turn out to be anything but monsters, as we struggle to subdue them against the currents, and in so doing make complete fools of ourselves? We've all met them, at first with tremendous joy: the piece of driftwood played out in the flow, the snag on the bottom that moved just enough to convince us we'd hit into something extraordinarily big. On one occasion, this turned out to be for me a child's fishing net, of all things, which added much to the mirth of my friends. Most memorable of all, however, was the phantom barbel I hooked on the Thames one night. Its stupendous fight for freedom was quite beyond anything I'd ever experienced before, and that led me to nurse a few doubts. Yet still I doggedly persevered with the tremendous tugs on the end, until that is the line suddenly went slack and I wound in the remainder of my gear, at which point an angler fishing in the next swim unbeknown to me, approached panting like a dog in heat to tell me about the massive barbel he had just lost. Okay, perhaps I should have come clean there and then but didn't have the heart to disillusion him, or to ruin the tale he's probably still telling about the one that got away.

A Change of Habitat

Whether or not certain fish have changed their habits, and also therefore their actual habitats over the years, I can't rightly say, but what some of the angling authors of old would have us believe in relation to the character of the water associated with them, does noticeably differ from what we observe today. This suggests that either they had it wrong or the needs of certain fish have indeed changed marginally during the passing decades, and I tend to think the latter is the case.

The bream affords us a classic example of this. It has been portrayed in the past as a stately, executive type fish favouring deep pools of still, or placidly moving water (which it does), and having an intense dislike of anything more than the most moderate of flows (which it most certainly doesn't).

With lessons learned from ageing literature like this in mind it takes no effort to imagine how surprised I was to find a large shoal of decent sized bream residing in the thunderous flow of a raging weirpool. That must have been nigh on forty years ago, and I've no reason to suppose they aren't still there, in a situation in which we have been conditioned to think is totally alien to them. I have since discovered their presence in all manner of unlikely swims, some very shallow, others very fast, from which barbel as well as chub have come out alongside the bream.

Carp were once said to abhor running water even more than bream, and once again that isn't the case. River carp appear to be fairly widespread; it is anglers prepared to seek them with the kind of determination required, who are thin on the ground, a position which isn't likely to change while so many other potentially more promising venues are open to them. Should they try, though, they'd find that even the lustre-lacking River Thames is capable of throwing up some decent carp, often quite large carp.

I learned my craft on the Thames, and yet not once during my apprenticeship can I recall the species earning as much as a solitary mention in connection with the Thames, let alone actually clapping eyes on one from the river. When I finally did, it came out from where a discharge of warm water from an establishment on the banks at Camberley Gardens flowed into the main river at Kingston-on-Thames.

These days the capture of carp is being reported from all over the lower Thames, with areas like Staines, Teddington and most stops in between becoming firm favourites among those who are prepared to keep an ear to the ground and then follow their hunches, however unlikely, with a resolution that does them proud.

Barbel are another case in point, about which I heard very little until actually catching one when aged fourteen. All previous reference to the species was confined to the tales my father told me concerning the catches he and his own father made from the Thames during a period which seemed like a lifetime ago to me, and yet there at last was one of my very own in the net! I don't know who was the most delighted, my father or myself.

I think it was significant that barbel then began to be taken all over the river, and while my critics have claimed this was a direct result of improved techniques, rather than a general relocation of the species concerned, I cannot subscribe to that. Had the barbel been there all along, then I must assume I'd have seen at least a few taken during my childhood, even if perhaps accidentally. Barbel do hook themselves often, I have since learned, so why not then? Why also, may I ask, did my father cease to catch them decades before and then quite suddenly begin to reel them in once more, using identical tactics to those he had grown up with?

It would be more puzzling if, unbeknown to us, the barbel had continued to live all the time in the areas of the Thames we knew best, than if in fact they vacated them as I had supposed, long ago, although for the reasons already mentioned I'm fairly convinced that they did.

Many drastic changes occurred on the lower Thames during the years immediately following World War II, any one of which could have had a profound effect on the barbel population of the river at that time and caused it to seek pastures new. A great deal of dredging took place, disrupting the bed of the river that had remained untouched for years, and playing havoc with the flow. Add to that the eventual effect on both river and fish that water abstraction must also have had, and we really ought to be asking ourselves not why the species concerned reacted in the manner that I think it did, by

Bernard Alfrey (to whom this book is dedicated), poses with a typical Thames barbel. Has the species changed its habits and therefore habitat, the author wonders?

moving house, but rather, how the hell it ever managed to survive Man's violation of its environment!

But the species did survive, to return gradually to its old haunts, having adapted remarkably well to new ones elsewhere, after the disruption of the lower Thames during the post-war years. Why it should return after such a long absence, I have no idea, unless its previous haunts in the Thames have reverted back in nature, to a level more acceptable to the species – or could its habits (and therefore needs) have changed over the years, to the point where those old locations could accommodate it better?

Maybe the characteristics of some species, including barbel, have changed, to fit them better for their supposedly new environment, having been so unceremoniously forced out of their old. This could explain why carp are now caught where they've no business to be, and likewise bream. It's an interesting theory, at least, that is worthy of further thought.

Be it right or wrong, however, the fact remains that bream, for instance, will continue to be taken from the text book swims of old – the deep unruffled water adjacent to locks, the equally deep water that glides stealthily beneath the bridges fording the Thames and other rivers. However, bream will also turn up in quite unexpected places, as will other fish, in complete disregard of our expectations.

In conclusion I can only add that if a river as mighty as the Thames can be transformed in such a way by the interference of Man, then it must naturally follow that waters of a lesser magnitude will have been influenced a damned sight more. Wherever you may be fishing, there may well have been changes to the natural habitat of fish of all kinds, some of which may have caused the nature of the fish concerned to have changed also, so that the species has veered slightly from the accepted norm to a point where it might be better equipped to deal with its altered surroundings.

For whatever reason, the Thames has changed from a water clear enough to see tiny gudgeon enter the neck of a milk bottle with bread inside to attract them, to one that is now too deep and murky in the reaches I know best to see even the bottle, never mind the fish inside. Therefore, on this and other rivers which have been affected by change, and they must be many, the angler shouldn't be surprised at anything he catches at night, because as much as some of us prefer to set our sights on a particular species, there's no knowing what we might encounter after dark. Bream, barbel, carp or chub – the choice isn't always ours to make.

The Battling Barbel

Although attempts have been made to introduce them to non-flowing water the barbel is first and foremost a species of the rapid stream. I am not therefore altogether in agreement with efforts to settle them elsewhere. Still water is not their true environment and experiments along these lines cannot fail to bring about a change in the characteristics of the species that we know best, if they haven't already undergone a change. I am tempted therefore to say at this point: why tamper with them in the first place? Fortunately for us, somebody did, without which barbel, along with a good few other species, would be nowhere near as widespread as we find them today. Indeed, some are not even indigenous to this country, including the highly-esteemed carp, so overall I suppose we must be content in the knowledge that experimentation of this kind does take place and that more good than harm is generally the result.

However, whatever the future may hold in store for them, barbel fishing will always remain for me a sport to be followed in rapidly running water – the faster the better I find when it comes to middling sized fish, although it was noticed long ago that some of the giants preferred to end their days (and nights of course) in quieter regions away from the full thrust of the flow.

To my great joy I was once convinced I had hooked such a fish, and for a good thirty minutes I gingerly played it while hardly daring to breathe. The usual spectators had gathered to cheer me on, but how quickly their cheers turned to jeers as I finally coaxed the great catch to the net. It weighed about four pounds and had been neatly hooked in the tail!

Now as it happens most of the barbel around are descended from those of the River Thames or, to be more precise, from the ancient fish of the Rhine, if we care to go back that far – and that includes those that reside in what some still see today as the true mecca of monster barbel, the Royalty fishery on the Hampshire Avon at Christchurch.

When I was very little I badgered my father to take me there, thinking that this superb water was in some way connected with the Christ Church just around the corner from me – no wonder I could never find it! I would suspect now, though, that the reputation the Royalty has enjoyed for many a year as being the best big barbel water in the country, is being challenged by the River Severn, among others, while the poor old Thames scarcely gets a look in. It affords me no pleasure at all to add that the Thames itself cannot possibly be termed as a big barbel water, as much as I may wish otherwise. In fact, you're doing quite well to net a barbel of much above five pounds on the lower reaches of the river and anything approaching a pound or two more must surely call for a round at the bar.

The best I personally can vouch for was a seven-pounder, from the island of Penton Hook near Staines, Middlesex – and that was almost forty years ago. Bigger ones have undoubtedly come out since, but I certainly haven't seen them. I like to think that because some rivers are obviously producing bigger barbel now than they have in the past, the lower Thames will eventually catch up with them.

The upper reaches of the Thames offer far better fish, but by no means as many as other, more prolific, barbel rivers, whereas the lower reaches are pitifully lacking in barbel of a size that more fortunately sited anglers would deem as only moderate, in spite of the fact that we all know that a former record of 14 lb. 6 oz. was taken from the lower Thames at Molesey, in my grandfather's day, which still equals the official record of the same weight taken from the Royalty fishery at Christchurch in 1934, even if it isn't acclaimed as such now. It must be stressed, however, that the Thames at Molesey has changed considerably since that great fish came out and much as I like to play with the idea of an even bigger barbel swimming in the deep water at that location, I must admit that it's rather unlikely.

Nevertheless, barbel are there for the taking, in more rivers than I could possibly count on both hands – and they don't have to be all that wide or deep to contain the species either; it's just a matter of finding them and then holding on grimly when you do, because not for nothing has the barbel earned the reputation of being a fighter right to the very rim of the net, after which they should be dealt with lovingly but hastily, so as to get them back into the water with the least possible delay, with head held upstream as they're cradled gently but firmly in the hands until they can move away steadily under their own steam.

Barbel should never be put in keepnets, not even to allow them to

Born to battle, this fine double-figure fish leaves no doubt about its ability to fight, as can be seen by its streamlined shape.
(Photograph: Peter Wheat.)

regain their strength. To suggest as much would amount to an open invitation to all and sundry to do just that, irrespective of how small their nets or the position in which they are placed. You'll be doing them a better service by returning them to the water in the manner advised, and that goes for all species.

Barbel swims are legendary, of course, described as they always are as being gravelly and well furnished with the inevitable streamer weed. 'Find such a swim and you're in with a chance,' so say the experts of old, while I must counter that with the question: where on the lower Thames would you find such weed? A few lonesome strands there might be, here and there, but nothing at all like we've been asked to search for. So we must seek swims that look right without the added attraction of long swaying swords of weed, and this takes me mainly to the weirs. Where this weed is present on other waters there can be no denying that in amongst it is the place to put your bait, usually, although I sometimes turn to deep water within the vicinity of it.

There are several ways of catching barbel at night, but the choice must be that of the individual angler. Some for example will never waver from their feeder tactics, while the first thing others do is to lay down a carpet of hemp then proceed to fish over this with something more substantial on the hook for bait. Both methods work extremely well at times, and I often make good use of them. I am not one, however, to become too engrossed in any particular approach and may well tempt barbel with just a sprinkling of chopped up meat, or whatever, and offer the same affixed to the hook. Much will depend on the situation as I see it at the time.

I prefer to barbel fish in winter, when the rivers are near to flooding and I can pick them off better by fishing close in to the banks. This is achieved by casting well downstream to the edge of the flow from where I am based and allowing it to sweep my bait close in. Here many barbel and other fish will have gathered to seek some respite from the force of that wicked water. Tackle needs to be adequate to cope with the conditions prevailing as well as the fish sought, which are in tip-top condition now, as one might suppose; I would suggest then a line of at least 4 lb. and more realistically one of 6 lb. if you're concerned about breakage, because these winter fish really go, believe me.

For bait I generally prefer a good helping of luncheon meat or a couple of fat lobworms. They do look huge, I grant you, but you'd be surprised at how confidently barbel take them: in one mighty gulp, judging by the way they take the rod round, which makes them difficult to miss, providing you've a betalight or such attached to the tip to see them. I still keep ledgering leads fairly light compared to what some anglers are in the habit of using and will rarely go above a half-ounce, unless really forced to by the wrath of the flow. I can sometimes manage with just a couple of large split-shot on the line. A running or link-ledger is what I mostly use now, finding it unnecessary to indulge in anything more sensitive, although in calmer conditions I may well at first experiment with a totally lead free line.

The maxim, when in Rome do as the Romans do, applies to fishing as much as anything else and only a fool would persevere with his favoured technique and catch nothing, while those about him are making hay with another approach altogether. This often becomes the case on waters unknown to the angler concerned, and when I find myself in that category you can be sure that I'm all ears and eyes. I like to know what's going on around me, what others are catching and how. More often than not I'll find that feeder fishing is the in thing here and won't hesitate to follow suit, at which point I'm relieved to know that I'm as competent with this arrangement as any other and hopefully will soon be catching fish. Nonetheless, I do view any adaptations I make with caution. For who is to say that the others have got their approach just right? Mightn't there be an even better way to produce the goods? We must entertain the possibility that there might be and consider the options on offer, after which some are discarded and others retained for further testing with the dedication warranted, not simply tried in a half-hearted fashion out of sheer desperation. Therefore don't be in too much of a hurry to mimic what others are doing, even if they are getting results. With a fresh and unbiased look at the situation you might just introduce something completely new to the scene, to be rewarded with dividends that leave you reeling in more ways than one.

Bream: the Most Ceremonious of all Fishes

Bream fishing always comes across as a very lazy pursuit to me, in which the angler's approach is leisurely. But that undoubtedly stems from the time when I used to chase them with a float at night and from the way the float would dither like a teenager on a first date before finally plunging out of sight. The setting for my quest for bream was also invariably relaxed – or positively dreamy, when looked at in retrospect, for during my younger days it was always followed on a wide, deep stretch of a pleasantly murmuring river that produced the kind of flow that allowed your bait to rest on the bottom and the float to sit as firmly as if it was painted there on the top, to be picked out by the beam of a torch that steadily got weaker and weaker as the night wore on and the batteries were slowly drained of their power. Oh, to have had rechargeable batteries then, just when I needed them most! They'd have made a hell of a difference to my early bream period, I can tell you.

Then there was a deep but much faster bream hole that was influenced by the driving force of a nearby weir from which I took many bream on the paternoster. Pale, sickly looking slabs of fish they were, and not at all like the bronzed beauties I came to prefer later, but they amounted to good sport in spite of their pallor. It was our practice then to use dough bobbins with a drop of at least three feet as butt indicators, and how sedately they would rise as the bait was taken; always a knob of breadpaste or flake, incidentally, in those far off days. So here once again was a dreamy situation in which haste played no part whatsoever. Is it any wonder then that I still think of bream fishing as a laid-back sport?

Thanks to the undivided attention given by a few individuals to the massive fish recently found to inhabit a handful of now well publicised still waters, we are experiencing a born again interest in big bream fishing at least. We are also enjoying a more modern approach to the sport that continues to be fuelled by the tremendous catches now being made of truly majestic bream. It's hard to imagine what a hulk of a fish a fifteen-pounder would represent, but bream of that size and bigger are now being targeted and caught according to plan, albeit less frequently than some would like. For big bream fishing has been described as very much a waiting game by those fortunate enough to have encountered them, during which endless nights and days are whittled away in pursuit of the monsters that so rarely show. When they do, however, there appears to be every likelihood of the angler in tune with them taking more than one such specimen during a single session. So how about that? Fish as big and every bit as beautiful as the bronze wonders we would expect to find in a museum, residing in a gravel pit – makes you wonder what might turn up next, doesn't it?

For the record, Oxford's Queenford Lagoon is the place to be, if you can get a foot in the door (as if you didn't already know that), with the nearby legendary TC pit still pitching in for top position on the list of the country's foremost big bream waters. It shouldn't be forgotten, though, that the biggest of the lot came out of a Staffordshire mere in 1986 at 16 lb. 6 oz., so who can hazard a guess as to when and where an even bigger bream will put in an appearance? Possibly the bream record will have tumbled again before this is committed to print, so fluctuating are records these days. When I was a boy most of the records were long-standing; as firm as the British Empire once was, like segments of angling history which we viewed more as folklore, since we never expected them to change. In stark contrast to those days, we now scarcely expect records to last for more than a season or two – not that I'm complaining about that mind, but where, I wonder, will it all end?

Normal bream fishing is a sport I don't pursue often these days, even if I do occasionally get caught up in it when trying for something that is to my mind more worthwhile. Okay, the odd four-pounder turning up in my tench swim I can live with, but when there's no deterring them, I'd much rather cut my losses and try elsewhere. I was doomed to this kind of unwanted attention from the species on occasion during the last season, and have no wish for a re-run of the torment I was put through. The last time it happened I brought to net in little more than an hour no fewer than seven bream, which were all around 4 lb., and they nearly drove me insane. Had I been using a feeder, I dare say I'd have taken lots more, but

The author with a four-pound bream. At times they can reach plague proportions.

since I was after tench at the time I found the intrusion of these bream very annoying indeed, and was forced to move in the end. There was an instance, however, when an 8 lb. bream turned up quite unexpectedly in the middle of the night to save me suffering a complete blank, and I was very delighted to see that one.

Feeder tactics probably offer the finest means of putting together a good bag of bream, which need to be fed constantly to keep them concentrated in a limited area, since they do tend to rove a great deal. Block-end feeders filled to capacity with maggots are more commonly employed to meet this end, with maggots also offered as bait, although the big bream specialist will more often pin his faith on open-ended feeders containing bread or cereal-based groundbait, with perhaps something entirely different on the hook. It all depends on the quality or quantity of the bream hoped for.

My own approach is more likely to be with a paternoster or link-ledger, on rivers, or a freelined bait on lakes, which will probably be a large helping of breadpaste or a fat lobworm, both of which can be cast without the aid of any additional weight. To grab the attention of a bream shoal, and hopefully hold it, I usually proffer a dozen or so balls of groundbait at the very beginning of the session which will also contain some samples of the hook bait. More of both is introduced later, should the need arise. Failing that, a lot of chopped up worms go in to attract them. For bite indication I invariably use either Optonics or Bitech Viper buzzers, having discovered a long time ago that bream can produce one hell of a run.

I first became aware of this when fishing a water unknown to me, in the forlorn hope of contacting a carp, a species almost equally as unknown to me at the time. When a fast run developed on my ball of paste, I could scarcely believe my eyes. I struck much too soon in my eagerness to react to it and could have bawled my eyes out when I realised I'd fumbled the strike and missed. I needn't have worried, however, because another run came almost immediately, to exactly duplicate the first. I made no mistake this time though, and was surprised and not a wee bit disappointed to reel in a bream of no astounding size. Bream will give you a good run on the take if allowed to, although I must say here that I personally haven't found them to be too concerned about resistance when taking a bait – once they finally decide to, of course.

Because of their excessive slime, which is easily removed, and also because of the fact that their dorsal fins are prone to becoming entangled in mesh, bream, like barbel, should never be kept in nets, no matter how pleasing to the eye a good catch is in the morning. So whether they happen to be your favourite species or not, return them safely to the water as soon as you can, and try not to handle them unduly. Finally, it must be emphasised that while five-pounders are common enough, bream of above that weight are not to be taken regularly by most. Also, while many fine specimens have come from rivers, the truly great bream are inevitably taken from still waters, any one of which could quite suddenly come into the limelight by producing mega bream of a size you wouldn't believe. This is definitely the kind of water to head for, if you feel like making your bid for an elusive double-figure bream.

Carp: Superior Species or Stupid?

Although they're an exciting species to fish for at night, and will without question produce the greatest thrills, carp do, unfortunately, represent something of a grey area to me. This is mainly due to the fact that during the period I was madly keen to learn all there was to learn about them, I could scarcely find an accessible water on which to pit my wits against theirs. Then, ironically, when I shifted my pitch to the other side of the world, I was literally surrounded by carp. They were free for the taking, provided you didn't put them back, at which point I believe some explanation is called for.

In the Southern hemisphere carp are classified as vermin, an obnoxious breed which when feeding disturbs sediment on the bottom to the distress of other, more native species, although this has never been irrefutably proven. Nonetheless carp were outlawed a long time ago and a price put upon their heads, to the effect that a fine of $2,000 (roughly £1,000 sterling, which has probably risen by now) is the penalty for being found in possession of live carp of any size or description, and that includes using them for bait or even keeping them in an aquarium or garden pond at home.

Such was the situation I discovered upon my arrival in those sunnier climes, which nipped nicely in the bud any notions I had of becoming at last a proper carp angler, for the law of the land decreed that any carp I caught were to be killed on the spot. Now as it happens I'm loath to kill any fish I catch – even trout for the pot – so on the few occasions when I did come into contact with a carp, either unexpectedly or otherwise, I'm pleased to say it 'accidentally' slipped the hook before reaching the net. This was the only way I could deal with a situation in which it was considered to be great fun to shoot good carp with a shotgun or hunt them down like big game with bow and arrow from a canoe!

I have written about this subject on several previous occasions and mention it again here only to emphasise what a tragic affect it had on my future carp fishing, both in this country and overseas. What it did was to dampen the enthusiasm and respect I hitherto had for the species, which I came to view as an easy target that couldn't wait to get caught on a hook – or that's the impression I gained from Australian carp, which resulted in my thoughts and feelings about carp generally becoming confused. I eventually readjusted to the possibility that perhaps they weren't all they were cracked up to be. I have yet to spend the time required in pursuit of them in this country to allow me to dispel such thoughts once and for all.

All being well, this will come in time, for I've already noticed how British carp put up a much better scrap when on the end of a line, and while I do appreciate that I'm treading on sacred ground here, I would beg the indulgence and understanding of all carp enthusiasts in respect to why this is so.

Having said all that, I have, as any thinking angler would, nevertheless kept abreast of new developments as they've taken place and tested not a few. Yet the idealisms of carp fishing which remain with me are of trying to tempt them on baits other than boilies and on rigs that don't need a mountain of lead to make them work. Don't ask me why, because I couldn't tell you; suffice it to say that I prefer to do things my way, and have never enjoyed following trends simply because they were there to follow. A large ball of bread, a cube of meat or perhaps a lobworm, is what you'd most likely catch me using for carp bait, freelined; and I make no apologies for that because surely one fish on any of those baits must be worth three on boilies.

My simple approach also spares me a lot of headaches; for such is the drive in carp circles these days to find new and completely revolutionary ways to present the bait (invariably boilies), that the time must inevitably come when an appropriate educational degree will be required to understand just the gist of them! You think I exaggerate? Of course I do. I appreciate this kind of diversified thinking – it is keeping up with it that creates the problems!

Therefore, if you want to try for carp without committing the rest of your life to them, keep an open mind; don't be put off by the aura that surrounds the fish. Approach them sensibly with one of your usual rigs, for they will all score at times. Boilies, if you must use them, are more likely to succeed when fished in conjunction with a hair-rig, as will most baits, but be prepared to feed the swim liberally when fishing with boilies. Several thousand put in to attract the quarry is not entirely unknown, but remember, there's a definite line between drawing carp to your swim and overfeeding them to the point where they might not even look at the bait on the hook, which will then remain untouched throughout.

A surface-fished bait in the margins still works, but this obviously calls for the greatest display of stealth. It's an exciting method with which to take carp, though, and is conducted well away from the water's edge. Should you insist upon a more technically involved advance to carp fishing, then you'd be well advised to join The Carp Society. Among its members are the top carpmen in the country, from whom some of the most innovative thinking of today flows. It is then generously passed on to all members via the society's *Carp Fisher* magazine.

I do question, though, the God-like worship bestowed upon the species for being the most intelligent thing adorned with scales and fins, now that so many of its number are regularly caught, photographed and returned, then promptly come back for more. So are we not, then, affording a carp's ability to think and to out-manoeuvre us, more credit than deserved? I sometimes wonder.

Whatever a carp's IQ, – and many are better qualified than I, to comment on that – there is no refuting its ability to fight when hooked, and for that reason alone it has earned tremendous admiration. I am in no way trying to put the species down – I simply want to view it objectively and in the right perspective. The comment contained in a recent letter from an eleven-year-old nephew in Australia, is worth repeating. 'They're stupid,' he wrote, referring to some small carp he'd just taken, and I was sorely tempted to agree with him. His comment is worthy of note because it is unbiased, formed entirely without being influenced by the angling press, which we all know can enhance or contaminate the credibility of just about anything concerned with fishing. So what then is the answer? Are carp gifted with the super-intelligence rating that so many credit them with; or is my small nephew correct in his assertion that they're stupid?

Cherubic Chub

One of my first memories of chub is associated with the sound of my father bashing their brains out in the middle of the night on a low railing behind me. I was very young at the time – about five – and the *coup de grâce* taking place would awake me to the certainty that Dad had caught yet another. He used to fry chub in batter and have them with chips, but I usually declined them because of the bones. This disgraceful treatment of the catch didn't disturb me in the least at the time, although I did grow up, of course, to be thoroughly ashamed of it, made my feelings known and henceforth the practice stopped.

In retrospect perhaps my own respect for the species was no better, since I was probably twice as old when shooting with an air pistol a big stuffed chub that my grandfather had caught and had obviously been very proud of when having it set up. I'd have been just as proud of it myself today, had I not knocked the stuffing out of it a lifetime ago. For I learned in time to afford chub and every other fish I came into contact with the courtesy and respect due to them, and have for many years kept a special place in my angler's heart for the species under the microscope here.

Chub have always held a deep attraction and fascination for me, mainly I suspect because I virtually grew up with them on the banks of the River Thames. I can in fact state quite categorically that after finishing with gudgeon and the like I cut my teeth on chub when first requiring a landing net to lift the catch out of the water at the grand old age of six or seven. The line we used then was 12 lb. cuttyhunk and coffin leads the sinkers, without ever a plea to my father as to why! Perhaps it was just as well then that I reached the age at which I could ask myself the very same question, after which I began to mend my ways and have since progressed to the stage where I approach chub quite differently on the various rivers I fish. And I've fished a few in my time, from waters as far afield as the Hampshire Avon, the Kennet and the Dorset Stour, from the Thames, the Medway and the piddling little ditch in Middlesex from which I have had chub.

This species is, I think, just about as near as you can get to what most people's conception is of what a fish should look like. Some other species are long and lean, while others are almost bloated, or even quite squashed in the case of bream, as though flattened by a heavy roller; not so the chub, however, which has almost perfect proportions for a fish. And somewhere, whatever the time of day or night you'll find them feeding. It's just a matter of getting to know a water really well and deciphering its every mood – which on reflection is no small thing, I suppose, but a requisite nonetheless, if you are to succeed.

I find that baits can be left almost to the angler's own personal choice; for when in the mood chub will carry off with glee almost anything of an edible nature and some things which aren't, but I guess I'm a bit catholic in my own selection of baits. Cheese paste is falling out of favour, yet for chub I still think it takes a lot of beating, particularly in the weirs. Luncheon meat is cheap and simple to prepare – you just cut it up into bait sized cubes. It continues to gain in popularity, and the chub love it. What's more, if used in conjunction with a hair rig, it stays firmly in place, although some anglers prefer to push the hook through the bait until the bend shows and then insert into this the fine sliver of a twig or whatever to prevent the hook ripping out of the bait on the cast. It's a trick that's been around for quite a while now and continues to work very well.

Bread flake (rather than paste) is one bait I'd never be caught chubbing without. I have great faith in the bait and, indeed, many contemporaries of mine insist that if a large piece of flake won't tempt a chub, then you're unlikely to catch one on anything. I would be inclined to agree with that: generally flake can almost be depended upon to get you into the fish.

Lobworms are another favourite chub bait of mine – more so in the winter, when I find that some baits, including cheese (and also flake to a lesser degree) lose a lot of their appeal. We also have the various berries which chub adore – elderberries and cherries for example, that are sadly these days so seldom given a try. Don't forget either that at certain times of the year, chub will zero in on a small livebait. Happily, this normally coincides with an influx of tiny fish of all kinds, and that's during the earlier months of the term. I have known chub to accept small live gudgeon at night even in winter, the period in which they feed most ravenously of all, of course. In fact,

I've recently turned over a couple of real beauties on a weed-choked little stream, but that was just before dusk. For some reason they ejected the live gudgeon as they left the water, but I'll be back; you can depend on it.

Maggots, it goes without saying, are responsible for many big bags of chub, usually via the feeder, at night. Here we might well be advised to take a lesson from a match angler, because these match types appear to have worked out very nicely the way to use the feeder rig to its best advantage – that much is made obvious by the results some attain. Feeder fishing has never made a great impression on me personally, but that's solely down to individual taste I expect.

Many moons have passed since the best bait of all for chub was considered to be a dead frog, as some angling writers decreed. The frog was arranged in such a way on the hook as to make its legs pump as it was worked back to the bank to give the impression that it still lived. And from frogs we finally turn to slugs and other such creepy crawlies that nothing at all would otherwise induce us to touch, if we did not want them for bait. The list of these is quite endless; suffice it to say that if a chub won't eat it, then it really must be out of this world. Fished on the bottom, or on the top at night in the manner with which one would present a dry fly, any one of these can produce additional sport, and what's more important to us, every bait mentioned here can be used to good effect after dark, although I must say I would draw the line at using frogs, and would never encourage others to do so.

My own approach is to ledger at night, with a reasonably light outfit comprising of a line of 4 lb. and rod to match, plus (if necessary) the very minimum of lead on the line. A couple of swan-shot is about as heavy as I like to go, but one cannot be too insistent on this point. The demands of the flow control the question of lead weights, not the whimsical wishes of the angler, as he will quickly discover. Remove that control and I'll be freelining a bait (again!), for I fully appreciate the effectiveness of these tactics. Indeed, in just the right setting one might fish bread flake or worm, using much the same principle as one would when long-trotting with a float, adding just a small split-shot to the hook-link perhaps to keep the bait nearer the bottom. Failing that, a link-ledger will be my next choice, or (if conditions cry out for it) I'll be just as content to 'roll' a bait along the river bed.

So techniques can be almost as varied as baits, but don't forget to adjust them as circumstances change. Bites may suddenly drop off, in which case some adjustments will probably be called for in respect to the length of tail between hook and sinker. This may also be desirable when changing baits, and while we're about it, does the swap warrant an alteration to the lead load as well? It might. In fact a more buoyant bait could end up in an entirely different spot, unless compensated for by some extra weight, so keep this possibility in mind. It also pays to follow up your bait occasionally with a few free offerings to encourage the fish to anticipate more.

There are only two modes of detecting a chub at the bait as far as I'm concerned, and one of these is to watch the rod top or quiver/springtip for takes with betalight or tin-foil attached. The other, and most sensitive of all in my opinion, is to actually feel for them using the touch ledgering technique, with the tightened reel line wrapped around the index finger. Why the index is always suggested I have no idea, the next in line being the finger I use because I find it more sensitive to a take. I also have a woollen glove with that particular finger cut away to keep me in more positive touch with the line.

If watching a quivertip for takes, make sure you're using one that's suitable to conditions. They vary in power from around an ounce to about 3.5 oz., dependent upon the distance the bait is fished as well as the flow. Get that wrong and you may have problems with setting the hook. So it's a good idea to have a selection of quivertips to meet most demands.

To find chub, look for fairly rapid water; calculate (as always) what the passage of the flow tells you, and base your attack on that. Weirpools will rarely let you down, although on more open stretches of water you'll doubtless find them frolicking in the midstream flow. A more concentrated effort should be brought to bear wherever trees line the banks, or rafts of rubbish collect to entrap whatever is carried along by the currents in the nature of food. Eddies will also develop around these rubbish rafts, which means that edibles travel round with them. Find such an obstacle in the middle of a small stream and you'll likely as not discover that it harbours most good chub within the immediate vicinity. Do keep in mind that you'll be fishing in the dark, though, so note well beforehand where the most dangerous snags lie, otherwise you'll be tying on fresh hooks all night long.

Eels that Never Surrender

A much respected quarry of the nightstalker, the eel is blessed with two well known specialised groups that exist for the sole purpose of studying and catching it in greater numbers and size. The species has not always enjoyed such attention. Until the formation of the National Anguilla Club in the early sixties, eels were considered as fair game for the pot. They were in fact often referred to as 'potsies', and seldom returned. This isn't so surprising when taking into account the high level of protein they contain and the price demanded for fresh eels; it's a wonder that any were ever put back.

There was also the future breeding aspect of the other species, to afford them protection, but since, as we all know, an eel doesn't reproduce in freshwater, this cushioning effect wasn't extended to it, so the angler could quite legally (and morally perhaps, dependent on your point of view) kill and take home for the missus to prepare for the table, any number of eels. Being such an unworthy creature it didn't then rate worrying about in respect to detailed study; for any damned fool could pull out an eel without even trying, or so it was thought at the time.

When it came to extraordinarily large examples of the species, however, all attempts seemed to run smack into a brick wall; only when technical advances associated with more worthy fish began to take shape and slowly embrace the eel also did we finally see the possibility of big eel fishing being approachable from a purely specialised angle. Specimen hunters of the day began to sit up and take note; they began to acknowledge the fact that there was after all a real chance of selectively seeking out big eels – and I was among them.

My thanks for that must go to the late Peter Mead, who was as eel-crazy as anyone possibly could be and would go to any lengths to deposit a few big'uns in a bath filled with fresh water for a few days to rid the catch of any lingering muddy flavour before cooking, since the slightest suggestion that he really ought to put 'em back would have him climbing the walls!

It was Peter who wised me up to using whole deadbaits instead of just the tail when I was in my early teens, a bait from which thenceforth I rarely strayed. These were affixed to the wired hook with the aid of a baiting needle and I soon learned that rather than being much too big, as I had at first suspected, such baits tended to discriminate between the big eels and the small, with scarcely any weighing in at less than two pounds (nothing at all to brag about now of course but worthy of comment at the time). Peter, though, along with a few other eel fanatics, had designs on something better – the eel record, no less!

Henceforth I was encouraged to join them in their eel–record-busting attempt, which stood at a paltry 8 lb. 8 oz. at the time, not that I ever gave the possibility much credence, mind; it was fun though to discuss the matter and to look at the real problem. This was that each time a really big eel was hooked, it was inevitably lost again because the gear expected to hold it was always hopelessly inadequate for the job. A further annoyance was that they were usually claimed to have been another species with a bit more credibility to it (which they may well have been of course, but we weren't having any of that).

These cases of mistaken identity often occurred, so we thought, and to ensure it didn't happen to him, Peter equipped himself with suitable tackle; I teased him, saying that he had the exploits of conger more in mind, looking at the special landing net he made. For the ring, he used the rim of a bicycle wheel, which I had trouble lifting when empty, never mind with the projected record eel inside. You had to hand it to the man, though; our only means of travelling then was by public transport, and off he would go with this huge contraption dangling at his side. The record eel? No, it never did materialise for us, but if one bloke did deserve to catch it, then it had to be Peter Mead. He spoke of actually hooking it once, but not even the gear he used could control it, so it must have been something special!

For my part I lost interest in serious eel fishing quite some time back. I can't exactly explain why, but the old impetus in relation to eels was no longer there. That was a pity because I really enjoyed seeing the old centre-pin go into a spin whenever an eel took, as I had occasion to when fishing for eels down under in Australia. Enormous they were, and that old problem of inadequate tackle returned again. Yet even when I used hefty saltwater boat rods they continued to be smashed, or literally grounded on most occasions, achieving at best a few eels of up to five or six pounds. They were not, though, as far as I could ascertain, the same species as we have here, not that you'd guess as much when coming into contact with them.

A friend (Bernard Alfrey, to whom this book is respectfully dedicated) managed a whopper in Sydney that weighed an astounding twelve pounds, but don't think for a minute that's as big as eels go, Down Under. Duck shooting with friends over a wet and windy marsh in the State of Victoria, my brother Paul (now living back in England) realised as soon as the first duck was brought down that some gigantic eels lived in the water. The shooter found himself wrestling with one of the beasts that had reached the bird first, and quite a battle ensued before the prize was held victoriously high, minus a few bits and pieces. But wait, there's more! When a far smaller eel was caught and cleaned for the pot, its head and entrails were thrown back into the water to disappear in a gulp and the wash of a miniature tidal wave; but it took the seizure of a gun dog's hind leg by one of the brutes to convince the shooting party that it was time to go.

To return to eeling in this country, I can recall quite clearly the first big'un I ever hooked. I was about ten at the time and had to make do with just the top joint of a rod stuck in the ground. Away went the dough bobbin and I struck, if one can call it that, on a four-foot length of greenheart, and was immediately pulled to the water's edge by the monster on the end. For some reason we had no landing net and so I had to watch helplessly as my father tried to beach the catch. You'd never believe the tears that rolled down my cheeks when the line parted – I was in a sorry state. Fortunately, others were soon to follow, culminating in what I guessed to be a four-pounder. I make no apologies for that, because even now eels of that size are by no means commonplace.

Modern methods haven't changed eeling a lot, as far as I can see, although the thinking behind it has altered. Attention to would-be resistant points is now carried out more or less habitually in an attempt to overcome them. Gear is more robust and often purpose-built for the job, which shows in the way that huge eels are now being bullied all the way to the bank, instead of breaking free when far from it. Baits are now more varied, with fish heads, rather than whole fish, in the forefront. I've done reasonably well on chunks of cats' pieces of fish obtained directly from the fishmonger's stall. I would go so far as to say in fact that if it's of a meaty or fishy substance, then an eel is bound to eat it, and that includes the angler's fingers – I know!

A stormy night is supposed to send eels into an uncontrollable frenzy, and has been acclaimed as the ultimate time from way back in which to set your sights on them. While I can't positively vouch for that, I have noticed on numerous occasions that exceptional sport has been had from eels during stormy weather; but equally so during a pleasant hot summer's night. Blistering hot days have produced them also, when they often turned out to be larger than normal. As for the suggestion I've come up against that eels feed freely throughout the year, I haven't experienced this. For sure, the odd one has come my way in winter, and that too has been abnormally large, but during those freezing nights on the banks, I do better with other species; notably barbel and chub.

When it comes to bite detection I simply keep an eye on the drum of my centre-pin reel. When an eel takes it revolves madly, and that I find very exciting. Should the reel run too freely at the pull of the stream, then a few pebbles placed on the drum will counteract this, without interfering with a positive run. On still waters I'll probably rely on buzzers; it is from here that history has taught us to expect the biggest eels of all. This was at one time linked with the captivity theory, in which eels were said to become trapped in lakes and the like with high banks from which they could never escape; they were supposed to grow into virtual monsters.

That theory for whatever reason seems now to have been dismissed, but it can't be denied that the largest eels do tend to come from still waters. This might be because we can present a bait more delicately on them to fool the big'uns, whereas on rivers we're constantly battling with the flow to achieve as much. This is just a theory of course, but one worth mulling over, since there's no logical reason that I know of why rivers shouldn't also support giant sized eels. Indeed, you'd expect them more, perhaps, on moving water, because wherever they end up it's a damned certainty they arrived there initially via a river.

Discussing eels recalls for me a friend of my father's called Warner. He was some angler, by all accounts, and his exploits were often mentioned by my father. He once insisted that Warner had caught an eel so big that when he hung it over a clothes line that was a good five feet high, both the head and tail of the eel touched the ground. I never did learn who was responsible for those whoppers, Warner or my father; but I suspect the latter of merely trying to enhance the image of an old angling friend – and how!

Beware of the Pike

So you want to catch a pike at night? Oh dear, you're a glutton for punishment. Nevertheless, pike fishing after dark is being done with mounting enthusiasm by those well versed in the ways of the species during the light of day. This is how you need to acquire the necessary qualifications before even thinking about embarking on night piking. The waterside at night is no place to learn the skills required for handling pike confidently and unerringly with the minimum of fuss.

Pike need to be dealt with efficiently for the sake of yourself as well as the catch (I nearly wrote victim, which is what it will become if not handled with due care), for you could end up with a very nasty gash in your hand if it comes into unnecessary contact with a pike's maulers. This is a simple mistake to make during the day, never mind at night. Hooks, too, may be swinging freely to ensnare you, so my advice must be to give *Esox* a miss at night until you are thoroughly conversant with it in daylight. You'll then be able to approach it in the net with the least misgivings and the pike, too, will be grateful for that.

It doesn't like to be mauled (what fish does?) and what's more it trusts you to do the right thing by removing the hooks (for obvious reasons preferably barbless at night) with the least possible delay by turning it on its back on the unhooking mat and retrieving them gently by way of the gills (with a long pair of forceps, if the hook is well down). Then it can be returned to the water right away; all of which is no simple task in the dark, with only a torch to guide you. Just thinking about it makes me shudder, and I've done as much in the middle of the night quite a few times, and countless more times during the day. If you haven't, then I suggest you postpone your night assault on pike until you have.

Just bringing one of those devilfish to net in anything but natural light can be an experience; but this is eclipsed tenfold when you've actually got it on the bank, for that's when the real drama begins. It's a scene re-enacted often now, as more anglers begin to focus on pike at night. Yet it does demand a lot of thought and preparation, since some unwritten rules apply.

To start with, don't put them to waste by trying to land pike with a net that's too small. Mine has 40-inch arms and I often wish they were longer; some I've seen swamp my own. When it comes to rigs, a pike float would be a devil of a thing to keep tabs on in the dark, and while most ledgering techniques will suffice, I usually rely on a running ledgered deadbait, fished on a very tight line to let me know instantly when the bait is taken. This is more easily determined on rivers, I find, where takes tend to be more positive due to the flow, which also enhances the river pike's more pronounced spirit in battle. Imagine too the sudden shock of a lure being taken at night! Now that's got possibilities surely. Livebaits are apt to encourage the smaller predators to strike, and I'd rather forego the chore of fiddling about with those in the middle of the night; at times they prove to be more difficult to deal with when on the bank than their betters.

For detecting takes, the usual bite indicators are employed, but they must be observed more diligently than ever to offset any chance of deep hooking should a fish run off with the bait; for the mind wanders at night, well away from the projected goal that coerced you to spend it in the open in the first place, but not, I trust, to the detriment of the wellbeing of the fish. A badly hooked pike may soon become a dead one and there's no limit to the steps I will take to prevent something like this, which would niggle at my conscience. A missed fish rather then a deeply hooked one is the kind of philosophy that I personally adhere to at all times, and I'm not alone in that respect.

But what thrills await the competent pike angler at night! He'll sometimes wonder what's hit him as he struggles in the dark to bring to heel that savagely exploding beast confronting him, for it's a poor pike that doesn't do its damnable best to buck that invisible force that's drawing it forever nearer the bank. Contrary to popular opinion, which dismisses the fighting qualities of pike until winter as inadequate, they are more than a handful to get to grips with at any time, including the summer months, when more response to a bait is generally to be had from them, and obviously when most night fishing is undertaken. But check first to be sure you're permitted to fish for pike during the earlier months, for (though it's hard to believe) the ancient ban on pike fishing before winter arrives still exists in parts.

A 22-pounder at dawn. Its captor would never have had baits out that early, but for the fact he was already on the scene, having fished all night.

Unfortunately you won't find much about piking at night in print, because it's still a relatively new approach to the species. Therefore the best further advice I can offer is, get out there and do it yourself. Discover how the pike in your own waters react to a bait at night, and above all, don't live in fear of them. They're just another species of fish after all, albeit one with particularly sharp teeth – they're just as sharp in the day! Here are a couple of points worth mentioning, in conclusion. Don't worry too much about bringing a powerful light to bear when netting the catch – better that than making a complete hash of things – and do determine long before dark exactly where you're going to return the catch. Pike are unusually big fish and putting them back into the water needs thinking about beforehand, requiring as it does a reasonable depth of water with easy access. It's unfair to the fish to be kept out of its natural element while its captor aimlessly wanders the bank in the dark, searching for a likely spot to release it. It could be dropped and irredeemably damaged, if hands begin to fumble or legs stumble; so take measures to ensure this doesn't happen by selecting a suitable site for the purpose before first wetting a line.

Roach – Pronounced with a Hush

Roach: now was there ever a more dainty fish to behold? I don't think so, and I am never disappointed to catch one, unless it is on bait intended for something else, when my feelings about them become somewhat mixed. They're not easy fish to fool by any means and there was a time when the true roach angler was hailed as the most skilful of all. That kind of adulation has long since died, however, but not the demands still placed upon the roach-fisher to go about his business discreetly, even furtively, so as to avoid the least suggestion to the fish that he is within a mile of them.

Such an approach can become a strain, quickly turned into a bout of frustration if one doesn't observe the roach fishing rules, for I can think of no other fish that can be put down so decisively at the drop of a hat, unless it is the chub. Win their confidence, however, by coaxing them to feed, and roach will continue to do so with the greatest of pleasure, until a false move is made on the angler's part; then it is back to square one again.

Little and often is the rule applying to groundbait, and usually it's of the cloud variety to avoid overfeeding the fish during the course of attracting them to the swim. This can be a very hit-or-miss situation after dark, and for that reason I tend to lure them to my swim with limited examples of the hook bait instead, put out gently by the catapult, if they cannot be introduced by hand.

Sensitive to any form of drag, roach are not to be lumped together with the other species that feed well at night. Sure, you'll occasionally take one on your chub, barbel or bream gear, but don't hold your breath while waiting. Roach have to be fished for purposely, with the right tackle and frame of mind, and by that I don't necessarily mean match gear, either, but rather a lightened version of what one would normally use for chub: a two or, at most, three pound line for instance, with just a whisper of lead. This I prefer to be attached directly to the tail of the hook, rather than on a separate link placed further up the line because there appears to be less evidence of any attachment when small quantities of lead such as I have in mind are used in this fashion, so the more popular trends of ledgering are best left to the pursuit of other species.

The very idea of ledgering rather than float fishing for roach will have the purist seeking psychiatric help – he'd need it, if wrestling with the dubious task of trying to use a float at night, not that you'd catch him fishing for roach in the dark in any case. For roach aren't usually thought of as a night species and are therefore rarely fished for in the dark, despite the fact that they do indeed on occasion feed very well right through the night, just like most fish. They also tend to come to net at a much better size than during the day; and the results might surprise you.

I ceased to be surprised years ago, having deliberately fished for and caught some very nice bags of fish, which the waters from whence they came would never have been credited with supporting. The lower Thames is a case in point, the particular stretches I have in mind being at Molesey and Hampton Court. Roach abound in these reaches of the river in large shoals, attaining at best a few measly ounces, judging by what you see taken on the float during the day. Try them with light ledgered pellets of cheese on a size 14 hook at night, however, and you'll soon find out just how wrong you were. The average weight of those I've taken over the years at night would probably work out at around a pound, though I have netted fish of nearly twice that size, and a fair few only slightly smaller. Obviously a two-pounder is always a real possibility, so don't underrate the roach of the Thames before approaching them after dark.

Still water roach will also oblige at night, but not to the same extent as river fish, I find. Yet they still appear often enough to become a nuisance when baiting with bread or corn for tench. Indeed, when recently fishing a very picturesque lake in the West Country for the very first time, I was quite convinced that the few bites I had unaccountably missed just had to be from tench, until the first fish I connected with proved to be a roach – a nice roach admittedly, of around a pound. I had though stopped admiring them by the time the fourth one arrived, for I was fishing for tench after all, and just what the roach score was by dawn I really have no idea now, but I do recall that the tench score was a very disheartening nil.

There's nowhere I'd rather take roach (or most other species for that matter) than from the frisky flow of a weirpool. Here I can enjoy to my heart's content the kind of fishing I like best. It is as active as it is interesting, not to mention the challenge it represents, for it calls upon all my resources as an angler to succeed. It makes me think about what I'm doing, just like a fish at times, to help me understand what's taking place beneath that turbulent surface and how the inhabitants may be reacting to it. Now this is the very meaning of fishing for me, and like a dumb trout forever rising to a fly on the top to increase its chances of one day becoming hooked, I too rise at every opportunity proffered to meet head on the challenge of the weirs. Unlike the trout, there's simply no question of me becoming hooked on it however, because that took place a great many years ago.

The song of the white water surging on its way excites me no end, while at the same time fostering within me a deep and most satisfying sense of peace, of idle contentment, and could any angler wish for more than that? I am left undisturbed to test different baits on what some might see as completely hopeless rigs; but I became cautious of accepting literally as gospel what others thought or said long ago. I prefer to dwell at length on advice offered, prior to following it up in my own way, with a little refined thinking here and there to marry it to my own particular needs.

Let it not be said then that I don't think about my fishing, because I do, a great deal, and so must you, in order to succeed. Think positively about the finicky fish you hope to intercept that's in the spotlight here. Think about its built-in radar system that can detect your approach long before you've made it in earnest. A roach will hardly drag its fins to ask, 'What's that?' when it detects your first footfall. It'll be long gone before you arrive. Therefore, think about the natural survival instinct of the species – all species – and allow for the irrefutable fact that what you hope to outwit is in every sense a wild creature, with more knowledge about its own environment and ways than any of us can ever hope to aspire to. Do that much and you're well on the way to making one of the greatest discoveries of your life. You will also begin to marvel at the manner with which, in spite of all the barriers to suggest the contrary, you manage to prove on occasion that you're just a wee bit smarter than the fish that does after all have so much more going for it.

Tench – the Jewel in the Crown

The tench is said to adopt the colouring of its environment, and it must surely be as symbolic of the classic, heavily mist-draped still water scene as is the carp, and I often look upon the aforementioned species as samples of emerald delight, while others describe them as the very jewel in the crown. And aren't they that and more, as droplets of water sparkle upon their flanks like so many gems as they lie beaten in the net? Now that's the kind of picture I never tire of, for each and every one serves to remind me of how beautiful the tench really is, even though I have had them as black as lumps of coal.

My interest in the species goes way back to the days when, try as I might, I simply couldn't catch a tench, not even the kind which the other kids fishing the pond on the local common after school kept pulling out with impunity. So minute were they that those kept in the proverbial jam-jar had room enough to spare; but their size did not matter one iota to me then – I just longed to catch one of these mystical mites – or 'doctor' fish, as they were sometimes called, because of the manner in which other species were thought to sidle up to the tench to cover their wounds with the other's protective slime. Old wives tales? Maybe, but not without some logic, I think.

Tench are gregarious fish and once contact is made with them you can usually expect more than one, although at night, in my experience, a catch of three or four is the best you can hope for on most waters; much will depend on where you fish, of course. As many as four in a whole week, would come as a pleasant surprise on some lakes I could mention, whereas the angler with less than a dozen tench in a single session would think he'd been hard done by on others. However, when thinking in terms of tench in excess of five or six pounds, as I am here, I can only add that quality rarely means quantity as well, but that concerns me not in the least.

A big bag of fish has never interested me unduly, no matter what the species. I'd be just as content with a catch of tench numbering three of between five and seven pounds, for example, than a dozen of similar size, and would doubtless appreciate them all the more for their individuality, which sadly gets lost under the weight of sheer numbers. I have in the past harvested good bags, and while the joy of catching them was very real I found I couldn't really relate to these rare occasions for what they were – red letter days – or rather nights.

I like to approach tench with the same delicacy reserved for roach, for the gentle approach appears to be most appropriate for the usual tench scene. In fact the tench itself comes across as a very mellow creature, demanding our full appreciation of the fact as we advance on tip-toe if necessary to offer a bait with such finesse that it scarcely ripples the water. How that gentle touch changes, however, once a fish is hooked. It's all systems go! For the appearance of a tench tends to belie the fact that it is first and foremost a damned good fighter, affording a situation in which no moves are barred as it tests to the very limit of endurance and beyond the skill of the angler as well as the credibility of his gear, as it struggles to part company with both.

To those unaccustomed to this battling breed, I strongly recommend a line of six pounds, even if the best you can hope for is a not to be sniffed at four-pounder – you'll appreciate the stronger line from the word go. My own reels are normally loaded with a line a couple of pounds lighter, unless the presence of heavy weed dictates to me otherwise, but I do know both my waters and the tench therein very well; which isn't to say that I don't often wish for a heavier line myself while struggling to bring a particularly big tench to net. But I do try to approach tench fishing as light as I can, irrespective of the strain it must at times have upon my old ticker.

For this reason I much prefer to present a bait on a totally lead free line whenever the chance arises, which is much more often than most experienced tench fishers would have you believe. Indeed, some are quite surprised when learning of my approach, simply because they assume, I suppose, that these tactics are now outdated and therefore judged to be of no further use. But don't you believe it! Freeline fishing still takes a hell of a lot of beating, as far as I'm concerned, for all manner of fish. It represents the most natural way of working a bait to a fish that I know of, other than the dry fly angler's approach, and in the right circumstances it's a joy to use for the reasons already mentioned in this book.

If ledger leads must be used then I suggest you keep them light, a half ounce being quite adequate for all but special needs, such as

Night time is tench time, as can be seen by the seven-pounder caught by the author on corn.

those required for punching the bait well out. These I invariably affix to a short link of a few inches, attached to the main line at a distance of about a yard or so from the hook, dependent on how sport develops. If it's not forthcoming, then adjustments are naturally made to the rig.

Baits are varied, and while bread can work very well on some nights, on others sweetcorn will account for the most fish, or occasionally a hook loaded with maggots or worms – even a lively lobworm. Luncheon meat also scores at times, so be prepared to ring the changes. Don't forget also that boilies of one flavour or another are now considered to be not just an option but a very desirable tench bait indeed; so much so that on some waters the challenge lies not in simply catching tench but tempting them on something other than a boilie.

For my part I'd much rather catch tench on a good dollop of breadpaste or a lobworm, but suspect that's because I can use them on a freeline. Nonetheless, it gives me an extra buzz to succeed with something a bit out of the ordinary on the hook, with or without the requirement of lead on the line to cast it out, and I'm often trying all kinds of would-be titbits. Ideally, these ought to be tried when there's evidence of fish feeding, not when all else has failed, as is so often the case. I think it must take a special breed of angler, however, to continue to persevere with the unknown qualities of one bait, while knowing he'd probably score well with another that's more familiar to him.

Hooks should always correspond to the bait, not merely in shape or size but also hopefully in colour. Peter Drennan for instance, produces hooks for corn that match faithfully the golden hues of the bait, and I can confirm that they really work a treat. The size I mostly use for tench baits is number 12, but don't, I hasten to add, stick too rigidly to that. I'd have difficulty in trying to contain a large lobworm on a size 12, but might just find it a bit big to accept a bunch of maggots, so the size of the hook in relation to the bait is the first factor to be kept in mind; a simple deduction, I agree, but one that is nevertheless overlooked by many.

On the question of groundbaiting I react to whatever gut-feeling I get at the time, whereas it was once common practice to bait the swim heavily for tench without the least bit of caution. It worked then and probably would now, although whether such concentrated groundbaiting is necessary to the degree that used to be recommended, is a matter for conjecture. I'm inclined to groundbait only moderately, putting in at the start of the session fewer than a dozen balls of well mixed bread or whatever, with samples of the hook bait added to enhance its appeal. I will also throughout the night introduce into the swim via the trusty catapult the occasional pouchful of whatever is on the hook.

Weatherwise, I like to see anything other than a completely flat calm for tench; a calm tends to forecast a total blank, I've learned, however pleasing to the senses. Should the sky be overcast with a warning of rain, then so much the better, in my book. Bites, when they occur, can come at any time – usually when you're least expecting them. Having put in a great deal of time on my own particular tench water I can safely say that at two and four o'clock in the morning my betalight bobbins and buzzers can almost be relied upon to call me to action stations. Before and after those times, developments are very much a case of Hobson's Choice. It's absolutely vital to be fully alert at all times, if humanly possible, which it isn't of course. That's why I like to make a brew-up during intervals throughout the night, not so much because I need one but simply because preparing it keeps me awake and on the move. I'm there to fish for tench, and if a single take develops in the night then the venture has, to my mind, been worthwhile, whether I make a connection or not. Should I connect, and bring the catch safely to net, then I'm naturally overjoyed. The mere sight of a good tench in the net is enough to accomplish that much, without the battle to get it there, for it truly is the jewel in the crown.

Capturing the Mug Shot

Treasures such as the fish you've just landed will doubtless be destined to have their images retained for ever more in photographs, with you drooling all over them. If you've taken good pictures you'll still be drooling over them in the years to come, because photographing the catch is the grand finale of the event for many anglers these days, myself included. It's a simple enough undertaking during the day, when, if you haven't got a companion with you to do the honours you can usually get a passer-by to operate the camera for you, while you're suitably posed with the trophy for a mug shot – that's assuming your camera has a PHD button (Press Here, Dummy). If it hasn't, you'll be presuming an awful lot if you think that everyone passing by is a born photographer with the know-how to work your camera. The chances are they won't be, and so what you get back from the processors is an out-of-focus image of yourself taken at the wrong speed or exposure – and where's the bloody fish!

Fortunately, I've had friends with me during the capture of most of my best fish who were at least half-way competent in the skills required to take a decent picture; albeit nothing better than the usual, uninteresting mug shot. Nevertheless, I'm thankful for every one, and never would I part with them. It's true to say, though, that whenever printing up shots that I've taken of my friends with their catches, I can't help wondering why they couldn't do an equally good job of capturing me with mine on film? Now I'm not a professional photographer by any means, having no training or qualifications in that field whatsoever. I have, however, been taking pictures since before I was a fourteen-year-old; initially with a little plastic thing I bought for my younger brother one Christmas for the princely sum of seven shillings and sixpence (a measly 37½ pence in today's money, so you can imagine just how sophisticated it was). I still have some of the results obtained, which I thought quite good at the time, lurking in a box somewhere at home, which brings the wisp of a smile to my lips whenever I come across them.

Since then, of course, I've learned a lot and gone through many cameras, each supposedly better than the last one. My first expensive and fully professional camera (?) was a Pentax Sla; the same model I believe that Dick Walker used at the time (the early sixties), so naturally I had to have one also; not so much because Dick had the model but because I was writing for the angling press then and needed a really first-class camera with which to illustrate my work; and who, may I ask, could offer better advice about such things than Dick Walker? It'll last ten years, he promised, and nearly twenty years later I thought the time had come to change it; not because it didn't still take good pictures but because I needed the through-the-lens exposure readings that more advanced cameras could now give me and so turned to a Pentax ME, which was said to be the smallest single lens reflex camera on the market and largely automatic. It is light and still has a very sweet action after about twelve years of abuse, although not the same professional feel as the Pentax Sla, which one well known angling scribe, I've just learned, is still using to wonderful effect – after a period of nearly thirty years!

The ME (sounds more like a military missile, don't it), I use solely for black and white work, and for colour (always transparencies, for reproduction purposes) I have a Nikon FM2, plus various lenses for both cameras, not that I use them much. Close-up tubes and lenses are brought more often into service for finicky detailed work of rigs and baits, etc. But by far the great majority of my pictures are taken with the standard lenses that came with the cameras, mainly because I'm too lazy to take my other lenses on every excursion to the waterside. When I do I rarely use them, and much the same can be said of tripods.

Nonetheless, a well exposed and composed picture taken with a telephoto or zoom lens mounted on a tripod, is one you'll never regret having taken, so if you're built like a cart-horse (and I'm not) then do yourself a favour and take such items of photography gear along with you whenever you go fishing, and not just when you're out for a week or longer. Then you won't sit bemoaning the great pictures you missed out on.

Should you be alone in the middle of the night and catch something you really must pose with, then you've got two choices. The first is to pop it in a carp sack till morning, and take your pictures then, when the light will be better. The second is to capture it on film directly after netting by using a flash. This is not quite as easy as it sounds, demanding as it does a bit of forethought.

The typical mug shot, taken at night with a flash.

First of all a suitable site has to be chosen within the vicinity of your pitch, on level ground, hopefully, with no humps or bumps to trip you up in the middle of the night. It should also be in a position in which your camera won't get damaged; especially if, like me, you're in the habit of leaving it in place all night, when safe to do so, contained within a plastic bag for protection. This saves the time it would otherwise take to get the camera up and ready for action. It also gets the fish back in the water sooner.

Next, having decided on where the photographs are to be taken, get down on your knees at the exact spot where you'll be posing with your catch and push a bankstick or some other marker into the ground at either side of you and level with your head; this will effectively frame the picture. Now, having done that, place another marker in the middle of the banksticks but still in line with them to focus your camera on (another bankstick, bag or brolly, will do for this). Then take a few steps back with the camera until your middle marker is perfectly in focus in its viewfinder and the outside ones are no longer in view. Set the camera on a tripod, or bankstick with a special adaptor, which can be purchased from most tackle dealers at a very reasonable price, and you are more or less ready to go.

In daylight you'd check the focus and exposure, roll the film on and probably activate the self-timer – it's now a mad dash to get back to your network of markers, remove the middle one and then strike a pose with your fish before the self-timer operates to photograph you. At night you'll need a flash, set to the requirements recommended in the instruction book that comes with it. You also want, if possible, a long air-release cable, with a fitting at one end to screw into the thread of the self-timer on the camera and a bulb at the other for you to kneel on when ready to take the picture. Pressure on the bulb operates the camera, of course. Easy? Who said it was? It does help to have a suitable camera for this lark, and if you haven't one then consider the secondhand market. It's simply filled with bargains that come within the financial scope of most of us.

The camera and flash should hopefully be set for operation long before dark, but it always pays to check the focus at night by the light of a torch, just to be on the safe side. Some anglers remove all markers before taking the picture, but if you take pains to ensure they're out of it when composing the shot, I see no point in that. Clever composing is nigh on impossible at night; we have to be content with mug-type shots. During the day, however, when we're better equipped to see what we're doing, it's far more interesting to

Angling photography shouldn't begin and end with the mug shot. Move in on the catch with your camera, adding 'props' to enhance the picture.

look for different angles from which to photograph the catch – still difficult when alone and holding it, I admit, but angling photography shouldn't end there.

Good pictures can be taken with the fish arranged on something suitable on the ground, such as a wet carp sack for instance. The additional prop, such as the rod and reel that the fish was caught on, will add much to the overall appeal of the picture and put the size of the fish more into perspective, as will weighing scales, a reel on its own, forceps or even samples of bait, if they look right in the viewfinder. Don't be limited with your camera; be inventive and move in for the shot.

Most of my best pictures depict other anglers with their fish, inevitably, but that I have to live with. I enjoy taking them in any case, from every conceivable angle; most of which get published somewhere at some time. I also need them, to add to my forever growing collection of literally thousands of negatives and slides, of which a fair percentage must have been published by now, in all manner of books, papers and magazines. Fortunately I have, for thirty years or more, developed and printed my own black and white exposures, which cuts down tremendously on expense while allowing me to crop prints in a more personalised manner. When it comes to film, I'll only entertain those which I consider to be the best; Ilford and Kodak materials, with an ASA rating of about 100 in summer and 200 in winter, when the light is bound to be weaker, hence the faster film. On the rare occasions when I use a tripod and cable release my film speed will be drastically reduced to achieve better results.

For transparencies I rarely use anything but Kodak's Ektachrome, which I leave with my photography dealer to pass on for processing. On one of the few occasions I didn't, when shooting colour in Northern Ireland, I had to make do with Kodachrome instead and it got lost in the post; so imagine how I felt about that. I was a guest of the Tourist Board for a week, and had every intention of writing a descriptive piece for a general magazine about that part of Ireland, as a thank you gesture. To be fair, films don't often get lost, but if they're as important to you as that one was to me, then once in a lifetime is once too often, by my reckoning. Fujichrome is worth thinking about also, over-emphasising the tone of colours as it does, to please some but not all. Yet that too, has to be sent away for processing, with the same risk of the film being lost. If you're prepared to take the gamble, fine. I rarely am.

Things that go Bump in the Night

We all hear them; all talk about them, those unaccountable things that go bump in the night, even though there is rarely anything at all ominous about them – I think, although so seldom do we learn from where the bumps originate that I'm probably being a bit optimistic there. Nevertheless, the more cowardly amongst us will be relieved to hear that very few weird noises have reached my ears during the dead of night. Indeed, I can recount only a few bad experiences that have come my way. One of the most memorable occurred on such a wretched night, weatherwise, that I should never have been caught out in it in the first place and would rather forget that I was.

The fish were in hiding and then down came the rain, leaving me with no alternative but to seek the sanctuary of a nearby covered weir, where I thought a bit of shut-eye might be in order; but I hadn't allowed for the wind. It soon joined forces with the rain to batter the weir's structure unmercifully as I tried to sleep, its woeful cries carrying along to where I lay in the dubious security of the foetus position praying for it to go away. I must have dozed at times because, like a persistent alarm clock, that wicked wind would arouse me, and each time it was in even more of a temper, whipping the water into a frenzy which the weir struggled to hold back as it raced downstream like an unleashed demon in an attempt to expend its rage.

But could the weir withstand this hammering? I began to think not, and if the weir should go then so would I, into that heaving caldron below. It was a frightening situation to be in, as I'm sure you can imagine, yet still the structure moaned, the sheer weight of water it tried to contain sent shivers down its spine – and mine. It was a bit like waiting for the devil to take me away, ha, ha, or so I thought at the time; then in complete panic I felt the wooden planking I lay on begin to tremble and creak, to be accompanied by a loud rumbling sound that, I'm thankful to say must have drowned out my petrified scream – as some damned fool rode over my feet on his pushbike in the dark.

Now in the cold light of day the above appears to be more amusing than scary. Live through the same experience on a night such as that described, however, and you'll doubtless soon be wondering how you ever did. But not so on a particularly dark night in Australia, during which I was determined to fish till dawn. My friends had decided to turn-in, leaving me alone with the more innocent noises one hears by the water at night, until I saw a pair of menacing eyes staring at me from the water's edge. No, they weren't six feet apart, as somebody has since suggested, but they may just as well have been for all the fear they injected into me, causing me to react in the way that anyone would, under the same circumstances, and that was by fleeing in pursuit of my friends.

My entire gear – everything – was left on the bank behind me, and there it remained untouched until the sun was well over the water on the following morning. But what had watched me out of those evil, unflinching eyes? I guess I shall never know the answer to that, having entertained not the slightest wish to return to the place to find out. It may well have been a harmless possum, since I'd seen enough of those around, often with a baby on their back, but in a country where a mythical creature can rejoice in such an absurd name as a Bunyip, surely anything can turn up.

Something certainly did on the night I fished the surf on the State of Victoria's celebrated Ninety Mile Beach. We had a fire going on the beach as usual and all sat around it with the billy on the boil. Seating arrangements were left to parking your backside wherever you could and, not to be out-done, a more determined member of our group went off in search of his own 'parking place' and returned with a large heavy log to sit on. Needless to say, as the night lengthened so did the yarns, and one by one we were all obliged to gradually withdraw from the heat of the flames – but not so the angler who still sat on his log. It was, he claimed, a mite too heavy to keep shifting about. We were most surprised then when he suddenly shifted in one hell of a hurry; taking off like a demented greyhound along the beach. Unbeknown to him a deadly snake had been coiled up in a peaceful sleep inside the log, until the heat from the fire had aroused it in panic to make good its escape between his outstretched legs.

It was a venomous black snake that my brother Paul chased across the ground one night, mistaking it for an eel that had slithered free from the sack. Only in the nick of time did something about the snake's movements register to prevent my brother from making what could have been the deadliest – and last – mistake of his life. So, on reflection I'd rather hear strange bumps in the night that amount to nothing at all, than endure some of the actual experiences I've lived through. It's a pity they too, weren't mere bumps; I'd have found them a lighter load to bear.

The ultimate nightmare, however, must have been lived by the fictitious character who was escorted to the estate lake by the Lord of the Manor, and there introduced to the head bailiff. Being of a friendly disposition our guest cracked a joke with the bailiff: 'I'll pay you a pound for every poacher's head you bring me in the morning,' he laughed, and paid up without a word of protest when the bailiff stepped out of the early morning mist with four heads tied securely to his belt.

The Long-Stay Angler

Just a weekend spent on a water is something to look forward to with tremendous delight – imagine then what the prospect of a whole week or longer would amount to. It's planned with infinite, painstaking care, leaving nothing at all to chance lest it ruin our expedition completely. Tackle is overhauled with a concentration rarely allocated to other, more pressing domestic matters, and rigs are re-fashioned or born anew, while baits are obtained in bulk. Anything in fact which you might just need throughout your extended fish-in, is piled in a corner of the den long before departure.

Only by preparing for such an event can you possibly know how high this pile of 'extras' will grow. There will be extra pullovers; socks; trousers and coats; extra this, that and the other; just in case they're needed, and that concerns only the extra clothing you'll probably want to take along, for no better reason than to be on the safe side – just in case. Now, add to all this questionable gear the really essential bits and pieces and you're well on the way to including the kitchen sink. Not quite? Well, at least a bowl to wash up in will be included, and why not, when you intend to be away from home for so long?

You'll probably regret having deemed so much as indispensable, when struggling along to your chosen pitch with it weighing you down to the ground, but a full week is a long time to survive without the convenience of a bathroom close at hand, a freezer, or even a proper cooker to prepare a meal on. So don't complain; be thankful for the fortitude you've shown to have included it all, even if a great deal won't be used. It's far better to be prepared for whatever fate decrees, than have your stay ruined by being inadequately prepared; and once there of course it requires no further attention until the time arrives to cart it all back to the car again.

Some items are indeed indispensable, waterproofs among them. They may be a burden to wear; but you'll be glad you brought them if the weather turns bad – and how! You'll still need waterproof leggings long after the rain has stopped, to protect your legs from the high grass that will remain wet and clinging for some time. Wellies will give you added protection, much as I'd rather forego them, preferring to wear trainers when fishing, in which I can step more lightly without alarming the fish. Come the rain though, and I'll take my chances in wellies every time. Thigh waders – now a normal part of the carp fisher's uniform – offer additional resistance to the rain and the damp. They do restrict one's movements, however; a disadvantage to be contemplated before deciding to wear them.

It goes without saying that a brolly is essential and better still a bivvy with groundsheet in place, giving at best, a fairly comfortable retreat and, at worst, a base from which to operate. It is also a shelter to sleep and eat in, and a safe place in which to store your supplies. Be sure to have it firmly pegged down to the ground, however, to help keep out uninvited guests. The pegs that come with most bivvies are generally quite useless; you'd be better advised to purchase from a camping store some heavy duty tent pegs, which will enter hard ground without bending. Make sure they'll go through the retaining loops of the bivvy first though.

Bedchairs and sleeping bags are included these days and, if you really feel like spoiling yourself, a blow-up mattress as well; the normal drill being to fish during the peak hours at dusk, throughout the night and at dawn, and to catch up on some sleep during the less promising hours of daylight. That I think is vitally essential if you are to function at full throttle as twilight approaches again, bringing the promise of better things to come. To burn the candle at both ends will find you firing on less than all cylinders at the least promising time of day and not at all when fast asleep in your bivvy at night, when you really ought to be fully alert and close to your rods.

In respect to bivvies, brollies, bedchairs and sleeping bags etc., I have tried to assess which might be the best, but the conclusion I eventually came to is that you do get what you pay for. Kevin Nash gear, for instance, is by no means cheap, but it is good and totally reliable. It is also the most revolutionary; you have only to look at his brollies to appreciate that. The Oval Brolly affords almost as much protection from the elements in reasonable weather as would a bivvy. As a measure of its dependability, the Kevin Nash Overwrap has become the best selling bivvy in the world. His winter clothing shouldn't be overlooked either; for gone are the nights when one was attired in several layers of garments to keep warm; it's all specially

Angler Len Arbury knows when to relax. To burn the candle at both ends is to achieve nothing at all.

designed one- and two-piece suits, nowadays, and if they've actually been designed by an angler, than so much the better, for who could have a greater awareness of our peculiar needs?

Personally, I find a one-piece suit too much like a straitjacket to contend with for long and will opt for a two-piece every time, but others may prefer to wear the former. With thermal gear in place, however, I normally manage quite well without the above mentioned garments until winter is upon us with a vengeance; it's then advisable to keep your head as warm as the remainder of your body. Otherwise, if you're anything like me, you'll find that if your head gets cold then so does the rest of you. Be sure then to wear a warm hat of some kind. I have several, one of which is a really warm fur-lined hood that covers my ears and the back of my neck to prevent any annoying draughts creeping in.

Fortunately, I don't suffer cold feet often, but perhaps that's because of the thick socks I wear with my wellies. I have two pairs, bought in Australia for a couple of dollars each a good fifteen years ago, and there's still scarcely a mark on them. I have also had for some years a long pair of seamen's socks, but have never seen the need to wear them, my Aussie socks and wellies keeping my feet warm and dry in all but arctic conditions, when probably nothing on earth will be completely satisfactory. Moon boots and such like I have no call for, while others swear by them.

If you're not too concerned about looking just right for the part of an angler, than you could do worse than to call in at your local Army disposal store, where you'll find all manner of garments to keep you warm and dry, for a very reasonable price. That's where I used to shop, and much of the cold and wet weather gear that I use today was purchased from this particular market a very long time ago. For, let's face it, top of the range angling apparel is very expensive; so why pay more than you have to in order to keep warm?

We have no option but to buy things like bivvies from the tackle trade, yet sleeping bags and even bedchairs can be purchased for half the price you'd expect to pay for a purposely designed fishing one. A friend paid £20 for his bedchair at a local marketplace some time back, and it's still going strong. Okay, nobody's saying it's as good as more fashionable and therefore more expensive bedchairs, but it nevertheless suits him fine. Way back in the sixties, another friend purchased from an Army surplus store the simple outer casing of an American soldier's sleeping bag, which was apparently warm and most definitely waterproof. All night he laid out in the open in it, completely disregarding the persistent rain, and I couldn't believe how dry he was when he finally vacated his bag in the morning. Don't be influenced by fashionable trends; if you haven't the cash to spare – go for something cheaper that will serve the same purpose.

However, if you can afford to buy the best, then why not? I would suggest you look at Fox International's bedchairs before any other. They're expensive but very popular, so are obviously worth every penny. With so many different designs on the market, though, it's almost an impossibility to recommend just one, and I hesitated before doing so. That applies to most items of gear referred to. For whatever some individuals will be looking for in a bedchair, or whatever, others may be searching for something entirely different. Lightness combined with durability are high on my list, and if they're finished in a washable material I'd consider that a bonus.

Sleeping bags I think of in much the same way, for they really do get abused and often covered in mud. A washable cover is most desirable. As to design, well, I have yet to see one incorporating a quick release system, to enable the angler to flee his bag in the middle of the night, in time to connect with a bite. His one chance of doing so now is achieved by leaving the sleeping bag unzipped to allow for a speedy exit, although ideally he shouldn't be in the bag in the first place with baits still out.

Now what else will be required for this extended stay? Insect repellent most definitely, during the warmer months. I use the highly recommended 'Shoo!' to keep the midges away. Produced by Cummings Ltd, it can also be had in the form of wipes. And don't forget the toilet rolls – oops. A tiny garden trowel is also taken along to keep things in that respect in order. It's also handy for grubbing around for worms. I'm also in the habit of dropping in my bag a few clothes pegs; not to hang my smalls on but to peg the flap of the bivvy in place when it refuses to stay put. There are many other uses for clothes pegs, and I would often have been lost without them; and the same can be said of a long length of string, which you're bound to need if you haven't got it.

Aspros, band-aids and such are forced into a small tobacco tin, and you'd be surprised at how often that's opened; not only on my own behalf but for the benefit of those around me, who invariably need something from my tin. A safety-pin? Yes, I've even been propositioned for one of those, before now, which just goes to show that you never know what you'll need next.

Fires being banned on most waters, I occasionally take fishing with me a galvanized bucket with holes punched in it (such as used by night watchmen of old). This, when filled with coalite on top of a fire-lighter to get it going, will continue to throw out enough warmth to keep you glowing all night. It's a boon, also, for keeping the kettle on the boil. Check with the appropriate authorities first, though, to be sure you'll be breaking no rules with your flaming bucket.

Other items worth taking, if you've got room, include a small radio with ear plugs attached. You'll then be able to listen to your favourite pop records without disturbing other anglers nearby. Remember though that you won't hear buzzers screaming their heads off, with the radio's ear plugs in place, so you'll have to concentrate on bobbins instead.

Another idea is to equip the entrance to your camp with an alarm, to give warning of intruders. One young angler I know rigs up a spare buzzer for this, which operates directly somebody approaches to set off the alarm. There is now a purpose built alarm for the night angler, the manufacturer of which I've been unable to locate. Should he contact me then I'd be delighted to review his product, because I think there's a need for it.

Finally, if you're fishing with friends who are stationed at the other

The author communicating with a friend. Such contact can lead to increased catches.

side of the water, and are fearful of the possibility that they might out-fish you, then splash out on a pair of walkie-talkies. They're not very expensive and can help you catch fish. How? Wait and I'll tell you. One of my fishing buddies and I much prefer to do our thing alone. We arrive at the water together and leave likewise, but in the meantime we select swims that are far apart – and keep in touch via the walkie-talkies.

At first we left these continuously operational, but to conserve power we then arranged to speak to each other at hourly intervals to discuss progress. And you wouldn't believe the number of times we have scored because of this exchange of information. 'Tried luncheon meat?' Matt would ask. 'I've had three out on it already.' If I hadn't, you can be sure I soon would be trying luncheon meat, hopefully to good effect. At other times the reverse situation would apply, and Matt'd take his lead from me; and it's all due to the contact we have on walkie-talkies. But quite apart from this obvious advantage to be gained from our contact, it's comforting to hear the voice of a friend in the middle of nowhere at night – and something to look forward to as the pre-arranged time of communication draws nearer. Our equipment is stamped: Sonic CB 27/81, Channel 14–30, and is Police-Approved. Some isn't, so be sure to check this point out, if contemplating the purchase of walkie-talkies.

Yes indeed, our night fishing necessities do tend to grow; even more so for an extended visit. I do, though, resist the temptation to add to them still further, and am more inclined to reduce them drastically – and to hell with the consequences. Fortunately, it's more likely to be loaded into cars, these days, but that wasn't always the case. Many years ago a dear friend decided he'd had enough of lugging gear around on his back, so made a trailer for it to be pulled by his pushbike. Great! I thought, when hearing of his plans. I didn't think it such a good idea after all, however, when he turned up at my doorstep, just a few blocks from his own. For he was already utterly exhausted from pedalling with the trailer behind him and there was no way he was going to take it to the fishing site, a good twenty miles away. So we unloaded the trailer, grabbed what gear we could carry and dashed off to catch the train. Happy days? Don't you believe it.

And Finally – Preparing the Meal

Food, along with the means to prepare it, probably presents us with the biggest headache of all when planning a fishing trip for a week or longer, because we have no way of keeping it fresh, and therefore fit for consumption, for more than a day or two away from home, unless of course the angler is fortunate enough to own a well equipped van, containing among other things a small fridge, in which case he's really got it made.

For most of us it's a matter of managing as best we can with a couple of frozen ice-blocks, if we're lucky, or a bag of ice (obtained, incidentally, from service station coin machines, in other parts of the planet earth), to keep perishables fit enough to eat for perhaps the first couple of days, after which we'll have to depend on canned or packaged food, so be sure to take a dustbin liner along with you in which to deposit rubbish as you make it. Some don't, which is why a few of the fisheries I'm familiar with have banned tin-cans on their waters altogether, to set the long-stay angler a most difficult poser indeed. Blame the lame-brains who caused the bans by their indiscriminate dumping of rubbish. And, should you witness such indescribable behaviour, take steps to ensure it doesn't happen again by confronting the culprits and showing them the errors of their ways. Probably they won't listen; that kind never does. They're not anglers, but pests, out for a few laughs at your expense; for it's your fishing and mine they're spoiling, not their own – they wouldn't know the meaning of it.

Having got that off my chest, let's look at some of the tinned food available to us that can be cooked in a jiffy. Apart from the more obvious tins (and packets) of soup – the creamed variety of which can be watered down slightly to enlarge the volume – and the ever-present can of baked beans that some manage to eat cold (ugh!) there are all manner of delicacies that come in cans, such as salmon for instance, which when served with ready-cooked potatoes from a

Brother Paul preparing breakfast.

tin that can be heated in a trice makes for a very pleasant dish, if canned peas are also added. In place of the salmon can be corned beef, ham, spam or whatever you fancy. The list is practically endless, but don't forget the salt and pepper.

The beauty of cold meat in a can of course is that it doesn't have to be heated, so saving on time and cooker fuel. Other ingredients taking no more than a few minutes to warm up are mixed vegetables, sweetcorn, sausages in baked beans, hotpot, stew, and whatever else you're likely to name, for there's no shortage at all in this respect. Look on the shelves of your local supermarket and you'll see what I mean. Even mashed potato is on call. Mixed to instructions it'll go nicely with fried eggs and beans. More's the pity American rolled bacon in a can is no longer available. Shortly after the Second World War that really was a treat.

Small, lightly boiled potatoes in their jackets, will keep for a day or two in a sealed freezer bag, and again take just minutes to heat before serving. Therefore, by selecting the kind of food you like best, a nourishing meal can be fixed quickly, if not perhaps a feast fit for a king. It'll taste like one, believe me, when eaten at your leisure, prior to getting back to your fishing in earnest. I'm in the habit of nibbling in the day and having my main meal in the evening, which keeps me going until I'm forced to nibble some more. Should I be expecting visitors during the week then I'll arrange for them to bring me fried fish and chips – and also a fresh carton of milk as a change from the tinned or powdered stuff I'm bound to be using by then. I'll request, fresh water, also, to top up my supply.

Many drinks are made during the course of a week – coffee, tea or whatever – and that calls for a lot of water, which you may have brought with you from home. For long gone are the days when you could rely on water from the river or lake to drink, and to find freshwater on tap near to where you're fishing is a convenience I seldom enjoy.

On really cold nights there's nothing quite like an Oxo cube dissolved in boiling hot water for hitting just the right spot, I've learned, and usually have some with me, kept in a small plastic food box. These Tupperware-type boxes come in handy for storing all kinds of edibles – cheese, butter, eggs, tea bags and sugar; I'd be lost without them. That's also applicable to the can-opener, small frying pan, saucepan and kettle I take along, with the equally obvious knife, fork and spoon, plus a tin-plate to eat from. A spare cup is sometimes needed to share a drink and a chat in the middle of the night with a neighbour, and perhaps to receive one in return.

To make the brew – or indeed, to cook a meal without lighting a fire for the purpose – we have to make do with a camping stove. A little methylated spirit stove was once used to boil water and for anything more substantial a paraffin pressure stove (usually a Primus). It was often a long-winded affair to light the Primus though, if the wind was blowing in the wrong direction, and the smell of paraffin was difficult to remove from the hands. If it wasn't removed, your baits became tainted by it and your fishing took a dive, so eventually I turned to a small camp stove that was run on gas, and that just about met my needs. I still have one in fact, but a poor example of the magnificent cooking equipment that Calor turn out nowadays, and have been doing for quite some time. In other countries, their refillable gas bottles can be conveniently dealt with at any service station, but to achieve as much here, can be a problem, I find. Therefore, if you discover a regular refilling source, stick to it like glue.

A Cotswold Baits double-burner camping stove has recently come into my possession, designed (it would seem) to fulfil my every wish, as far as camp cookers are concerned. The burners, divorced from the

The author with designs on a sample of Fred J. Taylor's cooking from the Dutch oven.

gas canister as they are, sit firmly on the ground, making toppling kettles, so readily associated with the more usual kind of camping stove, a thing of the past. Each burner, incidentally, is so small it can fit into a shirt pocket, and can be attached to the gas bottle in a matter of seconds. To light it, should your matches get sodden with rain, keep some waterproof matches in a tin. They'll come to the rescue when all else fails – even the rubbing together of sticks.

When it comes to cooking out in the open though, Fred J. Taylor has the whole business sewn-up. He uses a Dutch oven, which, if you didn't know, is a large cast-iron pot with three legs and handles. You need a fire for this, on which the pot is placed to cook all manner of super dishes. Place it in a hole in the ground and even bread can be made in it, which is saying something, I reckon. Fred tells me it needs a controlled amount of heat, and that the Dutch oven he uses now has been in his possession for twelve years. It has some history behind it, also, in that before Fred came by it the well known American angling journalist Ted Trueblood owned it. Sadly, Ted died some years back, and the Dutch oven went first to his son and then on to Fred, who is now known to enjoy his waterside cooking as much as his fishing. I predict that at some time in the near future, I'll be sampling some of Fred's cooking from his pot, and if it's only half as good a I've heard, I can't wait to indulge. So, eat yer hearts out, peasants – I'm destined for better things.

'68

Nicholas Royle was born in Manchester in 1963. He is the author of five novels—*Counterparts*, *Saxophone Dreams*, *The Matter of the Heart*, *The Director's Cut* and *Antwerp*—and one short story collection, *Mortality*. He has edited thirteen anthologies including *A Book of Two Halves* (Phoenix), *The Tiger Garden: A Book of Writers' Dreams* (Serpent's Tail), *The Time Out Book of New York Short Stories* (Penguin), and *Dreams Never End* (Tindal Street Press). He lives in Manchester with his wife and two children, and teaches creative writing at Manchester Metropolitan University.

Also by Nicholas Royle

NOVELS

Counterparts
Saxophone Dreams
The Matter of the Heart
The Director's Cut
Antwerp

STORIES

Mortality

AS EDITOR

Darklands
Darklands 2
A Book of Two Halves
The Tiger Garden: A Book of Writers' Dreams
The Time Out Book of New York Short Stories
The Agony and the Ecstasy
The Ex Files
Neonlit: Time Out Book of New Writing
The Time Out Book of Paris Short Stories
Neonlit: Time Out Book of New Writing Volume 2
The Time Out Book of London Short Stories Volume 2
Dreams Never End

’68

New Stories from CHILDREN OF THE REVOLUTION

Edited by **Nicholas Royle**

May 2008

SALT

CAMBRIDGE

PUBLISHED BY SALT PUBLISHING
PO Box 937, Great Wilbraham, Cambridge CB21 5JX United Kingdom

First published 2008

Printed and bound in the United Kingdom by Biddles Ltd, King's Lynn, Norfolk

Typeset in Swift 10 / 12

ISBN 978 1 84471 481 0 hardback

Salt Publishing Ltd gratefully acknowledges
the financial assistance of Arts Council England

ARTS COUNCIL ENGLAND

1 3 5 7 9 8 6 4 2

In memory of
Anna Kavan
1901–1968

&

Cornell Woolrich
1903–1968

Contents

NICHOLAS ROYLE

Introduction

GEORGINA HAMMICK WROTE an essay, 'In Defence of the Short Story', which appeared in *New Writing 3* edited by Andrew Motion and Candice Rodd. 'For although our history in the story is as distinguished as any,' she wrote, 'and while the story continues to flourish in the United States and Canada, in South America, in Eire and in other places besides, it must be true to say that notwithstanding a small band of supporters and enthusiasts in all corners of the book trade, the literary short form is no longer paid much (or serious) attention here.' *New Writing 3* was published in 1994 and the unavoidable observation to be made is that the situation, in general terms, far from improving over the next decade and a bit, almost certainly got worse. Of those authors looked after by the bigger publishers, only the most well established get to publish collections of their own short stories on a regular basis, assuming they still write enough to fill them, and then only if the deal includes the next novel as well. Authors languishing in what used to be called the midlist, and now has no name because it doesn't exist any more, can forget it. And if single-author collections are now fewer and further between, sightings of multi-author short story anthologies have become even rarer. Magazines have struggled, too, and in the wake of recent Arts Council cuts some have gone to the wall, while others are finding life even harder than they did before.

There are, however, recent signs that things may be improving.

While the conglomerates have, for the most part, had their backs turned, certain smaller publishers have been doing excellent work to support the short story. Serpent's Tail, for many years a strong supporter of the form, have continued to publish collections and anthologies. Comma Press, a small independent founded in 2002 and based in the north-west of England, has published an excellent series of anthologies named after punctuation marks—*Comma*, *Hyphen*, *Bracket* and *Parenthesis*—as well as other anthologies and author collections. The origins of Salt Publishing lie in poetry, but their commitment to the short story has been made abundantly clear from the number of fine collections they, too, have published and from the fact that their logo nestles on the spine of the present volume.

The news these days is increasingly good, as it happens. They started small, but Norwich's Elastic Press have now published dozens of story collections and anthologies, concentrating on slipstream fiction, neither quite genre, nor mainstream. Bigger, but still an independent, Faber are not afraid to launch a new writer with a short story collection. Other publishers are still either springing up or hanging in there and doing short stories, among them Social Disease, Crowswing Books, Night Shade Books, Gray Friar Press, Toby Press, Dedalus.

Even mainstream imprints have started putting out the odd anthology again, if the editor is someone like a Zadie Smith or a Nick Hornby, both of whom, fortunately for the short story, seem to have a genuine commitment to the form. Smith's *The Book of Other People* contained three or four brilliant short stories that might otherwise never have seen the light of day. If I were editing a new incarnation of Giles Gordon and David Hughes' annual reprint anthology *Best Short Stories* (Heinemann, 1986–94), as I often fantasise about doing, a couple of these would have walked straight into it.

When Gareth Evans told me that he and Verena Stackelberg were planning a season of talks, screenings and exhibitions, *All Power to the Imagination: 1968 and its Legacies*, to mark the fortieth anniversary of the events of 1968—the election of Alexander Dubček in Czechoslovakia and subsequent Prague Spring, widespread demonstrations in the US against the Vietnam War, strikes and student protests in Paris that almost brought down the government, worldwide resistance to the established order—I immediately thought we should do an anthology of new stories by writers born in '68. I started making a list, and pretty soon the list included names of authors born in '69, because I thought if you want the spirit of '68, maybe you want writers who were conceived in '68. Of course, you could have been conceived and born in '68, but I suppose by '68 we generally mean May '68, so anyone born in February '69 might well have been conceived while the paving stones were being ripped up in Paris, but then you start to wonder about babies born early and babies born late. If you include anyone born in '69, they could well have been conceived not in '68 at all but in '69.

So, '68 it was. Also, it's tempting to think that there was something in the air in '68. Maybe some of these '68 babies were born and took their first breath and swallowed along with it a waft of revolutionary idealism. I deliberately didn't ask contributors to tell me in what month they were born. I didn't want some to seem more '68 than others (by being born in May, for example). In the end you just have to make a decision and stick with it. And then, late in the day, when contributors start dropping out for one reason or another, and writers born in '67 or '69 get in touch and you eye their excellent credentials with something approaching desperation, you wonder if you should jettison your ideals and let them in. But then you remember that ideals were part of '68 and that you'd have excluded other writers unfairly if you allowed these ones in at this late stage.

And so began a hunt for a couple more writers. It was of vital importance to me not only that they be born in '68, but that they be good writers, good short story writers in particular, and that their work should appeal to me personally. Out of more than 250 stories I've been fortunate enough to be able to help into print as editor, in anthologies and magazines, there's not a single one I didn't like. I'm not interested in publishing stuff just because it corresponds to notions of what is 'good'. I've got to like it as well. One story I liked a lot, in an anthology for *Time Out*, was 'Spaces' by Cath Skinner, born in 1968, but short of hiring a private investigator, I couldn't work out how to track her down, once I'd exhausted the phone book and the internet, to get her to write a new one.

The word goes out, however, and people pop up. The gaps were filled. It was always going to be a short anthology and it was always going to be turned around very quickly (no other publisher could have been so flexible or such an enormous pleasure to work with). My invitation to the writers was deliberately vague. I wanted them to address the subjects of revolution and change, but to have the freedom to do it however they wanted. I didn't want them to feel tied to 1968 but nevertheless to produce a story with something to say about the legacies of '68, about the nature of revolution or rebellion, about utopias or dystopias, about dreams, change, potential.

Toby Litt's 'History!' reads like a creepy cross between *Desperate Housewives* and Michael Haneke's terrifying *Funny Games*. Justina Robson and Tricia Sullivan both show that science fiction is as good at ideas as it is at action; their future societies have both been formed through change, one violent, one less so. The violence in Marc Villemain's story is internalised; 'This Was My Flesh' is the French author's first work to be translated into English. The setting of Frank I Swannack's 'The Lovesick Womb' may predate '68 by four centuries but change remains the same. Christopher Kenworthy writes about the revolt against the natural and James Flint explores a pairing that one suspects will always be around: students and drugs. Paris and its *banlieues* make an apt appearance in Rhonda Carrier's 'Nine Cubed' and Marc Werner gets stuck into the quintessential '68 film *If. . . .*, while Kerry Watson, an Australian author, confronts her country's shame over its treatment of its Indigenous population.

Sharp-eyed readers will have noticed that the book is dedicated to the memory of two writers who lived almost exactly contemporaneous lives, Anna Kavan and Cornell Woolrich. Kavan was two years Woolrich's senior; they were both outsiders, both excellent writers and both produced a powerful body of work, including many short stories; they both died in 1968. It may be slightly fanciful to suggest that something of their talent or spirit was reborn in these ten writers the same year, but I'm going to suggest it all the same.

MANCHESTER, MARCH 2008

’68

TOBY LITT

History!

THEY MET IN the thickest part of the woods; also, the furthest from the edge. To get there, they had to hack through thick brambles, use compasses, check their synchronised watches and remember the routes of their country girlhoods. Radio silence was maintained, however. It was twilight, clement because late summer. This den within a copse had been their place of recourse, when the adults had made it plain they were becoming too alive to be tolerated—too alive meaning too fast, too loud, too vivid in thought and question.

All of them, all three, had had both original parents to respond to; since then, all three had lost one or the other. Later, it was speculated that this might have had something to do with their actions. Information was initially hard to come by, and what there was seemed contradictory.

First to arrive at the meeting point was Margaret—her usual distinguishing feature, an aureole of chestnut ringlets, now squashed beneath a black balaclava. Her eyes, if one had been able to see them, were underlined with brown semi-circles. Margaret had given birth five years previously to triplet boys, two of whom were hyperactive; the third was given to feigning death behind the sofa for no apparent reason. Margaret, who of course herself dies before the night is out, left behind a written statement saying she did what she did for them. The consensus among the villagers was, she was a bad mother, knew it, and took the coward's way out.

'Hello,' said a low voice from the cover immediately behind Margaret. 'I wondered whether I'd be able to sneak up on you.'

Margaret had at first given a real jump; the voice interrupted thoughts of whether she could trust the teenage babysitter with John, Jack and James. Her husband had funny business at the Lodge.

'Well, then, you succeeded,' said Margaret.

Out from behind the thick trunk of a tree stepped Beatrice known as Bee, who also dies. 'It doesn't matter,' she said, 'No-one else is going to be out here.'

'This isn't a game.'

'To be entirely serious is to play into their hands,' said Bee, who was theoretically minded in her opposition. 'I am maintaining an element of joy.'

Margaret smiled a sad smile, almost as if she knew they were going to die. 'It's good to see you,' she said, and the two women hugged. Both were aware of the crackling sounds of the woods around them—were they being crept up on?

'How are the boys?' asked Bee.

'They are very well,' said Margaret, willing herself not to cry. 'It's still all battles in our house, though. War-war-war.'

'Any sign of Liz?'

'Not yet,' replied Margaret.

The two women sat on the loamy earth of the woods. It was nice for once not to have to worry about dirt—tonight was a time for being deliberately dirty. 'She's late,' said Bee, who had turned thirty the week before.

'She'll be here,' said Margaret.

'What if she doesn't come?'

'She'll come.'

There was a moment.

'I like your hair like that,' said Margaret.

'Thank you,' said Bee.

Bee's hair was usually done in a neat black bob, but she had shaved this off earlier in the evening—down to a Number 1. Some have taken this as a sign that she was all along intending martyrdom. She had been anorexic for years, which was also taken as explanation—hatred of the self and of the world. But although she did not know it, at the time of her death she was three weeks' pregnant. Despite widespread DNA testing, the father will never be found.

'Do we go ahead anyway, if she doesn't come?' Bee asked.

'I think I hear her now,' said Margaret. If she heard

something, it wasn't Liz; perhaps a fox or a badger. After this, though, they waited in a listening silence.

Eventually, quarter of an hour later, Liz crashed out of the undergrowth and fell against them. It took her two minutes to regain her breath—during which time, both the others wanted to tell her to keep quiet but didn't feel it possible.

'I was followed,' was the first thing she said that they understood.

'Calm down,' said Margaret, who wasn't the leader—they didn't have a leader; hierarchies being part of what they wanted to destroy—but who often was first to introduce ideas into their circle: she had suggested tonight; the others had not been slow to agree. 'Tell us whenever you're ready.'

Liz—who dies—sat with her head between her legs, gasping less and less. At twenty-nine, she was the youngest of them. (Margaret was thirty one, Bee—as mentioned before—thirty.) 'I'm sorry I'm late,' she said.

'We have plenty of time,' said Margaret, but checked her watch anyway.

'Who followed you?' asked Bee.

'A policeman,' Liz said, her breath a little more even. 'He was dressed in civilian clothes, but I could still tell he was a policeman.'

'How?' asked Margaret.

'Because I hated him so much,' Liz said, then sniggered. 'And he walked as if he'd been taught how to march—you know what I mean.'

'Do you think they know anything?' Bee asked.

'No,' said Margaret. 'How could they?'

'I'm not so sure,' said Liz. 'He seemed to want to follow me—for no reason.'

'You managed to lose him, didn't you?' asked Margaret.

'Of course,' said Liz, sitting up straight. 'Or else I wouldn't be here.'

'How?' asked Bee.

'Well . . .' said Liz, and took a long breath.

It turned out she had gone to the house of a sympathetic female friend, knocked on the door, been invited inside and then, after a brief explanation (seedy man loitering, fear of rape), had climbed over the back fence and into the concreted area behind the cricket pavilion. From here, she had been able to make her way to the woods without breaking cover more than once—to cross the main road near the stables.

All three women kept horses there, and this was later the cause of much speculation. Perhaps it was a sign of sexual frustration—unhappiness in marriage. The husbands of Margaret and Liz denied this as libel. Singleton Bee was discovered (by the tabloids) to have been gratifyingly promiscuous. In the end, more than seven men came forward to testify to her total lack of frigidity. 'She was very intense,' one of them said. 'Almost too intense. I didn't like it.' Nymphomania became the favoured diagnosis.

Margaret coughed quietly. 'All set?' she asked.

'Yes,' said Liz.

'Ready,' said Bee.

They started walking, in single file. All of them were quite fit—Bee did yoga, Margaret did Pilates and Liz did a weekly salsa class—so they made very rapid progress. It took them half an hour to reach their destination: a gamekeeper's cottage in a small clearing, surrounded by a neatly kept garden—lawn, rockery, fruit trees. By this time, it was starting to get dark. The lights were on inside the cottage, the now infamous 'Bower of Bliss'; the flowery curtains of the sitting room had not been drawn. A Mercedes saloon and a Renault Clio were parked on the drive, which had long-ago been done in crazy paving.

The three women made a quick check of their equipment, particularly their radios. These were small and made of black plastic; across the top of them, the words *Action Man* were written in bright orange.

'Fine,' said Margaret. 'We follow the plan.'

She and Bee proceeded to the front door. Liz, keeping low, made her way to the kitchen door—around the other side. She could hear the sound of the television. It was the theme tune to the *Antiques Roadshow*. They were bang on eight o'clock.

From her rucksack, Liz took out two rolls of camouflage-patterned tape and a chunky pair of childsafe scissors.

Bee radioed to check Liz was in position.

'All present and correct,' said Liz, a phrase of her father's.

Margaret pushed the front doorbell with the middle finger of her left hand; in her right was a toy gun belonging to one of her sons. It was very realistic, as long as one didn't get too good a look—which was why she had chosen to use it.

A man answered the door—fifty eight, fat, dressed in a green tweedy suit but with leather slippers on. This was Colin Richardson, Mayor of the village, publican of the Queen's Head, left-arm orthodox spin.

'Margaret,' he said. 'What can I do for you?'

She pointed the toy gun close up to his forehead, where it would be out of focus.

'Do exactly what we say,' she replied.

'Is that real?' Colin asked.

'Yes,' she said. 'And if you don't get inside, I will demonstrate how real.'

Colin turned and walked back into the house.

'Hold your hands up where I can see them,' said Margaret. 'I know you keep a shotgun.'

'Not any more, alas,' said Colin. 'I had to hand it in—sop to the council lefties.'

'I think you're lying,' said Margaret, as they passed out of the hall and into the TV-loud living room.

'Numfon,' said Colin. 'Be calm. There's nothing to worry about.'

A Thai woman in her mid thirties was sitting on the left of the sofa, holding a glass of Australian riesling in her hand. The glass was made of cut crystal. Her fingernails were long and had paste jewels on them.

'Sit down,' said Margaret. 'Not next to her.'

'Hello, Numfon,' said Bee.

'Bee,' said Numfon.

'Please come with me, quickly, and fetch Roger,' said Bee.

The two of them went off through an adjoining door.

The name ROGER was spelt out on it with a rhino, an ostrich, a giraffe, an emu and another rhino.

'What's this about?' asked Colin. 'It's clearly not the usual parish council business. Is it planning permission?'

'It's about everything,' said Margaret. 'You'll find out soon enough. Now, please be quiet.'

She radioed Liz.

'Building secured. You may enter.'

Liz tried the back door. It was unlocked. A moment later, she had joined Margaret in the living room.

'You, too?' asked Colin.

'Oh, yes,' said Liz.

On the television, they were valuing a wig that was said to have belonged to Samuel Johnson.

Numfon reentered the room, carrying Roger, a five-year-old boy, half-Caucasian, half-Asian. He was still groggy.

'Sit down,' said Margaret. 'If you can keep him quiet, we won't need to gag him.'

'Margaret,' said Colin, 'the nearest house is half a mile away—half a mile of thick woodland. You could shoot the lot of us, and no-one would hear.'

'Yes,' said Margaret. 'We could. I just don't want to have any whining bloody kids around. I get enough of that at home.'

'So, what can I do for you?' asked Colin.

'You can call the police,' said Margaret. 'Tell them you've been taken hostage. Tell them we're serious. And that, when they get here, we can discuss terms.'

'Anything you say, Margaret.'

Margaret slapped Colin's face, with her non-gun hand.

'Don't be such a smarmy cunt, Colin. You can die painlessly or very painfully indeed.'

'Yes,' he said, his hair disarranged.

'Dial 999,' said Margaret. 'Tell them to get here as soon as they can. Tell them we'd like a helicopter.'

'What, to escape with?'

'No, just to fly around overhead, so we feel important.'

Colin picked up the receiver and dialled.

It took him five minutes to get through to the right person.

'Yes, they're very serious indeed, it seems,' Colin said. 'No, I don't know what they want.'

'Tell them we'll only speak to an officer specially trained in hostage situations.'

'Did you hear that?' Colin asked the policeman. Then, to Margaret, 'He heard, he says that might take some time to arrange.'

'Tell him we will shoot your wife in one hour,' said Margaret.

Colin soberly repeated the words.

'Now give me the phone,' she said.

Colin obeyed.

Margaret took the receiver from him. 'You can be quick when you want to be,' she said into it, then hung up.

'Back in there,' Margaret said, and shoved Colin into the living room. She was really enjoying this—more than she had expected.

On the sofa, Numfon was cowering and Roger was crying.

'Gag them,' she said. 'The police are on their way.'

Colin slumped into the armchair and sent a brave smile towards Numfon. 'Don't worry, darling,' he said. 'We'll be alright.'

'No, you won't,' said Bee. 'You'll never be alright.'

'You deserve this,' said Margaret.

Liz handed over one of the rolls of tape to Bee, who started on Numfon. 'Lift your hair out of the way,' Bee said.

'What does that matter?' Liz asked.

'Don't hurt my mummy,' wailed Roger, just before Liz sealed his mouth. Snot immediately began to run down the slick surface of the tape. Roger's eyes were no longer those of a five-year old.

Bee taped up Numfon's hands and feet. Liz left Roger's hands free, so that he could put them round his mother.

Then Margaret taped Colin's feet together, and his hands behind his back. His mouth, she left alone.

'Tea, anyone?' asked Liz.

'Yes, please,' said Margaret. 'And see if you can find some biscuits. I'm sure they keep some nice ones.'

On television, they were valuing a Queen Anne table with very fine cabriolet legs.

Margaret sat down on the sofa with the toy gun in her lap. Bee took the armchair on the left-hand side, after removing the antimacassar. She crumpled it up and threw it into the fireplace, where imitation coals sat ready to be gassed.

Apart from Roger's sniffles, everyone was quiet until Liz returned with the tea. There were mugs for the three hostage-takers, nothing for the family.

'So, Colin,' said Bee, 'why did you call your son "Roger"? It's such a stupid name.'

'We like it,' said Colin.

'Which only proves how stupid it is,' said Margaret. 'Almost as bad as Colin. Who wants to be five and be called "Roger"?'

Bee turned to the boy. 'Let's ask Roger. Roger, do you like your name?'

Roger looked at his mother.

Margaret leaned across and pulled the tape off Roger's mouth.

'Do you like your name?' asked Liz, with a gentle tone.

Roger shook his head.

'Does that mean you like it or you don't like it?' asked Margaret.

'Don't like it,' the boy said.

The three hostage-takers all laughed.

'You see,' said Bee. 'Even he hates it.'

'So,' asked Liz, 'what would you like to be called?'

Roger looked down into his chest.

'Optimus Prime,' he said.

'Right,' said Margaret. 'From now on, you're Optimus Prime. Which is going to sound pretty silly in twenty years' time—but I don't think there's much reason to worry about that.'

'Would you like some juice, Optimus Prime?' asked Liz.

He said, 'Yes, please.'

'Very polite,' said Margaret. 'That's good.'

Liz went and got him a beaker full of orange. He drank it very quickly.

'Do you still wear a nappy, Optimus Prime?' Margaret asked.

'No,' he said. 'I'm a big boy.'

'Then you must tell us if you need to go wee-wee,' said Margaret. 'Do you understand?'

'Okay,' said Optimus Prime.

'Look,' said Colin. 'What is it exactly that you want? Perhaps we can sort it all out before the police get here?'

'What we want,' said Margaret, 'is for the police to get here. Now, please, don't speak again.'

They watched the television for a while.

'Do you like this programme, Optimus Prime?' asked Margaret.

'No,' he said, becoming more confident. 'It's boring.'

'What would you like?' Bee asked.

'Cartoons,' he said.

Margaret passed him the remote, which had been sitting on Colin's arm of the sofa.

'Choose something,' she said.

Optimus Prime skipped through the channels until he came to a programme called *Robotboy*.

'Ah, yes,' said Margaret.

They watched it for ten minutes. Then Bee said, 'Optimus Prime, do you have any guns?'

Optimus nodded.

'If we undo your legs, will you go with me and fetch them?'

'Yes,' he said.

Liz came across and cut through the tape with the chunky scissors.

Bee took Optimus's hand and led him into the bedroom.

A few minutes later, they came back, arms full of imitation pistols, lasers and machine guns.

'Which is your favourite?' asked Margaret.

Optimus picked out a red and black laser.

'You keep that one, then.'

'And I'll have this one,' said Liz, choosing an old-fashioned-looking revolver. It had cowboys on the handle and a wagon train running along the barrel.

'And can I have this one?' asked Bee, picking up a business-like automatic in black plastic.

'Yes,' said Optimus. 'As long as I can have them back.'

'Of course you can have them back,' said Margaret.

They sat down to watch the TV—all much happier, now they were armed.

Colin had been looking at Margaret's gun. 'That one's not real either, is it? You came in here and held us up with a toy!'

'Shut up or we tape your mouth up,' Margaret said. 'What do you think about that, Optimus Prime?'

The boy looked surly.

'Then he won't be able to tell you to go to bed,' said Liz.

'Or tell you to do anything at all,' said Bee.

Optimus Prime said, 'I do anything I want all the time.'

'I bet you do,' said Margaret, and laughed. 'But, shall we tape up your daddy's mouth? Just for a game.'

'Okay,' said Optimus Prime, with a sideways glance to see the effect of his words.

'Roger!' Colin shouted.

He struggled as Liz and Bee wound the camouflaged tape around his head. His face was pink by the time they finished. It became even more pink when Bee pinched his nostrils for half a minute, to check his mouth really *was* sealed. When she let go, he snorted raggedly.

'I need a wee,' said Optimus Prime.

The hostage-takers looked at one another.

'I'll take him,' said Margaret. She went and picked him up from the sofa. He put his arms around her neck. Colin flinched at this.

Margaret carried Optimus Prime through the kitchen and into the toilet; she knew where it was. She pulled the boy's pyjama bottoms down until they were around his knees, then lifted him onto the seat.

He put his finger on his willy, to point it down, then peed almost immediately. They both listened to the small gush until it went quiet.

'Finished?' asked Margaret.

Optimus Prime nodded.

'You don't want a poo?'

'No,' the boy said.

'Come on, then.'

Margaret dried Optimus Prime's willy with a sheet of toilet paper, then hiked his pyjamas up.

'All done,' she said, carrying him back into the living room.

Just then, sirens came into earshot. They became louder quite gradually. And then blue lights flashed across the stripy wallpaper.

'At last,' said Margaret.

But it took another ten minutes before the phone rang.

Bee picked it up.

'We are surrounded,' she said, relaying the words to the other hostage-takers. 'We can talk about this calmly. Whatever issues we have can be addressed. We can come outside with our hands above our heads. No, we're not going to do that,' she said. 'Where's our helicopter?' She listened. 'That's not good enough. We wanted a helicopter. Half an hour? Okay, I want you to make helicopter noises. Yes, you heard me. Make helicopter noises, or we shoot the woman.'

She held up the phone so the others could hear the chunka-chunka-chunka sound.

'Very good,' said Bee. 'But we want the real thing.'

She put the phone down, then picked it up when it rang.

'What else do we want?'

Margaret and Liz nodded at her. The plan.

'We will exchange the woman for a policewoman. A straight swap. You have five minutes to decide.'

She put the phone down.

It rang again two minutes later.

'We can have a policewoman,' she said, after listening for a few seconds. 'But they want the boy as well. No,' she said, 'that's not the deal. One for one.' A pause. 'Alright. They'll come out the front door.'

Bee replaced the receiver.

Liz cut the tape off Numfon's ankles.

'Don't try to run,' she said. 'Not until the policewoman's inside.'

Margaret took her into the hall, then slowly opened the door. She was disappointed to see so few police cars—only three.

A WPC was standing beside the open passenger door of the nearest, her hands in the air.

'Come towards me,' shouted Margaret, who could feel herself tickled by the sights of real guns.

The policewoman walked steadily forwards, until she was halfway.

'I want you here,' said Margaret, pointing to the paving stones with the gun-barrel.

The WPC started moving again.

When she was close enough, Margaret pushed Numfon away and grabbed the WPC by the neck.

Numfon stood on the spot.

'Run, you silly cow,' said the WPC.

Numfon looked back, then started to walk away. She was bawling.

Margaret pulled the WPC inside.

'What's your name?' she asked, leading her through into the living room.

'Jane McDowell,' said the young woman.

'Would you like a cup of tea?' asked Liz.

'No, thank you,' said the WPC, assessing the situation.

What she saw, on the floor, was a pile of toy guns. Then she looked at the guns the hostage takers were holding. First Bee's, then Liz's and, finally, turning her head round as far as it would go, at Margaret's.

'Is this some kind of sick joke?' she said.

'Gag her,' said Margaret.

'We can talk,' said the WPC.

'Now, why would we want to do that?' asked Bee, before placing a strip of tape across Jane McDowell's mouth.

The phone rang, was answered.

'They want to know what else we want,' said Bee.

'Tell them "World Peace",' said Margaret.

'We want World Peace.'

Bee listened.

'He says, "Don't we all?"'

'No, we don't,' said Liz. 'That's the whole point.'

'World Peace, now!' shouted Bee, into the receiver. 'Stop the violence.'

She clattered it back onto the phone.

'So, Optimus Prime,' began Margaret. 'What should we do with the policewoman?'

Optimus Prime looked at the dark uniform.

'She hasn't got a gun,' he said.

'No,' said Bee. 'But we do.'

'Is she a real policeman?'

'I don't know,' said Liz. 'What do you think?'

'I think she's not a real policeman because a real policeman wouldn't just surrender and come in like that. They would fight and stop you.'

'I think you're right, Optimus Prime,' said Margaret. 'I think she's just pretending to be a policeman.'

'That's a very naughty thing to do, isn't it?' said Bee. 'Really bad.'

The WPC looked about in panic.

'Go on,' said Bee. 'Shoot her with your laser.'

Optimus Prime hesitated.

'She deserves it,' said Liz.

The boy stood up and pointed the laser at the WPC's face. Then, making a shoom-shoom sound, he fired off two zaps straight between the eyes. A red light glowed faintly on Janet McDowell's forehead; the thing's batteries were going.

'Good boy,' said the hostage-takers. 'Well done. Fantastic.'

Optimus Prime smiled a sideways smile. He did not look towards his father.

'Into the kitchen,' said Margaret.

She and Liz bundled the WPC through the door and slammed it shut.

Two minutes later, Liz re-emerged, a smudge of blood on her left temple. She was holding a carving knife.

'Margaret says you can finish her off, if you like.'

Colin looked through the doorway, and saw the black-stockinged legs of Janet McDowell lying on the wood-effect lino of the kitchen floor. They twitched, once, twice.

Bee took the knife and went into the kitchen, leaving Liz to watch Colin and Optimus Prime. The father was trying to say something, making an anguished humming sound. He had known Janet McDowell since she was a baby. He had several times slept with her mother.

'Did you kill the woman?' asked Optimus Prime.

'Yes,' said Liz.

'Why did you kill the woman?'

'Because there was no other way.'

This didn't satisfy Optimus Prime, but he had no more questions.

Liz, holding her toy gun, went across to the window and gazed out. Then she began to turn her head towards Colin, so the first shot ripped her left ear off. The second, coming almost immediately, took away the top half of the head to which the ear had been attached.

In the kitchen, Margaret and Bee only had time to look up from the WPC's blood-wet body before the window shattered and Bee's forehead exploded.

Margaret dived to the ground, pushed the kitchen door open and crawled through into the living room.

She could hear the back door collapse as the police battering ram smashed through it.

Optimus Prime was curled foetal on the sofa; Colin had managed to stand up, intending to hop across to his son.

Margaret stood in the middle of the room, legs apart, pointing the toy gun defiantly at the doorway.

The first policeman through took her out with a shot to the chest, then finished her with three to the head.

'It's alright, son,' he said to Optimus Prime, who had been spattered. 'You're safe now.'

JUSTINA ROBSON

1968: A ShortSpan Snackfood. Valid for Year 7 Student Use. Calories: 231

I SWALLOWED THE 1968 tablet with a cup of coffee at 10 a.m. and went into the Library Reading Room to wait. I hate writing essays. I particularly hate writing them about historical periods before the Map. I never know if I have to explain what it was like before the Map, when information that went into your mind was governed only by what you did and who you knew and not a guaranteed source or impartial quality control in sight. Imagine if everything was left to chance like that, to parents, to just anyone who had an opinion about anything. And don't even start me on the virulent horror of some of the ideas that circulated in those days. Never being able to purge your mind of negative energy, the pus of trauma, the wounds of bad ideas. It's just a hell, but at least even though it's possible to load simulated experiences of those old times and live the nightmare, I've only had to take 1968 as a quick one-hour dose of interactives.

They show up on time, after I've got myself a nice seat in an out-of-the-way carrel, far from anyone who looks like they might know me. The man is an intense, bearded white guy with wire-frame glasses and a tie-dyed shirt—they really went a bit overboard on him. The woman is a Mod, in what I understand intuitively is a regulation green army surplus parka which conceals her cheap but pleasant skirt and blouse. She fiddles with her earring. Her parka is covered in ska badges.

'Hey,' I say. It's always hard to know what to say to people who are essentially figments of your imagination. Well-crafted figments, full of historical metafictions and personalities as finely honed as fifty quid will buy you, but still products of some wetware running a goonshow in your head.

'Yeah,' said the girl, as if saying hello was too uncool to be borne.

'Geoff Wetweather,' said the man heartily, offering me his hand to shake.

I leant forward and shook it. It felt quite real but these things are never right, like another true human. They used to be, but it freaked people out, so they started to make them feel like plastic.

'Interesting name,' I said, wishing I could include that in the essay as it might have made it more readable. 'Family burden?'

He spread his hands out. 'I chose a new name.'

The girl snorted and turned her head half away to conceal a pitying smile.

'And you are?' I asked.

'Julie Bridewell,' she said. Her nails were all bitten down.

'So, tell me all about nineteen sixty-eight,' I suggested, sitting back with my notebook open to record. Sometimes you get a chatty one who barely has to be prompted, you never know your luck. It depends on the manufacturer, they say, but I prefer this brand—their people are more natural seeming and less like answer machines.

'Some bozos were born, a lot of people died, Martin Luther King got shot,' she said drolly, staring at me as if I were stupid.

'We're moving on from the old systems and bureaucracies of the past,' Geoff said, leaning his elbows on his knees, his face full of the enthusiasm of radicals everywhere.

It occurs to me that I hate the title I've been given. Writing essays is for dead people. Nobody reads them. Like the rest this one will be stuck in the bank, occupying some five kilobytes of otherwise inoffensive circuitry and surfed only by search agents scanning for phrases that can be recycled into some other student's presentations. 1968.

I composed—'Some bozos were born and some died, a couple of political shootings and a lot of talk about radicalism in that way people talk about radicalism of the past, as if it was something that actually happened, and mostly not a lot of talk. Which it was, because it didn't lead to anything, and there you have the hallmark of talk.' I'd put that, but I can't, obviously. It must have led to something and tutors don't like cynicism in students.

Geoff and Julie look mildly expectant, slightly bored. Beyond them I can see students in other carrels laughing, frowning and talking with people who aren't there. I wish I was doing one of their exercises. They all look more interesting than this one.

'Political thought is really changing,' Geoff said, snapping me out of it.

'How so?'

'It is not,' Julie snorted, rolling her eyes. 'He's just a hippy, he would say that,' she informed me, peering at my notebook as it scripted her words down on the screen all by itself.

'How can you say that?' He turned to her, full of amazement. 'Everything's changing. People went to the Moon. The Moon!'

'People went to Vietnam,' she retorted, all but sticking her tongue out. 'I don't think they thought it was all that different to any other place to die for no reason.'

'But the workers' consciousness was lifted,' he countered. 'Assemblies, unions, the proletariat are fighting the old structures. Things are going to get better.'

Julie rolled her eyes and bit her nonexistent nails. 'Listen to you talk like some crappy rag off the street in your Oxford voice. You don't know anything. I know what happened to all that and do you know what, I can't believe you fell for it. Women and workers royally shafted all the way into the seventies and beyond. Come the nineties and feminism is dead, the Soviets are gone and the Americans still haven't figured out that the only way to conquer the world is to buy it.' She glanced at me and half turned. 'And now? Are you gonna tell me it's different now?'

'It is,' I said.

Her lips thinned. 'Don't believe yer.'

Her anger and disappointment made me really want to persuade her. 'We have equality,' I said. 'And fair trade. Family Years of childcare paid for by the cooperative state structure. Free healthcare.'

'You see!' Geoff was triumphant. He turned to me. 'How did it happen?'

Now I've got to explain it. I take a deep breath. 'Let me start by saying I know fuck all about 1968 since I didn't live in it. I'm going on the history files. All I can say is, whatever you thought was going on, Julie is more right than Geoff: the song is always the same and it revolves around Money, Land and Power.'

I can't keep talking like that. They just stare. I show them what I've pulled up on the Notebook in a few minutes last night and appended. It was going to form my conclusion, or part of it.

'The means for acquiring power was not possessed by any radicals of the year 1968 because they were opposed to the kind of people who ran the institutions of the time and were stupid enough to say so directly and openly. The only radical alteration in the history of human thinking or acting and especially of social reform took place in 2031 with the covert, unilateral and widespread dispersal of inhalable viral-borne information and the mind-moulding software that has since become known as Map. They say one of the Western governments planned to use the Map to force global accord, but their own more radically and idealistically minded scientists stole it and got in first. They made it a public property, dispersed it freely and opened about a million software writing franchises. You can't trust anyone.'

It's hard to explain Mapped life as the entire thing sounds as mental as a box of frogs but I felt an obligation to show them that there was change, although not the way they wanted it. They weren't real, of course. So why bother? But you forget these things, or I do.

Geoff read aloud slowly, his face a picture of mystification. 'Before the Mapping of humanity everyone just got what they knew from other people. There wasn't any quality control, even for people who were well off and well educated and living in places where technology and subsistence were of very high standards. In those days there were several main routes for people to get their information: parents, peers and the social Everybody. All of the people in the first two groups and the imaginary people, media and randoms that made up the last were themselves the product of a wild ecology of information.' He looked up at me slowly and handed the Notebook back. 'You make it sound like we're all stupid or victims or something.'

Julie snorted.

'It wasn't your fault,' I said.

'But what's now?' he frowned. 'Where does your information come from?'

'Validation,' I answered. 'All absorbable information is graded for Validation so you know how true it is or how compromised . . . '

Geoff shook his head. 'And who watches the watchmen?'

'It's a global accord,' I said.

'And who can issue this . . . information?'

'Anyone can write Mapcode.'

Julie sat up. 'Anyone in the world?'

I held up my hands and started to explain it more slowly.

In the past, let's say, in 1968, you had to decide for yourself what to think about everything. But everything you knew came from other people who weren't validated. They were in the same boat. They didn't have a filter for scientific truth and one for opinions and one for suppositions and one for theories and one for beliefs. They didn't have any independent references and there was no way of purging bad information and rescaping if you found out that things weren't as you'd been led to believe.

You can say the same thing now, of course, about Validated items—they're only as good as the Validation test, but it's not as if people can pass off religions as literal truths any more, or that you can pick them up without knowing they're just an interpretation of internal reality possibilities filtered and corrupted through a lot of uncomprehending proxies. Filters these days you can dissect and remake yourself. With layers. Back in '68 there was no Onionskin capability to strip ideas and no Link Filter to map localised motivations that could be blurring your informational input. So a lot of people were poor judges of what to think and what to let alone. Then they became parents or peers and passed their bad judgements on. Hard to imagine how strange it must have been to be so alone in worlds of bad information!

Julie just stared at me. Geoff smiled. I put forward my essay thesis.

Sixties radicals wanted to go some way to alerting the population at large to the effects of widespread social injustices and the memes which perpetuated them. They did not create a revolution in the obvious sense of political overthrow or structural remaking, however, but in a subtle way which manifested generations later—a piece of legacy revolution. The social freedoms of the Nineties and Noughties were due to Sixties influences, but diluted and thrown around by the inherent turbulence of the wider and more formal social world. The usual resistance to change on the superficial mass social levels was fierce, however, due to the high pressure of economic wealth combined with uncertainty and the gross material legacy problems of disproportionate usage of resources over time. Known presently as the Ecosocial Weather Conditions, these pressures combined with the emergent individualism and spiritual development to produce conditions of acute self awareness combined with extreme insecurity. Ultimately, forty years of stormy conditions and technological development later, this was to give rise to the Mappa Mundi conspiracy that led us where we are today.

Needless to say most of the human population got no say in the matter, though as commentators have pointed out this was true throughout history. Also, huge numbers of people were stuck in Middle Ages mindsets, killing one another in Tit for Tat wars, even on the day that the plague began spreading Mapware uncontrollably. Resistance was futile. Mapware even said so in its introductory spiel as it unlooped itself into your head. The people who wrote it had been brought up on a diet of Daleks.

Geoff laughed. Julie stared. They understood Daleks but I could see the rest was lost on them.

'What's left of us today then?' Julie asked after a minute.

'There are two designer Memefaks based in 1968,' I said, 'Lutheralia and PiphanyTrance. The first is available as a biscuit and the second as a special download from the Educational Ministry. They offer potted histories of the era, plus music, culture and reportage symphonies that can give you a good idea of the time. They're both available as Immersions, Wallpapers, Backgrounds or Archive formats and include experiential effects of various consumables, including drugs and artistic impressions of what it was like to serve in the Vietnam War, be a member of any minority group or ruling class (Western Hemisphere only), and the prevailing Social Wind. Lutheralia is more political and takes a few hours to trawl. You can surf PiphanyTrance in just ten minutes though. As with all such products, we keep what we like and purge what we don't.'

'Purge?' Geoff asked.

'I unloaded the whole of the Prague Spring except the FAQ addon. Man, that was a depressing experience,' I said.

He nodded but his eyes were vacant. Julie smirked. 'All of history is this . . . edible entertainment?' she asked after a minute of watching Geoff nod and try to liberally digest what I'd told him.

'Any knowledge of any kind,' I said, but I was distracted as I saw Renee walking in to the carrels block, looking for me. She looked impatient. I tried to duck down but I was too slow. Both the sixties people turned around to see, as if they needed to. Renee came over and sat down on Julie's lap. Julie scowled and got up to shoo Geoff over.

'Are you wasting more money?' Renee didn't mince words. She snatched up the empty pack of 1968 and read the labels. 'You spend your whole damn life talking to people who don't exist.'

I smiled at her. Renee took education very seriously. She was also very cute, so I didn't mind it too much, in fact I study mostly because of her, to get my vocabulary up. She tucked a curl of honey-coloured hair behind her ear and glanced around, 'Am I sitting on them?'

'Not any more. Coffee?'

'I'm soaking up Marxist theory,' she said, waving off the suggestion, as if coffee were some kind of antidote.

'Hey,' said Geoff, impressed at once.

I shot him a black look. A pretty girl and the mention of old lefty politics and he was all on fire. Julie looked suspicious. 'What does she mean, soaking?'

'It's another kind of download,' I said. 'It puts information in your memory over time and then you sort of discover it for yourself using the trigger document, kind of like book study but you can't forget anything.'

Julie curled her lip jealously. 'So anyone can know anything?'

'I guess,' I said.

'But that's amazing!' Geoff burst out. 'Power to the people! Tell me how it works! Who runs the world?'

Renee was staring at me, snapping her fingers in front of my eyes. 'Jojo!'

'What?'

'It's lunchtime. Did you forget? You said we'd go to Pappa's. You're paying.'

'How could you forget?' Julie said, scratching her ear.

'I don't use calendar addons,' I said to Julie, watching Renee's expression get slightly snittier. 'I'm a Naturalist. We don't maintain any data structures by artificial means —it interferes with creativity.'

'Explaining yourself to fictional characters!' Renee exclaimed, rolling her eyes. 'They're supposed to be educating you, not the other way round.'

I shrugged, 'What's the harm? They were only curious.'

Renee glared at me. 'They're not real! You're talking to yourself about yourself again! And they ARE artificial data structures. You jerk.' She added the last rather late.

I looked at the time. Twelve-forty. My stomach growled. 'Do you think that the way things are now could be said to be power in the hands of the proletariat—

because of the Map?' I wanted to see if I could sucker her with the lure of knowledge.

'If the power to control all the Mapware was held by the people,' she said tartly, 'which it isn't. '

'It is,' I said. 'People write the stuff. It only occasionally gets corrupted in the wild. Everything is made by people. You vote by buying it or not buying it.'

She looked thunderous. 'Stop it. I'm not in the mood. Are you coming to lunch or not?'

'I will if you tell me who runs the world.' She isn't the only one around who has kudos as lunch date material. Besides, she likes me baiting her. 'Julie and Geoff here want to know before they have to go.'

Renee rolled her eyes. 'Nobody runs it. Everyone looks after themselves.'

'Anarchy!' Julie was finally impressed.

'Now we can go,' I said and slid out of my seat.

'But how does that really work?' Geoff was saying as we started to walk out of the building.

I'd like to write that the happy conclusion to the spirit and influence of 1968 is a peaceful anarchy in which everyone miraculously looks after themselves and doesn't bother anyone else because everyone is in a basic kind of agreement about what matters most but that'd be wrong. I don't want to pop Geoff and Julie's bubble, though, as they only have a few more minutes to exist, so when we pass the athletic woman in the black body armour with her sword and gun I let them think she's a lone vigilante existing in her own privately scripted drama. Everyone is, after all. I don't tell them she's one of the many Vindicators that are allowed to read minds, and on whom we rely for fair trial, judgement and protection. Why spoil their fifteen minutes of fun?

Renee stops and looks with admiration at the Vindicator's steady walk. She wants to be one when she's done. Me? I can hardly write an essay, let alone be bothered to march about doling out justice. Besides, what kind of an asshole job is that? Giving your life and sanity for the sake of people too dumb to stop themselves doing something stupid? We're all in a slightly smaller world than we used to be, and some choices just aren't allowed, but let's not go mad here.

'You can't be serious,' I said to Renee, for the nth time, as I closed the essay file on the notebook. It'll get a D or something—I can tell that myself, but a pass is good enough.

'I want to do something useful,' she said, turning into Pappa's.

'You see?' I said to Julie and Geoff, holding the door for their fading forms. 'Once a human, *plus c'est la même chose*. You can take the dumb ideas out of the zealots but you can't make them drink.'

They stood around by the table for a few more minutes, listening and watching and slowly they faded out completely. As they went they both smiled, one with surprise and puzzlement, one with what looked much more like relief.

MARC VILLEMAIN

This Was My Flesh

Never had it been so quiet in the house: so Géraldine Bouvier thought as she watched the latest polling figures appear on screen. No, she said to herself, studying the faces of her husband and children, I don't ever remember seeing my family so disheartened. The Bouvier house was well known in the area, partly thanks, of course, to the celebrity status of its owner, but also because of the good-naturedness of the family, their openness of spirit and general cheerful demeanour, which had transformed their home into a haven for the whole neighbourhood. People liked to ride their bicycles past the tall hedges bordering the garden, as the diva's voice exercises rose into the air intertwining with the smells of sage, lily of the valley, lilac, thyme and numerous other plants and flowers, all as tranquil as they are colourful. They would imagine catching a glimpse of the opera star, an unexpected sighting, perhaps an intimate one, but mainly they just took pleasure in giving a ring on the bell as they passed by or in shouting a greeting, their simple hearts cheered by the prettiness of the garden, said to flower in all seasons; some, the more refined and discerning, would leave a gift on the steps, a poem, a watercolour, a basket of fruit, a hand beribboned with honey, sugared ears or bone marrow from the tibia, simple offerings, anonymously left.

But for the first time in a hundred years, two hundred, since the beginning of time, the cannibal party was predicted to lose the election. The opposition, self-proclaimed revolutionaries and humanists, were polling 51 per cent, but the fact was unavoidable, like a worm in the apple: not only was the majority party crumbling, but the very basis of civilisation itself was threatening to collapse. The polls were taking everyone by surprise, including the revolutionaries themselves, the more rational of whom were startled by the promise of success. Julia, the youngest child, started sniffling, incapable of holding back the tears: she was frightened. Géraldine sat down cross-legged next to her and held her, unable to find any words of comfort to whisper in her ear, content merely to hold her tight, combing her long hair as if to send her off to sleep. Without stopping, but with the action of the caress becoming somewhat mechanical, she turned her head to look at Gabriel, who looked half-dead collapsed on his chair, his empty glass before him. At length her husband sat up and turned to look at her, trying awkwardly to assume a mantle of dignity, the bearing of a man who knows himself to be observed, but managing only to breathe, in a voice weighed down with despair, 'What's to become of us?'

As far back as anyone could remember, humanity had always been cannibalistic, for a long time in secret, often in hypocrisy or denial, but always cannibalistic. That very morning, Géraldine Bouvier had been designated, among a hundred citizens (lots were drawn every second and fourth Monday of the month, in advance of the ceremonies that took place each second and fourth Thursday). Notwithstanding the forthcoming election, which filled up the serious papers, the press was as keen as ever to report on the event: there was no denying the national glory attached to the ritual act of giving. Without being a militant, like so many others, Géraldine Bouvier had always voluntarily adhered to the fundamental virtues of cannibalism, in which the teleological gift of flesh constitutes the very finality of existence, the end stage in a moral nobility that no other society had ever reached or could ever reach; no previous civilisation had ever known the tranquillity that characterised our world, rid of malnutrition and famine, of overpopulation and terrorism, of the epidemics of religion and its substitutes, of all those plagues that in former times caused the greatest suffering to mankind and into which revolution was always threatening to send us tumbling back.

In the television studio, the debate rose by a notch, without quite masking the dumbfoundedness of those taking part. Géraldine caught only scraps, which seemed to break up further as they reached her. *Our fertility rates have never been lower: I do not deny the policy has brought us progress, but do you believe we can carry on exploiting the human body for food with impunity?—My dear sir, if it so happens that tomorrow you accede to the highest position of power and at one stroke wipe out the progress made by our ancestors—morally, spiritually and socially, as well as in terms of sanitation, food, demographics and economics—then I tell you at what price: you will be held responsible for the extinction of civilisation.—Can you not see that what you call our civilisation suffers from that which we should resolve to designate, if you will permit me to paraphrase, as the childish illness of cannibalism?—Ah, there you go again with your beloved references: but they date from a different millennium! And you're talking about staging a revolution?!* Somewhat stiff and formal up to now, the election campaign had suddenly ignited.

Without reacting, Géraldine made her way towards the bay window, which drew forth the last of the daylight. Her husband, touched that his wife was still there by his side, touched also by the feeling of being loved perhaps, contemplated her elegant appearance, which in these normal surroundings seemed to him more beautiful than on the loveliest stage of the most beautiful theatre. Slowly he went across to join her, leaving the three children gaping at the television. On his feet behind her, aligning his body perfectly with hers, he hesitated before taking her in his arms, which he did, finally, without a word. Her skin was fresh, her smell as light and profound as happiness itself, her dress revealing flesh feathered with the softest down. He shivered. They remained standing for a few moments, leaning against one another in silent contemplation of the street, which seemed to sparkle—the asphalt, trees, lamp posts, the road signs, the forms and shapes of the urban environment, in which everything seemed to be deep in slumber, intact and inaccessible, insensitive to the upheaval, subject only to the eternal essence of things. The little homes that lined the street seemed equally drowsy. Looking more closely, however, with the help of the rumbling lights that revealed their stylish interiors, the couple witnessed strange scenes: convulsive faces hanging from balconies, shadows fidgeting in living rooms, bedrooms and kitchens, some passing from one room to another, from one stage to another, going upstairs, and back downstairs again, sometimes surprisingly still, and all, to a man or a woman, failing to express anything either reasonable or intelligible. A muffled noise would sometimes escape, with neither discernible purpose nor outcome. A motorcyclist passed below their window at speed, making a crude backfiring noise, vulgar, half-drunk. Noticing them standing together in the window, he bellowed *Long live the revolution!* Quietly, Géraldine intoned an air from Verdi's *Rigoletto*, extracting a smile from the man whose warm and fearful breath she felt on her neck.

Stretched out on the carpet in front of the television, Julia sobbed into the arms of Loïc, who was far from happy himself, while Anna, the eldest, strove to comfort the two younger children. All three of them joined their parents around the table for dinner. While filling people's glasses, and affecting an air of enjoyment that fooled no one, Géraldine announced that she would take advantage of her celebrity—certain that she would get the opportunity to make herself heard—and call a press conference for the following day. She would strike a chord, catch the mood of the people. She would devote the three days that separated them from the election, and which separated her from the accomplishment of the ritual, to the civilised traditions of cannibal society.

The party in power used all the means at its disposal to counter the secession and force back the tide of history; working around the clock, utilising all its networks and sustained by the enormous majority of intellectuals, writers, artists and philosophers, in short by everyone that society regarded as eminent and sensitive figures, it published numerous reports, food statistics, economic documents, scientific brochures, religious treatises and dozens of tracts. On their own initiative, the leaders of the world's ten greatest orchestras, on five continents, wrote an open letter to the press to emphasise that the ritual act of giving, for which, every fortnight, a hundred citizens were selected at random, was a 'constituent part of civilisation', and they went on to say that in the case of Géraldine Bouvier, 'a citizen like the others, of course, but an outstanding artist, unique in the history of the world', it would constitute an honour to the arts, suggesting that if she sang so magnificently and if her voice was celebrated the world over, it was because her singing was 'born of an ideal'. They proclaimed their attachment to a world in which 'morality did not turn its back on history', calling at last for respect of the teachings of the founding fathers of democratic cannibalism. Alas, a new poll confirmed the findings of those before it, even taking into account a widening of the divergence between the two parties. The only riposte of the country's leaders was to denounce the polling institutions for selling out to the revolution, lest it pass them by, arguing that this alone proved that the revolution was nothing but a revolt, corrupted before it had even won.

Géraldine Bouvier's press conference had provoked a riot, in the minds of the people as much as in the streets. The government was accused of cynical appropriation, of media manipulation; it was reproached for exercising undue pressure on both the people and the pollsters. Above all, the singer herself was accused of not caring about the general interest, of mounting this rear-guard action only because the victory of the revolution would deprive her of her opportunity for national honour and would prevent her from being eaten by her loved ones; as evidence for her venality, the anti-cannibal party published on the front page of its national daily a copy of the bills the Bouvier family had paid for ritual feasts, using her as an example of the middle classes' eternal defects—their immorality, their criminality, the fact that they were an expensive luxury. The great artist, however, stood tall and proud. Surrounded by her husband and three children, she was reserved, collected, strangely relaxed. She didn't even see the forest of cameras and microphones in front of her, she evinced no emotion that might have affected the solemnity of the moment, heard nothing of the kerfuffle outside, where uniformed demonstrators gathered in their dozens and chanted the hideously banal slogans of humanist totalitarianism. There was a tremor in Gabriel's hand as it rested on her shoulder, while her three children appeared thrown into spasm by the momentous onslaught of people, lights and noise. As she spoke, her gaze was directed elsewhere, into the distance, extending beyond the crowd and soaring into another time; her voice, meanwhile, reached the depths of people's hearts. She was expected to be tearful, plaintive, disgusting: she was prophetic. If any tears flowed, they did so among the crowd gathered in the press room. Recalling the terrible struggle for survival that the ancients had had to lead, Géraldine Bouvier evoked the distant past in which men, emaciated, stinking, itching and bent under the yoke of misery and hunger, begged for a pittance in the streets and attacked each other to be first in the queue at the soup kitchen, before rotting on the spot in ditches and gutters, their flesh so far gone that even animals would turn away. She cited those revolutionary times, 'to which the revolutionaries would have us return', when men were left to die in hospitals, refused a simple glass of blood, a bit of fat, some human bone marrow or brain. Driving her point home, she addressed those revolutionaries who she said were gargling an ageless Christianity, and she quoted the words of St François de Sales: 'From death, which devours all, comes the meat of consolation.' Some applauded, others barracked her. Everyone present, for one reason or another, became somewhat hysterical. The stakes demanded it.

During Tuesday night the Bouvier residence was targeted by scattered groups of youths; Gabriel identified one who couldn't have been any older than ten or eleven. In less than half an hour they had uprooted most of the hedges, torn up the flowers, urinated and defecated on the front steps. The façade of the house was covered in blood stains and the garden had been transformed into a waste ground with piles of rubbish, leaflets, pornographic photographs and other questionable materials. The fun was over by the time the police arrived. Géraldine strove to calm Julia, and Gabriel tried to get through to Loïc, who had shut himself in his bedroom, while Anna was struggling to clean away the worst of the dirt. The family knew what to expect. But they also knew they could count on the support of thousands of citizens, and innumerable testimonies reached Géraldine Bouvier's residence. Each well-wisher, after assuring her of their thoughts and their prayers, invited her, if by ill fortune the revolution were to triumph, to go on and celebrate the ritual, whatever the cost.

Wednesday was characterised by a strange atmosphere. The media reported scenes of panic in the shops with people filling up trolleys with thighs, buttocks, shoulders, livers, ribs and brains, some coming back for more after stocking the freezer at home; as for country-dwellers, they were to be seen sitting in traffic jams as they returned from the towns and cities with supplies to survive the meagre days to come. The revolution, up to now mainly peaceful, took a deadly turn. However, in view of the profound shift in public opinion towards change, these events were scarcely more than isolated incidents. This very day, in fact, May 1st, a huge crowd filled the country's main avenue to show support for the revolution. *Down with the cannibal carcass*, you could read on the banners; or, in red letters, *Cannibalism is the opium of the people* and *Vegetarian happiness is a new idea*; or, on another, the once-famous *Run, comrade, the cannibal is behind you!* The demonstrators streamed through the streets, abandoning their organisers and marshals, encouraging onlookers to join them, in some cases forcing them to. As for the president, his ministers and their families, they had withdrawn to safety, protected by the army and a hundred or so plainclothes police officers. From both sides, calls for calm were issued and greeted with more or less disdain by militants white hot with revolutionary fervour.

It was in this explosive context that the elections duly took place; there were few irregularities to deplore and only a handful of violent incidents to tarnish a poll that, as well as for its result, was historic for its turnout. The leader of the revolutionary party this Thursday was sporting a gaudy short-sleeved top on the back of which was drawn a basket filled with vegetables—courgettes, peppers, carrots, spinach, haricot beans, soya . . . He voted very early in the morning, surrounded by his principal lieutenants, explaining that the nights were short for those who dreamed of change. As for the president, he carried out his electoral duty in the company of his wife and their five children, before declaring soberly that he was placing the destiny of civilisation in the hands of the people.

A few minutes after the announcement of the results, the new president made a declaration of appeasement. Certainly, his first utterance was to proclaim the abolition of the cannibal society and specify that any act of cannibalism would be considered as contrary to the values of normal society and punished accordingly. Certainly, he announced the creation of a committee of public welfare charged with bringing to justice those who might contravene the decree to be issued in the hours that would follow. He announced that with the support of the people he would ask his newly elected representatives to reinstate the death penalty as part of a legal framework to be submitted without delay to the critical scrutiny of parliament. But he also offered the opportunity to the opposition to play its part in this process, and in the shaping of the future of politics. Above all, he was swift to say that the new law was not retroactive: in fact, this as good as authorised the hundred citizens designated the previous Monday, according to the ancient ritual, to honour the institutional roll of the dice and observe the cannibal ritual. No allusion to Géraldine Bouvier was made, unless indecipherably, as he slipped in a coded reference to 'those ordinary citizens who refuse to turn the page of history'. Revolutionary indulgence was nevertheless begged to allow those final ritual feasts to go ahead, controlled by a representative of the government health department and taking place strictly within the family. The crowd applauded at last, the opening chords of a fanfare rang out, champagne corks were popped and the signal was given for the party to start. At the request of the new government, it went on until the early hours of the morning.

Géraldine has inserted the disc of her final recording with the state philharmonic orchestra: Mozart, *Don Giovanni*. A recording thought by connoisseurs to represent both the summit of the singer's career and the purest homage ever to the maestro of Salzburg. Gabriel, sitting in the leather armchair next to the open fire, watches her while sucking on his pipe, moved by the extraordinary beauty of this woman whom he has never stopped loving since the age of seventeen, moved also by the voice that can now be heard throughout the house, a voice of such purity barely touched by humanity, heard by countless strangers all over the world, and still to be discovered by so many more. He is somewhat feverish and senses in his joy a kind of empty perplexity, a response perhaps to the weight of destiny. Upstairs the three children are alternately playing and bickering. They are getting ready for the party, putting on their Sunday best, just like grown-ups.

It was a lovely evening, a wonderful night. Gabriel and the three children communed with her body with the passion of lovers since time immemorial, glowing with the happiness of those who surrender themselves to life's hidden tragedy, intense beauty and extraordinary magnificence. Julia and Loïc roar with laughter when their father recalls their early years, his clumsiness with their nappies, the first baths he gave them, in the kitchen sink, and how he would laugh when they scampered around the house on all fours, then, later, the mad chases on the beach and games of hide and seek at their grandmother's house. Each child put on their favourite of their mother's records, the Requiems above all, which always resonated for them with an unexpected combination of hope and peace. No sadness was allowed to darken the moment, even if they all knew that henceforth they would never again be allowed to eat their loved ones, which was a sad thing in itself. They all ate well, and Gabriel drank more than he ought to. Midnight had sounded more than two hours ago when he decided it was time to put the two youngest to bed, since they had fallen asleep at the table, dishevelled, with sticky hands and sweaty brows, their heads resting on their forearms. Afterwards he came back downstairs to tidy up the living room and kitchen. Before going up to bed himself, he kissed Anna, who sat daydreaming in front of what remained of the fire. They held each other and hugged with tenderness and modesty in the dark silence of a perfect night. Then he went up to bed, advising her to do the same. She breathed some life back into the fire in order to hear the crackling of the embers and she stayed by the hearth for a long time, a very long time. Her eyes heavy from the extraordinary day, her mind and her senses drunk on a surfeit of emotions, she went into the kitchen and took from the fridge the mouth and lips of her mother, which she placed delicately on a little plate. Finally she climbed the stairs, slowly, carefully, then lay down with her eyes wide open and consumed the final remains of she who, even that very evening, had helped her to grow.

Translation by NICHOLAS ROYLE

TRICIA SULLIVAN

Plan C

THE ANGELS' SNIFFER dog tracked Ruqqayah from her father's lab to the hospital's pharmacy, where she shut the door in its face. It started barking, so she made an improvised escape through a warren of basement storage rooms. A couple of cameras had to be disabled. She used the corkscrew tool of her Swiss Army knife, hacking at the wire so that when she was done it looked like a mouse had chewed through the insulation. She timed her way past a third camera and reached the west elevator bank, where Amir had long since disabled the camera. Then she stopped in her tracks. Somebody had put a spanking new lens in.

Shit. She couldn't go back. She wouldn't stand a chance in the stairwell. It was either fool the lens outside the elevator, or get caught. She didn't want to get caught. If she decided to deal with the Angels, she would do it on her terms.

Ruqqayah took out Amir's flashlight and eyed it sceptically. She had never used it before in this context. Her father had sworn backwards and forwards that the script he'd loaded in that flashlight would render anyone holding it invisible to cameras as well as humans, but Ruqqayah thought that this was theoretically impossible and therefore didn't trust it.

'Cameras don't have a pineal gland or a visual cortex,' she argued. 'Cameras don't have an endocrine system. You can't script a camera like you can script a person.'

'Which one of us is among the top four script Riders in the entire country? You or me?'

'You. Used to be. But —'

'But, but trust this light. Because it could save your butt.' And he'd laughed at his own feeble joke.

No choice now. Shining the flashlight on the lens, she forced open the doors of the dead elevator far enough to slither through the gap. The childhood she'd spent watching parkour on YouTube had been put into practice many times in the post-Blink city. Now in the elevator she braced on the hand rail, swung her legs up to kick out the emergency hatch, and swarmed through the hole. It was easy.

Amir must have been right about the flashlight, because no alarm sounded and no one came. Ruqqayah lay on the roof of the elevator, sweating in the hot darkness. It was a bad place to stay, but she stayed anyway. She had to think.

Some people were endurance athletes; Ruqqayah was an endurance thinker. She believed that if you thought long and hard enough, you could solve any problem. Now she was stuck. Her father had vanished. She had found no sign of his recent presence in his basement lab. No note, no clue; not even the most subtle trace.

Ruqqayah had feared many things, but this one had never crossed her mind, not once. Even in the past three weeks, when he'd been out of touch, she'd put it down to his psychological volatility in the face of the scripts that he fought to control. But never, never would he abandon his lab.

Something had happened to him.

Amir had told her what to do.

'Never try to think in a crisis. That's why we have Plan B,' he told her. 'Plan B will save your life if the shit hits the fan.'

Plan B was fleeing the city and getting outside the light quarantine zone. It was a responsible plan, made by a parent for a child. But it would mean giving up the cause. Not try to think in a crisis? She had to think. Blind obedience, that was for the blue line. That was for the scripted.

If the dog had not come she'd probably still be sitting in the lab, tracing lines in the dust on Amir's laptop cover. The cushion of her father's chair was dented from where his ass had pressed all those times; even the pile of the fabric was flattened and starting to get shiny. Ruqqayah had sat on her haunches, knees drawn up to her chest, and let her head fall back so that she was staring at the ceiling. She followed its lines with her eyes. She studied its grubby fingerprints. She saw faces in the knots on the plywood.

She could pretend that he'd just stepped out for a minute. Would be back later, with all his tics and his stammering and his funny way of holding his hands behind his back when he lectured—which was pretty much the only way Amir knew how to talk without being tripped up by speech impediments. She felt herself choking up, remembering all the things about her father that had used to annoy her. When he held court, he could fool you into thinking he was still teaching and Mitch was still running a restaurant and everybody had all their marbles. That the Blink never happened.

'We're all the same,' Amir had used to tell her, like he'd told his first-years. 'Two arms, two legs, one cortex slaved to an endocrine system designed in primeval times. So limiting. We're doomed to an essential apehood unless we can change our deepest programming. And let's face it: people have very little self-control. We're mostly a set of biological levers waiting to be pulled. But we can change that, and that's what scripts can give us. Better neurochemical paths. New ways of being. They can literally change our minds for the better without the side effects of drugs, because all of the chemicals are made by our own brains.'

It had been a speech. A performance. Then he'd say:

'With light therapy we can cure schizophrenia and bipolar disorder and OCD. But it doesn't have to stop there. The scripts that play their best music are the ones natural selection overlooked. Script Riders are discovering paths and potentials that we haven't even dreamed of. It's an exciting time. Why would you want to go bumping around in the darkness of your species' history when you could take matters into your own hands? Tell yourself what to think, be, feel. Humanity has an opportunity to transcend its own biological limitations.'

And here he'd pause dramatically.

'Of course, power is power. People like having their levers pulled; it's how they know they're alive in an increasingly wired world. With scripts, the opportunities for corruption and abuse are as great as the opportunities for growth. That's why I stopped Riding and joined the University. In the course of seeking the perfect lightborn for weight control or sexual satisfaction we must exercise great care that scripting remains safe and under our conscious control. After all, some scripts being developed in the Field now are as complex as the AIs that regulate them. Imagine a zoo where the animals are as intelligent as the wardens.'

Many of her father's Rider colleagues had lampooned his conservatism. Amir had twitched and stammered and said that they hadn't been where he'd gone. Then the Blink had made them throw themselves out of windows and in front of buses, tripped them out like overloaded circuits.

Yes, Amir had seen it coming—for whatever that was worth. In his wisdom he had been left with a city in chaos, a paranoid nation outside the light quarantine, and a Field whose AIs had run amok. He had gone underground.

'We can't leave,' he'd told Ruqqayah. 'The city's been cut off to prevent the Blink from spreading. But some form of Blink will happen out there anyway, sooner or later. It's Murphy's Law. So either we roll over and die, or we deal with it.'

'Deal with it?' Ruqqayah had said, astonished.

'Y-yeah,' he said. 'I'm c-c-coming out of r-re-retirement. I'm g-going to Ride a cure.'

Ruqqayah had done her best to help. Amir had told her that the population of San X needed to be primed to receive it. You couldn't just beam the lightborn out in one shot. The cure was something that had to be passed through people and back to the Field (what was left of it) and re-scripted and re-administered.

'It's a process,' he'd told her again and again. 'Curing the Blink isn't like taking a pill. There's feedback involved. That's why we need to keep the lights active all the time. New scripts every day. Get people synched up to what we're doing. The healing of San X has to be orchestrated.'

How could that happen without him? Ruqqayah was fifteen, the only person in the whole city unable to respond to scripts, and Amir had played his cards too close to his chest. She was trapped inside a hospital administered by government-controlled blind people and their sniffer dogs, populated by the most dangerous scripted, with nothing left of her father's work but his laptop and its coded contents.

And she needed to pee. *Orchestrate that.*

Ruqqayah covered her eyes and wondered what her mother would say. Mitch, smoking flagrantly and cooking chicken Madras and drinking wine at ten in the morning as she sang along to an old Queen Latifah CD. Mitch the rebel, intentionally fat in a town that boasted the best weight-loss scripts in America. Mitch, who had lit up a cigarette one night with a cheap Bic lighter and caught a script so damaging that she'd ended up on the fifth floor of this very hospital, where she had stayed until the Blink brought the city's infrastructure down.

Mitch wouldn't have squatted in an elevator shaft trying not to pee her pants until the Angels found her and shipped her to Albuquerque. Mitch would say, 'If I'm going down, I might as well go down in flames.'

Ruqqayah stood up. She unclipped from her belt a little gizmo that one of the Gila River Indians had traded her for melatonin. It looked like just a loop of braided rope, but it had a catch on it that worked like a ratchet. Ruqqayah always carried hers, even though she hardly did any salvage work anymore, because it was perfect for shinning up streetlamp poles, lolly columns . . . or greasy elevator cables. Now it took her up the shaft.

The top level of the hospital was deserted. She suspected that the searing heat up here had played a role in the failure of the cameras; the Angels certainly didn't frequent this floor. The toilets were repulsive, so Ruqqayah peed in a janitor's bucket. Drawn by habit, she went to her mother's old room overlooking the main parking lot. She recalled the anguished weeks between her mother's disappearance from the hospital and Ruqqayah's rediscovery of Mitch, half-alive, in the prana house. A fat woman, reduced to skin and bones, tricked by scripts into believing that the universe would feed her.

Ruqqayah blotted her eyes, swallowed. Told herself she still had a mother. Not a perfect mother; not a functional mother. But Mitch was alive.

She cradled the laptop against her chest. If Ruqqayah gave Amir's cure script to the Angels, would they let her bring Mitch out with her?

Amir had been a legendary Rider in his time. The script he'd created to fight the Blink, it might not be a silver bullet, but it was working. She'd seen that with her own eyes, on the streets below. Amir had been paranoid; but surely the government would pay for a cure. And Mitch. She was only in the city because Amir hadn't pulled any strings to get her out. She could be isolated, taken to a secure hospital the way that VIPs had been removed in the early days and weeks of the Blink.

Ruqqayah opened the door of room 6638 and went in. The air was dead and hot, but the room was made up as if awaiting a new patient. Everything was tidy, and if it was not actually clean, then the dirt was not obvious. There was a large window that opened from the top, and here she stood, irresolute, watching the sun go down amid a tussle of storm clouds, gold and grey. Thunder and lightning marched across the city. Trees bent over. Then a cacophony of rain hit the hospital roof.

Ruqqayah knew she could find a way to do this. She would use her radio show to make the arrangements. She could take Mitch and the feeding tubes that kept her alive, bundle her in a coat because Mitch would need that even in the heat. Get her out of the prana house and on to secure transport. They would give her that much, when they saw what was on the laptop. *They*. Any Rider, any lightborn company, especially Sweet itself, would pay for Amir's scripts in any currency she demanded. Even clemency for Mitch. She could bring her mother to Sonoma, to her grandparents. The contents of the laptop would be analysed. Everyone would praise Ruqqayah for her role in protecting the outside world from the Blink.

And it wouldn't be a betrayal of Amir. It was just a variation on Plan B.

Something had happened to him, but his work could carry on. Surely he would want that?

Darkness now, the silvery glint of rain fading to black. In defiance of government bombings, lights came on here and there across the city. Even in the flash storm, the blue line powering the city would carry on. It might go faster. Ruqqayah pictured the men's bent backs, droplets banging down on their skin, bringing relief from the heat. Theirs was a world of pure physicality, and now she envied it. They didn't have to think; just respond. They were keeping the city alive against all odds.

Then she jumped in her skin. Something had moved in the doorway of the hospital room. Instinctively she cringed.

'Ruqqayah. I thought it was you,' said a man's voice.

She could see his silhouette in the doorway. How did he know her name? This was not Amir. He was a big man, with a black voice and a strong Louisiana accent, and she could smell him from here.

She began to tremble.

'You don't want to stay here, Ruqqayah,' he said, very quietly. 'Angels won't hurt you but they'll drug you up, make you an inmate. Go back to the street. The program's all set up for you. You'll be OK.'

Ruqqayah licked her lips.

'Who are you? How do you know me?'

'I'm your friend,' he said. 'Just as you are mine. I can't stay. It ain't easy to fight the scripts. So much interference, but you could fix that.' He looked pointedly at the laptop tucked under her arm. 'Get out of here. Tonight. Don't you give them that computer, whatever you do. Don't give them the lightborn. They'll only use it against us.'

Sound of sneakers on the corridor outside. Small lights, bobbing down the corridor. Angels.

Ruqqayah dove under the bed.

'Bobby!' a woman's voice called, beckoning. 'We've been looking everywhere for you.'

She could see the Angels' feet. There were five of them, all carrying therapy beams whose illumination crossed and doubled, washing Ruqqayah's room in bands of colour and shadow. 'Bobby' was silhouetted against the lights, and he looked even bigger. He started towards the Angels. He carried one shoulder higher than the other, and even walking slowly he subtly shifted his head from side to side, tracking. Predacious.

'How did he get out of sedation?' said a male Angel. The woman's whisper hushed him.

She said, 'It's OK, Bobby. You want a beer or something?'

Bobby just kept walking towards them, not even trying to shade his eyes from the therapy beams. Ruqqayah saw the Angels' feet shuffle as they slowed down. They were in no rush to confront him.

'He should be down by now,' said another male. 'I've got mine on full.'

'Try another script,' said a third male. 'Looks like the usual patterns aren't working anymore.'

'This is fucked,' said the second male. 'It always works. You could take down an elephant with—'

'Bob-by!' sang the woman. 'Come on, it's all right. I'll get you a beer. Or a joint? Is anything hurting you? We're here to help.'

The lights flickered as the Angels changed patterns. Ruqqayah wondered how much of Bobby's face they could perceive with their tongue-cameras.

'Run, Ruqqayah!' Bobby's voice boomed. 'Take the script. Don't be afraid. Just do what you have to do.'

The Angels stopped in their tracks.

'Uh, Mary?' the third male said. 'We got a situation on the upper floor. Better seal the exits, just in c—'

Bobby lunged forward. Ruqqayah saw a pair of feet lift off the floor. Bobby's legs quivered; then there was a crash and a man's body went flying across a cart carrying resuscitation equipment and hit the wall beyond. The man slid to the floor, limp.

'Bobby, there's no need to hurt anybody,' the woman said. 'Do you remember me? Kristina? We've played Super Mario Brothers together? Come on, just tell me what I can do for you.'

'Bitch,' said Bobby, and lunged again. The men tried to protect Kristina but Bobby held something gleaming in his right hand—scissors, maybe—and he went charging in. Angels ran; Bobby pursued them around a corner. Ruqqayah could no longer see them, but she could hear one of the men screaming.

'Mary! The lights aren't working on him. Get everybody out of his way.'

There were cries, thumps. Then silence except for Bobby's footfalls as he came back around the corner.

'Ruqqayah!' he barked. 'Execute Plan C.'

There had never been a Plan C.

'Plan C?' she croaked.

'Plan Fucking C. The future. It's your Ride. Take it. *Now.*'

She crawled from beneath the bed, terrified into obedience. Bobby made a peremptory gesture toward the stairs with the bloody scissors. There were dark stains on his sweatpants and his black t-shirt looked wet.

'Hurry up!'

Ruqqayah slunk along the wall, past the unconscious Angel with his mouthpiece fallen out on the floor beside him: without it, he'd be blind. If he woke.

'Go!' roared Bobby as she reached the stairs, and he charged at her as she went through the door.

Ruqqayah never moved so fast in her life. Down the stairs, three and four at a time, all but flying. She was dizzy. He came hurtling down behind her.

At the bottom she forgot all about her usual devious routes into and out of the facility. She made straight for the exit, pelting through the ER with its stale air and semi-comatose incumbents. People reacted to her blearily, seemingly in slow motion.

'He's killing the Angels!' she screamed. 'Look out! Run!'

She didn't wait to see what they made of Bobby coming after her.

The air outside was wet and smelled of tarmac. Wind

and rain smacked her in the face, whipped her hair back, and she was weaving among parked cars. Behind her, people were spilling out of the hospital in herd panic. She glanced back once and saw Bobby come through the front entrance. Her heart felt twice its normal size, swollen with exertion, and her lungs ached. Her legs were wobbling beneath her. She leaned on a people carrier and tried to get her breath back. A guard robot woke up and rolled ponderously towards the hospital, guns swivelling towards the doors. People screamed and dove.

Bobby stood before the doors of the hospital, facing the robot. He turned his head and looked at her. She saw his mouth open. He made no sound, but his lips said, 'Run, Ruqqayah!'

Then he turned back to the robot and charged it. Shots went off. She saw the fabric of his t-shirt tear; saw his head whip back on his neck as something struck him in the face. A small woman in the crowd behind him crumpled to the ground. Bobby launched himself at the robot and grabbed hold of the central gun barrel, wrenching at it as if to tear it off. The gun went off into his midsection and sprayed pieces of him around the parking lot.

Ruqqayah could think nothing. Helicopter noise drowned out the screams of people and Angels, and Ruqqayah lost track of herself for a while. She must have moved. Some time must have passed. The next thing she knew she was on the ground beneath a Durango, prone on oily macadam that smelled of diesel and cat pee. She was retching, and there was vomit dripping from her nostrils. She began to crawl. Search lights plastered the hospital parking lot from overhead. Military aircraft. They would be shining subjugation beams. Ruqqayah didn't dare put her head up, lest she get shot. But she knew what people would be doing. They would be lying down in the beams, going to sleep.

And when they woke up, they would be crazier. Worse than before. She had seen it all before, in the early days of the Blink, when the submission beams had been used routinely.

She crawled from car to car. Trying not to think about Bobby. Her memories of Amir were talking to her now.

Keep your head, Ruqqayah. Fear is just a script.

But she heard her father's words in Bobby's voice and she could not shake the sensation of it.

She reached the edge of the parking lot and climbed a small, rocky rise bisected by security fencing. She found the cut-out place in the bottom that Amir had made for her. They had chosen a spot that was already overgrown with wild brush so that the security weakness would stay hidden. By the time she'd scrambled through the gap, she was scratched and bleeding and muddy all over, but she had to continue climbing until she reached the top of the ridge. She now stood above the cutting where the interstate ran, adjacent to the hospital. The highway below was dark and empty.

She could look down on the hospital from here. A helicopter had landed on the roof and there was a lot of Angel activity up there. Robots encircled the hospital and controlled the parking lot, but the scripted were now following Bobby's lead and hurling themselves at the machines.

Only a handful of people had slumped to the ground, obeying the subjugation beams. Angels were struggling to carry these few inside, skirting around Bobby's head and torso that lay in the ambulance zone.

He had staged the attack to make her run. The most bizarrely altruistic violence Ruqqayah had ever seen.

Why?

How did he know her?

Who had he been?

It's your Ride.

One of the robots opened fire on the rebellious crowd. Ruqqayah cringed and turned away. At the same time, the helicopter took off again—a pilot wouldn't be risked in San X for more than the briefest missions. Bent double, Ruqqayah took cover behind a stanchion supporting a *Perfection* billboard facing the interstate. The helicopter's light swept the whole area once more as it lifted; then it banked to the east and headed up, out of range of the Blink's script lights.

After the chopper had gone, the night was too quiet.

Ruqqayah shut her mind to Bobby's last moments but she couldn't stop replaying his voice in her head. *Take the script . . . Just do what you have to do . . . it's your Ride.*

Crazy. Ruqqayah had never Ridden a script in her life.

Get out of here. Now.

That, at least, made sense. She slithered down the embankment to the interstate and set off across the road, turning her back on what was becoming a massacre. Heading back to the Hide.

The rain felt intimate, almost alive, on her skin. Lightning made scorpion tracks across the sky.

The bile still in her mouth was bitter.

FRANK I SWANNACK

The Lovesick Womb

THE WOMB IS an insolent creature. Afflicted with uncontrollable sexual desires, it thrashes about with great motility causing the Lady to behave irrationally. The womb possesses her with amazing strength and a beguiling tongue, which strikes serpent-like at every given opportunity. If the Lady were let loose, she would copulate with half of London and give birth to all kinds of monstrosities. Not to mention that her gossip would bring Earls to the gallows. The Lady must be kept safe indoors and her mouth strapped tightly shut until her wedding night.

I must stipulate, however, that *all* women are enslaved by their wombs, which is supposedly chained to the woman's lower abdomen by the Devil's horns like a primitive savage. Men must control this wild creature and be rewarded by a healthy baby boy who will continue not just the noble lineage but will prevent the birth of monstrous unions such as murderers and other beasts who will overrun our fair land, while womb and Lady face death; a reward that frees them both from terrible pain.

I surface from the absorbing narrative. My hand is tired from writing. I stretch my legs and move to face the far wall of my study, which is flanked by shelves of clothbound books. The concerns about my book's medical merits are dissolved in the family portrait. The oils recall a sitting where my mother, Elizabeth, is always accompanied by my father, my three elder brothers and two sisters. She is always sat down, her face turned up towards my father, the Earl, who stares out belligerently beyond the canvas. Sometimes, when I look carefully, I can see my own reflection in those diamond eyes.

Until recently, I would have written that the womb never reveals itself. Not in its live bedevilled state but exposed only by dissection—inert and glistening with a faint hue of its former splendour. Yet, when I read over my words carefully inscribed on the animal skin parchment, I see the adjective 'reluctant' has crept in; a tentative gesture towards believing the revelation that the roaming womb had reached a certain woman's mouth. A disturbing encounter I find myself recalling as the din outside becomes more intolerable.

Mist rose constantly from mud tracks like the plague manifest exuding an uncomfortable humidity and a noisome stench of decay. It constricted my throat; hot sweat ran from my choleric brow. I lifted my nosegay, a small posy attached to my lapel, and inhaled deeply its fragrant bouquet as I stepped down from my carriage. With a sharp whipping from the driver, the horses turned it round, scattering the mist in their wake. Dark pinched faces were briefly unveiled, shuffling back into the shadows. Rows of houses stood firm. Nothing more stirred. The sheathed sword running down the length of my leg swung in tandem with my brisk strides.

The tavern parodied the Queen's court. A juggler attired garishly in a patched costume of rags spun through the rancid air what, I first perceived, were severed fingers to the raucous ballad being roared by merry rogues banging long wooden trestles with their fists. Whores and drunkards jigged arm in arm, clashing elbows as their pace quickened to an impossible speed.

My leather boots banged purposely on the wooden floors as I cut a path through the inn. Wenches assailed me. They seemed to appear from all angles, shoving their pale, generously fleshed and, might I add, deliciously cold paps in my fevered face.

With acidic ale in one hand and a weighty whore balanced precariously on his knee, Tom, with sudden recognition as I approached, threw the wench to one side and sent her on her fornicating way with a cheerful slap to her backside. His face was ruddy from ale and excessive merriment. He stood unsteadily as we shook hands. His face serious with our gentlemen's agreement, or the nearest a peasant like Tom could pass likeness to a gentleman's countenance.

'Where is my wench?' I demanded, more fiercely than intended. Tom beckoned me to follow. We weaved our way single file to a short flight of narrow stairs. Once ascended, we entered the first room on the left. It was small and empty, thin grey light sieved through a tiny window. My throat turned dry. Tom approached the wall opposite and, with the wide expanse of his stretched arms, felt with his fingertips. He grasped ridges imperceptible to the eye, and moved a wall section to one side. A new odour attacked my nostrils. At first, I thought it decay but it also had a strong musty stench of semen. No doubt layers of smell accumulating from the whore's myriad clientele.

Tom lit candle stubs, their wicks sunken grotesquely into deep pits, placed strategically around the room. Burning wax alleviated the noxious odours, and cast monstrous shadows on the walls. The woman was prostrate on a filthy bed animated by lice. I felt her stiff arm punctuated with numerous sores. She had been dead a long time.

'She was all right a couple hours ago,' Tom protested, 'The plague must 'ave got 'er.'

I lifted a candle, trying not to singe or drip wax on her flowing tresses, which were like spun gold. In stark contrast her face was swollen and scabrous, slender neck blackened purple. Tom's plague diagnosis masked a multitude of sins. She could not have been much older than twelve. I gently probed her throat.

'This is the girl,' Tom gestured, sensing my disapproval, 'as prom'assed.'

I paid him to ensure his silence. In order to solicit the word around this disgraced part of London, I had to blacken my noble blood to counterfeit a looking-glass image of roguish trust. I became a supporter of Robert Devereux, the Earl of Essex, and was entrenched in a terrible plot to dethrone the aged Queen. As if God's will approved of my designs, Essex had recently been placed under house arrest for returning too soon from Ireland. He failed to defeat the savage wood-kern Hugh O'Neill, and so came scuttling back to the protective space of the English court. The beginning of Essex's downfall, though 'supporters' like me were still impressed by his spectacular defeat of the Spanish at Cadiz. He had exuded the qualities of a true general who would follow the successes of other Protestant noblemen including the Earl of Leicester and Sir Philip Sidney, who were also, at one time, all close to the Queen. However, Essex was more like Phaëton, who stole his father's chariot, harnessed to the sun, and lost control of the horses. His youth denoted by bashfulness and incompetence. Essex was consummate in bringing trouble to other people's space. Gossip has it that Essex used his players, the Earl of Essex's men, to perform Shakespeare's history play, *The Tragedy of Richard II*, in London's Inns and on its streets to gain support for his Machiavellian plot. In Shakespeare's play, the weak, feeble, effeminate and anointed King Richard II is deposed by the better suited but illegitimate Bolingbroke who became the newly crowned King Henry IV. Essex, therefore, invited comparisons between the Queen and Richard II, and himself and Bolingbroke, to justify his treasonous actions.

Essex's very name broached infamy as John Hayward discovered to his cost. Simply by dedicating his book *The First Part of the Life and Raigne of King Henrie IIII* to Essex resulted in him being sent to the tower. Hayward also had unwittingly evoked, in the Queen's sombre eyes, the political analogy between King Richard II and her Majesty, which Essex paraded all over London. Through this delicious infamy, I gained the rapid trust of the likes of Tom. Essex was splendid villainous currency.

The conflict within my heart is that the Queen is the only monarch I've known. The scarce times I had seen her, my eyes had been enveloped by a milky hue. Her face was pure as ivory, and her stance as starched and fervent as her elaborate dresses glittering with jewels signifying her divinity. She was also the epitome of chastity, her abdomen an iron cage for her womb whose rebellious desires had been quashed long ago. It remained dry and barren in the desert of her sexuality. Essex had once gained the Queen's affections. They had enjoyed long and passionate kisses. He'd once been close to her heart, but his mistake was not being close to her womb. This is because the delicate heart is easily ruled and the Queen is no man's fool. She has eyes and ears not only all over London, but Europe. My betrothed, a cherished maid of honour also named Elizabeth, also furnished me loquaciously about the fate of a once highly regarded spy and playwright named Christopher Marlowe in a Deptford tavern. The murderer pardoned by a Privy Council emboldened by God's obvious displeasure with Marlowe's much discussed debauched life. Now Essex was following in those tragic footsteps.

I took the ferry that was rowed through the Thames' waters thick with filth. The wind was in my face wherever

I sat. The Ladies held on to the huge plumages from which their heads appeared to emerge. Beyond the city walls, playhouses were spared the Mayor's wrath unlike the taverns that had to hide their illicit trades. Yet, how I felt that day, my penny would have been better spent whipping a blind bear. Nevertheless, the monstrous scale of my deceit had me contributing with other Essex supporters the total sum of forty shillings to the Lord Chamberlain's men for the night's special performance. It promised good omens that I thought would inspire my own search.

London was a honey pot for players and the hive swarmed with peasantry. They gathered round the square oak stage and appeared to be piled on top of one another in the tiered galleries. Above the stage, just below the Heavens supported by two huge pillars, were the Lord's rooms. My usual haunt, except I needed to be inside this metaphoric womb, rubbing shoulders with pickpockets and murderers, in order to find its live exposed counterpart.

Bilious laughter and trite chatter was amplified in this enclosed space seemingly carved into the earth's bowels. What fermented within this amphitheatre was not simply the threat of the plague. Ideas were brewed, sparked by performance. The Queen did not fear the deaths of thousands of peasants, but that the body politic would be overrun by these parasitic caterpillars.

Through the arras covering the stage's central discovery space, a clown poked out his head. He moved it up to an impossible height, almost to the Heavens, then back down so that it was almost touching the stage. His head was tilted to one side; eyes rolled, tongue lolled as the audience cheered and laughed. Then the mirthful banter ceased.

Trumpets flourished. Boos and hisses accompanied Richard Burbage, the actor who is playing King Richard II. Through the arras he has swept aside, he leads a procession of servants out towards the baying audience. Burbage carefully takes his place on the raised throne situated centre stage. *The Tragedy of Richard II* had begun.

The build-up of discontent towards the King is tangible. The audience entranced as the dramatic action escalates through rapid scene changes. The excitement barely contained as King Richard II is dethroned, divorced, imprisoned, then murdered. The typical Aristotelian flawed nobleman whose tragic fate is sealed from the opening scene. King Henry IV is eternally triumphant. My unquiet heart-caged thoughts, however, were for the girl at the tavern. Her only tragic flaw was having a womb. I left the growling throng to enrich the soil of discontent. No longer were they caterpillars munching on the body politic's luscious greenery, but were intent on pruning the dying head of a particular fair flower.

The Globe is near London Bridge and a short walk away from the ferry. I rounded a corner and in the moonlit gloom of an alley I spied an older Tom. His unnaturally pale skin-tight face was devoid of flesh, and glowed in the pale dark. He stood bare-legged. A wench was knelt down in front of him. Both absorbed in a performance of their own. The pungent stench of sexual joy was overpowering. I lifted my nosegay to discover it had absorbed those venomous fumes. I coughed and this caused the wench's head to bolt upright, wide rubious lips speckled white. I then, quite unexpectedly, glimpsed my prize and started forward. Tom attempted to pull up his hose as my hand reached for the wench's pale slender throat which unbalanced her. But I was too late. Sated, it had already taken Tom's seed back to its lair.

I stand, with arms behind my back, absorbed in my mother's portrait. It feels like I've never moved. The past two years coalesce within my mind into a single moment. Essex and his supporters are already marching through London's streets to depose the Queen, my Queen. I hear their footsteps, swords being drawn, excited on-lookers hungry for a public beheading.

My servant has no time for announcements. Elizabeth flies into my arms. Somehow she'd managed to escape the court. This should have alerted my suspicions. She allows me a minute or two of kissing and fondling before forcefully driving her weapon through my garments.

'Traitor!' my betrothed gasps tearfully, her countenance torn between anger, pity and uncontrollable affection.

'A traitor to whom?' I whisper, harshly. 'To the Queen, to nobility, to Ladies, to God, to myself?'

Elizabeth is no murderess. The blade misses my delicate sensitive heart by a wide mark. I hold her close, her face dampening my chest as her own weak heart has no appetite for hate. Yet, I still have my purpose and imperceptibly manoeuvre her so her nostrils touch my nosegay.

Immediately, her body convulses and arches violently

back. Black venom leaks like treacle between her yellowing teeth, drips from her fair chin. I glance up, noticing the family portrait has changed. My father, the Earl, is looking down belligerently at my mother, who smiles at me with approval; her swollen belly visible beneath her clasped hands. I gently open Elizabeth's mouth as far as it will go. I can already see it emerging at the back of her throat, pulling itself up by peristaltic movements. I cram my face into the cavity, and feel it sucked further into viscous moisture.

I have returned home.

CHRISTOPHER KENWORTHY

Young

THREE DAYS AFTER Sarah Parkinson was buried, somebody unearthed her coffin and cracked it open. She was found the next morning, sitting up, a hairbrush in her lap, hair freshly brushed. I think people would have been less shocked if the corpse had been stripped and raped. The brushing of hair is a tender act, and nobody should be tender with a body. And who has the right to be tender with a fifteen year old, other than her parents?

By the time the story had spread around the village, it was assumed her father had dug her up, unable to cope with the finality of it all. Around the grave he'd left nothing but boot prints and nine plastic water bottles. They weren't sure whether he'd brought the water to drink, or to melt the freeze from the soil. He must have dug furiously, because it takes two men over three hours to dig a grave, at the best of times. Being on the edge of the village, he must have worked in near silence, and almost complete darkness. There was one church light that could have betrayed his efforts, a lone outdoor bulb that he'd carefully unscrewed and set aside. Before he left, he'd screwed the bulb back in. People in the village were impressed by this display of calm, but I was disturbed by his need to restore the light. He was happy to leave the bottles, so he wasn't exactly tidying up after himself. So why the need for light? Did he think Sarah would be afraid, sitting there in the dark?

She was found, as bodies always are, by early morning dog-walkers taking a shortcut. The sun hadn't risen high enough to get into the grave, so Sarah was covered with frost. Nobody touched her until the police arrived, and by then she was soaked with dew.

There were only three police in the village, and all three were there when I arrived. They were hanging around the edge of the grave like schoolboys having a secret smoke—casual and tense at the same time, heads lowered, almost slouching. There were onlookers, a handful of middle-aged couples who didn't come near enough to see into the grave, but near enough to take in the scene. The police took no notice, and the small crowd was held back by nothing more than embarrassment, but they whispered constantly.

I'd knew I shouldn't go near, but I rushed to get there, assuming they'd just put the lid back on and bury her again. But they had to find out whether he'd done anything to her, other than brush her hair. Whether he'd taken anything away.

Most of what I heard over the next day was based on rumour. The police made no statements, and the local paper—so unused to dealing with actual news—relegated the story to an embarrassed paragraph on page two. But people talked, and it took only a few visits to shops and pubs to hear what was being said. Apparently, the police made an inventory of her body and clothes, but found nothing missing, as far as they could tell. But they continued to investigate.

I went home and sat there waiting for somebody to find out that I was responsible. Every time a car pulled up, I looked out to see if it was the police. Every time something banged in the night, I was sure they were coming to arrest me.

It was the second time I'd been through this. When Sarah had first died, although the cause was a brain haemorrhage, I still thought there'd be an investigation. Children don't just die without an investigation. I was certain they'd look into her past. That I'd be tracked down. But nothing like that happened, and she was buried out of my sight. I'd considered hanging around in the background watching her funeral the way they do in films; a clear view of the coffin without anybody noticing you're there. It isn't like that in real life. You get near the graveyard and everybody looks at you. Especially if you're standing behind a tree, trying not to be noticed. So I left, and pretended I'd never even heard of her.

There are so many ways to hurt people, by accident, by design. And although I neither killed nor dug up Sarah, I couldn't believe her death happened completely by chance. Sooner or later they'd find out what I'd done, and there would be a way to trace me. I'd known Sarah for such a short time, but I must have left a trail of evidence all over her.

I wanted, as always, to blame Paul. He was the one who saw Sarah and her sister at the bus stop. They were obviously heading into Lancaster for a night out. Two young girls looking for fun. We were in our early thirties, but blessed with looks that made us look like we were in our mid-twenties. So Paul had a plan. We'd drive back to my cottage, then nick around the back field to cut onto the main road. This meant we could walk past the bus stop, and see the girls. We'd just walk past, smile hello and keep walking. Then, once they were on the bus, we'd leg it back to my house for the car and try to beat the bus into town. We'd park, and ever so casually time it so that we walked past the bus as they were getting off. We were obviously at least seven or eight years older than them, so they'd let us buy them drinks. And then, finally, once they were drunk enough to trust us, we'd say we had free drinks back at my place. How could a couple of seventeen-year-olds resist?

We didn't know they were sisters at the time. Once we found that out, it was obvious they couldn't both be seventeen. One of them had to be sixteen, at most. But we didn't find that out until it was too late.

Everything happened exactly as Paul had pictured. It was as though he'd scripted it, and none of my protestations about being too old or boring made any difference. Sarah and her sister stepped off the bus, saw us, smiled hello, and instantly Paul said, 'Sorry, we should have given you a lift.' After that it didn't take more than a minute for them to admit they were under eighteen, and it would be helpful if we could go into the pub with them. Perhaps buy the drinks.

The pairing-off began within seconds. Paul started talking to Sarah's sister, and I talked to Sarah. I knew she wasn't eighteen, and that she was the younger sister. No matter how I tried to justify it later, I knew she was no older than sixteen. But I did everything I could to make her feel safe. I listened to her, no matter what she talked about, to maker her feel interesting. Because I wanted to get off with her. If you saw somebody like me in a film, doing that, he'd be the villain.

By the time we got back to my cottage, Paul and Sarah's sister were ready to disappear into my bedroom without hesitation. Which left me with Sarah. That was the point at which I should have asked how old she was.

never heard the phrase 'made it' except in films, and that caught my attention more than anything.

Paul was livid, because Sarah burst in on them and dragged her sister into the night. 'She was like a fucking corpse anyway,' he said later.

The peculiar thing is that I didn't think about this as a crime until she was dead. She was alive for one more week after the night I touched her, and I did everything I could to track her down, to get in touch. Not to apologise, but because I wanted to go out with her. Even if it meant waiting until she was older.

The only time I saw her was when she came out of school. I was driving past, and there she was in her uniform. It made her look younger. That night I kept thinking that when they show 'schoolgirls' in porn, they never look as young as actual schoolgirls. Actual schoolgirls are children.

But once she was dead, I was sure they'd find me. They'd check the CCTV from Lancaster, they'd find my skin on her body. My spit. Instead, they buried her. Then somebody dug her up, and they buried her again.

People said there were plans to send a patrol car around once a night, to make sure she stayed down there. And every night I sit here, listening for that car. It brakes as it comes past the house, and then revs up to climb the hill. I always wait for those revs, knowing that sooner or later they won't come.

JAMES FLINT

Carl

CARL WAS A mathematics genius and could play the piano well. He made a point of telling me over and over that the two attributes often went together, and when I replied one time that yes, I knew (thanks), and could he please shut up, he went into Blackwells and stole me a copy of *Gödel, Escher, Bach* to drive home the point.

We were in The White Horse drinking Diamond White and Stella Artois snakebite and he went next door to the bookshop and came back with a copy five minutes later. I didn't doubt he'd nicked it. First, despite his parents being completely loaded and living in some ancestral pile in Norfolk he never had any cash at all. And second, he liked to steal for fun.

I'd seen him do it. He had a whole technique. Choose a rainy day, so you could wear a heavy coat without alerting immediate suspicion. Browse a couple of random volumes before going over to the one you actually had your eye on. Take two adjacent copies from the shelf, hold them together in your hand, and open the cover of the top one to peruse the contents page. Have a quick flick through then close and replace the top volume on the shelf while swinging the other down inside your coat. Move along, browse another book or two while manoeuvring the hidden copy upwards until you had it pinned between your elbow and your hip. Exit the shop, both hands empty by your sides.

Done.

It was classic misdirection. When I discovered that Carl could do card tricks too, it didn't come as a surprise.

We had our tutorial at 11 a.m. on Tuesdays, which made Tuesdays the end, rather than the beginning of the week. Weekends were generally spent—in my case, at least—breaking personal promises to actually get some reading done and pissing the whole 48 hours away. Mondays were when the work really happened—or, to be more accurate, Monday nights. And Tuesdays were the moment of truth. After which it was only right and proper to go straight down the pub again.

So. 12.05 every Tuesday morning, in the below-decks ambience of one of the town's smallest pubs, in the company of washed-up dons and footsore tourists, we made our date with the lovely ladies Stella and Diamond. Always on my tab.

The me-always-standing-the-drinks thing wasn't just down to my being the only one to ever have actual cash. It was more intricate than that. Carl and I had somehow tacitly agreed that whichever of us performed better in the tutorial didn't have to pay. And despite his rarely getting down to work before 3 a.m. the night before (at which point I'd long since given up and gone to bed) and producing three sides at most of semi-legible scribblings (compared to my carefully notched eight to ten sheets of clumsily geared arguments and quotes), that was always Carl, and never me.

By the end of our first term, I no longer wrote my essays for the tutor. I wrote them for Carl, with the express purpose of one day getting him to buy me that drink. Carl was my target. He was the one I was trying to out-think.

Oh how I would crow when it finally happened. But however much I pored over Frege, Whitehead, or Dennett, however much I tried to puzzle through their lists of propositions or carve out the complex citadels of meaning enfolded within the axioms of their origami prose, however much I thought I'd got it, Carl always somehow collapsed my pretensions at understanding within a few minutes of the discussion opening up.

He did it without apparent malice, but that didn't mean he did it without glee. He danced around me happily, scoring easy points, jabbing lazily through my guard. If I was frivolous he'd be serious. If I was passionate, he'd be light. If I was metaphysical, he'd be ontological. If I became a master of ontology, he'd switch to semiotics and laugh at me from there.

Occasionally the tutor challenged him but it was like lobbing paraffin on a flame. Carl would always have an answer ready. Not only did he have a mind like some kind of beautiful brass mechanical calculating machine, he could also be fucking funny when he chose. Very rarely was he unable to turn an apparent defeat into at least a social victory.

He was infuriating and awe-inspiring in equal measure. The only thing that stopped me strangling him was my vague belief that there was something flawed with the entire enterprise that was Philosophical Logic. That in its attempt to formulate a language with which one could banish equivocacy from explanation it was doomed to failure from the start. And if I knew this, Carl must have known it too. Point being that even if I'd been able to prove him wrong beyond all doubt and refutation on any of the issues we debated, I wasn't sure he'd care.

Carl wasn't like the rest of us. With his bone white skin, hollow flesh and rinsed-out eyes he looked more like the front man of a punk band than someone likely to subject you to a diatribe on the baroque. He had a couple of second-hand suits that despite being too short in the arms and legs he managed to wear with some panache, but whenever he ventured into casual wear he ended up dressing like a girl—hideously coloured sweater tucked into a pair of hip-hugging, half-bleached jeans, socks with sandals, that kind of thing. Most of his clothes looked like they'd come out of a skip.

I'd never really met anyone like him before. There were geeky boys at school—geekier than me, I mean, which was pretty geeky. They wore trousers that were too short in the leg and too high on the hip. But their clothes were new, and clean, and they wore them because they were told to do so by their mothers and they hadn't figured out that they could do any different. And they had pale skin, but their hair was neat, and parted. And they were good at music, or maths, or languages, or all three. But they had no sense of humour. Or depth of personality. And they didn't drink. And they wouldn't dream of taking drugs.

Which was not something you could say of Carl.

It was around the time of our third or fourth tutorial together that I found out just how seriously Carl took the ingestion of narcotics. I really didn't know him very well at this point. I'd seen him around college a bit but he wasn't on my party circuit, which mainly consisted of stoners, theatre-types and musicians. I was a musician too—to earn my drinking money I spent at least a couple of evenings a week playing student venues in a succession of jazz-funk bands, and music had been the one conversation I'd had with Carl, at the Freshers' Bop. He'd made some comment about being able to find the basics of all jazz improvisation in Monteverdi and I had told him he was talking utter bollocks. We had a beery argument which proved one thing only: that Carl knew more about Monteverdi than I did about John Coltrane. It was a harbinger of arguments to come.

It might have been a consequence of this crossing of swords that he invited me back to his room that Tuesday morning. We'd been spat out, dazed, from our hour with the good Dr. Khadri, with whom we were already locked in mortal battle over the issue of whether or not mind and body were one and the same or totally distinct. The tutor, though he hadn't strictly told us what he thought, fell pretty clearly into the latter camp (a paper of his on Emergent Materialism was, after all, on the reading list, which somewhat gave the game away). Being an arty type I naturally took the former stance, though as I was also taking a module in neuro-anatomy I felt entitled to bolster my arguments (mainly stolen from Smart) with reference to what we knew about how the cortex actually behaved (an approach which, I was to realise much later on, would cost me crucial points in Khadri's eyes, as a strict logician should never advance a point with its foundation in the shadow realm of the mere empirical). And Carl, being Carl, disagreed with both of us, offering instead an I-haven't-actually-done-the-reading attack on the whole notion of propositional attitudes, which he backed with ammunition he'd dug up from Davidson and some esoteric American paper on computational neural network theory that clearly even Khadri, for all his sage nodding, didn't understand.

When it was over we stood together shivering on the worn stone step at the bottom of the staircase, contemplating the February drizzle.

I murmured something about needing a spliff.

'Great. Let's go to my room,' Carl said. 'We can have some KM as well.'

'Alright,' I said. And so off we set, Carl leading with his funny, loping walk, me following on behind, as much to find out what the hell KM was as anything.

❖

Carl's room turned out to be right in the very south-western corner of the college, overlooking the back quad, at the top of a winding staircase. It wasn't a particularly nice room, rather long and thin, but that didn't seem to trouble its occupant, who'd done nothing at all to make it remotely homely.

As far as I could tell he was still living out of the suitcase he'd arrived with: at least, that's where all his clothes lay heaped. There were no posters or hangings on the walls, no personal effects beyond the most basic toiletries, no stereo or clock radio, and hardly any books. The few that there were were stacked rather than standing, and they shared the shelves with empty beer and coffee mugs, dirty plates from hall, a battered pair of trainers and a single plimsoll, various boxes and bottles of pills, and several standard-issue aluminium foil ashtrays, all of which were filled to overflowing.

The single individual touch was an expensive Yamaha keyboard that stood on a simple collapsible black trestle alongside the bed.

'That's my piano,' Carl said, as soon as we walked in. Without bothering to remove his coat he pulled up a plastic chair, sat down in front of it, shifted a clinking Sainsbury's bag stuffed with god knew what away from the pedals, and began prancing out the Handel study that was propped up on the stand.

I sat on the bed and listened politely as snatched flurries of notes rippled into the room. Carl could clearly play, but he played like the geeky maths nut he was. All logic. No patience.

As if to demonstrate he stumbled at a tricky passage, tried again, then ripped his hands from the keyboard and raised them skywards, laughing as if it was all one terrific joke.

'Thank Christ it's Tuesday. No more Khadri for a week, ha ha!'

I agreed with the sentiment, and we bitched about the tutor for a while.

'He's such an idiot.'

'It's like he has an affliction.'

'It's an aphasia, an inability to process any concepts formulated after 1930.'

We spoke as condemned men, as if we hadn't not just chosen but fought and studied and sacrificed to be here now, in this room, in this college, on this course. But that was part of our joy. We were the cleverest. We were smarter even than our ditsy tutor, a full professor in one of the top universities in the world. We lived in relative luxury, wanted for nothing. People saved for a lifetime just for a chance to come and see the sandstone fantasies in which we jostled and cavorted. The toil and capital of ages had been extruded in these buttresses and parapets; the majesty of great forests arched above our heads, lay prone beneath our feet. Our libraries held within their vaults the feast of human knowledge, any morsel of which was available to us on a whim. We were blessed. We were gods. Of course we had to pretend that we despised every last glorious minute.

'Skin up,' Carl said.

I nodded and delved into the pocket of my jeans for the hard lump of black north African hashish that I'd bought from some friend of a friend. Carl produced papers and a crumpled Silk Cut and taking a lighter I began the task to which, despite my multiple O-levels and A-levels and honorariums and diplomas, my friends judged me best suited. Rolling a joint.

This, in case you've never done it, is one of the various ways in which to perform this useful task.

1) *Take three papers.* Wet the right-hand half of the adhesive on the first and join it to the second at an angle, so, with adhesive of the second outermost and uppermost. A triangular flap of paper will hang free; set fire to this, blow out the flame, and a golden rim will eat away the flap before being extinguished by the line of still-damp glue. Fix the third paper perpendicular to the other two, at the wider end. Place this construct close at hand, away from draughts and animals.
2) *The cigarette.* Hold it upright by its filter using the thumb and first finger of the left hand (assuming you're right-handed). Find the seam of the cylinder and moisten it with a stroke of the tongue. Peel the seam downward, and the cigarette will fall neatly open.
3) *Heat the gear.* It's hard and compact, black hash. Heavily compressed, mixed with all kinds of adulterants. I didn't really know much about how it was made, other than it was the resin of the plant cannabis sativa. What it was didn't really matter. What it represented, did. The

surreptitious and slightly salacious atmosphere enveloping its purchase. The perfume, velvety and exotic, the scent of baked earth beneath an equatorial sky, of souks, and silks and slippers, of extended calm, of elsewhere, of libertinage; the sexual feel, that hot crumble from veneered impenetrability to peaty moistness at the slightest lick of flame. That small black lump: it was the spirit of the 60s ossified, a coded message sent to us from that decade of true hope, free love, streets running with democracy, that time before the inexorable decline into oil crises and management theory and focus groups and the rise of the markets. The last gasp of romanticism, of those poets and dreamers about whom our sensible parents, who were surely somehow implicated in the rise of this terrible new order, had warned us. And to travel back, to release that spirit like a genie from a lamp? All you had to do was hold it between thumb and forefinger, warm it with a lighter or a match, then softly grind the heated nub with the inside of your knuckle and catch the falling flakes in the natural cup created by your upturned hand.

4) *The mull.* Keeping the fragments of hashish in the palm, add a portion of the tobacco extracted from the cigarette in (2). Then mix ('mull') the tobacco with the hashish, breaking down the strands of tobacco slightly in the process. When an even distribution of drug and vehicle has been obtained, lay the construct made in (1) face down over the whole. Placing palms together, quickly invert, leaving the melange in the centre of the

papers. Then set to one side, again taking care to watch for draughts and animals, for now it's time to:

5) *Make the roach.* Cast around your space for anything that might afford a small piece of cardboard. Leaflets, junk mail, packages, cigarette packs—all are ready sources of roach material. The number one choice, of course, is the Rizla pack itself, though beware: roaching someone else's Rizlas can offend. The advantage of the Rizla pack is that its faces are already the ideal width for roach material (i.e. between 10 and 15 millimetres), as well as being the ideal weight, viz., of sufficient thickness to provide structural support, without being too heavy to curl into an easy tube.
6) *The roll.* If your preparations have been thorough, the roll should be a relatively simple matter. Arrange the mull and the roach in position on the papers, adhesive edge uppermost. Using the thumb, fore and middle fingers of both hands (forefingers topside, middle fingers and thumbs below) hold the construct taut and fold the two sides upwards to create a gentle valley. Roll to and fro once or twice, barrelling the mixture, and when you're satisfied that all is well roll the nearside downwards, tuck inside, and roll back upwards into a tight, gentle cone, finishing the roll with the left hand and using the right for guidance and control.
7) *Finishing postures.* Holding the joint upright by the roach stroke it rapidly with bunched fingers once or twice along its length to settle the contents. Using the discarded filter of the cigarette eviscerated in step (2), nip the extra paper at the wide end of the cone inwards

on one side, capping and containing the mull inside. Taking a lighter, singe away any extra paper left around the roach. Then sit back and admire your handiwork.

I think I preferred rolling joints to actually smoking them.

I'd run through the little procedure outlined above a thousand times. I could do it in my sleep and, sometimes, I did. But on this occasion I'd only reached step (5) when Carl stopped me.

'Wait a minute, wait a minute . . .' Like a crappy string puppet he hopped up from his keyboard, dangled his way across the room, retrieved the solitary trainer from its place upon the shelf, and shoved his hand inside. It came out clutching a small foil parcel. Hunched and intent, he carefully unwrapped it and held the small pile of gritty grey dust inside for me to see.

'KM.'

'Right.'

'Put some in.'

'Er, OK. How much?'

'A bit.'

'Right.'

I took the foil and hoping that a bit was about a third I sprinkled that much of the pile into the mull then rolled the cone.

We smoked it, and it ruined us. Or it ruined me, at any rate. For Carl, it was just an *hors-d'oeuvre*. I'd barely stubbed out the embers of the spliff before he'd produced a glass tube that he'd presumably purloined from one of the science labs and started using it to chase the dragon of the remaining KM directly off the foil.

He offered some to me. I declined.

'What is this shit, in any case?' I pushed the words through the cushions of cotton wool that had enveloped me, post-joint.

'KM?' Busy with his hands, Carl flicked his eyes towards the sink. There, among the usual clutter of toiletries, stood a bottle of what looked like cough medicine.

'This?'

He nodded.

I reached for it. It wasn't cough medicine at all. It was Kaolin & Morphine. I hadn't seen it since I was a child. My mother had dosed me with it occasionally, when I'd had diarrhoea. It was possible that my parents still had the same bottle sitting in the back of their medicine cabinet. It was one of those things, those strange 1950s brands, that they bought, used three times, and then let sit around for years, nondescript apart from the brown/grey division into which its contents always separated out.

'This?'

He gave me an impatient look. 'Yes.'

A light came on. I'd never given the stuff a second thought before. But the name said it all. This over-the-counter diarrhoea remedy, this strange product that was associated in my head with hot water bottles, days off school and Ovaltine, was literally clay and laudanum. That's why it separated if you left it standing for more than a day or two. The grey was the kaolin, the clay. The brown must have been the tincture of morphine. Carl was siphoning this top layer off and drying it to concentrate the drug. He was getting home-made smack out of something he was buying down the road in Boots.

Christ.

This was a step beyond the Johnny Rebel recreational soft drug use that I indulged in. This was hardcore. Or a big step in the direction of hard core. Carl, my fellow student, my tutorial partner, the bloke I argued jazz v. baroque with in the college bar, was a junky. Next he'd be asking me if I wanted some glue.

'Hey,' said Carl, polishing off the last coils of his dragon's tail. 'I've got some awesome solvents if you want.'

❖

I avoided Carl's room after that, and tried to make sure that on our pre- and post-Tuesday sessions we stuck to drinking alcohol—in public. However much Carl's wild-side lifestyle may have fascinated me, his homebrew heroin was not something I wanted to be associated with. Carl may not have cared whether or not he got discovered and sent down, but he was rich (his chronic lack of actual cash somehow seemed indicative), and therefore insulated. I was firmly middle class, and the first of my family to go to Oxbridge. We were comfortably off, as the saying goes, but the precariousness of those comforts had been bred into me from birth. I had no intention of leading a life that was entirely safe and dull, but I wasn't completely crazy, either. I had no desire to risk my university career.

Others, it seemed, were not so cautious.

Carl's predilections had kept him largely out of normal college circles—he foraged in more febrile fields—and for those first couple of terms he'd been to some extent my secret, dismissed by the fashionable cliques that dominated our social lives as something of a freak. But once word got round that Carl had a hotline to quality drugs at reasonable prices, suddenly he was everyone's new friend. Never underestimate the ability of public schoolboys to sniff out and consume intoxicants. Not that Oxford was exclusively public school—in those days the split was around 50/50. But the posh kids, because they had more fashionable clothes, prettier girlfriends, more exciting holidays, cars—because they had more money, basically—tended to dominate. And if their expensive education had taught them one thing, it was how to do drugs not just right under the nose of authority, but with its apparent sanction. Perhaps that's why Carl and his new friends weren't scared: they knew that the establishment looks after its own, they were secure in the knowledge that they were part of it, and they knew that flouting the rules made for the lower orders was a rite of passage, part of the ritual by which one demonstrated membership of the club. As for me, as far as they were concerned, I'd always be a wannabe. My dope-smoking: was it rebellion against conformity, or was it in fact an attempt to pretend I was one of them, a somewhat pathetic attempt to adopt the code, pronounce the shibboleth? Both—and neither. Maybe it had fuck all to do with class; maybe I was just a hopeless lightweight. I didn't know myself. Whenever I tried to think about it, I ended up confused and paranoid. Being semi-permanently stoned didn't help, of course.

Anyway, Carl's new friends. They weren't particularly interesting in his scuzzy KM, though there was a brief fashion for it for a while. What they wanted was the top-notch speed he brought back from his frequent bus trips to Banbury. Or the cocaine he claimed he could get for them in London.

Ostrich that I was, I didn't know any of this until Johnny asked me if I wanted to go halves with him on his corner of the deal.

'Deal? What deal?'

'Didn't you hear? Carl's getting a big order in.'

'No. I didn't hear.'

Johnny shrugged.

This was Monday; when I saw Carl the next day, I asked him what was going on.

'I'm getting some supplies in for the end of term.'

'You didn't mention it to me.'

'What are you, my mother?' I would subsequently meet Carl's mother, as it happened. A posh, pleasant and slightly scatty woman, she had the other-worldly air of someone who's not accepted the full consequences of her teenage son having a small poppy plantation in a distant corner of the estate. 'Anyway,' he continued. 'You don't do anything stronger than that nasty hash you smoke. I didn't think you'd be interested.'

'I wouldn't mind a bit of charlie,' I moped. This despite the fact that I had ambitions to be some kind of left-wing intellectual, the kind who would build a gleaming career predicated on the pursuit of justice and the truth. I knew perfectly well—who didn't?—what the cocaine trade meant for the rule of law and democracy in Colombia. I could probably have had a pretty accurate stab at the number of judges and government officials who were shot or kidnapped out there every year. But here I was, about to miss out on something special, something new. My career, and Colombia, suddenly seemed very abstract and far away. As did the chance of being caught and thrown out of college. Cocaine. It just didn't seem as bad, as serious, as heroin. It doesn't still today, mild tabloid shocker that it's become, part of the standard-issue celebrity survival pack.

'All you had to do was say. How much do you want?'

I had no idea. I'd never taken it before.

'Er, one?'

'No problem. That's fifty quid please.'

Fifty quid! That was nearly a third what I had to live on for the month.

'Right.' Pause. 'You need it now?'

'I'm not a bloody bank, if that's what you mean.'

So after our tutorial I walked with Carl to the bus station, stopping at the cashpoint in Cornmarket on the way, all the time trying to rid myself of a terrible sense that Carl was somehow disappointed in me. And who the hell was he to judge?

❖

The end of term college bop was scheduled for that Friday night and word went round on Thursday that Carl was back and that his mission had been successful.

I found out because Johnny told me so at lunch in hall, and after we'd eaten we went over to Carl's room to see what was what.

Carl was holding court. I'd never seen him so animated. There were three or four others already there; the usual suspects. The room was thick with dope smoke, and the other goods were laid out on the table. A red CD case—Yo Yo Ma's unaccompanied cello suites—was already scratched and smudged with a mess of lines. They clearly had decided not to wait to start the party until the following night.

Carl was in the midst of telling some tall tale about the guy he'd scored off, something about how when he wasn't dealing drugs he worked as a stand-in for actors in porn movies.

'What, like, you mean a *stand*-in?' someone tittered.

'That's right. If they can't perform he does the money shot. He's a stunt cock.'

This was admittedly very funny and the stoned company heaved with mirth. I laughed as well, though somewhat less enthusiastically, partly because I was sober and partly because I'd never heard Carl make any reference to sex at all before and it was jarring.

As the laughter died away Carl leaned forward, lifted one of the small rectangular paper wraps from the coffee table and passed it to me with exaggerated ceremony.

'This, I believe, is yours.'

I took it and slipped it in my wallet. 'Thanks.'

'Aren't you going to try it?'

'Think I'll save it for tomorrow.'

'Ah, the self-restraint! How admirable.'

More giggles from the floor. Who was this guy? This wasn't the Carl I knew. But then how well did I know him? Not, apparently, very well at all.

But maybe I was being unfair. It was the end of term. Carl was happy. He was popular, for once, the centre of attention. No one thought he was a freak now, or if they did they kept it to themselves. Maybe I was just jealous because he'd been my friend and now I had to share him.

Carl. He was on a roll. At the peak of his trajectory. See him smiling, see him joking, see him laughing, see him letting it all hang out. Good luck to him.

'Now!' he said, standing in the centre of the room, conducting, grin splitting his head in two. 'Who wants a speedball?'

❖

Popularity. It's like a drug. Get too much if you're not used to it, and you'll nearly always go too far.

No one, except Carl of course, wanted a speedball. No one except Carl, probably, knew exactly what a speedball was.

'Come on you lightweights. I thought you wanted to p-a-r-t-y!'

Well we did, but not like that.

'Bit early for me, Carl.'

'Think I'll pass.'

'You go for it, mate. I don't want to peak too soon, if that's alright.'

Carl glanced around the faces of his friends, and shrugged. 'You don't know what you're missing.'

Carl being Carl, that didn't really bother him. Bending over the coffee table, his thin frame arched like a croquet hoop, he opened one wrap of coke and one wrap of speed and scraped roughly equal quantities of each of the drugs on to a single square of foil.

I thought naïvely that he was going to do what he'd done the day he'd introduced me to KM, and smoke it. But instead he went and sat over by his keyboard. Here, back half-turned on the room, he rolled up his sleeve, pulled a manky old tie from where it hung over the edge of the bed and with the help of his large, slightly jaundiced teeth he tied it around his naked upper arm. Then he reached up, took down the solitary trainer, reached inside for a cigarette lighter, a syringe and spoon and fetched a half cup of water from the sink.

'Oh yes yes yes,' he sang softly, half to us, half to himself. 'Yes yes yes yes yes.'

The laughter died away. We watched him, watched ourselves watching him.

This wasn't quite what anyone had expected.

'Guys, I've got a lecture. See you tomorrow, yeah?' That was Sammo. Gone.

Suresh too. 'Yeah, I've got some stuff to do as well. Thanks man. Full power.'

'Yeah, thanks, Carl.'

Bang bang. Now it was just Johnny, Bingo, me.

'I'm kind of busy too. Essay crisis. Thanks mate. And take it easy, yeah.'

Correction. Me and Bingo.

So.

Why did I stay? Why did he?

Because we cared? Because we didn't want Carl to hurt himself? Because we were excited? Because we were intrigued by this chance to push the boundaries, to venture into the unknown? Because it was less frightening to stay than go?

I didn't know, and while I was wondering which it was and which, if any, were either redundant or mutually exclusive Carl was smacking his wrist, raising a vein, and sticking a needle into his arm.

Bingo and I started talking rapidly about absolutely nothing.

Carl half depressed the plunger on the needle, waited, and exhaled. 'Aaaaah,' he said, like Kim Basinger was sucking on his cock.

'Good?' I asked, slightly truculently. Wanting to shoot up was one thing. Wanting us to witness it was quite another.

'Ex-stasis,' he hissed, somewhat creepily and—it has to be said—somewhat pretentiously.

Then he depressed the plunger a little more and four seconds later he was juddering.

I mean exactly that. Juddering. Like ten thousand volts were coursing through him. Like someone had just upended a pneumatic drill and shoved it up his arse.

It might have been quite funny if it hadn't been so completely terrifying.

Remember that scene in *Jacob's Ladder*, where the guy just starts vibrating and cannot stop? It was just like that.

I looked at Bingo and Bingo looked at me. Neither of us had the remotest idea what we should be doing. No one had ever juddered on us before. At least not like this.

Bingo's eyes were like shotgun barrels, they were so dilated.

I was, I realised, the only sober person in the room.

Both of us looked at Carl. He juddered for a good few seconds more, maybe as much as a minute. Then he spasmed and his limbs splayed out so fast the back of his right hand caught Bingo in the face. Flung out of its vein in the other arm, the needle shot across the room and pinged against the wall. His chair fell back but as it did so he seemed to almost rise out of it. I remember the angle as impossible, maybe 50 degrees from horizontal, tops. But somehow, up he came, arms and legs pumping like a techno dancer's. Unable to think of any better course of action I grabbed him by the waist and swung him over to the bed. Then Bingo jumped on his torso and I jumped on his knees and we held him like that until the juddering had subsided, by which point he had started foaming at the mouth.

'Carl! Carl!'

'Hmnnnghgh.'

It was the only time I'd ever known him not to have an answer.

'What the fuck are we going to do?'

'I don't know.'

'He could fucking die!'

'I know!'

Carl started to convulse again and thrashed his head from side to side. I tried to think of something to do, but I knew nothing about first aid. The life-saving courses I had done in swimming class at school were a long long way away.

My eye fell on, of all things, a shoehorn lying on the floor, over by his suitcase. That was typical Carl. He didn't have a decent pair of shoes, but he had a bloody shoehorn. I dived for it.

'What're you doing?'

'Trying to stop him swallowing his tongue. We've got to get his mouth open. I'm going to hold his head; you pull on his jaw.'

Carl didn't seem at all keen on this idea. He raged and bucked, twisting from our grasp. If our efforts hadn't been so desperate they would have been quite comical. But at length we got him pinned, forced his teeth apart, and slipped the damn thing in. Like a bridled horse he seemed to acknowledge that we'd won an important victory, and immediately grew calm.

His breath sputtered in and out around the plastic blade. His eyelids fluttered intermittently. When they did, we could still only see the whites of his eyes. The pale blue irises were gone.

'We're going to have to get him to a hospital,' I said.

'And how the bollocks are we going to do that?' Bingo, I sensed, was panicking.

'Well I don't know. Go downstairs and call an ambulance?' This was, of course, in the days before the sub-brick-sized cell phone. Student telecoms were limited to a pay phone at the bottom of each college staircase.

'If an ambulance turns up at the front gates we are fucked.' Bingo was striding round the room now, clutching his own head. 'If anyone finds out what's been going on here, we are all completely fucked.'

'And if we don't do it Carl might fucking die! How about that on your conscience?'

We glared at each other. We both knew we couldn't afford the consequences of discovery, whatever else might happen. But we had to get Carl some proper care.

'Back gate,' I said.

Still with his hands clasped around it, Bingo shook his head. 'Still too risky.'

'We have to. They could park outside, come across the upper level, take him out the same way.'

'We can't! Look, why don't I go and get Matt Deacon. He's a medic . . .'

'We need more than a fucking medic. We're getting an ambulance. I'm going to call one now.'

I started for the door.

'You're not leaving me alone with him.'

But I'd already gone. Down the stairs as quickly as I could, fumbling in my pockets as I went, not for change—I didn't need any—but for reassurance.

The phone was occupied, of course. Lucy Barton, in the middle of some kind of long-winded family chat.

She waved at me, as if it was a perfectly normal Thursday afternoon. I grimaced and hurried out the door and round to the next staircase along. Its phone was also occupied. Two more tries before I found one that was available.

'Ambulance, please. Yes, emergency.'

I'd expected to have my pleas for them to come to the rear of the college and wait for me to show them in totally ignored. But the operator was understanding and attentive. Maybe she'd done this before.

On the way back upstairs to Carl's room I stopped by one of the toilets. Pulled out the wrap of coke, opened it, flushed the lot. It looked like I was going to have to wait to try cocaine.

To my surprise Bingo was still there when I got back. He was seated, puffing on a cigarette.

'Where the fuck have you been?'

'Phones were busy. How is he?'

'Better than he was.'

Carl was shivering now, rather than convulsing. Foam was still gathering at the corners of his mouth. His skin, which already verged on albino, was now the same delicate shade of blue his eyes used to be, before they vanished somewhere inside his head.

'You took the shoehorn out?'

'He didn't seem to need it any more.'

I took a hand towel from the hook beside the basin, wet it slightly, and used to it wipe the sweat and saliva from Carl's face.

'Are they coming?'

'Who?'

'The ambulance.'

'Yes.'

'When?'

'Dunno. Maybe twenty minutes. I asked them not to use the siren and to park at the back gate.'

'How we going to get him down there?'

'I think that's their job.'

He nodded.

'Alright. You go out and wait for them. I'll stay here.'

'You sure?'

'Haven't got much option, have I?'

I asked him for a cigarette and he offered me his pack of Marlboro. I took one and lit it, then went to the window and looked out over the quad.

There was no one about. We were at the centre of the storm now and it was calm, just like it's supposed to be. I felt nervous, but not uncontrollably so. Maybe everything was going to be okay.

I smoked for a minute or two, then stubbed the cigarette out on the window ledge.

At the door I paused. 'I ditched my drugs,' I said.

Bingo looked utterly morose.

'Me too.'

We'd never been exactly friends, me and Bingo. But now, perhaps, we were.

'This is fucked up,' I said.

'I know.'

The ambulance came to the back gate as planned and the crew—and this was nothing short of a total miracle—stretchered Carl down the stairs and right through the back quad without anybody noticing.

Off they trundled him to the John Radcliffe, a drip in his arm, while Bingo and I found a couple of bin liners and cleared the drugs paraphernalia from his room. Four Sainsbury's bags of empty Kaolin & Morphine bottles we found, stashed in the wardrobe and under the bed, plus a dozen or so packs of disposable syringes, several small foil packets filled with nameless substances, and a couple of half-empty tins of the industrial solvent he'd once offered me. Out it all went, into a roadworks skip parked three streets away.

Carl didn't thank us for it. Not at all. We went to visit him that evening and he seemed pretty out of it, but he clearly wasn't going to do anything quite so drastic as die on us. The next day he was up and about, arguing with the nurses because he wanted to discharge himself and they wanted to keep him in for observation. He eventually capitulated, mainly because he was so weak he could barely stand. But the day after that he was back in college, giving us an ear-bashing for over-reacting and chucking all his shit away. Bingo, who as it turned out had stashed his drugs instead of flushing them, wasted no time in telling him it was all my fault.

I saw rather less of Carl after that. Our tutorial course was finished, and I didn't really fancy getting drunk with him any more. Ms White and Ms Artois stayed behind the bar on Tuesdays, and The White Horse became a slightly saner place. As for doing drugs together, that wasn't very likely. I now thought Carl a maniac and he thought me a lightweight, and neither of us, for different reasons, thought the other was really to be trusted. And I don't think Carl was particularly shy about his new low opinion of me when around the monied public school kids who continued to score class As from him, as I quickly found myself all but dropped from this tight little clique, for which no crime was more profound than that of being sensible.

Well, whatever. None of it proved of any great consequence in the long run. And it wasn't like I lost touch with Carl completely. Our paths continued to criss-cross, even after college, for some years—he had a habit of cropping up in unlikely places. He remained as much of a disaster as ever, living off his trustfund, unable to find any kind of job, but permanently cheerful, hopeful and brilliant. And he still kept his poppy farm in that corner of his parents' enormous garden, though he had, by all accounts, long ceased shooting up, so maybe the incident that day did have some effect.

Last I heard of him he'd married some European princess even richer and crazier than he was, and the two of them were employed full-time wreaking chaos on their poor extended families.

But then that was Carl.

RHONDA CARRIER

Nine Cubed

'ALL CITIES HAVE scars . . . wounds that are unique to them,' mused the old man, lips papery as the unfiltered Gaulois wedged in the corner of his mouth. He spoke, it seemed, to no one in particular, and certainly not to me, two tables away. Me in my usual spot, stirring sugar into my coffee, writing notes in my old lined *cahier* while my baby son dozed in his pouch on my chest, head turned away from me as if, already, he were dreaming up a separate future, formulating plans that didn't involve me.

I nodded to myself, thought of Rachid. I had come to Paris and fallen in love. It's a cliché, but that doesn't make it any the less true. I'd fallen in love both with the city and with one of its inhabitants, not knowing the conflict that would ensue, the bitter choice that would be demanded of me.

The 'city of light', that's what they call it, and as I'd

walked around on brittle December nights, my eyes had blazed with the lights of several hundred Christmas trees, had reflected the twenty thousand bulbs illuminating the Eiffel Tower, its lightbeams sweeping the skyline like a golden broom. Clean and crystalline, Paris shone, even at dawn as I headed back to my rented room, dodging the little machines that swabbed the city, made its streets and pavements gleam anew. And I felt new too.

I wasn't in Paris for any reason other than that it was elsewhere. Blinded by its light, I decided to stay, enrolling on a bilingual law degree at Paris X. That's where I met Rachid. He called by on an errand for his mother, a cleaner at the university, and it was him I chanced upon when asking for directions. We ended up taking coffee together in the canteen, and while we chatted, of this and that, he mentioned the campus's nickname, *Nanterre La Folle*—a reference to its role in the sixty-eight uprising. His eyes shone like dark pools as he talked. I felt again the by now familiar pull of the unknown, the lure of difference.

'Life is elsewhere,' he muttered at one point, then said more loudly. 'You know that phrase?'

'It's the title of a novel. Kundera, wasn't it?'

He nodded. 'Yes, but taken—in a slightly wayward translation—from a Verlaine poem, which was in turn quoted in Breton's *Surrealist Manifesto. Quelle vie! La vraie vie est absente. Nous ne sommes pas au monde.* Students daubed it on the walls of the Sorbonne in May sixty-eight. It became their slogan.'

I watched his lips, his beautiful womanly lips, as he spoke, and I wanted to kiss him. His eyes, almost black, reflected my own image back at me, just as his thoughts and preoccupations seemed to mirror mine. And so I fell in love with Rachid and let him take me elsewhere.

It wasn't far. Just as far as Sartrouville, a suburb to the north of the campus, where he lived in a squat with some other *beurs* and assorted hangers-on. I became one of the latter, sharing Rachid's mattress on the floor, sharing the joints passed round nightly in the makeshift candlelit kitchen, listening to them all talk, relentlessly, as if picking at a scab, of ninety-one, when one of their friends, eighteen years old, was shot down by a policeman while hanging out in a local mall. Shot dead while killing time.

I listened to them talk of how things hadn't improved since then, not really. During a New Year visit the previous week, Sarkozy—minus his new pop star girlfriend—had paid only lip service to the frustration of the people living there, they said. To their fury over unemployment and racism, over the incessant ID checks and frisks, their sense of helplessness in the face of marginalisation. It was so many empty words from a man who, just three years previously, had called rioting youths 'scum' and suggested that the *banlieues* be cleaned with a Kärcher. The fact that these industrial-strength pressure washers were made in Germany gave his comment sinister overtones.

'Like so much dog shit,' said Rachid's friend Tahart, toking on a spliff. 'He's a fuckhead, that Sarko.'

Afterwards, in the utter blackness of his room, against a backdrop of sirens, Rachid would whisper to me of the need for action, of renewed resistance. After all, he reminded me, it was the fortieth anniversary of sixty-eight. One of the latter's failures, he explained, was that though it ushered in a more liberal attitude towards immigration, there had been no provision for the newcomers. Most were rounded up in ghettos surrounding Paris's heart, which became even more of a place for the privileged. Arriving in areas rife with unemployment and sub-standard housing, how had the immigrants been expected to make a decent life for themselves? How could they not feel rage, even aggression, herded away as they were, like animals into enclosures?

I listened, and I thought of the life I had been trying to make in Paris, in the cosy eyrie of my *chambre de bonne* in the Latin Quarter, a stroll from the river. I loved Rachid, loved him for the flame of his righteous anger as much as his physical tenderness, or perhaps even for this duality in him. But I missed the city itself, missed strolling down its long broad boulevards bordered by glittering shopfronts, wandering through the courtyards of the Louvre by night, browsing the secondhand bookstalls along the Seine as sunlight danced on the water. The grime of the suburbs was hard to get accustomed to, after so much light.

'It's because you're a bourgeois,' said Rachid, a rare bemusement twinkling in those sad black eyes. How had he come to fall in love with a girl like me, from a middle-class family, product of a private education, he seemed to wonder? And I wondered too.

'You don't realise,' he continued, 'but you've been raised to fetishise order, rationality. That's why you revere the Paris you do, the Paris of pomposity and self-aggrandisement.' He sighed into the darkness. 'All that money,' he said, 'spent on one man's paean to himself. One man's desire for immortality.'

'Who do you mean?'

'Mitterrand, of course. Mitterrand and his *grands projets*. Billions of *francs*—15 billion to be precise—spent on extending the pointless straight line of the *axe historique* and other fucked-up projects, while the suburbs continue to rot. And having the gall to claim that the monstrous cube of the Grande Arche de la Défense is a monument to humanitarian ideals rather than to military victory like the Arc de Triomphe, yet to inaugurate it with military parades to mark the bicentenary of the French revolution! And the Louvre Pyramide? Hah! Mitterrand's megalomania again. Thought he was a pharaoh, did he?

'And he wasn't the first control freak. The Paris we see today was created by Haussmann, a self-styled 'baron' working for Napoleon III. Sure, he created safer streets, better housing and traffic flow, and more sanitary conditions. But Napoleon's real aim was streets that were too wide for rebels to build barricades across, linked to large train stations so that army troops from the provinces could be quickly drafted in.'

'Why?'

'To stop the *communards*, of course. And like now, the poorer elements of society, those who had truly suffered under the previous medieval living conditions, were pushed out to the suburbs when bourgeois apartments replaced their slums.'

Rachid was so intelligent, so convincing in his arguments, that I wondered at the fact that he hadn't gone to university. But when I mentioned it, he just snorted.

'Don't talk to me about education,' he said, his tone even more acrid than usual. 'I wanted, from an early age, to be a mathematician. I had an almost autistic talent for it. Ask me anything and I can do it: algebra, geometry, you name it. But you try getting educated when your school is continually vandalised by its own pupils, by ten- and eleven-year-olds already soured by disillusion. It's like the riots that started in Neuf-Cube.'

'Neuf-Cube?'

'The kids' name for Seine-St-Denis. Because it's *département* number 93. Anyway, the youths were burning cars belonging to their own parents, friends and neighbours, turning their hatred inwards. You try getting educated when your school is so damn rough that only newly qualified teachers will agree to teach there, and only then on the condition that they won't have to stay long.'

If he'd learnt anything from the experience, he went on, it had been to question the official line, to resist being spoon-fed. And as such he had left school at the earliest opportunity and became become an autodidact, reading widely but never believing anything, always interrogating it.

I asked him how he could stand to live where he did, stand the bleakness. It was getting me down, and I often stayed in bed all day, loathe to venture out onto the drab, scarred streets, livened only by the now-familiar graffiti of rage. Rachid had persuaded me to ditch my studies, but I hadn't discovered anything else to live for, beyond him, and I didn't know if that was enough.

He snorted again, asked me where else he would go.

'Perhaps I'm naïve,' he said, 'but I was born here, and —I don't know—I feel I owe it to the place to stay, to try to make things better. For me there's no alternative.'

He gazed out of the window, into a sky devoid of sun.

❖

Our contraception failed, and with it our relationship. I couldn't, I said, bring up a child in Sartrouville. Couldn't raise it for a dead-end life of dirty precincts, mutilated schools, boarded-up shops. And much as I admired Rachid for staying true to his ideals, I wished that, for our child's sake, he would accept the necessity of giving up the fight and getting a job.

He wouldn't. And naturally, he wouldn't hear of moving to Paris with me.

'You need your straight lines, Clare,' he said. 'The axe, the *grands boulevards*. Your illusions of order, of sanity. But real life—*la vraie vie*—is here, beyond the *Périphérique*, the ring road built as yet another way of cordoning off the undesirables. Real life is in the urban sprawl around Paris, its scar tissue. Real creativity is here, amidst the chaos, in the spreading ink blot of the *banlieue*, the Rorschach test of France's psyche. Read the literature, listen to the rap, if you don't believe me.'

But I did. I did believe him. Yet still I left, and started anew once more, in another *chambre de bonne*, from which, if I stand on tiptoe on my bed and push open the mansard window, I can glimpse the river, the slow stately glide of it through the city's corrupt heart. I miss Rachid, and he misses the son he has never known. But he's a man of principle, and he won't come to see us in Paris. On principle, therefore, I can't take the boy to Sartrouville. And so we've reached an impasse.

I throw a handful of loose change into the saucer, watch as some of the coins spin and then clatter down onto the porcelain. As I leave the café, I look back at the old man, still muttering to himself at his table by the window.

I step outside, into the dazzling light, and walk, my still-sleeping son on my chest, halfway over the Pont des Arts, where I stand looking down at the water. The barricades are long-gone, the paving stones have been replaced, the tear gas has dispersed. Sixty-eight left its psychic wounds, but the city remained unscathed. Yet Rachid taught me to see that Paris is disfigured, disfigured by those who sought to leave their mark no matter what the cost to others.

When my son wakens, I look up at last and find that the light has begun to die, grey clouds massing on the fringes of the city like so many threats. For a moment my child looks at me, and then he lifts his eyes and fixes them on the horizon.

MARC WERNER

Someone Take These Dreams Away

WHEN *CONTROL* OPENED at the Cornerhouse, the nights were getting longer. Most days, it was dark by half past four. Anton Corbijn's biopic of Ian Curtis was the film of the year; everybody went to see it (apart from me), even Nick. But while the rest of our colleagues from English & Film would have allowed themselves to become immersed in Corbijn's recreation of late 70s Manchester, marvelling at Martin Ruhe's black and white cinematography, Nick would have been sitting there in the dark thinking of another British film with only a handful of scenes shot in black and white, the rest in colour.

Nick has a thing about black and white. He's fond of quoting Christopher Walken's line from Donald Cammell's

Wild Side. 'Life is black and white. Have you ever seen grey squares on a chessboard?'

I'm sitting in front of his computer in the office we've shared since I recommended him for a vacant lecturer's post, and I'm wondering where to look first. I don't even know how much stuff he keeps on his desktop machine. I hardly use mine at all, preferring my laptop. The office is tiny—the university has a problem with overcrowding—but it's surprising how sitting at Nick's desk gives me an entirely different perspective on it. The difference between it and the view from my desk is like the difference between the way *to* somewhere and the journey *back*. I spin slowly round to look at Nick's shelves. Two books by Roy Armes, *A Critical History of British Cinema* and *The Ambiguous Image*. Roger Manvell's *New Cinema in Britain*. Danny Peary's *Cult Movies*. (I have a copy of that somewhere, too.) A few annual-sized hardbacks—*Thriller Movies*, *A Pictorial History of Crime Films*, *Photoplay Film Yearbook 1976*. I was struck by how many of these titles dated back to the 1970s. Among the newer stuff: Chris Darke's *Light Readings*, Ali Catterall and Simon Wells's book about British cult films *Your Face Here*, and a recent edition of the *Time Out Film Guide*. An eclectic library.

It's very quiet in the office, which it rarely was when Nick was around. He'd either be banging away at his keyboard ('Touch-typing's for puffs. No offence') or complaining loudly into his phone about the standard of the technical equipment in the lecture theatres. Or he'd have a student in for a tutorial. Three people in an office designed for one. Admin, teaching, dealing with students

—that's only half of what we're supposed to be doing. The rest—our so-called research—is what brings in the real money. But if we want a quiet space in which to write, there's no point looking anywhere near the university.

18.8.87 [morning]
In a TV studio where I've been interviewed. The Queen turns up. Then we all go out to a tube station. The Queen looks nervous. On the train a man is smoking a cigarette and a cigar. His fat cigar looks like a knob with the foreskin pulled back. Arriving at Cambridge University (!?) I am shown with one other person (?) to my room, which is room B at school. I am given keys, though the door is of the saloon bar type.

On the upper shelves behind Nick's desk, the beautifully tactile, plastic-sheathed cases of DVDs. *Elephant*, *Old Boy*, *If. . . .*, *Zéro de Conduite*. Beautiful things, DVDs. Simple, full of promise. How many have you bought and never watched? In case you ever needed to see something again, to write about it, you told yourself, but really it was just to possess them. Like a director hoarding prints of his own films. A sense of ownership, a piece of marketing genius. At least half the DVDs in anyone's collection have never been watched.

I notice the line from *Wild Side* written on a yellow Post-It stuck to the side of Nick's inkjet printer. Also, on another Post-It alongside: 'When do we live? That's what I want to know.' I knew the quote. It was a line spoken by Mick Travis, the Malcolm McDowell character in *If. . . .*, near the beginning of the film. I might not have known it had it not been for Nick's interest in the film. His obsession with the film.

I've been covering for him for a week now. Delivering a lecture to undergraduates, running a workshop with his MA students. His absence has been noticed, but has not yet become a serious problem. It will, though. The conference he's organised—*Run in the Corridor: the Politics of School Shootings on Film*, which he's been working towards for several months—is only a week away.

A couple of times in the last few days I've been convinced things have switched around on his desk and have wondered if he's been in during the night. I know he has a good relationship with Byron, the dreadlocked security guard who wanders in from Moss Side towards the end of the afternoon. I've seen the two of them sharing a roll-up, huddled against the autumnal chill and standing a cautious distance from the main entrance to the building. One of them sources the gear and supplies the other. My guess is Byron is the supplier, if only because Nick, for all his strengths, is not very streetwise. But he can turn on the charm. One afternoon while he was waiting for a female student to turn up for a tutorial, he told me she was dyslexic. Listen to this, he said, reading from the student's Learning Support Document, '"Linzi has difficulty with planning work, prioritising tasks and concentrating when there is background noise. She has poor short-term memory and may lose flow when interrupted."' He looked up at me. 'For fuck's sake,' he said, 'Do you think *I'm* dyslexic, then.'

'Sounds like we all are,' I said.

When Linzi came in and sat down across the desk from Nick, he held up a print-out and said to her, 'This is your Learning Support Document.' He immediately crumpled it into a ball and threw it at the bin. When she looked shocked, he said, 'It's bollocks. I don't care how you spell encyclopaedia—consensus—liaison. Whatever. I'm interested in the *content* of what you write, not its *appearance*.' She looked uncertain. 'Don't worry,' he said with a resigned smile. 'I can always print off another copy.'

In the quiet of the early afternoon, the phone rings on Nick's desk. I look at it, wondering whether to pick it up. I don't look at it for very long.

'Hello? Nick's phone,' I say, strongly hoping the caller will not respond by saying, 'Hello, Nick's phone.'

'I'm looking for Nick,' says a female voice.

You and me both.

'He's not at his desk at the moment, I'm afraid,' I say. 'Would you like to leave a message?'

'That's OK,' she says, and before I know it she is gone.

I press 1471.

We are sorry. We do not have the caller's number.

I remember my own student days. One of my lecturers, Roger Huss—one of the few I really liked—had invited me to call him by his first name, and maybe I did a couple of times, but it never felt right somehow. *Excuse me, Roger. Thank you, Roger*. Now it's different. It's *Hey Nick* and *Laters dude*. Student reps sit on staff committees and complain bitterly if they think they're not getting their money's worth.

7.1.96
At school, a gang of lads gathers round. I bristle but say nothing. Another lad comes in and tells us what we have to do—look back over all the films of the year and see which one God would have made differently(!).

In my mind, as I hang up the phone, is a picture of Helena Swan, one of Nick's postgraduate students, a well-built and undeniably attractive woman in her early fifties. I've noticed her hanging around at the end of Nick's seminars, laughing at his jokes during a staff-students social event. I've had to start leaving the room when she comes for tutorials. It was her voice on the phone, I'm sure of it.

I switch his computer on. I know Nick's log-in because he dictated it to me over the phone one day when a system error was blocking mine and I couldn't use the photocopier. I enter it and the prompt asks for a password. I have a few weak guesses—anderson, mcdowell, oldboy, elephant (if. . . . doesn't have enough characters, even with the four-dot ellipsis)—but don't get lucky.

I stand up and go over to the window. Looking out at the windswept junction of side roads, I am reminded for some reason of another time I stood in exactly the same position and looked out to see Nick sauntering towards the building and talking on his mobile. He was smiling. I didn't often see him smile. As he approached the barrier, which was lowered to keep out unauthorised vehicles, he ended the call and dropped the phone into his jeans pocket. In front of him, the barrier suddenly rose as if, grandly, permitting him to enter. Nick looked up and gave a great guffawing laugh, which was even rarer than a smile and made him look a lot younger than his 45 years. I could hear it, two floors up and through double-glazing. I laughed as well and felt momentarily lightheaded as well as lighthearted. It felt like the first time we'd really connected in years, perhaps since school, though of course he hadn't seen me watching, and by the time he'd reached our office, his face had settled into its semi-permanent grimace of disapproval.

I go to the department admin office on the third floor. On the left as you go in is a series of filing cabinets. I open the one labelled S–Z and flick through until I find what I want. I leaf through a file, make some notes, and leave.

I stop by our office to pick up my bag and am about to leave when I have a thought. I walk over to Nick's shelves and take down the DVD of *If. . . .* and a couple of books and slip them into my bag.

22.1.96 [morning]
Attending hospital. Very soon it's become our old school —it's assembly time. We're all in uniform. There's a boy in a wheelchair near me. He's got a glass of Coca-Cola with ice in it. Another boy comes along and sits in another wheelchair, sliding a big brown suitcase underneath the chair.

The bus is full of students. I stare out of the window and find myself thinking about Iain Constable's recent lecture on research methods. He was coming across as rather pedantic with his insistence on correct presentation. Footnotes, quotations, bibliographies. Everything had to be just so, or the student would lose marks. 'Right down to the number of dots in an ellipsis,' he said, and Nick spoke up, saying, 'What about *If*. . . .? What if you need to mention the title of Lindsay Anderson's 1968 film *If*. . . ., which famously has four dots in its ellipsis? What then?' Iain laughed and Nick said he wasn't joking, it was a serious point. Taking Nick's interruption as a challenge, Iain entrenched and said an ellipsis with four dots was a mistake and would be marked as such in any work he came across. 'Good job I'm not your student, then,' Nick said, as he got up and walked out of the lecture theatre.

I found him later in our office, in tears.

'What is it?' I asked, shocked.

'Nothing. Leave me alone,' he snapped, then softened slightly. 'Just give us a minute, Mike.'

I went to see the head of department about a timetabling issue. When I came back, Nick had dried his eyes, but his face was red as it jutted towards his computer screen.

'Are you going to tell me what's wrong or shall I mind my own business?' I asked.

'Something I read in here,' Nick said, picking up Ali Catterall and Simon Wells's *Your Face Here*, which I knew had a chapter on *If*. . . . He opened the book and flicked through the pages. 'Page 64,' he said and chucked the book across the office.

I caught it and turned to the right page.

'Last par,' Nick said. '"There were plans for a school reunion".'

Writing about Anderson's idea for a proper sequel to

If. . . . (as distinct from the fluff that was *O Lucky Man!*), the authors caught the reader up on what had happened to key cast members. Christine Noonan (the Girl) had left the profession and gone into teaching, David Wood had become a children's writer and McDowell, of course, had moved to Hollywood. Two, however, were dead. Richard Warwick (Wallace) had died from an AIDS-related condition in 1997, and Rupert Webster (Bobby Phillips) had been knifed to death on the New York subway in the 1980s.

I felt a lump in my throat as I instantly recalled one of their scenes from the film, shot in black and white, in which they slept side by side in Wallace's bed. Although Malcolm McDowell's scene with the Girl at the Packhorse Cafe, in which they had ended up play-fighting naked on the floor, again in black and white, had been remarkably effective in its insistence that fantasy was very much a part of the film's reality, it was clear where the director believed the emotional heart of the film was to be found. The camera's slow glide across the dorm, showing first Bobby Phillips and then revealing Wallace lying next to him, had made that very clear. Earlier, Phillips had watched admiringly as Wallace, after flashing a smile at the younger boy, performed slow-motion acrobatics on the high bar.

Although the scene in the Packhorse Cafe was sexually explicit, even allowing a glimpse of pubic hair, the film's erotic peak was to be found later, Nick had once patiently explained to me, in another black and white sequence. The one in which the blonde Mrs Kemp, housemaster Arthur Lowe's wife, played by Mary McLeod, walks naked down an empty corridor towards the camera, and then, away from the camera, through a boys' dormitory, trailing a hand along a line of washbasins and turning, finally, to look back over her shoulder at the viewer, her stance recalling that of the Girl in the cafe as she looked round from under a curtain of thick, dark hair while making coffee for Mick and Johnny. Mrs Kemp looked over her right shoulder, the Girl over her left. One of these shots looked as if it was meant to be erotic, but was merely a tease, a stock pose, a nod to the classic black-and-whites; the other, exploiting the full-figured vulnerability of the childless and lonely Mrs Kemp, actually was and powerfully so.

'If only Mary McLeod knew how many adolescent boys' wanks she was responsible for,' Nick said.

This comment comes back to me as I get off the bus in West Didsbury. The anonymous Edwardian conversion across the road, once home to Factory Records, reveals no trace of its cultural significance. I cross Lapwing Lane and keep walking. The address I'm looking for is located within a grid of quiet residential streets to the west of Palatine Road. Helena Swan is not quite another generation, as Mrs Kemp had been to Mick, Johnny and the other boys ('Do you need this, Mrs Kemp,' Mick had asked, in one of the refectory scenes, with a provocative thrust of the sauce bottle), but she is an apparently available woman some ten years older than Nick, of a similar build to Mary McLeod in 1968. She could easily be a stand-in, a body double.

Dusk is turning the lit front rooms of these imposing

three-storey Victorian terraced houses into sound-stages, sets dressed and waiting for actors. A narrow footpath runs down the side of Helena Swan's property. Barely wide enough for two people to squeeze past each other, it offers a convenient spot from which to observe the back of the house. Some lights are burning; no noise can be heard. There must be a better way to go about what I'm trying to achieve. Do I really expect to see Nick suddenly appear silhouetted in a bedroom window? To knock on the front door and explain my quest would embroider unnecessary complications on to an already elaborate tapestry. I decide to wait for a while.

Wednesday 15 January 1997
At a swimming baths, there are three pools but they're short and narrow, barely bigger than normal bathroom baths. The one in the middle has two people in it: someone on the left who remains still, and a young black man who is swimming lengths. There would just be room for me to swim to his right. I'm perched on the rim about to dive in but I worry that my arms or legs might disturb other diners because now it's a restaurant as well. Also the black lad has just smiled at me and he's naked and I'm worried there isn't enough room.

My thoughts turn to the DVD in my bag. Assuming a lack of success in my current endeavour, I will play the film when I get home. I've seen it a number of times and my familiarity with it has been enhanced by Nick's frequent allusions and references, but to watch it again under these particular conditions might just throw up an idea or two. I could never forget the grey echoing corridors down which Mick, Johnny and Wallace confidently stride, three abreast, to meet their punishment at the hands of the Whips. Vicious lashes of the cane in the school gymnasium, the wooden floor pounding with the lengthy run-up of the sadistic Rowntree. How similar that gym was to our own, in the grammar school. How different were the relationships of abuse, yet how familiar, really.

I take out my notebook, then my mobile, and key in a number. I hear a faint ringing, then another light comes on in the kitchen window and Helena Swan appears. She picks up the phone.

'Hello?' she says. 'Hello?'

I hold my breath.

'Who is this?'

Still I say nothing.

Then, her voice shrinking to a whisper: '*Nick?*'

I thumb the red button to break the connection and breathe out and quickly breathe in again. I watch as Helena Swan turns away from the phone and stares into the air in front of her face, which looks as if it has just been slapped. I wish at that point I hadn't done what I have done, in spite of the information gained from it.

I asked Nick once if he was frustrated by the confusion surrounding the use of black and white sequences in *If. . . .*, for the most part a colour film. Every commentator seems to have a different take and all claim to be reflecting the position of director Lindsay Anderson. Some say it was done to save money, others that a consistency of colour tone in the chapel, with its great stained-glass windows, could not be achieved. Still others argue that the choice was aesthetic, that it had to do with reminding the viewer of Anderson's links to Free Cinema, that it was part of a general push for Brechtian alienation, that it was intended to heighten the tension between fantasy and reality.

'It's all of those things and none of them,' he'd said. 'Art's impossible without ambiguity.'

4 May 1997
Standing at a urinal in our school, but in Scotland. A man stood too close to me so I moved along and he muttered that the only person I'd have something to worry about in that department would be Ian somebody. I challenged him. He shook water at me, which I soon realised was his piss. I grabbed him and demanded to know his name and where he worked—Iain Grant, lab technician, he said. Somehow I knew they were two different Ians and that this one spelled his name the Scottish way.

When I get back home, I pour myself a large glass of wine and watch the film again. Every shot of the school reminds me of the one Nick and I both attended, he five years ahead of me. A couple of years ago there was a reunion. It was the last opportunity to visit the school, as the governors had finally admitted defeat in a long battle against time and announced that the school would move to new premises at the beginning of the next academic year. I asked Nick if he was going.

'Am I fuck.'

I went; I was curious. You were supposed to get a boy to show you around, but I slipped up the back stairs and prowled the upper corridors on my own. I wasn't hugely keen to catch up with old faces and was attracted more by the fabric of the building itself. There were textures and shapes I had forgotten, but which came back to me with startling clarity once I saw them again after two decades. The painted noticeboards pierced by thousands of pin holes. The grey plastic roller doors on boys' lockers outside classrooms.

The swimming pool was unrecognisable. Gone were the cold, green tiles, the constant drip of freezing water from the concertina glass ceiling. The pool had always been my most hated part of the school, even after optional wearing of trunks was introduced half-way through my time there. Until I was 14 or 15, all boys swam naked, and all boys found it humiliating and degrading. Mature adolescents, late developers—I was never sure which subset found it more embarrassing.

In the refectory I saw Corky—Mr McCorkindale, games master—and felt a sudden jolt of discomfort. I hovered on the edge of a group of old boys to overhear the conversation between them and Corky, who looked older (obviously), but also considerably smaller, than I remembered him. I already knew that he had left teaching, and I heard him say he had retrained as a psychotherapist. One of the old boys burst out laughing. Corky laughed, too, but then asked what was funny.

'Well, you created your own client base, didn't you?'

said the former pupil. 'With the school's policy on swimwear.'

We could see the funny side now, but it had been nothing to laugh about at the time. Some had got over it, others were left with intimacy issues. I know one old boy turned Sunday league footballer who has never felt comfortable showering with his team-mates after a game. *I just can't get naked in front of other men*, he told me, paraphrasing Woody Allen. Not a problem I've ever had.

Nick never asked me about the reunion and I didn't volunteer anything. Part of me wanted to tell him that I had tried the door at the back of the school theatre, but that it had been locked.

Rewatching *If*. . . . reminds me of the importance of Bobby Phillips. Not only do he and Wallace share a bed, but the younger boy finds himself up on the roof with Mick, Johnny, Wallace and the Girl at the end of the film, bristling with guns and ammunition. A loaded gun won't set you free? Depends who you're pointing it at.

Sunday 31 October 1999
[Halloween.] I was back at school. The corridors and great hall were familiar, but everywhere there were orange plastic girders and supports appearing to hold up the ceilings. I knew these would be unsuitable to bear any loads, yet they could have no other use that I could fathom.

The film has given me no clearer idea how to find Nick. From my bag I take out the books I borrowed from his shelves—a short BFI monograph on the film and his copy of *Your Face Here*, which falls open at page 64 and the paragraph about Rupert Webster and Richard Warwick. I have a look at the chapter on *If. . . .* and then the BFI book, by Mark Sinker, which is intelligently written and packed with ideas and different approaches to interpretation. I notice that *Your Face Here* records the location of the motorcycle showroom, from which Mick and Johnny steal the motorbike they drive to the Packhorse Cafe, as being in South Wimbledon, whereas the BFI book and other sources, both print and internet, maintain it's in Shepherd's Bush. I look up *Your Face Here* on Amazon and am interested to see it has nine five-star reader reviews, all posted by 'A Customer'. None of them goes into much detail. On a hunch, I google Richard Warwick: died at the age of 52 with a form of dementia brought on by AIDS. For Rupert Webster, however, I find a couple of sources claiming he's still alive. Either Anderson or McDowell spread a rumour that he'd been killed, they said. The internet is notoriously unreliable and it's only sentimentality that makes me place more trust in the printed page. I don't know what to believe, but I do hope that the boys who wrote *Your Face Here*, a lively and enjoyable read, are wrong and that Rupert Webster, who for a short time 40 years ago was Bobby Phillips, is alive.

More to the point, I hope Nick is alive.

I'm narrowing down my options. I realise I have to do something I should have done days ago.

I grab my stuff and leave the house.

The building containing Nick's flat is only a couple of streets away from Helena Swan's house. I'm wondering if she knows this, as I tell a resident on the top floor I'm delivering pizzas. The door clicks open while he's still asking his girlfriend if they've ordered any.

Sunday 27 November 2005
Looking through old copies of the school newspaper, I see one with a picture of a girl on the front page. I recognise her, but the name given—something Schneidor—is not familiar. There are pictures of me, black and white, milking the applause from a huge crowd. There are other pictures of crowds on the fields at the front of the school, among them a young Mike, looking at me and waving. He moves as the picture comes to life.

I've never been to Nick's place—he's never invited me—but I know he lives on the first floor. There are two doors on the first landing. The one on the right has pounding music coming from within, so I knock once on the door on the left, wait a moment, then lean my shoulder against it. I feel it give very slightly, so I treat it to a shove, then another, and I'm inside. I push the door to behind me and lean against it as I wait for my heart-beat to return to normal.

Straight ahead is a tiny bathroom. To the left of that an equally small bedroom. Facing the bedroom is a combined kitchen and living room. The size of the flat, a professional would be able to toss it in two minutes and leave with either what they came for or the knowledge that it wasn't there to be found. I'm not a professional, but I do know Nick. I check out the bookshelves. More film books.

Novels about cinema: *Flicker*, *Throat Sprockets*, *The House of Sleep*. A *Halliwell's Film Guide*. I take it down and look up *If. . . .*, which Halliwell appears to admire but still attacks for its 'fashionable emphasis on obscure narrative', concluding that 'the film as a whole makes no discernible point'. Halliwell just couldn't help himself.

On the next shelf down are copies of Nick's books. His studies of Westerns and Eastern European SF and fantasy cinema for Wallflower Press and the experimental novel that was published in a limited edition by a local independent outfit. There are not many of us who have read it.

There's a decent-sized plasma-screen TV, but nothing leaps out at me from Nick's collection of DVDs and tapes, and there's no sign of a laptop (and no room for a desktop). The bedroom is dominated by an unmade double bed, on the far side of which a fat, well-thumbed notebook sits on a little set of drawers. It appears to be a dream diary. I flick through it and read random entries.

24 January 2006
In school, towards the end of the day, I find myself near an empty staircase leading up, so I go up, thinking I'll just have a look around. I end up in a maths classroom full of small boys. The uniform is different and there are variations. I see one boy in a tight-fitting blazer and trousers that's very dark grey with silver symbols in a regular pattern all over it. The boys are getting up to go. I want to leave before them. I pass the teacher who has grey hair and who I think I recognise from my time at the school. He has his back to me. Then I'm looking for the door and I can't

find it. Finally I do, but it's hidden and to get through it you have to push drapes aside and step over a threshold of broken bits of wood—it feels like a trap.

They're not *all* about school, but enough of them are.

I put the notebook back down. On an impulse I open the top drawer and immediately wish I hadn't.

I was going to hail a cab, but when I get back to Palatine Road there's a bus coming, so I stick my hand out. I imagine everyone on the bus can see the way my jacket is weighed down on one side, but I doubt I'm the first person to catch the 43 bus with a loaded gun in his pocket. I wonder how he got hold of it, though when I think about it, there must be a hundred ways to get tooled up in Manchester these days.

I get off a couple of stops early and walk. I haven't been back since the reunion. The fence by the old biology block never was much of a barrier. I approach the main buildings from the side. Much less conspicuous than using the front entrance. I don't know what plans exist for the disused school. Demolition and a highly lucrative land sale, I presume. For now it stands empty. I enter via the ramp down to the basement on the west side. One of the double doors at the bottom opens at my touch. If the signs posted by a security company are anything other than an empty threat, I'd be surprised. I pick my way past a line of toilets, not a single door remaining, broken glass on the concrete floor flashing in the weak light of my mobile phone. I climb the stairs to the corner of the maths and geography corridors, where I stop and listen.

All I can hear is the thumping of my heart and a steady drip-drip-drip somewhere behind me.

I creep past the Great Hall and main stairs. The shadows are grainy, alive with glittering motes. I hesitate outside the Masters' Common Room, the smooth stones of the corridor floor carpeted with white dust and flakes of paint. In the theatre, the individual wooden blocks that make up the parquet floor are all loose. The door at the back is no longer locked, but Nick is not inside. I enter a room I have not been inside for almost thirty years, at least not outside my dreams. Night after night, sometimes, for several days at a time, I have found myself back here. Twice, at the most, we were here together, but in my mind the narratives of those two occasions have become intertwined with the many, many times I have dreamed myself back. If the closest I can get to Nick in reality is sharing duties and an office, in my fantasy life we have remained locked into an infinite variety of positions on two turquoise vinyl-covered chairs pushed together as a makeshift couch in this tiny room—props cupboard? Wardrobe department? —at the back of the theatre. The first time, early May 1980, he had a little Philips cassette player and a badly recorded tape of bass-heavy music, dark and threatening, but utterly compelling. I asked him what it was and he smiled as he said it was called *Unknown Pleasures*. Even with the unsophisticated musical tastes of a twelve-year-old, I could tell it was special. The way the drummer played just off the beat, the fact that the bass player carried the melody more often than not. Nick described the singer to me, told me he suffered epileptic fits, sometimes during performances.

When he touched me, it felt both wrong and right at the same time, but he was tender and patient. I liked his smile and the smell of his neck. When he held my face with his hands and kissed me, I imagined the east and west wings of the main school building somehow wrapping themselves around this tiny room at the back of the theatre and keeping us safe.

The second time, just before the Whit week holiday, Nick told me that the singer from the band had killed himself. He played the album again and we sat in the dark listening to it, the lyrics scattered with clues that should have foretold the singer's suicide. Nick also told me about a film he had seen on television just over a year ago in which four schoolboys and a girl staged a bloody revolution at their boarding school, shooting the headmaster and killing dozens of pupils and teachers. *We're in that film,* he told me. *You and me. One day you'll see it and you'll see what I mean.*

As I reach out an arm to steady myself against the wall, I feel the weight of the gun in my pocket.

I re-enter the auditorium and head for the swing doors that lead back to the main corridor. The eroded hollows in the steps cushion my footfalls as I climb the main stairs. The upper corridors are lit by moonlight. I stop and look out across the quad towards the windows of the adjacent corridor where a moving figure catches my eye. The pale, wide-hipped body, silvery white hair. Black holes for eyes. I don't need to be any closer to know that Helena Swan is playing Mrs Kemp, which would place Nick most likely at the end of her corridor at the junction with mine.

I keep walking, the weight of the gun tugging at my right shoulder.

When I reach the junction of the two corridors, Nick is not there. I figure he'll be half way up the next one, so that in a moment he can have Helena Swan walk away from him and look back, just as Mrs Kemp does. I doubt he's gone to the trouble of bringing a camera, but am aware that if I approach now I will ruin his shot. So be it.

He steps out from behind a bank of lockers twenty yards away.

'I wondered when you'd come,' he says.

Helena Swan falters and stands still, uncertain how to react.

'You shouldn't be walking around with that in your pocket,' Nick says calmly. 'Give it to me.'

I take the gun out of my pocket. Helena Swan, on seeing the dark shape in my hand, turns and runs towards the far end of the corridor.

'Who is it for?' I ask.

Nick smiles. 'You brought it,' he points out.

'I couldn't leave it in your flat with the door off its hinges,' I say. 'But if I give it to you, I'm worried you just might use it. Whether here and now or next week at your conference, in a dramatic re-enactment of a certain film.'

'"One man can change the world with a bullet in the right place",' he says, quoting Mick Travis. 'I'm not sure I can face that conference. All those academics.'

I remain silent, thinking. He has a secret he can't live with. I am it.

'So,' he says. 'Stalemate.'

Slowly, I bend at the knee and place the gun carefully on the floor. I straighten up and place the toe of my shoe against the mouth of the barrel and give the gun a gentle kick so that it slides several yards along the corridor to a position roughly half way between us.

'Indeed,' I say.

KERRY WATSON

The Sorry Years

1968. I AM born in Bendigo, a sleepy provincial town in Australia. My mother is thirty-five. She has grey showing at the roots of her dyed brown hair. There are no other babies in the hospital at this time, and the nuns are able to spend more time than usual with her and the baby. She knows most of the nuns from previous visits, and enjoys chatting with them. She is kept in the hospital for two weeks. She has six other children at home.

When my mother returns home with me, my older sister Linda is taught to change my nappy. Linda was too young to change nappies when the other babies were born. Now she is ten years old, and she is given charge of me. My oldest sister is given charge of my two pre-school sisters.

There is a lot going on in 1968, but Bendigo doesn't pay much attention to it. Its daily newspaper gives the bulk of its attention to local concerns such as the price of wheat, the transportation of cattle, and the alarming, albeit delayed, popularity of the mini-skirt among local women.

The first two big news items of 1968 in Bendigo are the troubled construction of its Prince of Wales Show-grounds, and the anti-climactic announcement that the search for missing Prime Minister Harold Holt has been called off. He had gone swimming in the dangerous waters off Point Nepean. His body is never recovered.

I am told I am the seventh child, but I am really the eighth. The baby that died six years earlier is not spoken of. Where I'm from, it is common to be silent about bad things that have happened.

In 1968, the year I am born, Aboriginal babies and children are being forcibly removed from their mothers and families by the government, according to legislation that has been in place since the nineteenth century.

Aboriginal people in Australia had been fully acknowledged as Australian citizens by being included in the national census only one year earlier, after a referendum called for by the now missing Prime Minister Harold Holt.

When I am three years old, my next sister is born in a hot December. The next year a group of Aboriginal people assemble a city of tents outside Australia's Parliament House and call it the Tent Embassy. They want to regain the rights to the land that has been taken from them. Australia's first Labour Prime Minister since 1949, Gough Whitlam, is elected, and he is agrees to visit the Tent Embassy and talk.

I am four now, and I know nothing of this. What I know is the sunny back-doorstep away from the mayhem of the kitchen, which is shaded in the afternoon by a walnut tree.

Aboriginal children and babies of mixed-race descent are still being removed from their families by the government, chased through scrub-land and herded into trucks. This will continue until well into the seventies.

When I am five, my youngest sister is born. Now we are nine. I am sent to stay with a neighbour named Mrs Wicker while my mother is in hospital with the baby. She feeds me Weetabix and lets me pet her rabbit. Her daughter Rosalee has purple cords tying up her pigtails.

In 1977 Elvis Presley dies at his home in Graceland on the same day as my father's birthday. Three months later Gough Whitlam, Australia's Prime Minister, is dismissed from office by the Governor General, the Queen of England's representative in Australia. I am aware of these events but I do not fully understand them.

As I grow older, I ask my mother to explain things. I learn from school that Aboriginal children were taken from their families. I am not informed that this continues to be the case. My mother explains to me that mixed-race Aboriginal children are rejected by their full-blood Aboriginal families. This turns out not to be the case.

I ask why there are no Aboriginal people in Bendigo, and my mother tells me they left. As I have never seen an Aboriginal person in Bendigo, I imagine this to be true.

My mother teaches me to knit, but I am a lazy knitter, and I only get half way through a scarf. Linda teaches me to sew, but I take shortcuts and she finishes the clothes off for me. My mother teaches me to peel potatoes, stew apples, compare supermarket prices, stir gravy, tell stories and bake biscuits.

When I am in high school, my mother bakes a casserole for the school's family night. Other people's mothers also bring casseroles. My mother has made a tuna casserole, with white sauce and tuna and pineapple pieces. I see two of my school mates pulling faces, and hear them making jokes and saying rude things about my mother's tuna casserole. I feel sadness and shame, and look around quickly to see if my mother has heard them. I'm not sure if she has or not. I feel hot all night at the thought that she might have heard them. I don't remember what kinds of food the other mothers brought. My mother is very proud of her ability to feed a family of eleven on a limited budget.

When I am thirteen, I wait and wait for my mother to tell me about periods. All the other girls' mothers have told them about periods. Even our teachers have told us about periods. I wonder when my period will come, and I worry about how I might tell my mother if it does, when she hasn't broached the topic with me. I know what a period is, but I don't know what to do when it comes. All I know is to visit the school nurse and she will tell me what to do. I am afraid of getting my period, but I hope that when it comes, it comes at school so I know who to talk to about it.

My sister Linda is a very fine horsewoman. One day I ask her what a gelding is. She explains to me that the horse she is currently brushing doesn't have balls, and that it is the balls that have the seeds to make the babies. And that a stallion or a colt does have balls, and that when they are removed, the horse becomes a gelding.

I am fascinated by how easy this conversation is, and by how much it has made many of the other pieces of my slowly assembling jigsaw of sexual information come together.

My mother finally, in an awkward drive home from the supermarket, introduces the topic of periods by saying, 'I s'pose you've already heard about periods.' She doesn't say much else, just that they are a nuisance, and that she's got some 'things' ready for when I get mine. She goes on to tell me that I will get my period when I am fourteen, because all my other sisters had their period at exactly fourteen. I am relieved to hear this information.

I have an awkward adolescence. It has become clear my mother is uncomfortable about talking about womanhood. She dismisses all topics, from boys to bras, and the topic of sex is never broached. I am glad I had the conversation with my sister about the horse.

We have sex education at my Catholic girls' school, and the progressive Sister Patsy promises she will attempt to answer any sensible question we have. Finally the last pieces of the mysterious puzzle are fitted together, and I get it.

I can see why my mother has never, and will never, get to this bit.

My mother is proud that I write poems. She enlists me in a local competition, where I have to stand on stage in a borrowed dress and read out a poem I wrote. The other girls in the competition are from the competition circuit.

They seem to know what is going on, and use terms and do breathing exercises I am unfamiliar with. My mother asks me if I would like her to stay with me back-stage, and I say I would rather be alone with my nerves. She agrees without a fuss. I see her before I start my poem sitting in the audience. My sisters have not been allowed to come. There are not many things we get to do together without everybody else. I am proud, because I can see that she is proud. I am also more afraid than I have ever been in my life. I win the competition, and receive a medal with two masks on it, one happy, one sad.

As I grow older, I plan to leave home. I will do this by getting a place in a university in Melbourne, the city that lies a hundred miles to the south. This will be a relatively simple transition, not like my older sister's unbearable arguments for wanting to get her own flat in Bendigo.

My mother encourages me in my efforts to get a place in a university. None of my brothers and sisters have ever been to university. My great-grandfather, my mother's grandfather, had gone to university. He had been a poet too. I can see by the way my mother talks about him she is very proud to be related to him, and I feel she is investing her hopes in me.

After I leave home, I visit Bendigo weekly at first, then fortnightly, then occasionally. When I do visit I have plenty of my mother's time to talk, but my interests have changed, and I find her conversations repetitive.

I start to become aware of the things that have been happening throughout my lifetime. I feel appalled by how much I don't know about Aboriginal Australia, its history, its recent histories, about people and places and things that happened. That here, at this time, life expectancy is so much lower for Aboriginal Australians. That the infant mortality rate is so much higher. That babies are dying in the same country where I live comfortably. That so many Aboriginal people were stolen from their families during my lifetime. That so many Aboriginal people die in police custody. That so many Aboriginal people are in prison. That third world conditions exist in remote Aboriginal communities, communities that are part of a rich country.

I ask my mother again about the state taking Aboriginal children away from their families. This time she says people had thought it was for the best. I query this, and she shrugs and says, 'They weren't bad people. They thought it was the right thing to do.'

I get angry and frustrated. I quote Martin Luther King Jr at her. 'The ultimate tragedy is not the oppression and cruelty by the bad people but the silence over that by the good people.'

I discover that there are Aboriginal people living in Bendigo, that this has always been so. I ask my brother, who is well informed about these things, how this can be so, when I have seen so little evidence of it. He suggests that it might have been seen to be in everybody's interests for the Aboriginal residents to lay low. That it might have been safer in the past to not be seen. And that you see what you want to see.

My brother goes on to point out that his childhood friend, who has been a regular visitor to our house throughout my life, has Aboriginal ancestry. I think of his friend's face. It seems possible. He says he has only found out recently, and has finally realised why the other boys called his friend 'Blacky' at school.

A good friend of mine who has lived all her life in Melbourne discovers that her father had Aboriginal parents. He was brought up by a white family, brought up to be white. He waited till his children had grown up to tell them. He doesn't know his Aboriginal family.

I do not know if my brother's friend had an Aboriginal mother or father, but I do know that none of this matters now. I am from a country where a systematic programme to dilute an undesired gene pool was endorsed by government and actively carried out for most of the twentieth century. Words like full blood and half blood do not belong here.

Similar stories of people separated from their families, from their heritage, from their culture, have been emerging for many years. I think of my brother's words, that you see what you want to see. I start to see differently.

In May 1995, a National Report is commissioned, into the separation of Aboriginal and Torres Strait Islander children from their families by the then Prime Minister. When it is tabled in Parliament two years later, there has been a change of government.

One of the report's findings was that the programme of forcibly removing Aboriginal children from their families was an 'act of genocide, aimed at wiping out Indigenous families, communities and cultures'. The recommendations of the report are that 'Australian Parliaments offer official apologies and officially acknowledge the responsibility of their predecessors for the laws, policies and practices of forcible removal'.

The new Prime Minister John Howard refuses to say sorry to the Aboriginal people who have been forcibly removed from their families. He continues to refuse to do this until the end of his political career more than ten years later.

These years waiting for a sorry make the country of my birth grow sour and ugly in my eyes. People appear to grow meaner. Those that continue to fight seem to lose some of their enthusiasm. Those that support the fight move into disparate areas to make small differences in small places, rather than take part in the unequal fight and dirty tricks on the main battlefield. I, along with probably millions of others, am very sad about what is happening to our country.

When I am thirty, I am visited by an Aboriginal friend from the Northern Territory, a woman in her fifties, who I invite to stay for some weeks at my house. She asks if her partner, Freddie, and her two children, aged 9 and 12, can stay. I say they are absolutely welcome. June and Freddie are uncomfortable in my small loungeroom, and ask if it is alright to set up a bed under the carport, and if it is okay to light a fire in the disused garden bed. I say that is absolutely okay.

Two weeks later my landlady, a Greek-Australian woman in her seventies, asks her daughter—whose English is better than hers—to communicate a complicated complaint that she has received from my neighbours, who are also her tenants.

Christina, the daughter, is a nice young woman who works in a pharmacy across town. I have talked to her before, when the tenant-landlord discussions have been more complicated than collecting rent. She says there has been a complaint. I ask what it is. She says the complaint is that 'people have been coming and going' from my house.

I tell Christina that that has indeed been the case, that I had friends staying, a family of four. 'I'm allowed to have friends stay, aren't I?' I ask her.

'Of course you are, Kerry,' Christina says. There is a pause in the conversation. I realise the neighbours have made things difficult for her and her mother, and that she is merely passing on information, and trying to resolve a dispute she does not understand.

'Do you think it's possible . . .' I start to say. 'Do you think it might be because they are Aboriginal?' I say to Christina. The small gasp and silence on the other end of the phone tells me that she didn't know this, and that the nature of the complaint has just become clear.

She says, with heartbreak in her voice, 'Oh, Kerry . . .'

We are both sorry to have had this conversation.

These are the sorry years, and I will always think of them as a time of near defeat for many, many good people. A friend of mine who is a novelist is having a profile written about him in a national newspaper. He is photographed holding a sign that says 'Say Sorry'.

The word 'Sorry' is written by an aeroplane across the

blue skies of Sydney on National Sorry Day, a day that is not endorsed by the government. On this day a quarter of a million people march across the Sydney Harbour Bridge. It is the largest public demonstration in Australia's history. At the same time, I take part in a march through the streets of Melbourne.

My mother takes part in a ceremony in Bendigo on the same day.

When I am thirty five, I give birth to my first child by caesarian section. I am the same age my mother was when she gave birth to me. My mother catches the train down from Bendigo to visit me and the baby. She has brought a small jumpsuit, size 0000. It is the only thing we have that is small enough for the baby to wear.

In the ward of six mothers, the woman opposite me is an Aboriginal woman. Her new baby boy is named TJ, presumably after the Aboriginal teenager who was killed after being chased by police in Sydney's Redfern district two months earlier.

The teenager believed that police were chasing him. The police involved maintained they had nothing to do with his death, despite three witnesses claiming the boy was riding a bicycle while being chased by a police car. The next day, whilst still maintaining the police were not involved in the death of the teenager, large numbers of police officers and the riot squad are sent into 'The Block' in Redfern, the neighbourhood the teenager was from. There are riots and a nine-hour clash between the riot squad, police officers and the Aboriginal residents.

The baby who is opposite me in the ward has exactly the same cry as my baby. The mother has her male partner by her side almost constantly. She is joined during most daylight hours by a mother, a sister, a brother, and another friend or relative. She does not want to have to stay in hospital, and talks at length about her plans once she gets the baby home. She has all the baby things set up ready. She is eager to start her life as a mother.

When her baby cries in the middle of the night, I sit up to see mine sleeping soundly.

The woman opposite me in the ward has been in the hospital for longer than me. I'm not sure how much longer. She doesn't want to eat the hospital food, asks for some 'soup or something' instead. I hear the ward staff complaining about her while she is in the shower.

I don't know how long she has been in here, but I have been in here for two days and I am desperate to go home. I keep asking if I can go home. I have had a major operation, I am told, and they want to monitor the weight of the baby before they let me go home. On day three, I think they are about to let me go home, but I am informed that my baby has lost weight, and until she starts to gain weight, I will not be allowed to leave the hospital with her.

After the Aboriginal teenager died, his mourners laid flowers along the metal fence upon which he had been impaled during the chase, and then marched to the Redfern police station. They couldn't get close to the building, though, as the police had erected crowd control barriers, and Special Operations Group officers, plus additional police officers equipped with capsicum spray, stood in formation outside the police station entrance. A police helicopter hovered overhead.

A decision to release the teenager's father from prison to allow him to attend his son's funeral was overturned.

On the day I am told I can take my daughter home from hospital, I pull the shielding curtains away from around my bed, opening the cocoon of new motherhood that I have kept around me in this clinical and unfamiliar place. I see the woman opposite me, with her partner holding their new baby. I smile. We have seen each other before, but were locked into our separate worlds of intense experience.

'Our babies have got the same cry,' I say.

'Yeah. It's exactly the same, eh?'

'Yeah.'

My things are piled on the bed, with my baby sleeping in the crib beside me.

'I hope you get to go home soon,' I say. 'It's not good in here, is it?'

She smiles.

I look at her baby boy. He is sleeping. I pick my girl up and wait for my partner, who is coming in a taxi to take us home.

I know why they are keeping her in hospital.

The Australian Bureau of Statistics reported in 2004 that in 2003, 6.2% of total Indigenous male deaths and 6.5% of total Indigenous female deaths were infants.

This is compared to 0.9% and 0.8% of male and female deaths for non-Indigenous Australians.

Her baby was two to three times more likely to die than mine was.

❖

In 2006 my partner, our not yet two-year-old daughter and I move to England. It is true that part of what has driven me here is shame and a feeling of helplessness towards my country's treatment of its Indigenous people. In England I meet a man who is a travel writer. He tells me a traveller feels a 'pull'. He says a migrant feels a 'pull', but they feel a 'push' as well.

In November 2007 my partner and I sit up all night in our English house watching the live stream of the Australian Federal Election results on the internet. My friends in Australia and I exchange enthusiastic texts as it becomes apparent there will be a change of government.

There is a new Prime Minster. Many Australians, at home and abroad, wait anxiously to hear what action he will take to improve the lives of Australia's Aboriginal people, and when he will say sorry on behalf of the Australian Government for forcibly removing Aboriginal children from their families.

2008. On the night of February 12th, in Australia the morning of February 13th, the Prime Minister is going to say sorry to all Australian Aboriginal people forcibly removed from their families. My partner and I sit up till late in our English house watching the live stream on the internet.

People gather at public screens all over Australia. My sister Linda is watching, my other sisters and brothers are watching, all my Australian friends. My friend who I am texting during the broadcast is with a large gathering at Federation Square in Melbourne, where they have been waiting for the announcement since dawn. When it finally comes, the sound of the Prime Minister's repeated 'sorry' is like a mantra. I feel a heaviness begin to lift.

I feel relief. Some shame has lifted. It might one day be possible to go home. This is what I feel at the time. This and a terrible sadness.

Three hundred Aboriginal people and many other supporters gather in the dusty country town of Bendigo to view the announcement being made on a big screen that has been erected. Most of them have lived there all their lives.

Others watch the announcement on their televisions at home. My mother is one of them.

Forty years away from 1968, I almost feel that one day there will be a place to go home to.

But I can't help thinking of the truth, the truth that is backed up by statistics.

And the truth as it stands now, if statistics are correct, is that my four-year-old daughter is likely to live to eighty-two or longer, and four-year-old TJ, who had the same cry as my daughter, is not expected to reach sixty.

Biographical Notes

RHONDA CARRIER was born in the Midlands and educated at the Sorbonne, among other places. Her short fiction has appeared in *The Time Out Book of London Short Stories Volume 2*, *French Literary Review*, *Image*, *Neonlit: Time Out Book of New Writing Volume 2* and elsewhere. A new story is due to appear in *Paint a Vulgar Picture: Fiction Inspired by The Smiths* edited by Peter Wild. She now lives in Manchester with her novelist husband and three sons.

JAMES FLINT is the author of the novels *Habitus*, *52 Ways to Magic America* and *The Book of Ash*, and the short story collection *Soft Apocalypse—Twelve Tales from the Turn of the Millennium*. One of his stories, 'The Nuclear Train', has been filmed for Channel 4, he scripted the London Fieldworks film installation *Little Earth*, and for some years he has run the film tent at the Port Eliot Literary Festival (www.port eliotlitfest.com). A former editor of *Wired* and *mute* magazines, his journalism has appeared in many national newspapers and he currently works full-time for the Telegraph Media Group. He is a member of the Writers in Prison Committee of English PEN (www.englishpen.org) and his own website can be found at www.jamesflint.net.

CHRISTOPHER KENWORTHY is the author of two novels, *The Winter Inside* and *The Quality of Light* and a short story collection, *Will You Hold Me?* He was born in the north of England but has lived in Australia for over a decade. He is married with two children and now works as a film director.

TOBY LITT is the author of *Adventures in Capitalism*, *Beatniks*, *Corpsing*, *deadkidsongs*, *Exhibitionism*, *Finding Myself*, *Ghost Story*, *Hospital* and *I play the drums in a band called okay*. He was named as one of the Granta Best of Young British Novelists. His website is at www.tobylitt.com.

JUSTINA ROBSON is the author of seven science fiction and SF/fantasy novels and her work has been shortlisted for many awards in the UK and USA. She was born in Leeds.

TRICIA SULLIVAN grew up in New Jersey, studied in Benjamin Boretz's Music Program Zero at Bard College and then worked as a teacher in Manhattan before moving to Britain in 1995. Her novels include *Lethe*, *Someone to Watch*

Over Me, *Dreaming in Smoke*, *Maul*, *Double Vision* and *Sound Mind*. She has three children with her partner, the martial artist Steve Morris. She lives in rural Shropshire.

FRANK I SWANNACK was born in Kingsbury, north-west London, but has lived most of his life in the north-west of England. He has previously had a story published in the Barrington Books anthology *Sugar Sleep*, and has published stories in the small press magazines *Strange Attractor* and *Grotesque*. He has also published poetry widely. He is currently working on a PhD on the Renaissance poet Edmund Spenser at the University of Salford. He is due to be married on 28 June 2008.

MARC VILLEMAIN lives in the Saint-Germain des Prés district of Paris and Etretat in Normandy. He is the author of *Monsieur Lévy* (Plon), a book about Bernard-Henri Lévy, and a novel, *Et je dirai au monde toute la haine qu'il m'inspire* (Maren Sell). In October 2008, Le Seuil will publish his collection of short stories, *Et que morts s'ensuivent*. He writes literary criticism for a number of French magazines; his website is located at www.marc-villemain.net and he has a blog at www.villemain.canalblog.com.

KERRY WATSON is an Australian writer currently living in the UK. Her poetry and short stories have been published in magazines and journals in Australia, and have been broadcast on the ABC, Australia's national broadcaster. She also works for the Arvon Foundation.

MARC WERNER was born in London and has also lived in Paris, Berlin and Brussels. His short stories have appeared in *The Time Out Book of Paris Short Stories* and *The Time Out Book of London Short Stories Volume 2*, and he has published art criticism in *Art Review*. He lives in London where he works as a journalist and photographer.

CAREERS IN
THE POLICE FORCE

CAREERS IN **THE POLICE FORCE**

Jean Joss

Third Edition

KOGAN PAGE
CAREERS
SERIES

Acknowledgement

Particular thanks are due to Chief Inspector Bunce of Thames Valley Police for his help in updating this new edition.

First published in 1982
Second edition 1986
Third edition 1991; reprinted with revisions 1992

Kogan Page Limited
120 Pentonville Road
London N1 9JN

British Library Cataloguing in Publication Data

A CIP record for this book is available from the British Library.

ISBN 0-7494-0202-4

Typeset by DP Photosetting, Aylesbury, Bucks
Printed and bound in Great Britain by
Clays Ltd, St Ives plc

Contents

Part 2

Foreword to the Third Edition

Policing has never been an easy career option and over the past decade it has become an even greater challenge for the new recruit. The public of the nineties demands a great deal from its police officers and an increasing amount of media attention has tended to focus on incidents which have detracted from its appreciation of basic everyday police work. Becoming a police officer today will therefore require not only dedication and commitment, but an even greater breadth of social awareness and sensitivity - particularly of the interdependence of police and public. The police service as a whole is responding to this with changes in organisation and training but the individual officer will still carry the ultimate responsibility for the police's reputation every time he or she steps out on to the street.

Part 1

Introduction - A Police Officer's Life

Being a police officer in the world of the 1990s is one of the most demanding careers you can follow. Not everyone is physically or emotionally suited to the challenges it presents, but those who are will tell you that their work has become very much more than a mere job; it is a way of life.

The police are responsible for looking after the community as a whole, by keeping it a safe and ordered place to live in. They are appointed by the community they police and are responsible to it for doing their job properly. This can frequently cause problems since it means that although a police officer has to enforce the law in the manner of a guardian, he* is at the same time employed as a servant of the people he polices. As a result a police officer can never be certain of what the public's attitude towards him might be - if they need help he may be treated as a friend; if they are under suspicion for some offence he may be regarded as a hostile foe. If you join them you will be expected, on duty and off, to have relevant knowledge at your fingertips and give advice and assistance to anyone who requires it. You must know the correct procedure to take under any circumstances, whether dealing with fatal accidents or murders, or taking charge of lost dogs or straying cattle. You must be prepared to be the carrier of bad news to relatives of an accident victim or even, on rare occasions, be prepared to act as a midwife! It is not a career for the faint-hearted or the squeamish - the public expects you to take charge immediately and decisively on every occasion - but a high degree of sensitivity and a great deal of patient understanding are also needed. Above all, you must want to work with people, all kinds of people: you will meet the timid, the cunning, the honest, the dishonest, the well-meaning but

---

* Policewomen are on a totally equal footing with their male colleagues and consequently every time *he* is used in this book, *she* is also intended.

misguided and the actively hostile. It can, on occasions be dangerous work – police officers can, and do, get badly injured (or even killed) in the course of duty, though this is fortunately a rare occurrence. You may be called on to face a rioting mob or the aftermath of a terrorist bomb, without panic, and to endure long periods of inactivity without getting bored or frustrated. You will certainly know the meaning of the phrase 'working under pressure'. In return a career in the police force can offer you an endless variety of incident, unrivalled experience of what goes on at all levels of everyday life and a unique opportunity to understand and stretch your own capabilities, as well as a great personal sense of satisfaction in belonging to something worthwhile.

Joining the police force means that you become one of a team, a team whose members place a great deal of reliance upon one another. Not that all the members think alike and have stereotyped personalities; far from it (take them out of uniform and police officers become individual personalities like everyone else), but the force as a whole has to appear to act with consistency. You have, for example, to mask your personal feelings even when under a lot of provocation. Imagine how you would react if someone started hurling abuse (or even bricks) in your face and you knew you had to remain cool and clear-headed. You might well feel disgust or anger at some of the characters you come in contact with (child batterers, muggers of old ladies, hit-and-run drivers, for instance) but it is not your job to judge them, only to deal with them as the law allows. Individual police officers are trained to assume a definite role of neutral authority and it helps to realise that, should the public criticise or show hostility, it is directed towards this image, not towards you personally. Every time you step outside you also assume a great deal of responsibility towards your fellow officers and the police service in general. Many people rarely have any contact with the police except in moments of personal crisis and this makes it all the more important that, whereas they are likely to be emotionally upset, you must remain calm.

It is up to each individual police officer to let the public see that he is as human as they are, despite his special role in society. Children, of course, are the easiest to convince (either way!) and most forces have schemes for school visits and encourage youngsters to ask questions about the work and the men and women who do it.

Your personal life has to be above reproach if you join the

police. No one is going to respect the authority of someone whose conduct off duty is suspect. You are not allowed to take up any part-time work for payment without permission (although many police officers do voluntary unpaid work in the community, such as encouraging local youngsters in sporting activities). There are other regulations, too, which affect police officers and their families. For instance, they are not allowed to keep a shop or a public house.

Becoming a member of the force has a marked effect on your family life too. The police, of course, are subject to the Official Secrets Act and frequently you cannot talk about various aspects of your work, however much interest your family shows. You and they will also have to come to terms with shift work, uncertain hours and last minute cancellations of your social plans. Some of your friends may lose patience with your irregular hours and the fact that you are never available at what they regard as 'normal' times. You are often at work when others are out to dinner, at the cinema or socialising in the pub; you have to sleep off night duty when life around you is going on its normal, noisy way (particularly at weekends or in school holidays). And when friends and families plan get-togethers at major holiday times such as Christmas and Easter you will most likely be on duty. But it's a life-style you adjust to and it does, in fact, have compensations: you are off when there are fewer crowds at the shops or on the beach; you have free mornings on late duty and long afternoons/evenings on early duty to pursue sports or hobbies. The irregularity in hours and the restrictions on personal conduct often mean that police tend to make friends among themselves much more than, say, officer workers or teachers. There is a great sense of camaraderie between serving officers, both on and off duty. On duty they know they may owe their safety (or in extreme cases, their lives) to their colleagues; off duty they are sure of a sympathetic listener who understands the frustration and stress, the highs and lows of police work. All forces have social facilities where you and your family can relax and meet others and there are frequent social events organised to fit in with your particular hours.

Few jobs are more closely concerned with people, and a police officer needs the ability to talk to and get through to vastly different characters. In the same week you may be dealing with a royal visit, the local 'dossers', a mob of unruly football fans and an old-age pensioner who has lost her cat. Policing is a totally unpredictable job and rarely follows a set pattern. But, although the situations and the principal characters may vary, your role does remain constant. You are always expected to show your professionalism and take charge of any incident in an authoritative and unbiased manner; you must know the law, understand people, protect the public and prevent crime, while all the time keeping the delicate balance between the maintenance of law and order and the freedom of the individual. These days, with the increased coverage of police activities in the media, the individual is often quite aware of his or her rights.

'Every member of the force must look upon himself as a servant and guardian of the general public', the New Police were told at the very beginning of policing in this country. And the same words hold good today. The policeman of the nineties is, more than ever, required to be many things to many people. His role in fact has three major elements - enforcing the law, keeping the peace and serving the community.

You are not responsible for making the laws of the land - that is the task of Parliament. But you must be prepared to enforce them, whether or not you personally agree that, for instance, smoking cannabis is wrong. Frequently you may sympathise with people you have to arrest, if they have broken the law without meaning to or if they are genuinely sorry, but this cannot be allowed to affect your professional conduct.

In practice enforcing the law is only a small part of a police officer's day (or night), contrary to the popular belief that the police are there solely to catch thieves and speeding motorists! You will encounter crimes such as carrying or pushing drugs, possessing offensive weapons, robbery and burglary, assault, murder and rape, theft and handling stolen property. You will find, however, that you do not have to arrest everyone for the slightest infringement of the law - if you did, the police stations and the cells would be overflowing. Generally speaking, a police officer is trained and expected to use his personal discretion in deciding whether or not arrest is the answer in each individual case. Some offences, such as serious crimes like mugging, must necessarily mean arrest and the subsequent processes which will ultimately lead to the punishment of the offender. But where a crime has not actually been committed a verbal warning is frequently sufficient to deter. Such discretion can only come with experience.

Keeping the peace often entails solving personal or community problems. You may have to act as a mediator in domestic disputes, between husband and wife, parent and child, for instance, and civil disputes, for example if neighbours have a violent disagreement. You may have to deal with threatening and insulting behaviour, with drunken and disorderly conduct, with hooliganism and rowdyism or, in extreme cases, rioting. It is the police officer's task to restore peace and order for the majority of citizens whose lives might otherwise be disturbed.

The third element in a police officer's day-to-day work is essentially serving the community by giving advice and assistance to all manner of people in all manner of predicaments. You will have to deal with missing persons or pets, with lost and found property, attend with other emergency services at fires, accidents, burst water mains, gas leaks and the like, comfort the bereaved and the attempted suicides, or see schoolchildren safely across busy roads. In London, particularly, you may well feel you spend most of your time being a tourist guide during the busy holiday months! You will certainly have to face the seamier aspects of life, the wretched, the drop-outs, the depressed and the victims of violent crime or accident; you will have to get used to dealing with dead bodies and the various procedures in the mortuary. But professional training helps equip you for all these eventualities. And, of course, you will also deal with the brighter side of human nature too – the bravery, the generosity, the gratitude and the humour.

So there it is, a career in the police is not for someone looking for an easy option. It is a career which demands discipline (including self-discipline), independence, initiative and adaptability. If you are the right kind of person you will find it both absorbing and fulfilling, and it also offers a secure future – the police will always be needed. The following chapters will tell you in more detail how the police work and you will be able to judge whether or not it would suit you personally as a career.

Chapter 1

The History of Policing

Origins

The idea of making certain people responsible for keeping the peace and pursuing law breakers is an ancient one. Its roots reach back to Anglo Saxon times when every member of society was held equally responsible for maintaining a peaceful and safe community. King Alfred is traditionally credited with organising such collective responsibility with the use of groups known as 'tythings', made up of ten families and led by a 'tythingman'. Under this system if one member of the group committed a crime then all the others were bound to bring him to justice, or be held liable themselves. This sort of collective arrangement continued after the Norman Conquest and was known as the 'Frank-pledge': once a crime had been committed a 'Hue and Cry' was raised and the wrongdoer pursued by the 'shirereeve' and his 'posse-comitatus' (terms perpetuated in the American West).

By the thirteenth century the towns had grown very much larger and there was a common legal system with professional judges. A system of 'Watch and Ward' was instituted by statute; every citizen was made liable to serve his turn at guarding the town gates during the hours of darkness and parish constables were elected each year to supervise this duty and to keep the peace. The system was unpopular, largely because it was unpaid and interfered with other business, so more and more people used to avoid such duties by finding deputies to stand in for them (while paying them as little as possible). By and large only the old or incompetent were willing to accept the meagre sums offered and so the position of constable quickly fell into disrepute. (Shakespeare, for instance, ridicules it with such characters as the doddering Dogberry and Verges.)

By the eighteenth century as towns grew still larger the system had become ineffective and unwieldy. Despite the severe penalties for relatively minor crimes it was unsafe to walk the streets alone, particularly at night. In London, where crime and disorder were especially bad, the Fielding brothers brought in the Bow Street Patrols and the Bow Street Runners to try to combat lawlessness. These proved successful both as a deterrent to would-be criminals and in tracking down robbers and murderers. It was not until 1829, however, that the idea was extended - it was in this year that the Metropolitan Police Act was passed to 'make the streets of London safe for everyone' and Sir Robert Peel's 'New Police' came into being.

New Police

The policing of the community was now the job of paid professionals although, unlike police forces in other countries, they were organised along civilian rather than military lines (even wearing high hats and tail coats) and were answerable to justices of the peace, as their predecessors, the parish constables had been. The ordinary man in the street was not totally absolved from his duty to society, however and then, as now, could make a citizen's arrest if he saw a crime being committed.

The patrolling constables soon made their presence felt in London but the provinces were slow to follow, mainly because of the costs involved. In 1839 the County Police Act allowed the counties to form their own forces, if they wished to, but relatively few did so and by the 1850s only half had new police forces and many of the largest towns had none. Then, in 1856, Parliament eventually passed the County and Borough Police Act making the institution of police forces compulsory and allocating government payments towards their running costs. The number of separate police forces (nearly 350 at the end of the last century) has gradually been reduced until today it stands at 43 in England and Wales, eight in Scotland and one in Northern Ireland.

Objectives

The police, then, grew up from society's need to protect itself from discordant elements and its main objectives have stayed the same over the years. If you ask the man in the street what a police officer does, he may well reply, 'Catch criminals', but a constable's duties are very much wider than this. In Peel's original instructions of 1829 he laid down that:

> The primary object of an efficient police is the prevention of crime: the next that of detection and punishment of offenders if crime is committed. To these ends all the efforts of police must be directed. The protection of life and property, the preservation of public tranquillity and the absence of crime, will prove whether these efforts have been successful, and whether the objects for which the police were appointed have been attained.

This role of crime prevention and peace-keeping is seen as even more crucial in our highly industrialised and volatile society. As most police officers would be quick to point out, the public are very vociferous about their 'rights' but frequently forget their own 'duties'.

The 1962 Royal Commission on the police found that:

> Basically their task is the maintenance of the Queen's Peace, that is, the preservation of law and order ...

This view point was echoed in 1981 in the Scarman Report which followed serious street rioting and disorder in Britain. Lord Scarman concluded that the first duty of the police should be 'the maintenance of public tranquillity' - one of the main objectives of Sir Robert Peel and the motive behind the original 'tything' system.

Role of Women

Women were not allowed into the Police Force until after the 1919 Sex Disqualification Removal Act under which they were given the vote and permitted to enter virtually all the professions. Their usefulness was viewed with suspicion for some time, however, both by the public and their male colleagues. In fact before the outbreak of World War II there were a mere handful of women police (about 250), half of whom were in London, and only one in four of the provincial forces employed a few 'token' women.

During the 1939-45 war women volunteers were necessarily called in to help with police work and a Women's Auxiliary Police Corps was launched. Not all of these were true policewomen since their duties did not demand full police authority, but as the war continued a certain number were attested as constables and some of these were kept on in regular service when the corps was later disbanded.

In the fifties and sixties the numbers rose steadily and policewomen became generally accepted, reaching the higher positions, but tending to be employed in activities considered more 'suitable' for their sex. They worked slightly shorter hours than the men and received less pay.

Now the policewoman has become a completely equal partner with her male colleague. She enters the force on the same conditions, performs the same duties, accepts the same responsibilities and takes home the same pay. She can also, theoretically, attain the same ranks. There is little doubt that women have had to suffer discrimination in the police, as in every other profession and the number of women in top police posts is relatively small. Barriers are, however, being gradually broken down and although we have yet to see a woman chief constable, it can only be a matter of time ...

There are women dog-handlers, motorcyclists and mounted police; they are also integrated with their male colleagues in riot units. In some forces a whole unit may consist of female officers where it is felt there is a need for this type of resource.

Case Study

A WPC (Woman Police Constable) reviews her career to date.

> I always wanted to join the police, ever since I was at school. I lived in the north of England at the time and left school with eight CSEs, including shorthand and typing; I'd also done a course in commerce and business studies. After I left school I thought about joining the cadet corps and got as far as sending for their recruiting literature but then I thought I should really take a job outside first to let myself get some experience of meeting people in general. So I went to work for a local menswear firm as a shorthand typist. I stayed there for 18 months and then went on to a finance company for six months. Both were pretty boring jobs and I found it very tedious being in an office all day being told what to do.
>
> I decided not to join the local police force because I was told that, at that time, there were better opportunities for women in the big city forces so I moved down south and was accepted when I was 18½. Even though I was well qualified academically, I found the training course hard work, but I really enjoyed it on the whole and found it most exciting learning so many new things. After I passed out I was posted to the busy urban station where I've served for several years now. Like every new recruit I started on the shift system and found the work quite fascinating. You are under a lot of pressure and are supervised closely to make sure you are getting the hang of things properly and there are regular interviews and reports with senior officers. But I found most people really helpful and encouraging and

the work itself was rewarding. You never knew what was going to happen next - quite different from dictation and typing letters!

When my probation ended (after two years) I got the opportunity to work on a crime squad (uniformed officers working in plain clothes detecting local crime) and then I went on a prostitute squad (working in uniform this time). Both proved extremely interesting. Recently I also spent some time in the obscene publications section and now I'm back on the shift where I started, patrolling the city streets.

People are always asking me what it's really like being a woman police officer. Well, when I first joined the force I admit I found it quite difficult to be accepted by my male colleagues. There was a lot of pressure on the women to prove that they really meant business. I think things are changing now. There are more of us for one thing and the majority of officers on the streets today tend to be fairly young and have always been used to working with WPCs. I've noticed other changes over the last few years too. The public the police have to deal with these days seem to be getting younger and younger. We're mainly preoccupied with juvenile crime and young people in general and I think they accept women officers more easily. Some years before I joined, women police were employed mainly in specialist departments particularly working with children and young persons but now, of course, we get out and about a great deal and do everything that our male colleagues do, just about. I don't think we should ever go back to the old system; I prefer the new system and so do most of the other women I work with. I think that WPCs are often better at talking to people with social and emotional problems, particularly rape victims for example.

I find I get on well with the public and, generally speaking, I can cope with most things as well as any of my male colleagues, although obviously I turn to them from time to time whenever I have very violent men to deal with. I'm quite good at self-defence but sometimes you do need a bit more brute force to get an unwilling suspect to accompany you to the station! I'm often asked whether I have become more cynical after the years I've spent in the force. I don't think I have, in fact I'd say that I'm more understanding and sympathetic to people's problems, particularly the social problems that can create so many difficulties. When I first started in uniform I must admit that I did find it hard to deal with some of the dangerous, dirty or unpleasant jobs. The police have a number of difficult things to do, for instance going round to relatives of people who have been found dead and telling them that their son or someone very close to them has died. From time to time obviously we also find dead bodies. Then, of course, not all the people we have to deal with are particularly clean or come from very good backgrounds. The way I've always managed to face things like this is by telling myself that the public rely on you in those situations and you have to be seen to be doing the job efficiently and with professionalism. When you bear those points in mind you usually find you can cope in an appropriate manner.

I've just got married last summer, to a sergeant who is currently working in a more rural area. Unfortunately, we're not often on the same shifts, so sometimes he is going to bed as I get up and vice versa! I know I could get a transfer to his area to have more compatible working hours if I asked, but because I know there wouldn't be any difficulty I don't feel that there is any pressure to do so at the moment. I like working in the heart of a city; it's always busy and interesting and there are so many different things going on so I don't particularly want to move to a quieter area.

I don't personally see the force as a career, inasmuch as I don't envisage myself staying on for 30 years, but at the moment I enjoy it so much that I wouldn't think of leaving, unless of course I had children and then I would consider rejoining when they started school.

Chapter 2
Structure

The Police in Britain

Britain, unlike many other countries in the world, does not have a national police force under the overall control of one person or government. There are currently 43 separate forces in England and Wales, eight in Scotland and one in Northern Ireland (see Chapter 9 for details), and although they naturally maintain close contacts with one another, each force enjoys local autonomy under its own chief constable. He has the authority and responsibility for policy-making within his own particular area and reports to his local Police Authority, made up of local councillors and magistrates. This does not, however, mean that the police are the servants of the local authorities. They remain servants of the Crown and chief constables have also to report to the Home Secretary at regular intervals. The Metropolitan force in London is run on slightly different lines since the district it covers includes too many independent local authorities to make the Police Authority system workable. It is, therefore, directly responsible to the Home Secretary through its chief officer who is known as the Commissioner of the Metropolis.

The cost of running an efficient police force is considerable. Not only do police officers themselves and premises have to be financed, there are also vast armies of back-up staff (see Chapter 6) to be employed to keep things running smoothly. Local authorities have to pay a proportion of the sums involved through local rates: local organisations (such as football clubs) who use police services also pay for the amenity. The remainder is made up from government grants. The chart on page 23 gives some idea of the costs involved in running the country's largest force – the Metropolitan Police, some 28,000 strong.

The police are not a political body and the way they are run is unaffected by changes of government. Individual police, of

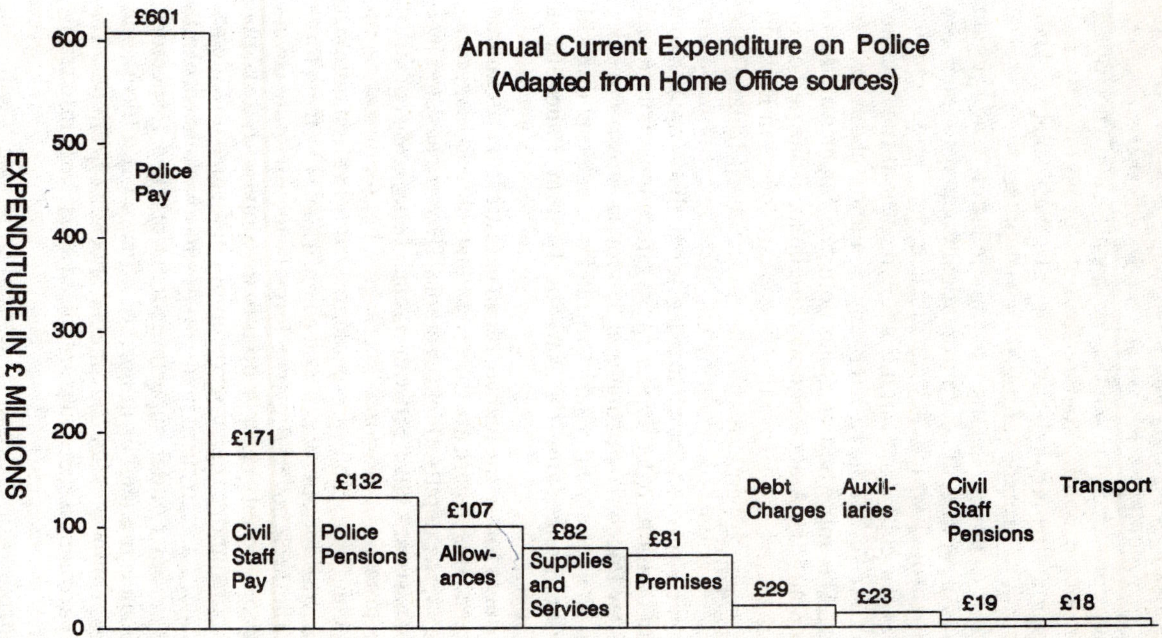

Figure 1. *Metropolitan Police 1989/90*

course, have their own political views (which they can express, like any other citizen, by voting in local and general elections) but these are strictly for off-duty hours. On duty a police officer's job is merely to uphold the law as it stands, whether or not he personally approves of it in political or moral terms. When police are called out on political demonstrations or go on duty at a polling station during an election, they are there solely to keep the peace, not to promote any specific viewpoint.

Nor do the police belong to any militant trade union movement. All serving officers automatically belong to the Police Federation through which they can air their views and exchange ideas with their colleagues but it is a union without the ultimate weapon of strike action to back any demands about pay or conditions. The more senior ranks join the Superintendents' Association and the Association of Chief Police Officers.

Rank Structure

The rank structure has not varied a great deal (apart from adding sub-divisions to the higher ranks) since the introduction of Peel's New Police. The promotion 'ladder' is shown opposite, headed in the county forces by the chief constable and in the Metropolitan Police and the City of London Police by a commissioner.

In the county forces the highest ranks operate from the county headquarters. Based here are the chief constable and his second-in-command, the deputy chief constable. They are assisted by a number of assistant chief constables, each being responsible for a specific area of operations. There may be, for instance, an assistant chief constable for personnel, another for support services, a third for operations and so on. Titles vary from force to force. The area covered by the force (which usually covers more than one county) is split up into divisions with divisional police stations under the supervision of chief superintendents. These divisions are, in turn, made up of sub-divisions with sub-divisional stations under superintendents or chief inspectors. Each division is manned by uniformed officers, CID officers and sometimes members from the smaller specialist branches. The traffic department is generally organised separately into traffic areas.

The Metropolitan Police is structured in a slightly different way to take account of the complexity and density of London and the surrounding area. Based at the Scotland Yard headquarters

Counties	*Metropolitan*
Chief Constable	Commissioner
Deputy Chief Constable	Deputy Commissioner
	Assistant Commissioner
Assistant Chief Constables	Deputy Assistant Commissioners
	Commanders

Chief Superintendent
Superintendent
Chief Inspector
Inspector
Sergeant
Constable

are the commissioner and his second-in-command, the deputy commissioner. There are also a number of assistant commissioners who are in charge of the main branches at the Yard - Territorial Operations, Personnel and Training, and so on. The Metropolitan Force is responsible for some 800 square miles within a 15-mile radius of Charing Cross, with a residential population of over seven million. This is divided up into eight areas each under the command of a deputy assistant commissioner, assisted by a commander (Operations) and commander (Support). Each area is split into divisions - these include Thames Division, concerned with the policing of the river. Each area also has mounted branch stables.

Identifying Ranks

As in any other uniformed organisation rank is shown by insignia worn on the jacket and subordinates show their respect for the ranks above sergeant by addressing them as 'Sir'. A constable carries a number on his epaulets (accompanied by a letter to signify his district in the Metropolitan Police); a sergeant has three stripes on his sleeve; an inspector wears two stars or 'pips' on his epaulets, a chief inspector three. Superintendents have a crown on their epaulets, chief superintendents a crown above a single pip. Assistant chief constables and commanders carry crossed batons inside a wreath of bay leaves on their shoulder; deputy chief constables and deputy assistant commissioners add a single pip above this. Chief constables have a crown above the crossed batons and bay leaves, while the Metropolitan Police Commissioner can be identified by his particular insignia of a crown above a single pip above the crossed batons and bay leaves.

The CID have the same ranks which carry the same responsibilities as the uniformed branch. Their officers are known as detective constables, detective sergeants and so on.

Duties

Generally speaking, the police officer the public is most likely to encounter is the constable who spends the majority of his time on the beat. The higher up the rank structure you go the more you become involved in supervision and administration, which necessarily entails more time in the station or behind a desk doing paperwork. Sergeants and inspectors also go out on the streets patrolling to supervise their officers and particularly to attend serious or contentious incidents where their authority and experience may be needed.

Because of the seriousness of some of the offences dealt with by the CID, the higher ranking officers are more likely to be involved in operational work than their counterparts in uniform. The uniformed chief inspector, for example, spends most of his time in administration while his CID counterpart frequently has to go out on serious crime inquiries. In murder investigations detective superintendents or detective chief superintendents are frequently in charge; virtually the only occasions when a uniformed chief superintendent becomes involved in operational work are public order events such as demonstrations or major incidents.

Sergeant

Sergeant is the first rank of the management ladder in the police. It is the sergeant who is responsible for supervising the uniformed constables on his shift and they will look to him for help and advice. There is usually more than one sergeant on duty (three or four in the larger stations under the supervision of an inspector). A sergeant may find himself either in the station as custody officer, or outside patrolling on foot or in a police vehicle, making sure that the constables are performing their various duties correctly and giving them assistance if they need it or personally dealing with any unusual or potentially difficult incident that might arise. In addition, all reports, paperwork and correspondence completed by the PCs in the course of their duty must be checked by a sergeant (prior to checking by the inspector). Sergeants, in addition, supervise probationers, make recommendations about them, and must be able to answer any of their questions on points of law. A sound knowledge of their own force is essential.

Inspector

The inspector is personally responsible for whatever happens during the hours his particular shift is on duty. Should one of his constables or sergeants get involved in a difficult or potentially dangerous situation then it is up to the inspector to sort it out. He has to supervise both the activities in the station and out on the beats as well as dealing personally with serious incidents such as fatal road traffic accidents or incidents involving serious personal injury. He also has to organise and supervise the policing of small local parades or public order events (such as minor demonstrations).

Management, particularly staff management, is what the inspector's rank is all about. He has to deal with internal discipline, career and welfare matters and forward planning; in addition he must keep well informed about new legislation and case law so that he can give authoritative advice. The special procedures and organisation of his own particular force must be second nature to him because he must deal with an enormous amount of internal paperwork. And he must know his local area well, its crime trends, its problem families, its potential trouble spots, as well as keeping up close contacts with outside organisations through representatives such as social workers, probation officers, housing officials, doctors, nurses, youth club workers and local press reporters.

In addition it is the inspector's task to give written annual assessments on all his officers, as well as probationers' reports, and it is on his recommendation that members of his shift are put forward for consideration for specialist work, such as CID or Traffic.

Chapter 3

Recruitment and Training

Introduction

There is no short cut to a career in the Police Force - no matter what your background or qualifications. Everyone must begin by serving a minimum of two years as a uniformed constable on patrol work at a police station. This is how the dog-handlers, the home beat officers, the top CID detectives and the chief constables themselves began.

How to Join

You may apply to join any of the 43 forces in England and Wales or those in Scotland or Northern Ireland (for addresses see pages 82–84), no matter where you live at the time. You may find your choice is determined by the fact that there are vacancies in some forces and none in others at the time you wish to join, or you may be attracted to country policing, or to the idea of working in one of the big cities. Many people feel drawn towards London in the first instance. The choice is wide and you must give some thought to the type of area in which you would like to live. There is no central clearing scheme for applications to the police (because there is no national police force), so if your first attempt is unsuccessful you can always try again elsewhere. There are certain general requirements you must satisfy, however, and it is as well to make sure you can meet these before setting your heart on a police career.

Age. Before applying to join as a constable you must normally be aged 18½. (Some forces prefer candidates to be 19 or over.) There is now no upper age limit and more mature candidates may apply to all forces.

Nationality. You must be a British subject by birth or naturalisation or a citizen of the Irish Republic or the Commonwealth whose stay in the United Kingdom is not subject to restrictions.

Education. Most forces now require candidates to take a written entrance examination with several papers in English and mathematics. This initial recruitment test is not like a traditional examination; it is concerned with intelligence, reasoning powers and comprehension rather than formal English and mathematics, so do not worry if your knowledge of these subjects is a bit rusty. Providing you are reasonably intelligent, you should not find the test beyond you, even if you have not been in formal education for some time. You can send for examples of test papers beforehand to get some idea of what is required. The actual test is standard throughout the forces in England and Wales (Scotland has its own), although the pass mark may vary, as this is set by the individual forces. Some forces may waive the entrance test altogether if you have certain academic qualifications. Other forces insist on all applicants taking it, no matter how many formal qualifications they may have.

Height. The old height limits were abolished in 1990 and no longer apply in any force.

Health. Physical fitness is crucial for a police officer - after all, he may be called upon to do things which require the maximum of exertion and effort - and you will have to fill in a detailed questionnaire about your personal medical history. Acceptance is then subject to a satisfactory medical examination. One of the most rigorous requirements concerns your eyesight which has to be of a high standard. Different forces have slightly different standards; some accept both glasses and contact lenses, some neither, some one but not the other. (These are detailed more fully on page 84.) If your eyesight is not perfect you may need to have your eyes tested and send in an optician's certificate. Good colour vision is also important, so if you know you are colour blind then your chances are not high. (After all, who would believe a constable who talked about red and green traffic lights in court, if it later turned out that he could not distinguish the colours mentioned?) Excellent hearing, good feet and legs and no dental problems are also essential. Nor must you be greatly over- or underweight for your height.

Once your application has been sent off it may take several weeks before the next stage, and you must be prepared to wait patiently while various references you were required to give are taken up and security checks run. A candidate must be found to be 'of good character' and without a criminal record since, if accepted, he would be in a position of great responsibility. However, in many forces, a relatively minor offence as a juvenile (shoplifting when you were younger, for example) may not be a bar to acceptance, dependent on the time elapsed and subsequent conduct of the applicant.

The next hurdle is the selection procedure where you have to satisfy a board of assessors that you really want to be, and have the potential to become, a good police officer. Most forces now run extended interviews for potential candidates to observe them in a variety of situations. The standard is high to avoid excessive wastage because, once accepted, your training will be very expensive. This may sound intimidating, but remember that people from all walks of life enter the police, many after spending several years in totally different jobs, and so the board will be looking at you as an individual, not as a 'type'. The person sitting next to you in an assessment exercise may have a totally different accent, education and background from yours, yet in the end you both might be accepted as recruits. It is personality and character that count.

Case Study

A young recruit nearing the end of his initial residential training course.

> I am 20 years old and I'd lived in the same place all my life until I joined the force I'm with now. I am not married but have been going out with the same girl now for nearly a year and might well be thinking about settling down if everything works out. I went to school at a comprehensive near home and got four CSEs, not particularly brilliant, I suppose, but then it wasn't a very good school and I didn't find studying easy. I left after the exams and went to work in a local factory as a packer. The work was even more boring than school! They got into difficulties with the recession and everything and a lot of us were made redundant last year. While I was sitting at home on the dole I got to thinking about what I'd really like to do with my life. I saw what was happening to a lot of young people round our way - just drifting around all day, getting into trouble, fighting and the like. It made me feel that I wanted to do something more with my time, in a job that was going to mean something. It occurred to me that we could be thinking about getting married soon so I would need some sort of steady income, and then, of course, the police give you housing which can solve a lot of problems. In the end I had a chat with the father of one of my friends. He's been in the police for years (the

father, I mean) and he told me a lot about the work. So I wrote off for all the literature and filled in the forms.

Training school has been far harder work than any of us thought it would be, there's so much to take in and it's all so new. At least we don't have a final exam to pass now though; I was never any good at exams, just went to pieces I suppose. The continual assessment here keeps you working all the time and it helps a lot to talk over what you're doing and assess yourself.

I really enjoy the practical stuff we do. I'm much better at that than the theory. You know they've got a video here; it gives you a really funny feeling to see yourself in uniform on it - makes you realise what you'll look like to the public when you get on the street yourself! I can't really see myself walking around on my own yet, but I'm quite confident that I can do a good job in the end. It seems to me that the police are in one of the best positions to help people with their problems and I am looking forward to that. It will make me feel that I'm doing something useful at last. No one round my way seems to do anything to help people, particularly young people. I would really like to get involved in helping at youth clubs and things like that. I'm very keen on motor bikes - I've got one of my own and I also ride in trials. I think it would be great if the police could get involved in helping to train young riders. They go mad when they get their first bikes. It would be nice if I could do something like that. When I've finished my probation I think I'd like to try to join the Traffic Division.

Joining the police has meant a few changes, I suppose. Some of my mates at home are a bit suspicious when I go back for the weekend. You can almost hear them: 'That's so-and-so; he's a copper now'. But it doesn't worry me. I feel really glad that I have something important to do and that's great after all the boring times I've been through. So I lose a few old mates - I've made lots of new ones here and I'm sure I will make a lot more at the station when I get there. I'm no different now from what I was before, really, and I think things will settle down at home a bit, anyway, when they get used to the idea. My girlfriend is really pleased that I've a good job at last. Overall, I am glad I've joined the police and that's the main thing, isn't it?

Cadets

If you are too young for normal entry (ie at 18½) but are as certain as you can be that this is the career you would like to follow, then you can apply to join one of the cadet schemes that some forces run. These schemes are designed to give you further education and relevant training until you are old enough to enter the police service itself. Again you need to match up to the general requirements already mentioned. If you are accepted into the cadets (after a two and a half day selection process and a medical examination) you will, in some forces, be required to live in a residential school or training centre during the week - at weekends you will be free to return home. Other forces can only accept cadets who live at home or in approved lodgings so it is advisable to ask the force you are interested in joining for details of their particular scheme. Cadets generally work a 40-hour week, wear uniform and receive pay (a proportion of which is deducted for board and lodging, if applicable). Rates of pay vary according to age and force. (In the Metropolitan Police, for example, the annual rate is £4,947 if you are over 17 but under 18, and £5,427 if you are over 18.)

Apart from having the opportunity to acquire further academic qualifications (such as A levels and GCSEs) you also learn about the police in general and the force you hope to join in particular, its history and present state, as well as the nature of the work involved in modern policing. Apart from studying, cadets participate in physical and adventure-type training under the leadership of trained officers. You are encouraged to reach a high standard of physical fitness and taking part in the wide range of sports offered gives you more self-confidence. Activities available include: camping, canoeing, rock climbing, swimming, athletics, cross-country running, to name but a few.

As a cadet you also go out on community service to help broaden your outlook on society and to meet some of the people with whom you may well be dealing in your future career - the aged, children, the handicapped and so on.

Finally you may get a taste of police work itself, with visits to courts, specialist branches and places of interest, as well as periods helping out in an actual police station under the care of experienced officers. You will learn about the running of the station and also go out on patrol to observe what is expected of the police by the general public. You will be supplied with a uniform similar to that worn by regular constables.

By the time you reach the entry age of 18½ you will have a working knowledge and practical experience of the career you wish to follow, and if you complete the course satisfactorily you are then formally attested as a constable and join the normal training course with other recruits.

Not all forces now run cadet schemes. Currently there are only nine forces recruiting cadets – the Metropolitan Police, Dorset Police, Durham Constabulary, Essex Police, Gwent Constabulary, Norfolk Constabulary, Staffordshire Police,

West Midlands Police and West Yorkshire Police. The Metropolitan Police and Dorset Police recruit cadets from all over the country: the other forces accept applications only from candidates living within the area covered by their force. Vacancies are few and competition is keen.

Some police forces outside London run volunteer cadet schemes for young people generally in the 15-18 age group. Such schemes are primarily designed to help youngsters understand more about the community as a whole and how the police fit into it, rather than preparing them for a career as a police officer.

Youth Training

A few police forces offer Youth Training, in clerical work, for example, which would provide opportunities for interested youngsters to experience what actually goes on behind the scenes. YT is not, however, offered in all parts of the country and it would be necessary to contact individual forces to check their current policy.

Graduate Entry Scheme

If you are under 30 and in your final year at university, studying for a degree, or if you already have a degree, then you may apply to join the police in England and Wales via the Graduate Entry Scheme, no matter what subject you are studying. (Until recently Scottish forces operated their own graduate entry scheme but most have discontinued this and graduates have to apply in the normal way.) This method of joining does not exempt you from the general entry requirements, nor from the initial two-year period as a constable - no one, no matter how highly qualified academically, can enter the police at any other rank - but it does mean that once your preliminary probation period is over you have a good chance of accelerated promotion.

Provided you prove yourself competent during these first two years and, you are successful, at the first attempt, in the written sergeant's exam (see Chapter 5), then under the Graduate Entry Scheme you will be allocated a place on the next Special Course at the Police Staff College at Bramshill in Hampshire. The Special Course is a sandwich course with three months at Bramshill (Part I) being followed by one or two years' developmental training on the job, after which members of the course return to the College for a further four months (Part II). Once selected for the Special Course you are promoted to sergeant six months before joining Part I and stay in your own force until the course begins. This means that you could be a sergeant in your third year of service. The first three months of the course are designed to allow you and others to assess your leadership potential and to pinpoint the areas in which you need to develop if you are later to become an effective supervisor. Management skills (including team building, problem solving and inter-personal and communication skills) are introduced, as well as modern technology, such as computing.

During the subsequent one or two years back in your force you will have to pass the qualifying examination for promotion to inspector and continue to satisfy your supervisors (from your own force and from the Police College). Once this developmental period is over you return to the college as a temporary inspector for Part II. When you have completed these four months satisfactorily you will be appointed as an inspector (subject to a year's probation back on the job). This effectively means you can attain the supervisory rank of inspector at a relatively early age.

Competition for the Graduate Entry Scheme is fierce and the selection procedure rigorous. Only a handful of places are available each year but many graduates who fail to enter via this special scheme decide to join in the normal way and some, by sheer personal determination, may gain promotion at the same rate by winning a place on the Special Course later on (see Chapter 5).

Graduates interested in this scheme should initially apply to the Police Graduate Liaison Office at the Home Office (Room 553, Home Office, Queen Anne's Gate, London SW1H 9AT) or contact the Police Graduate Liaison Officer at their own university or polytechnic, who can also arrange for attendance at a familiarisation course if graduates are not completely sure that the police is the career for them.

Ethnic Minority Recruitment

Over the past decade or so the police, along with many other employers, has had to face up to the fact that certain sections of society have - for one reason or another - not been adequately represented in its ranks. Racial violence and accusations of racial prejudice from a wide range of critics have resulted in courses on racial awareness being included in police training to try to combat discrimination, both inside the ranks and on the street. The number of black people (male and female) in police uniform however, remains relatively low and there would appear to be little enthusiasm among young blacks to join the police service; there are, for instance, currently (1990) less than 500 members of ethnic minorities serving as Metropolitan Police officers in a force of around 28,000. The same force was the first to abolish height limits in an attempt to encourage applications from ethnic groups of slighter stature, although they were quick to point out that shorter white applicants would also benefit from the changes.

Several recruiting campaigns are currently being run specifically targeting such ethnic groups. Their success, however, might well depend on convincing the young would-be applicants that they can advance their careers within police ranks. So far no British police officer in the higher ranks is black - in contrast to America where blacks are seen in top positions not only in the police but also in the armed forces.

Case Study

A newly appointed sergeant awaiting a posting.

> I was 22 when I decided to join the police. First of all I took a Law degree and thought I might practise at the Bar but I didn't enjoy it and could see no future without the right contacts. My family weren't very enthusiastic about my joining the police service but I haven't regretted it. I've moved pretty swiftly in the four years I've been an officer in spite of the fact I didn't join on the Graduate Entry Scheme - personally I feel that graduates who get in this way lose a lot of credibility; you've got to be accepted into the 'canteen culture' and it's easier if you start from the bottom. I've just completed the sergeant's course and I'm waiting to see where I'll be posted.
>
> Obviously being from a different background from the majority has attracted comment over the years. I'm a Muslim and I found from the word go on the probationary course that a good many people have a stereotyped image of what they think that means. Sometimes the misconceptions have been humourous, sometimes offensive. And there have been times when I felt things had gone too far and that I had to stand up for my rights. My senior officers have generally agreed and supported me. I don't mind racist comments from people on the street so much, and I've had a fair number over the years. All police officers have to learn to cope with abuse as part of the job, we get paid to do it - but I won't put up with it from inside. A few of the older officers seem particularly bad in this respect, the younger PCs tend to be more open-minded, but it would be untrue to say that there is no

racial prejudice inside the police - after all the police is made up of members from all walks of society and no one would deny prejudice exists at all.

I don't think it is only the unpleasantness of racial prejudice that has kept young black people from joining the force, it's been the lack of career prospects too. But I personally feel that things have changed a lot over the past couple of years and that the opportunities *are* there if you want to take them. Policing isn't a hobby, though, you have to be dedicated and work hard. If you're not prepared to do that you won't survive, whatever your background. It's never easy being in a minority, and I really feel that the police definitely need to be more integrated, not only to be more credible with the people they are policing but to compete with industry who have realised that there is a lot of potential going spare. Black police officers today are rather like pioneers; some day there may well be a black chief constable and no one will find it particularly remarkable. But it needs positive input from within the force, we need more black people to join and the police need a better image in the ethnic communities. There should be much more training about the racial mix of an area to be policed and more racial harassment officers to deal sensitively with complaints. One unpleasant racial incident can put back integration that has taken years to achieve, not just in the area where it happened either - with the media coverage it gets these days it can affect a much wider section of the community as a whole.

Training

Once you have been accepted as a recruit then it is up to you to prove you will make a good police officer. The first step is getting through the concentrated and comprehensive foundation training course.

Initial training for new recruits has undergone substantial changes in recent years. There is now much more emphasis on learning by doing rather than listening, and continuous assessment has taken the place of the old 'make or break' end-of-course examinations. In county forces, for example, the old 14-week residential training course at the beginning of the probationary period has been replaced by a foundation course of some 31 weeks. New recruits alternate between residential training centres, where traditional teaching methods may be used in the classroom, and periods on attachment at the Police Station to which they are posted. These so-called training 'modules' ensure that theory and practice are combined; in other words you will learn about what to do, see it being done and then do it yourself (under supervision) right from the beginning. Throughout the process you will be assessed and encouraged to assess yourself and your colleagues - by the end of this foundation period you and your trainer should have a fair idea of your strengths and weaknesses and whether you are ready to go out on patrol independently. The post-foundation course, which covers the remainder of your two-year probationary period includes several week-long residential courses to consolidate the practical experience being gained. (The Metropolitan Police training is conducted slightly differently, with an initial 20-week course at Hendon preceding the first posting to a station.)

Most policing skills need to be refined by experience and observation and there is a daunting amount to be learned. Many recruits feel swamped by the demands made on them and the information they have to assimilate. Some drop out early, others don't finish the course, but generally trainers, supervisors and tutors all give great support and encouragement to overcome any problems which might arise. No one is expected to have any prior knowledge, no matter what their previous occupation and everyone in training is treated equally, whatever their age or previous background.

The list of topics covered during training is long and varied: the history and social context of policing; the role of the police today; the British legal system; court procedure; human relations awareness and communication skills; specific areas such as vehicle documentation, missing persons and lost property. There are practical classes on crime with demonstration arrests, court appearance, charge and bail procedure. Recruits are taught how to use a pocket book; how to give evidence clearly in court; what powers of arrest or search they have in given circumstances. The list is, of course, constantly changing to keep abreast of current trends and new legislation.

A good deal of learning is done with the help of audio-visual aids, particularly video-recording. A mock arrest, interview, or trial, can be simulated and then analysed and discussed so that you learn by example and by your own mistakes. There are written and practical tasks, both individual and in groups throughout the training period and you are expected to work hard.

Physical skills are also important. Police must know how to move as a disciplined body - important when controlling crowds at sporting events or on peaceful demonstrations; vital when faced with an unruly or hostile mob. There are drill periods and practical exercises in crowd control to learn how a relatively small number of officers can hold back a much larger number of people. In recent years also more attention has had to be paid to riot shield training and how to cope with an increasing level of violence. Every police officer must be able to life-save and this is taught in the swimming pool. Every police officer is expected to know how to administer first aid in an emergency and so this too is taught and tested. Self-defence is another vital skill which may save the life of a lone police officer. As relaxation recruits have a wide choice of sports to help them let off steam - police officers generally work hard and play hard throughout their careers.

Training in the station itself is an additional new experience to cope with. The first few days can be confusing as you become part of 'the system'. You have to learn the correct procedures, how shifts work, where to go for various activities or supplies, and, of course, you have to meet the colleagues you will be working with, all of whom will appear in your eyes as fearfully experienced and competent. Gradually, however, all will become familiar and routine and as most people will have been through the same process they will sympathise.

Initially you will go out on the beat with experienced officers (generally Tutor Constables) who will show you 'the ground' (as the area covered by a station is known colloquially). You will also go on attachment to various offices and departments within your station and on your division to see who does what and how. Eventually, when you are considered ready, you will be out on your own - stopping and questioning members of the public, giving advice, making arrests and giving evidence in court. This 'on-the-job' training is interspersed with further courses to consolidate your increasing fund of knowledge. Gradually a probationer becomes more experienced and accepted. You gradually become familiar with the local streets and the local people. You get to know other members of your shift on and off duty. Police procedures and jargon become second nature.

Throughout your probationary period you will be assessed at three- or four-monthly intervals by a sergeant and an inspector who will submit written reports on your progress regularly to their senior officers. The sergeant will observe your work on the beat, your performance in court, your judgement and success in making arrests and your ability to write reports. You will then have assessment interviews with your inspector and chief superintendent. It is very important to maintain a satisfactory standard, both in these reports and at the training classes. This may sound a daunting series of hurdles but the system is designed to pick up any problems as early as possible.

Finally, at the end of the probationary period your progress is assessed. If this is judged to be satisfactory then you are confirmed as a constable and remain in the force. From then on your future career is up to you; promotion and specialisation depend solely on individual merit.

Case Study

An inspector in his thirties looks back on his 11 years' service.

I didn't join the Police Force until I was 26, which is quite late compared to most recruits. I left school with two A levels and got a scholarship with a large wholesaling and retailing concern as a junior manager. After completing my training with them I became a salesman. I enjoyed this particularly as I could get out and about and meet people, but I quickly decided that there wasn't much opportunity for promotion or any real responsibility. I then worked for a time as a salesman with a firm of brokers who specialised in insurance. After several years I decided that I wasn't getting anywhere and a couple of friends of mine suggested that I might be interested in joining the Police Service. I didn't particularly want to work with another company which would entail working indoors, as I've always been more of an outdoor person, so I thought policing might be a good job to do.

As I say, I joined when I was 26 and after my initial training I was posted to a very busy inner city area where I worked for two years while I was on probation. I passed the probation exams at the end of this period with very high marks and I was encouraged to sit the sergeant's exam quite soon afterwards. I also did quite well in that examination and as a result I was considered for the accelerated promotion scheme. I got through the interview boards for that and went on the Special Course at the Police College where I held the rank of sergeant. When I came back to my force from Bramshill, I served another year as a sergeant, again at a busy city station, and then I was promoted to inspector. Because I had done well on the Special Course I was offered a Bramshill Scholarship to go to university for three years on a full-time degree course. I read psychology at university and came back to the force with a first class honours degree. I have now served three more years as an inspector working on a shift and am hoping to be considered for a board to chief inspector very shortly.

I must say I've thoroughly enjoyed my time as a police officer. It's important that if you intend to join the Police Service you have to recognise that it places some limitations on your social life. Most operational officers, for example, work three weekends in four. Their hours of duty include night shifts and are often changed at quite short notice to meet additional force commitments. However, shift work does have some compensations, since having days off during the week means that things like shopping and outings can be done when places are not very crowded. You also have to realise that there are some limitations on your own personal behaviour. Even when you are off duty you can't get involved in anything that might bring discredit on your force. When I first joined I found that I lost one or two friends through this but I made many more new friends inside and outside the force who appreciate the position I am in.

Once you accept these facts it is difficult to think of any other job which offers so much variety and personal satisfaction. This is so whether you elect to stay as a uniformed operational officer or whether you specialise.

At my station there is one inspector in charge of each of the four shifts. On my shift I have four sergeants and 33 constables to look after. When we are on duty I have responsibility for everything that happens in my area. On night duty, after midnight, I am the most senior officer on duty. When you think about the kind of things that can happen, it's quite a responsibility. Since I have been an inspector I have been the first supervising officer at the scene of two murders, three fatal road traffic accidents and a serious rape. At these sorts of incident the decisions made in the first few minutes are crucial to any subsequent investigation. Of course much more senior officers are called out to take over the incident but initially the local inspector is often on his own.

In the last 50 years or so, increased educational attainment, together with better mass communications and a veritable explosion of vociferous pressure groups has made the general public much more aware of their legal rights. I am not sure however that they are all as equally aware of their responsibilities. The police these days are always walking a tightrope. They must police in such a way that they curtail the activities of an anti-social few in order to ensure the peace and freedom of the great majority. However, if the police are unsuccessful, they may find that the proportion of the public engaged in anti-social behaviour rises and the level of police-public co-operation falls. This could mean the police having to engage in ever more forceful tactics to maintain law and order. It's a difficult trend to reverse. Traditionally in this country we have always policed with the consent of the public at large and with the minimum of political interference. I feel that maintaining this system begins and ends with the front-line constable. He has tremendous responsibility towards the local community he polices and it is upon his everyday actions that the force as a whole is judged.

Chapter 4

On the Job

In the Station

During the first few years of your service the police station to which you are posted will be the centre of your activities. It will frequently be under the control of a superintendent, assisted by at least one chief inspector, several inspectors and a number of sergeants. You will gradually become familiar with all the people employed there, both police and civilian staff, but the most important to you personally will, naturally, be the other members of the shift or section on which you work. Policing is a 24-hour, seven days a week job and, in order that sufficient officers are on duty at all hours of the day and night, a system of eight-hour shifts is the general rule. Usually the hours work out something like this:

Night duty	10 pm to 6 pm (or 11 pm to 7 pm)
Early turn	6 am to 2 pm (or 7 am to 3 pm)
Late turn	2 pm to 10 pm (or 3 pm to 11 pm).

Each eight-hour spell is manned by a shift (a 'relief' in the Met) – a number of constables under the supervision of an inspector and two or three sergeants. These are the most influential officers as far as the new recruit is concerned. You may have periodic interviews about your progress with the superintendent, but your day-to-day work is scrutinised by your individual inspector and sergeants. It is they who will give you your instructions, teach you your duties, watch your performance in and outside the station and praise or criticise you, as they see fit.

At the start of each tour of duty you will be paraded and briefed by your inspector (or sergeant) and each member of the shift will be assigned to his individual duties, having first been told what in particular to look out for: stolen cars, missing persons, wanted criminals, for instance, or potential trouble spots. For the first few months, at least, you will most likely find yourself 'out on the beat'. The beat system - dividing up the total area covered by a station into specific patrol areas covered by one or more officers on foot (or in a Panda car) - is as old as the police itself, although it has been developed somewhat since those early days. Constables no longer have to keep to the regulation 2½ miles per hour as they patrol, nor do they have unvarying routes and times - this proved too easy for criminal elements to plot their progress and wait for the constables to go by! Today you have more discretion and independence to work out your own timing and your supervisors can check your movements via your personal radio, instead of the old system of reporting in at set intervals from the now obsolete police boxes.

Beats vary in size depending on how busy they are. In central London, where you may be stopped every few yards (particularly at the height of the tourist season), they are smaller than in a less densely populated country area. Generally you will be posted to the same beat for some time, at least a month, to allow you to become familiar with the local geography and the local characters. Gradually you will get to know the regular people and normal activities which go on every day - and you, in turn, will become known by the local population.

Home Beats

Sometimes an officer is posted to one particular beat on a more permanent basis. He is, in effect, taking on the role of the old parish constable and the later village 'Bobby', only today he is generally known as a 'rural beat', 'home beat' or 'permanent beat officer'. There has recently been an upsurge of interest in this type of policing, following the serious street rioting in recent years, and several chief constables are firm advocates of its effectiveness. It is felt in many circles that the public like the reassurance of a familiar policeman and that his presence alone helps to prevent some crime. The home beat officer becomes part of the community he patrols: wherever practicable he actually lives among the people he polices and keeps in very close contact with local community leaders, schools, youth clubs and churches. His task is to involve the local people in helping him prevent crime and he must be experienced in his job as well as genuinely interested in people since he may well find on occasions that he himself is a key factor in preventing local tension from boiling over into full-scale hostility.

Case Study

A permanent beat officer (known as a home beat officer in the Metropolitan Police and a rural beat officer in the county forces), with two long spells of work in the community.

There was no dramatic reason really why I joined the force. I was 20½ when I joined and I was thinking of getting married at the time. I was on the look out for a good steady job with security and housing. The police fitted this bill. In fact it was a toss up between the customs and the police, and the police sounded much more interesting. I had left school without any qualifications so I found the initial training very hard work. The length of the course in those days was shorter than it is now and there just didn't seem to be time to cover all the work. Anyway I got through and was posted to a very busy inner city station which had all the problems you can imagine – high unemployment, poor housing, the beginnings of a large black community, many of whom were just coming to terms with living in a strange and different culture. The local people too were having to come to terms with their new neighbours.

I served for nine years on shift work with the other police officers at the station and then I was given a permanent beat in the local community to look after. It was one of the busiest and most difficult beats in the area and it was mine for four years. I didn't live on the beat but I spent almost all my working time there. I don't actually think that it's a good idea to live where you work in this job. You need to be able to get away from the work for a breather. It might be all right in a rural area but it was so busy where I was that I wouldn't have had a minute's peace day or night. Also, although it is important to get to know the local people and everything about the goings on locally it's just as important to be seen to remain absolutely unbiased and fair to all sections of the community. That could be difficult to do if you were constantly in the area, dealing with the same people every day.

The main difference, I suppose, between myself and the other officers was that I had more time to get involved in community affairs and have a go at sorting out local problems including crime before formal police action had to be taken. Of course I often used to get good local information on crime as well, but I am more interested in preventing crime where possible than having to detect it after it has been committed.

Another difference was that I had responsibility for eight local schools ranging from the very young (five-year-olds) through to senior schools with pupils aged 16 years and over. I used to do regular school visits, giving talks on policing and taking part in discussions about social problems and community affairs. Of course the older kids are more difficult to approach and foster good relations with but it's an enjoyable challenge.

After four years on that particular beat I felt I wanted a change and I went into the recruiting branch for 18 months before moving to my present station where I again have a permanent beat. It's a similar beat to my last one, though not quite as busy or difficult to police, but we do have our share of problems. I have five schools here to look after and two are particularly rewarding to work in. One is for children with special educational needs and one for emotionally disturbed children.

What about the future? Well, I'm not looking for promotion. I think job satisfaction is the important thing and I get a lot from policing my own beat. Over the last few years we have lost some credibility with certain sections of the public - particularly from 'fire brigade' policing with Pandas. I call them steel boxes - the police inside having little contact with ordinary members of the public. We have to get back to a system of locally based, permanent foot patrol officers in whom the public can confide and feel that they can call on for help whenever they need it.

On Patrol

You never know what may happen next on the beat and this, to many people, is the attraction of a police career. You may have to cope with a fight, give directions to a foreign tourist, step in to sort out a traffic jam when traffic lights have failed, go in pursuit of a thief, administer first aid and call an ambulance at the scene of an accident, or even just tell someone the time. On night duty you will also be checking the security of premises, making sure that shops and office buildings are locked up properly, calling key-holders to deal with burglar alarms that may go off and, at closing time, keeping an eye on the more drunken elements who reel out of the pub looking for trouble.

Should you find yourself in a difficult situation, confronted by several hostile members of the public perhaps, you can call for assistance on your personal radio. But the initial action is up to you. A police officer is trained and is expected to use his initiative in defusing any situation he may come across; he also has the discretion not to interfere or merely to warn on suitable occasions. His independence of judgement and responsibility is far greater, for instance, than that of a private in the army, although at first sight they appear similar in that they are the first and most junior ranks.

Beat duty is not always exciting; nor is it always congenial. Crime does not stop on cold, wet, miserable evenings when most people are snug indoors, nor in the freezing early hours of a winter's morning - and the police must be there to deal with it. But the outdoor life can be pleasant, too. During those summer days when the office workers are panting inside, you are out in the fresh air and sunshine dealing with people rather than pieces of paper. During your eight-hour tour of duty you are usually allowed a 45-minute break in the station when you can relax, eat and have an informal chat with your colleagues.

Car Patrols

Later on in your probationary period you may find yourself going out on patrol with an experienced driver in a Panda car (though you yourself will not usually be allowed to drive one yet). The use of motor vehicles means, of course, that you can cover a great deal more ground that the officer on foot patrol but there is less direct contact with the general public. Or you may go out in the area crime car which has direct communication links with force headquarters and which, among other duties, deals with urgent calls, pursues stolen or suspect cars, searches for wanted persons and goes to the aid of colleagues requesting assistance. Officers must attend driving courses at one of the police driving schools before being allowed to drive police vehicles.

In-Station Work

Some members of your shift remain inside the station to deal with the day-to-day administration and the public demands for assistance or advice. A higher ranking officer (normally a sergeant) is in charge, generally assisted by one or more constables, depending on how busy the station is likely to be. (There is also a number of civilian staff, such as typists, to provide the necessary back-up services, although they generally work regular office hours and their duties are taken over by police officers at other times of the day and night.)

Each station has a 'front desk' to which members of the public come, and those in charge have to evaluate the urgency of the complaints and be able to assist with the variety of questions posed. They must also deal with the formalities associated with lost property which is handed in, vehicle documentation presented for checking and motor accident reports. Patience, tact and a sense of humour are all needed, since the people coming in and out are from all walks of life.

Also inside, and a vital part of the station's operations, is the communications room. In here are situated the personal radio console, the telephone switchboard, the teleprinter and, in many cases, the police computer link (which holds full information on criminal records, vehicle records, wanted and missing persons). Every officer carries his personal radio to keep him in constant contact with his colleagues so that he can call for immediate assistance, check on suspect cars, report his handling of an incident and generally keep in touch. He is also given instructions by radio and it is up to the officers in the communications room to see that he gets efficient help and as full a picture as possible of the incidents to which he is sent. They are also responsible for responding to calls for assistance from the public and must try to gauge the urgency of these. Many radio operators nowadays are civilians but they are always supervised by a serving officer who makes the decisions and directs the operations.

Case Study

A uniformed sergeant in one of the county forces talks about his years in the police.

> I was 19 when I joined the police service with three A levels and six O levels. It was a toss up between the Armed Forces and the Police Force and I decided on the police.
>
> For my first two years I was a uniformed PC at Divisional Headquarters. It was an interesting and busy time during which I found myself patrolling in town both on foot and driving, as well as going out on the usual attachments to other branches. The following year I spent on duty in the general administration office of force headquarters, dealing with duties ranging from the wholly clerical to driving the mobile canteen and acting as secretary of the force welfare fund. Then I was promoted to sergeant and was posted to an urban station where I had about 20 constables under me. During this time I spent eight weeks at the Central Planning and Instructor Training Unit at Harrogate on the Student Instructors' Course. A year later I started as an instructor at a district training centre and afterwards was seconded on Central Service as an instructor at our regional training centre.
>
> After two years I returned to my own force to a different division but again to a town section as a patrol sergeant. I also spent some time in charge of the Inquiry Section and sub-divisional administration office, as well as standing in for other sergeants on the

section. I have now spent some months as an acting inspector in charge of a shift.

I have enjoyed all of my time in the service, perhaps largely because I haven't stayed in the same place doing the same thing for too long at a time. I find that if I do I get bored. Something I realise now, but probably didn't at one time, is that police work, with all its excitements, can be rather boring at times. Having been a section sergeant twice, with an interlude in training, I also now realise how much better I was at it the second time around.

The value of my experience in training was very important. The role of the section sergeant is, or should be, largely as a trainer and I think this is appreciated by too few sergeants. Only after I returned to operational duty after teaching recruits was I sufficiently aware of their short-comings and difficulties and the amount of help they need on the street.

I have some regret that, due to being promoted early in service and there being no real interchange available in my force, I missed out on CID experience. I don't see it as a major problem but I would have liked the opportunity to have served some time on CID, for variety if for no other reason.

I can't say I have any strong desire to become a very senior police officer, but would certainly like to attain sufficient rank to practise my own ideas reasonably unfettered by immediate supervision, so I suppose I am talking about divisional command at least. But I shan't be particularly disappointed if it doesn't happen, providing that whatever I do, regardless of the rank it carries, is interesting and I can change roles fairly frequently.

Village Police Stations

A village police officer lives in a police house with a sign and a noticeboard outside, and, like a doctor or a vet, can be called out at any hour of the day or night. He is generally an experienced officer, with several years of service behind him, responsible for policing an area which may include more than one village and a considerable area of territory. Usually he is a family man and he and his family are very much part of the community. Like the home beat officers in the more urban areas they know everyone and everyone, knows them. He has to be familiar with the particular by-laws and requirements pertaining to rural life – gun licensing and Foot and Mouth regulations, how to deal with sheep-worrying, straying or rustled cattle, Colorado beetle and the like.

It can be a quiet life for much of the time but when something does happen you have generally to cope with it alone for longer than a station-based constable. Assistance can be summoned, of course, from your supervising station but this may be a considerable distance away. Consequently you often do much of your own detective work which is where your knowledge of local people and conditions helps.

Public Order Events

Very often you may be called upon to take part in the policing of public order events - ranging from anti-nuclear demonstrations to royal processions or duty at the local agricultural show or race meeting. If a large number of police are needed then extra officers are drafted in from outside the immediate area. This type of activity frequently means weekend work and can involve you in marching with a good-natured crowd, sitting for several hours in a coach (in reserve just in case there is trouble) or actually having to restrain a troublesome mob. It is on occasions like these that you begin to appreciate the training and drill which makes police officers act as a disciplined and effective body. The 'thin blue line' of police can prove very strong indeed when tried!

Recently the police have had to contend increasingly with organised and hostile violence, making them resort to tougher measures for their own protection. Britain has not yet followed many of our continental neighbours in keeping a special force of riot police, armed with batons, CS gas, water cannon and the like, and wearing protective clothing resembling armoured spacesuits rather than uniform; but we have seen squads of highly trained regular police with riot shields out on the streets. You would only be asked to take part in such incidents, however, after adequate basic training, with regular refresher courses. It is a sad reflection on our modern society that such force is needed but, as the original New Police were told:

> By the use of tact and good humour, the public can normally be induced to comply with directions. If, however, persuasion, advice or warning is found to be ineffective, a resort to force may become necessary, as it is imperative that a police officer, being required to take action, shall act with the firmness necessary to render it effective.

Arrest and After

When you make your first arrest out on the beat you will begin to understand the relevance of the practical work you did at your training school. The British judicial system is based upon the premise that a man is innocent until he is proved guilty and there are a great many procedures to follow to ensure that he is treated in accordance with the rights of every citizen (even if you personally have caught him in the act of committing an offence and have no doubts as to his guilt or innocence!). Before you arrest someone you have to caution him by reminding him of his right to remain silent, a formality with which just about every television viewer or cinema-goer is familiar. But after this there are countless other equally vital formalities to be complied with in the station - he must be interviewed and charged, his property must be listed meticulously, he must have access to legal advice, there are bail procedures if he is allowed bail and, finally, there will be a court appearance (or sometimes several spread over a lengthy period).

As a probationer, you will not be doing the actual work in many of these cases - more senior supervising officers (generally the custody officer) are responsible for charges and bail for instance - but you will be present at these interviews and your evidence will be of paramount importance.

Appearing in court for the first time can be slightly nerve-racking, but you will have done various 'mock trials' and evidence-giving exercises on your training course, so the procedure and courtroom atmosphere will not be totally strange to you. You will appreciate, too, the vital necessity of keeping your notebook in a clear and concise fashion so that you can give evidence from it without hesitation.

Court appearances can be frustrating affairs. Cases can drag on for months, interrupting your ordinary duties, and the eventual verdict may not please you. But this is all part of being a police officer, and after a time you should be able to accept it with equanimity.

Chapter 5

Promotion and Specialisation

Promotion

Promotion in the police service depends solely on personal merit since everyone starts off in the same way with the same basic training and the same opportunities. By the time your probationary period comes to an end you should have a fair idea of how you would like your career to continue. You may wish to concentrate on getting promotion as early as possible in the uniformed branch, or you may prefer to try transferring to one of the specialist branches you visited on attachment.

Many officers choose to remain in uniform where the responsibilities and day-to-day challenges offer the most variety. No two days are alike on uniformed patrol duty - one day you might be dealing with a terrorist bombing, the next pursuing an old-age pensioner's escaped budgie (or incidents equally diverse). Invariably it is the officer in uniform who is first on the scene, and the other branches who are called subsequently are there to give specialist support and advice.

The first step up the promotion ladder is to sergeant. In the normal course of events you could gain this rank within five years or so, providing your progress is satisfactory. In all forces you must pass the written sergeant's examination; in the Metropolitan Police only those within the top range of marks in this examination qualify. In the provincial forces candidates are not in competition with one another but, should they pass the exam, promotion is subject to a successful selection interview.

Promotion to inspector is also by individual selection and written examination and, in the ordinary way, you could expect to attain this rank about nine years after first joining the force, should you show the required ability.

There is, however, a quicker route up the ladder for those constables who show outstanding potential. This is the Accelerated Promotion Scheme. It is open to everyone but the standard is exceptionally high and only a few succeed in gaining a place on it each year. First you must qualify for promotion to sergeant in the normal way, at the first attempt and gain extremely high marks while doing so. Then, with the approval and backing of your senior officers, you must satisfy a selection board from your own force that you are indeed worthy of consideration.

If you succeed in this preliminary interview then you are put forward as a candidate on a three-day extended interview for the Police College. These interviews, which are the same as those used to select graduates for the Graduate Entry Scheme, are run by the Home Office and are closely modelled on the selection methods used in the higher Civil Service. If you are successful you join the next Special Course at the Police Staff College, Bramshill and are promoted to sergeant six months before Part I of this sandwich course begins. Part I consists of a three-month residential course at the College, followed by one or two years' developmental training back in your own force. You then return to Bramshill for Part II of the course, lasting four months and, if you complete this successfully, you will be given the substantive rank of inspector, which is confirmed after satisfactory completion of one year's probation.

Competition for the Special Course is fierce. There are applicants from each of the 43 forces and only about 80 places available each year, approximately a third of which are allocated to graduates joining under the Graduate Entry Scheme (see Chapter 3). Similarly, in Scotland only about 12 serving officers from its eight forces are selected for accelerated promotion each year. If you are one of the lucky ones then, barring accidents, your future career prospects are extremely bright.

At the rank of both sergeant and inspector there are also a certain number of scholarships awarded annually for full-time university degree courses (on full salary) to outstanding students at the Police College. These can be taken up at any university (applications being made through the universities' central clearing scheme) in subjects which are considered to be relevant, such as sociology, psychology, law and business studies.

After the rank of inspector, promotion is made by internal recommendation and interview boards and is dependent on personal merit and consistent progress. Throughout the higher ranks, officers attend special Command Courses at various levels.

The relatively low retirement age within the police (see

Chapter 8) means that vacancies are continually occurring, providing opportunities for promotion and advancement. There are, for instance, approximately 20,000 sergeants, 6,500 inspectors and 2,500 chief inspectors within the various forces in England and Wales. You can also apply for transfer to a different force at any rank (the higher posts being advertised in publications such as *Police Review*). You may choose to remain within a busy urban area or opt for a country posting.

Specialisation

Those officers who consistently show special aptitude or interest will be encouraged to pursue these within the specialist branches, but no one may enter direct without first completing the two-year probationary period successfully. Generally speaking there is a good deal of competition to get into the specialist branches as there are relatively few places available each year.

The CID

To the uninitiated the Criminal Investigation Department conjures up all manner of excitement and adventure. You may have visions of joining the glamorous and dangerous world shown on television or cinema screens. The true picture is one of a job which does have its exciting moments but in the main is usually more concerned with painstaking routine. It can, however, give you a great deal of personal satisfaction in that you are able to follow a case through on your own efforts. Most of the CID's work at the police station is concerned with the investigation of serious crimes (such as burglaries, robberies, fraud, sexual offences, serious assaults and murders). They also assist the uniformed officers in investigating the less serious crimes, such as theft. CID officers deal mainly with crimes that have already been committed, since the increase in crime, and the pressure of work it has generated, has made preventive patrolling by the CID virtually impossible in urban areas.

Within the CID itself, however, there are certain specialist departments which deal with the prevention and detection of large scale organised crime; such as the Fraud Squad, the Drugs Squad and the Regional Crime Squad. But before anyone may be considered for a job in any of these he must have proven experience in the more routine aspects of detective work.

The CID do not work the regular three-shift system like their uniformed colleagues. The hours are frequently long and irregular, with a good deal of evening and some night and weekend work. If you get involved in a murder inquiry, for example, you may spend several weeks or months on a minimum of sleep and see very little of your home and family. You must be prepared to collect and sift information by means of slow, painstaking and often frustrating inquiries. A good memory, an eye for detail and the ability to assess people's characters accurately are all particularly useful in this work.

The rank and pay structure is identical to that of the uniformed police, with an additional plain clothes allowance (see Chapter 8).

A great number of police constables apply to join the CID but few are selected. Every force has its own department but only one in eight of all police officers belongs to it and a proportion of these are in the specialist branches, such as photography or fingerprints, so vacancies are few. A preliminary step to transferring may well be to go on temporary attachment to a local crime squad made up of officers from the uniformed branch (in plain clothes) under the supervision of a CID officer. If you show obvious talent for this type of work you may then be encouraged by your senior officers who will recommend you for consideration by an interview board. If selected you are sent on an initial training course at one of the six detective training schools (returning for further courses as your career progresses). Here you will learn what is expected of a CID officer: investigation and interview techniques, detailed study of criminal law, how to prepare paperwork and evidence for use in court, to name some of the requirements.

In the Metropolitan Police there is currently a system of interchange between the CID and the uniformed branch regarding promotion in the ranks of constable, sergeant and inspector. A detective constable who is successful in the sergeant's examination must serve at least a year in uniform in his new rank before choosing whether or not to return to the CID. The same system holds good for promotion from sergeant to inspector. This interchange sometimes takes place in the county forces also, though generally on a less formal basis.

Case Study

A detective constable with nine years' experience.

I've been in the police since I joined the cadets when I was 17½. I was born in Northumberland but moved to Scotland when I was nine and went to school in Glasgow. I left school at 16, with O level maths, and applied to join a Scottish cadet corps but their course was too academic for my taste, with too little sport and outside activities. So in the end I joined the cadets in an English force and got O level English during the course. I did plan to go back to Scotland but one thing led to another and I decided to stay on down here. I'm married now, with two young children (and another on the way) and we have a very pleasant police house out in the country, so I can't see myself moving at the moment.

I don't really know why I joined the police in the first place; it just attracted me at the time, I didn't want a boring nine to five office job and wanted to do something with more variety... After cadet training for 18 months I went on recruit training. I can't say I found that being in the cadets first was much of an advantage in my particular case. I still found the recruit training pretty hard going and had a tough time trying to discipline myself to study. After that I did my two years' probation in a busy inner city station, followed by 18 months on ordinary shift work before joining a crime squad (uniformed officers working in plain clothes) for a year. The work appealed to me so I decided to apply to the CID. I failed the first board but managed to get through the next time and became a DC (detective constable). I started out on the Robbery Squad, then three years later I joined the Regional Crime Squad where I am at the moment.

The job has more than lived up to my expectations. I love it and can't see myself doing anything else. You get more out of it the more you put into it, like everything else really ... I enjoyed my time in uniform and I think it takes at least four years gaining experience in uniform before you can really be sure you want to specialise in any particular branch. I know even after I had been on the Crime Squad I wasn't 100 per cent certain that the CID was for me ...

Since I joined the CID I've been involved in some 15 murder investigations and in two rather nasty riots, among other things. I particularly enjoy being given a difficult and protracted crime investigation. It's often frustrating and needs a lot of painstaking work, but it's worth it in the end. I enjoy dealing with the hardened professional criminals. I find it's much more difficult to deal with the silly opportunist type who does something on the spur of the moment without considering the awful consequences for his job and his family. Of course, we still have to take action but you don't get so much satisfaction or enjoyment out of a case like that.

I thoroughly enjoy CID work and can see myself staying on in this branch in the future. But I am beginning to feel that I have done as much as I can as a DC and that it's time to move on. I am studying hard at the moment to take the sergeant's exam next year. It's very hard work, particularly if you are actively engaged in operational work as I am. All the studying has to be done in your own time. It's not too bad if you have a nine to five job but I work quite a bit of overtime

- it's necessary on the job I am doing at the moment. It's hard on my wife, too, especially as she's expecting a baby this year, but she is very understanding and by this time is used to my long hours. Hopefully, things will be easier for her if I get through the exam.

Traffic Police

Most people think of the traffic 'cop' as someone concerned solely with the harrying of speeding motorists. His actual task is much more comprehensive and should you join the traffic department you will quickly discover that it is concerned with every aspect of safety on the road; from keeping the ever-increasing flow of vehicles moving through the towns to dealing with motorway 'pile-ups'; from checking that cars and lorries on the road conform to the safety requirements laid down by law, to escorting abnormal loads from one end of the country to the other. You do, of course, deal with motoring offences such as speeding but you also deal with the victims of accidents, which makes you aware of how necessary such safety limits are. At the same time, of course, the traffic officer is still a police officer and gets involved in all manner of non-traffic incidents.

Drivers of traffic cars (not to be confused with drivers of the Panda cars which belong to the police station) and motorcycles operate independently out of special centralised traffic garages, from where they go out on patrol and are called out to incidents requiring police presence (such as accidents, road blocks, major hold-ups and so on). Each driver has been highly trained at one of the regional driving schools to enable him to drive at speed but in safety, and has also taken courses in the specialist knowledge required, such as the various vehicle regulations governing height, weight, speed and so on. Traffic officers also learn how to deal with road accidents efficiently, how to keep the traffic chaos at a minimum when the road is blocked by damaged vehicles and how to assess the positions of vehicles involved in accidents for future court evidence should there be any question of prosecuting for careless or dangerous driving. You will also, of course, become familiar with the procedure for breathalysing and reporting someone for alleged drunken driving.

There are various back-up services in the traffic department and you may wish to go on to join one of these later; the intelligence section, for instance, where they analyse traffic problems and seek to remedy them.

Dog-Handlers

Police dogs have been used regularly since the end of the Second World War and they have proved invaluable at finding missing persons and property and at catching criminals. The 300 or so operational dogs in the Metropolitan Police, for instance, are responsible for some 6,000 arrests each year. If you become a dog-handler, then you must be prepared for a long-term commitment since you and your dog will become an inseparable team. You may well 'puppy walk' him until he is old enough to begin work; you and your dog will certainly train together and he will usually be taught to answer only to your commands; he will live with you and become part of the family and on retirement (at about nine years old) he will generally stay on and become your personal property and pet.

You cannot apply to work in the dog section until you have first proved yourself a good police officer by successfully completing your statutory two years on shift work. Then you may be given a trial course with a dog trained to accept commands from more than one person. You need to show a genuine love of animals, infinite patience and be fit enough to keep up with your dog on the various exercises involved. Then you may be placed on a waiting list until a vacancy occurs.

Police dogs and their handlers are very highly trained and attend constant refresher courses throughout their active service. The dogs must learn obedience so that they are always under complete control, even in the heat of a chase or when confronted with strange noises (such as gun shots); nose-work, the tracking of people or objects without being distracted by other more attractive scents (such as food or cats); and manwork, the pursuit and capture of a suspect by gripping, but not biting, until the handler arrives. In addition some dogs are taught how to sniff out drugs and explosives. Handlers are not only taught how to give clear commands but also how to care for their dogs and keep them in the peak of condition necessary for such active work.

German Shepherd Dogs (Alsatians) are most widely used with individual handlers in British police forces. Other breeds used are Labradors (particularly good as 'sniffer' dogs), Weimaraners, Dobermanns and Rottweilers. Dogs and handlers have to be available at all times and so they too work one of the three shifts, either on foot on in vans or on call at the station.

Many police dogs are now specially bred in police kennels so that forces can keep up a constant supply of the right sort of dog (both in breed and temperament), although a certain number are still bought in, or given by the public, while young enough to be trained properly.

Mounted Police

Not every force has a mounted branch and those that do generally have a long waiting list of would-be applicants. You do not however, have to be an experienced rider to apply (not like the old days when most recruits had been in cavalry regiments prior to joining). If accepted you will receive expert training in riding and caring for your horse at one of the special training centres, with regular refresher courses usually every year. You are, however, expected to stay within the branch for a number of years and, because branches are generally quite small, opportunities for promotion are necessarily limited. Of course, you are still first and foremost a police officer, so you have to have shown yourself competent at normal duties during your first two years if you want to be considered for the mounted branch.

Horses can be invaluable for crowd control during demonstrations and sporting events. There is always something formidable about a mounted man which the man on foot generally respects, and the horses are trained to remain calm even under the noisiest and most violent of conditions. In rural areas, such as parts of Scotland, horses are also useful during searches of wide areas of moorland. In London the Metropolitan Police horses still form part of all ceremonial occasions.

Mounted police go out on regular patrols, too, generally walking or trotting sedately, with frequent rests. You are responsible for the care of your horse before and after taking him out and probationers are expected to pass an examination in stable management as well as horsemanship. You generally have to groom your own horse, take it for shoeing and be responsible for your own harness and equipment - although above certain ranks these duties are done for you.

River Police

Some forces with large rivers or coastal waters within their boundaries need special contingents of men to police them. The Thames Marine Police (created in 1798 by magistrates Harriot and Colquhoun in an attempt to safeguard the trading companies in London's dockland from marauding gangs of thieves) was in fact set up before the Metropolitan Force into which it was incorporated in the 1830s. The Thames Division (as it is known today) is responsible for the river from Dartford Creek as far as Staines (excluding the docks which are covered by the Port of London's own force).

The number of vacancies for such specialised work naturally varies according to the amount of waterways to be policed so if you are attracted to a career afloat, choose the force you apply to with this in mind. Again competition is keen and you cannot go into the waterborne division without the initial two-year period on foot patrol. Candidates need to show themselves above average swimmers while competence in the handling of boats (such as sailing experience) is bound to be considered an asset. Patrol boats and motor launches deal with thefts from ships, warehouses and houseboats, help craft in difficulties, examine wharves, dock entrances, riverside premises and landing places; they also rescue people (or salvage bodies) from the water, secure drifting boats, derelict timber and the like which can cause navigation hazards and monitor water pollution (such as oil spillages). They also work closely with Customs and Excise to prevent smuggling or the illegal importation from abroad of animals which may carry rabies. They can also be called in to help in the pursuit of those wanted by the uniformed branch or the CID.

Underwater Units

Quite a few forces have underwater search units manned by highly trained divers. You need to be extremely fit to be considered for a posting to one of these teams as you may well be called out in the depths of winter to search under half-frozen ponds or other stretches of water for missing people, stolen property or suspected murder weapons. Units are usually very small and opportunities are limited.

Armed Police

The British police force is famed throughout the world for not carrying guns as a matter of routine, as the police do in many other countries. They pride themselves on trying reason and persuasion rather than resorting to threats and pitched battles with flying bullets and inevitable casualties on both sides. On some occasions, however, the police need to show that, as a last resort, firearms are available and will be used if necessary. At incidents such as hijackings of aircraft or when hostages are being threatened (for example, during the notorious Iranian Embassy siege in Kensington) the firearms branch will be called in. The officers who carry guns are all experienced policemen (and women) and highly trained marksmen who undergo constant refresher courses to keep them up to scratch.

Another section, who carry guns as part of their normal duties, is the Diplomatic Patrol Group - part of the Metropolitan Police. Their duties include the protection of foreign embassies and their staff, as well as high-security buildings and public figures who may be at risk (for example, politicians threatened by terrorist groups or letter bombs).

Special Branch

The Special Branch was started by the Metropolitan Police at the end of the last century to deal specifically with the threats of the Irish Fenians who were causing explosions in the city. It subsequently expanded its activities to encompass any foreign national who might possibly be a threat to Britain or to British subjects. (Karl Marx and Lenin, for instance, came under surveillance while they were studying here.) During the two world wars Special Branch worked with MI5 keeping an eye on possible spies. Today they carry out surveillance duties on anyone suspected of being a security risk and there is a department in every force. In some forces you join Special Branch via the CID so you have to prove yourself there before you can apply to transfer. In the Metropolitan Police its members are generally recruited from the uniformed branch direct. Knowledge of foreign languages, particularly the less-widely taught, such as Arabic, Russian, the oriental tongues and the Indian dialects, can be a great advantage.

Mobile Police Support Units

Experienced officers may apply to serve for a limited period in the Mobile Police Support Units of their force. These are highly flexible units which can be brought in at short notice to assist local officers should more manpower be needed for specific purposes - to police football matches, demonstrations or to combat a particularly high incidence of burglaries, shoplifting offences or robberies by organised gangs. They are also used for large-scale searches for missing persons, murder weapons etc and play a prominent part in sieges and similar incidents.

Juvenile Bureaux

The Metropolitan Police and most, but not all, of the county forces, have a special system for dealing with juvenile offenders.

(A juvenile is defined as someone who has not yet reached the age of 17.) Instead of being charged in the normal way they are referred from the police station to the area's juvenile bureau which is manned by uniformed officers, usually under the supervision of a chief inspector. Not every juvenile is automatically referred in this way; it depends to a great extent on the seriousness of the crime involved. If, however, the offence is relatively minor, it is possible to avoid a court appearance and sentence (and thereby avoid a criminal record). Providing the offender admits his guilt and the parents, complainant or victim and the police agree, he has a formal 'caution' meeting with the officer in charge in which he is told in no uncertain terms exactly what will happen next time. This is generally found to be an effective deterrent for many first offenders.

Officers working in such bureaux are responsible for home visits to assess the offender's background and family circumstances. They also keep close contacts with the social services, dealing with care and control cases which may arise when uniformed patrol officers in the course of their normal duties come across juveniles at risk. In these cases parents may be arrested or children removed from home for their own safety.

Court Officers

Some officers are employed full-time by Magistrates Courts and Crown Courts to supervise the organisation of paperwork and prisoners in order to ensure that cases run smoothly. The court officer is nominally attached to a police station but in practice he spends all his time at court. In some forces higher ranking court officers (such as inspectors or chief inspectors) act as prosecutors and present cases. To fill such posts you need a great deal of working knowledge and generally only experienced long-serving officers are appointed.

The Collator

The collator, called in many forces the 'local intelligence officer', is usually an experienced constable who works out of the local station. His job is to keep a detailed record of all the happenings in his area. With information and intelligence coming in from many sources, he provides a central point for analysis and dissemination. Most collators put out a daily or weekly crime bulletin for the reference of other operational officers. He provides an essential link between the CID and uniform officers in the area in matters of serious crime. Indeed it is when a serious incident occurs, such as a murder, that officers descend on the collator for local information. In these days of highly organised mobile criminals he will liaise with other police stations and other forces, keeping track of the movements of known offenders and their patterns of criminal activity.

Crime Prevention Officers

All forces have crime prevention branches and the larger forces usually have local crime prevention officers. They are experienced and highly trained, with considerable specialised knowledge in crime prevention techniques. They are on hand to give information to local officers and to the public on security of personal property. This ranges from information about house and vehicle security for private householders and car owners right through to large security systems for industry. They also give advice on personal protection, community crime prevention and identifying people or property especially at risk. This advice may be at a local, informal level, or through national campaigns such as the much advertised anti-burglary campaigns. CPOs, as they are known, work closely with local crime prevention panels and other community groups on local crime problems.

Operations Room

All forces nowadays have a highly sophisticated system of communications. Apart from the normal communications room which is a vital part of any police station, each force has a central operations room where 999 calls are received and information fed out to the local patrol cars and stations.* One of the main functions of the operations room is to be ready to deal with a major incident, such as a bomb, a plane crash, a derailment or a major street riot. The operations room has the facilities to set up operational control points on the spot with mobile major incident vehicles and the technical expertise to keep in touch with all relevant services.

To work in this department you need to be clear-thinking and have the ability to work under pressure. Traditionally it has been manned by experienced police officers although now, particularly in the county forces, civilian staff are also employed under

---

* Emergency calls may be renumbered in the near future, and the familiar 999 disappear.

the supervision of a serving officer. A clear speaking voice is obviously an asset.

Chapter 6

Working with the Police

Allied Occupations

There are various groups of people who work very closely with serving police officers, both in and out of the station.

Special Constables

'Specials' are part-time police officers who are employed full-time in a variety of other jobs but who spend a certain amount of their free time in uniform. Generally they do so because they enjoy working with people and feel this is a worthwhile way of helping the community in which they live. They are in fact following in the age-old tradition of the original parish constables (see Chapter 1), fulfilling their duty as citizens in taking their turn at looking after their own community.

The amount of time you can devote to policework as a special naturally depends on your job and personal commitments. You generally do what you can, when you can - anything from a few hours a week to a few hours a month. Each tour of duty is normally about four hours and while on duty you have the same responsibilities and powers of arrest as regular police officers.

Special constables are unpaid but do receive certain allowances and out-of-pocket expenses, as well as free uniform and equipment. Your work will be as varied and unpredictable as that of a full-time policeman - patrol work on foot or in a Panda car, dealing with inquiries or administrative work in the local police station, helping out at major incidents, on royal visits or at sporting events.

To join the specials you should call in at your local police station for an application form. You must, however, fulfil certain requirements. You must be a British citizen - natural born, naturalised or registered as a citizen of the UK and colonies. You should also be physically fit. You are not acceptable if you belong to one of the other essential services, the Fire Brigade or Ambulance Service, for instance, or if you are a doctor, a nurse or a midwife. Similarly, entry is barred if you belong to any of the Armed Forces, the Territorial and Army Volunteer Reservists, or if you are employed by a security organisation.

Once accepted you will be formally attested and attend a basic recruits' training course at a local training centre. This course is generally spread over a period of about three months, with weekly evening classes, supplemented with instructional duty on the streets. While training you will be accompanied by a regular police officer or an experienced special. Like the regular police your objectives are preserving public peace and protecting local inhabitants and property. A thorough grounding in police authority and duties is given in such matters as: your powers of arrest, local by-laws, traffic regulations, licensing laws and court procedure. You will also learn first aid to give practical help in an emergency.

Specials are drawn from all walks of life - from teachers, stockbrokers, factory workers and shop assistants. But, as one of them puts it:

> Once you put the uniform on, the public do not know - or care - how long you have been in the force. All they know is that you are a police officer and they expect you to act confidently and decisively.

Traffic Wardens

Traffic wardens sometimes describe themselves as 'an extra arm of the law' and their work is increasingly important in urban areas where it is vital to keep the traffic flowing smoothly. The police officer on the beat needs to concentrate on his primary role of preventing crime and maintaining law and order and obviously cannot be expected to deal with the mass of routine parking infringements (such as over-staying at meters or parking on double yellow lines) at the same time. And so, although the police remain responsible for the control of traffic both on the streets and behind the scenes, an act was passed in the early sixties to authorise the appointment of traffic wardens to take on the more routine tasks under the direction of the chief officer of the various police forces.

As a traffic warden you need to be fairly thick-skinned and extremely tactful - irate motorists are not the most pleasant of customers. You must be able to resist the most plausible of excuses by offenders and, occasionally, be the target of downright abuse. But your work is necessary; without traffic wardens there would be chaos, particularly in the bigger cities.

You generally work on the streets during the hours parking regulations are in force (usually 8.30 am to 6.30 pm Monday to Saturday) although the cover may sometimes be split into two shifts so that on some days you might go on duty at 7.30 am and on others finish at 7.30 pm. The system varies from area to area.

Traffic wardens are issued with easily identifiable uniforms to wear whilst on duty and their main task is to supervise the parking of vehicles at parking meters and to attach tickets to cars which contravene any of the relevant parking regulations. They also advise members of the public where they can and cannot park and issue parking tickets to vehicles found in illegal parking spaces. There are other ways too in which wardens may assist the police to control traffic. You might, for example, be asked to do school crossing patrols or traffic control duty, which requires considerable formal training, skill and self-confidence. You could also find yourself responsible for receiving vehicles that are towed away to a police car pound. And, of course, you are expected to keep your eyes open for out of date motor vehicle licences as well as other motoring offences.

To become a traffic warden you need to show that you are in good health and have a good standard of eyesight. You should also be fond of outdoor life and like the idea of working closely with the police. Before you go out on the street, you will complete a training course which will provide you with the necessary grounding in a traffic warden's duties. Instructors on these courses are generally drawn from both traffic wardens and police. After training you will know how to cope with the technicalities of the job; the regulations and laws governing traffic, the completion and issuing of parking tickets, how to direct traffic, how to give evidence in court. You will also learn first aid so that you are competent to administer it in an emergency.

When you first begin as a warden it is generally in an unestablished capacity for a trial period of around 12 months. Once established, you can gain promotion to more senior grades (such as supervisor or controller) with corresponding salary rises. Salaries depend of course on the area in which you work. In Thames Valley, for example, starting pay is £8,007 per annum. There is equal pay for men and women, who share the same duties, and also overtime and special allowances.

For more information you should apply to the traffic warden

section of your local force or (in London) to the Metropolitan Police Office, Department E8 Branch, Room 214, 105 Regency Street, London SW1P 4AN.

School Crossing Patrols

To relieve police officers from the routine but vital task of supervising busy road crossings points when children are going to and from school, most police stations rely on the services of a civilian school crossing patrol (sometimes familiarly known as 'lollipop men' or usually, 'lollipop ladies'). They are generally employed on a local level through a schools liaison officer and are supplied with easily identifiable clothing (including wet weather covering) and signs. For further information and availability of such posts in your area you should contact your local police station.

Civil Staff

Not many people outside the police force appreciate the vast numbers of civil staff who are employed in the various departments to relieve serving officers from the burden of routine or to perform highly specialised tasks which are a necessary part of police work. The Metropolitan Police alone, for instance, employs some 12,000 of these support staff. And so, even if you are unable, or would prefer not to become an actual police officer, you could still work with the police in a different capacity. The civil staff employed cover a wide range of duties: among them are typists, telephonists, teleprinter operators, clerical officers, data processors, radio engineers, scientific officers, photographers, fingerprint officers, catering staff, accountants, electricians, motor mechanics, architects and legal advisers. To cover them all in detail would require more space than this book allows, but here is a brief outline of some of the jobs available.

Scientific Officers

Forensic science is playing an ever-increasing role in police work and so there is always a demand for highly skilled scientists. Some forces have their own laboratories, others share resources. The Metropolitan Police, for instance, employs some 200 staff in its purpose-built laboratory which also serves the City of London Police. Scientists do not join the police force itself but are employed under terms and conditions similar to those of the Civil Service.

You can join at one of four grades and positions range from assistant scientific officer (requiring GCSEs or preferably A levels), through scientific officer (requiring a degree, a higher national certificate or higher national diploma), higher scientific officer (with a degree and postgraduate experience in a laboratory) up to senior scientific officer (requiring at least four years' postgraduate laboratory experience after qualifying for an MSc or PhD). Exact requirements for each level can be obtained from the individual forces concerned.

Police laboratories deal with a wide variety of cases and, of course, no two are ever exactly alike. Different divisions cover different tasks. Chemistry divisions, for example, deal with contact traces on suspects or at scenes of crime (material fibres, human hair, paint scrapings, etc), drugs and toxicology. Analysis techniques often involve scanning electron microscopy and atomic absorption as well as chromatography and spectrometry. More routine is the analysis of alcohol levels in breathalyser cases. A biology division deals with evidence originating from a living source such as bloodstains, and they are mainly concerned with violent crimes such as murder. Botany too plays its part. Safe-blowers, for instance, have been tracked down through traces of sawdust which is sometimes used as a ballast. The firearms division is where bullets are identified and matched with suspect weapons and the increase in crimes of violence has led to increasing activity on their part. The documents division investigates, among other things, forgeries of documents such as credit cards and cheque books, frequently making use of infra-red, ultra violent and visible radiation techniques. Specialised techniques such as photomicrography are also employed by the photographic division.

Police officers, or specially trained civil scenes of crime officers, usually bring back the evidence but sometimes scientists have to observe or investigate at the scene of a crime for themselves. Occasionally they may have to appear in court as independent witnesses, although evidence is often prepared in the form of statements and is read out to the court. For further information you should contact your local force or (for the London area) write to The Director's Staff Officer, Metropolitan Police Forensic Science Laboratory, 109 Lambeth Road, London SE1 7LP.

Fingerprint Officers

Most forces employ civil staff to work in the criminal records department identifying and matching fingerprints taken at the scene of a crime with those already on record. In addition to local records there is a national fingerprint collection which was started at the turn of the century and is still held at Scotland Yard. There are various grades of fingerprint officer so there is scope for promotion within this department. Fingerprint experts may sometimes be required to attend courts to give evidence or attend scenes of crime. No special qualifications are required but GCSE passes are preferred and generally you must be over 18 to apply. You must have good sight, both distant and near vision and also good colour vision. You also need patience, determination and integrity as the job involves painstaking and confidential work even though it now makes use of modern computer technology.

Data Processors

There are various grades of data processors employed by the police who make use of the latest techniques and sophisticated office machinery. Trainee data processors generally need no formal qualifications, although typing skills are an advantage. You must be at least 18 years of age. Data processors must have previous experience of a modern computer operated system, while senior data processors must be highly skilled; supervision of a data preparation pool is often part of their work.

Computer programmers need A levels and (in London) are recruited through the Civil Service Commission.

Clerical Officers and Assistants

There is a wide variety of work available in all departments and you have the chance of moving around as you gain promotion and experience so that in the course of your career you might get to know the workings of such different branches as CID, Traffic, Criminal Records, Personnel or Finance. You might be based in force headquarters or at a local station.

To be considered for the post of a clerical officer or assistant you need GCSEs, generally including English language. You also have to satisfy the force about your nationality and character since you will be employed in confidential work, as well as your health. Further particulars are available from your local force.

Photographers

If you have photographic qualifications you may be appointed in an established capacity, otherwise you can train, taking an approved course of study. Duties will include macrophotography, line and continuous tone copying, negative processing, bromide printing and enlarging, print finishing, cine and colour transparencies and camera operation. As a rule only senior photographers go on outside duties. There may also be a certain amount of overtime involved as well as a stand-by rota when you may find yourself 'on call' at home.

Law Clerks and Legal Assistants

The solicitors' department of the police employs a team of staff to prepare cases for trial and undertake prosecutions. Law clerks are employed at Crown Courts and work closely with police officers and barristers. You need GCSEs or equivalent qualifications and some skill at typewriting and should be at least 18 at the time of application.

Legal assistants are qualified solicitors who prepare, advise on and conduct criminal prosecutions, including advocacy in the Magistrates Courts as well as other legal work.

Personal Secretaries and Typists

Most police officers can (and often do) type some of their own work but there are many openings for typists, shorthand typists and audio typists within the various branches. Candidates generally must be over 16 and pass a typing test of 30 words a minute.

Senior police and civil staff officers also have their personal secretaries who must be over 18 and have satisfactory academic qualifications as well as proficiency in secretarial skills. Character references are also required because of the confidential nature of much of the work.

Radio Technicians

These are employed in the vital Telecommunications Branch which is responsible for the electronic equipment used so much in the modern police service - mobile VHF/FM transmitter/receiver equipment, personal R/T sets, tape recorders etc. Forces generally have depots where such equipment is serviced and repaired. Some formal qualifications as well as proven practical experience in telecommunications are required and there are often opportunities for further education and training.

Photoprinters

Photoprinters are involved in photocopying processes, microfilm work, offset litho operations and other print room duties. Generally training is given on the job and no formal qualifications are needed, though you must be at least 16.

Teleprinter Operators
Teleprinter operators receive and transmit the all-important inter-station and inter-force messages which keep police stations in touch with one another and abreast of local and national developments. The teleprinter needs to be operational 24 hours a day, every day, and so in some forces civil staff are required to work shift duties akin to those of serving police officers. In others they work normal office hours and police officers themselves operate the teleprinter during the other periods. It is advisable to check the requirements of your local force before applying.

Telephonists
The telephone system in most police forces is becoming increasingly automated but trained telephonists (and trainees) are still required in numbers. Like teleprinter operators telephonists may well find themselves working a shift system with occasional weekend and public holiday working, depending on the specific requirements of their local force.

Maintenance
The maintenance section of a force employs a great number of civil staff concerned with looking after the variety of police properties. For instance, technicians, electricians and fitters are employed to install, maintain, service and repair plant and equipment at such buildings as police stations, married quarters (police houses and flats), hostel accommodation, courts and probation offices. Their duties are widespread and generally you need specific academic qualifications and experience to join the team.

Catering
Policemen on duty frequently take their meal breaks in the station and often facilities are available round the clock. In addition to normal canteens catering for such officers there are also many occasions when great numbers of officers have to be fed off their normal working area - take, for instance, a major demonstration or public order event when large numbers need refreshments while on duty, and provision has to be made in premises other than normal catering centres. Some

qualifications and experience in the catering trade are often required although training is also given and there are opportunities for promotion.

Civil staff requirements vary from force to force. For other openings, current entry requirements and pay scales you should consult the Personnel Section of your local force. For general enquiries relating to employment (scientific, technical or administrative) in areas which give direct support to the police, contact The Establishment Officer, Home Office, Grenadier House, 99-105 Horseferry Road, London SW1P 2DD.

Chapter 7

Other Police Forces

British Transport Police

The British Transport Police is responsible for policing the railways, docks, harbours, stations and other premises used by the British Railways Board, the British Transport Docks Board and London Transport Executive. In the early 1800s with the rapid growth of the rail network, the various railway companies found it necessary to appoint their own private police forces; the first being on the Liverpool and Manchester Railway (1830), the London and Birmingham Railway (1833) and the Great Western Railway (1835). This system continued until nationalisation of the railways. The British Transport Police grew up from these and is now a national force, organised and run in accordance with the British Transport Police Force Scheme 1963 (Approval) Order, 1964. They currently deal with some 80,000 crimes a year, many serious offences and innumerable incidents where police advice or assistance is given. With the continued rise of rail travel and the boom expected with the Channel Tunnel their job promises to be even more challenging in the future.

The ranks in the British Transport Police are the same as those in the civil forces - constable, sergeant, inspector, chief inspector, superintendent, chief superintendent - with similar uniform and insignia. Basic rates of pay are the same, and there are also reduced rate travel facilities on British and continental railways.

The force is split into geographical divisions with centres such as Birmingham, Cardiff, Glasgow, Hull, Southampton; each division is made up of uniformed officers and detectives. There are also specialist officers who deal with highly organised professional gangs, mail robberies, thefts at and between London termini, thefts of bullion and cash and serious raids on freight trains in sidings and in transit. Major stations are also policed by dogs and handlers.

To join the British Transport Police you must fulfil certain general entry requirements (which are similar to those listed for forces in Chapter 3) regarding eyesight, nationality and so on. Then, if accepted, you will undergo a period of 33 weeks' initial training. This is currently a sandwich course with on-division training alternating with residential courses at Home Office training centres.

For further information and application forms write to:

Chief Constable's Office,
British Transport Police,
PO Box No 260,
15 Tavistock Place,
London WC1H 9SJ.

Ministry of Defence Police

The Ministry of Defence is responsible for policing its own establishments such as research centres, naval bases, ordnance factories and armament depots and to do so it employs its own police force. To join you must fulfil certain physical requirements and pass certain security checks (detailed information will be provided on request). Pay and conditions are similar to those of other police forces with free accommodation or rent allowances usually available.

The MOD police are divided into eight divisions which between them are responsible for over 140 establishments. Security is one of the main considerations as much of the ministry work is secret and must be confined to authorised personnel. Dogs are used extensively and there is also a CID branch including a Fraud Squad.

For further information, contact:

Ministry of Defence Police,
Recruitment Department,
Medmenham,
Marlow, Bucks
SL7 2ED.

Parks Police

Public parks, gardens, commons and open spaces are subject to special acts, regulations and by-laws, generally exhibited at the entrances. In London the largest parks are policed by their own patrolling constables who deal with such offences as trespass, wilful damage, theft and nuisance. These are very small forces and recruitment opportunities are therefore extremely limited. For further information contact:

Royal Parks Constabulary HQ
Room C11/12
2 Marsham Street
London SW1P 3EB
071-276 3762.

or

Wandsworth Parks Police
Admin Units
Battersea Park
London SW11 4NJ
081-871 7636.

Part 2

Chapter 8

Pay and Conditions

Salary Scales

A police officer these days is well paid and salaries are subject to annual review (generally in September each year). But it would be a mistake to choose the Police Service as a career in the belief that the money alone makes it worthwhile. You may, for instance, earn over £10,000 a year as a 19-year-old recruit in London, an attractive sum compared to various other starting salaries, but make no mistake, you will earn every penny. No other apprentice will be asked to take on the responsibilities and authority which the young probationer has from the minute he steps out on to the street in uniform. No matter how young or inexperienced you are, you will be expected to have the knowledge and capability to take charge of virtually any situation you can imagine.

Pay scales are standardised throughout the county forces and are slightly higher in London. The table on page 80 shows how they rise with rank and experience.

Housing

In addition to your basic salary, there is the considerable addition of free accommodation or rent allowance. Single police officers are generally allocated places in section houses where they have their own rooms and comprehensive facilities for recreation, laundry etc. However, due to a continuing shortage of force accommodation, Metropolitan Police probationers are likely to be required to live at home following completion of their initial training. Married officers may be offered police flats or houses, where maintenance of all kinds is carried out by service contractors. In most forces you must live in approved accommodation at least during your initial two-year pro-

Pay Scales (September 1991)

	£
Constables on appointment	11,790
After 1 year	12,606
After 2 years *	14,841
After 3 years	15,192
After 4 years	15,693
After 5 years	16,233
After 6 years	16,749
After 7 years	17,268
After 8 years	17,778
After 12 years	18,819
After 15 years	19,674
* *Entry point for those aged 22 or over, who will move to the next point after 3 years' service*	
Sergeants on appointment	18,819
After 1 year	19,674
After 2 years	20,367
After 3 years	21,039
After 4 years	21,588
Inspectors (Provincial) on appointment	21,588
After 1 year	22,263
After 2 years	23,133
After 3 years	23,820
After 4 years	24,510
Inspectors (London forces) on appointment	22,749
After 1 year	23,382
After 2 years	24,210
After 3 years	24,820
After 4 years	25,686
Chief Inspectors (Provincial) on appointment	24,510
After 1 year	25,197
After 2 years	25,881
After 3 years	26,571
After 4 years	27,264
Chief Inspectors (London forces) on appointment	25,686
After 1 year	26,316
After 2 years	26,994
After 3 years	27,714
After 4 years	28,431

bationary period. In some forces - Devon and Cornwall, for instance - house owners are required to move into a police house which may not be in the area in which they presently reside. (Exceptions are made of course and each case will be sympathetically and individually treated.)

Many police officers go on to buy their own homes. They are generally considered 'good risks' by building societies, since the police force provides stable employment and is not affected by financial recession, as, for example, are manufacturing industries. House owners receive a rent allowance in lieu of free accommodation and this addition to their monthly salaries helps considerably in paying a mortgage. This allowance ranges from £2,080 to £5,864 a year, depending on the area. You do, however, have to apply for the approval of the chief officer of your force before finalising the purchase of your own home (though this is, in most cases, a formality).

Terms of Service

When you join the police, you do not 'sign on' for any fixed length of service. You may leave, at any rank, by giving one month's notice.

Hours of Duty

Police officers work an eight-hour day, usually on a shift system, and are entitled to rest days at the rate of two a week. It is not always practicable to arrange duty rosters so that you get two days off every week so, for instance, you may well work seven consecutive nights when on night duty and then have three full days off. Rest days are usually taken mid-week and, generally speaking, you get only one weekend off each month. After all, police are more frequently needed on Saturdays, Sundays and bank holidays. Overtime and rest-day working is compensated for by time off in lieu or payment at enhanced rates (double rate for working on Christmas Day or a bank holiday Monday).

Holidays

Constables in their first five years of service are entitled to 20 days' annual leave, on full pay and allowances. This rises to 22 days after five years' service, 25 days after 10 years, 26 days after 15 years and 28 days after 20 years. Leave also increases with promotion - a chief inspector with over 10 years' service has nearly six weeks' annual holiday.

Pensions

Retirement comes earlier in the police service than in most occupations, because of its strenuous mental and physical demands. After 25 years' service you may retire having qualified for a pension payable at 50 years of age. This is normally equal to half your pensionable pay received during the last year of your service. If you retire after 30 years' service then your pension rises to two-thirds. Pension contributions amount to 11 per cent of pay for men and 8 per cent of pay for women. If officers choose to join an alternative scheme the benefits and contributions will, of course, depend on that scheme. If you join the force at 18½ then you may retire at 43½ and take another job. Many people nowadays, however, opt to complete the extra five years since the pay scales are so competitive. But even at the age of 48½ you are young enough to make another career and many ex-police officers join private or public companies as security officers, store detectives and the like where they can make use of their experience and knowledge of people and the law.

Sickness and Injury Benefits

Full pay (less National Health benefits) is given to a police officer absent from duty because of sickness or injury. Gratuities or pensions are paid according to length of service to those who have to retire early on medical grounds. Pensions at special rates are given to officers disabled through illness or injury resulting from duty.

In addition you are entitled to have any dental or prescription charges reimbursed. There are also special nursing and convalescent homes for police officers who are suffering from serious illnesses or injuries.

Uniform and Equipment

Uniform and equipment are provided free and this is a considerable saving when you consider how much an accountant or a bank employee or a secretary has to spend annually on suitable clothing. (Officers working out of uniform, members of the CID, for instance, are given a plain clothes allowance each month, which is added to their basic salary.) Uniforms vary slightly in different forces, some wear white shirts, some blue; there are different patterns of helmets (compare, for instance, the Roman style helmets worn by the City of London Police with those worn by their Metropolitan Police neighbours). You will be issued with several uniforms, of varying weight for winter and summer; in very cold weather you will wear a greatcoat, when it is very hot you are allowed to go on duty in 'shirt-sleeve order' (which means neatly folded short sleeves and special detachable epaulets to show your rank and number). Gone are the days when policemen were issued with regulation boots - you can now buy your own to suit your own taste.

Many people still think of policemen as being armed with truncheon, whistle and handcuffs. In fact he gets much more use these days out of his personal radio. Truncheons are seldom used since officers are taught how to subdue difficult customers with a persuasive tongue or, failing that, specially taught arm-locks. Should a truncheon be used then the fact must be reported at the police station where a detailed record is kept. Patrolling officers do carry handcuffs in pouches and training is given on how to apply them to cause minimum injury, and in what circumstances.

A more recent innovation is the use of riot gear with specially reinforced helmets and riot shields. But this type of equipment is employed only as a last resort and only specially trained officers are allowed to use it. The same can be said for tear gas and guns which are rarely seen, let alone used, in this country.

Sport

Policemen tend to enjoy sport of all kinds and police teams and individuals have made names for themselves in the sporting world. This is probably because in a job as challenging and demanding as police work sport offers a welcome opportunity to let off steam and relax from duty. Every force has its own sports clubs with excellent facilities (where families can also come along) and the service as a whole has the Police Athletic Association which organises inter-force competitions.

Chapter 9

Police Forces in the United Kingdom

England and Wales

Metropolitan Police, Selection Centre, PT3 Branch, 6 Harrow Road, London W2 1XH

City of London Police, 182 Bishopsgate, London EC2M 4NP

Avon and Somerset Constabulary, PO Box 188, Bridewell Street, Bristol BS99 7BH

Bedfordshire Police, Woburn Road, Kempston, Bedford MK43 9AX

Cambridgeshire Constabulary, Hinchingbrooke Park, Huntingdon, Cambridgeshire PE18 8NP

Cheshire Constabulary, Castle Esplanade, Chester CH1 2PP

Cleveland Constabulary, PO Box 70, Ladgate Lane, Middlesbrough, Cleveland TS8 9EH

Cumbria Constabulary, Carleton Hall, Penrith, Cumbria CA10 2AU

Derbyshire Constabulary, Butterley Hall, Ripley, Derbyshire DE5 3RS

Devon and Cornwall Constabulary, Middlemore, Exeter EX2 7HQ

Dorset Police, Winfrith, Dorchester, Dorset DT2 8DZ

Durham Constabulary, Aykley Heads, Durham DH1 5TT

Dyfed-Powys Police, Police HQ, PO Box 99, Llangunnor, Carmarthen, Dyfed SA31 2PF

Essex Police, PO Box 2, Springfield, Chelmsford, Essex CM2 6DA

Gloucestershire Constabulary, Holland House, Lansdown Road, Cheltenham, Gloucestershire GL51 6QH

Greater Manchester Police, PO Box 22 (S West PDO), Chester House, Boyer Street, Manchester M16 0RE

Gwent Constabulary, Croesyceiliog, Cwmbran, Gwent NP44 2XJ

Hampshire Constabulary, West Hill, Winchester, Hampshire SO22 5DB

Hertfordshire Constabulary, Stanborough Road, Welwyn Garden City, Hertfordshire AL8 6XF

Humberside Police, Queens Gardens, Kingston-upon-Hull HU1 3DJ

Kent Constabulary, Sutton Road, Maidstone, Kent ME15 9BZ

Lancashire Constabulary, PO Box 77, Hutton, Nr Preston, Lancashire PR4 5SB

Leicestershire Constabulary, Recruiting Dept, Police Training Centre, Blackbird Road, Leicester LE4 0AR

Lincolnshire Police, PO Box 999, Lincoln LN5 7PH

Merseyside Police, PO Box 59, Liverpool L69 4AB

Norfolk Constabulary, Martineau Lane, Norwich NR1 2DJ

Northamptonshire Police, Wootton Hall, Northampton NN4 0JQ

Northumbria Police, North Road, Ponteland, Newcastle upon Tyne NE20 0BL.

North Wales Police, Glan-y-Don, Colwyn Bay, Clwyd LL29 8AW

North Yorkshire Police, Newby Wiske Hall, Newby Wiske, Northallerton, North Yorkshire DL7 9HA

Nottinghamshire Constabulary, Police Careers Office, North Church Street, Nottingham NG1 4BH

South Wales Constabulary, Bridgend, Mid-Glamorgan CF31 3SR

South Yorkshire Police, Snig Hill, Sheffield S3 8LY

Staffordshire Police, Cannock Road, Stafford ST17 0QG

Suffolk Constabulary, Martlesham Heath, Ipswich IP5 7QS

Surrey Constabulary, Mount Browne, Sandy Lane, Guildford, Surrey GU3 1HG

Sussex Police, Malling House, Lewes, East Sussex BN7 2DZ

Thames Valley Police, Kidlington, Oxford OX5 2NX

Warwickshire Constabulary, PO Box 4, Leek Wootton, Warwick CV35 7QB

West Mercia Constabulary, Hindlip Hall, Hindlip, Worcester WR3 8SP

West Midlands Police, PO Box 52, Lloyd House, Colmore Circus, Queensway, Birmingham B4 6NQ

West Yorkshire Metropolitan Police, PO Box 9, Laburnam Road, Wakefield, West Yorkshire WF1 3QP

Wiltshire Constabulary, London Road, Devizes, Wiltshire SN10 2DN

Scotland

Central Scotland Police, Randolphfield, Stirling FK8 2HD

Dumfries and Galloway Constabulary, Loreburn Street, Dumfries DG1 1HP

Fife Constabulary, Wemyss Road, Dysart, Kirkcaldy, Fife KY1 2YA

Grampian Police, Queen Street, Aberdeen AB9 1BA

Lothian and Borders Police, Fettes Avenue, Edinburgh EH4 1RB

Northern Constabulary, Perth Road, Inverness IV2 3SY

Strathclyde Police, 173 Pitt Street, Glasgow G2 4JS

Tayside Police, PO Box 59, West Bell Street, Dundee DD1 9JU

Northern Ireland

Royal Ulster Constabulary, Brooklyn, Knock, Belfast BT5 6LE

Individual Force Requirements

These details are subject to alteration and you are advised to check with the force of your choice before applying.

Eyesight Requirements

The normal standard of vision requirement for forces in England and Wales is an unaided distant vision of not less than 6/18 in each eye (Snellens' test). The distant vision should be correctable (with either glasses or contact lenses) to a standard 6/6 in one eye, 6/12 in the other and 6/6 binocularly. The test for near vision with approved vision aides should be in accordance with the standards set by the Faculty of Ophthalmologists. Some forces require a higher standard of vision, some accept a slightly lower standard, and so it is advisable to check with the force in question before visiting your optician. Scottish forces demand similar high standards of vision.

Before Joining

If you have not quite made up your mind whether joining the Police Force is what you would really like to do, then you can visit a local station and chat informally to the officers there prior to filling in your application form. For details of how to arrange these informal interviews and for any further specific information not covered in this book, you should contact the main recruiting office.

For England and Wales

Police Recruiting Department, Room 624, Home Office, Queen Anne's Gate, London SW1H 9AT.

For Scotland

Police Division, Scottish Home and Health Department, St Andrew's House, Edinburgh EH1 3DE.

In addition to those forces already listed there are separate police forces on the Isle of Man and in the Channel Islands. The limited size of these forces means that there are only a few vacancies each year and these are generally recruited from local people through local press advertisements. For further information and specialised requirements contact:

Isle of Man

Recruiting Officer, Isle of Man Police, Police Headquarters, Douglas, Isle of Man.

States of Jersey Police

Recruiting Officer, States of Jersey Police, Rouge Bouillon, St Helier, Jersey, Channel Islands.

Guernsey (and Alderney)

Recruiting Branch, Island Police Force Headquarters, Amherst, St Peter Port, Guernsey, Channel Islands.

The Kogan Page Careers Series

This series consists of short guides (96–160 pages) to different careers for school and college leavers, graduates and anyone wanting to start anew. Each book serves as an introduction to a particular career and to jobs available within that field, including full details of training qualifications and courses. The following 'Careers in' titles are available in paperback.

Accountancy (*3rd edition*)
Alternative Medicine (*2nd edition*)
Antiques
Architecture (*2nd edition*)
Art and Design (*5th edition*)
Banking and Finance (*2nd edition*)
Catering and Hotel Management (*3rd edition*)
The Church
Civil Service (*2nd edition*)
Computing and Information Technology
Conservation (*4th edition*)
Crafts
Dance
Fashion (*2nd edition*)
Film and Video (*2nd edition*)
Floristry and Retail Gardening
Hairdressing and Beauty Therapy (*4th edition*)
Holiday Industry (*2nd edition*)
Home Economics (*2nd edition*)
Journalism (*4th edition*)
Land and Property
The Law (*4th edition*)
Librarianship and Information Science (*3rd edition*)
Local Government (*3rd edition*)
Marketing, Public Relations and Advertising (*4th edition*)
Medicine, Dentistry and Mental Health (*4th edition*)
Modelling (*2nd edition*)
Museums and Art Galleries
Nursing and Allied Professions (*4th edition*)
Photography (*2nd edition*)
Politics
Printing
Psychology
Retailing (*3rd edition*)
Secretarial and Office Work (*4th edition*)
Social Work (*3rd edition*)
Sport (*2nd edition*)
Teaching (*3rd edition*)
Television and Radio (*3rd edition*)
The Theatre (*2nd edition*)
Using Languages (*4th edition*)
Using Mathematics
Working Abroad
Working Outdoors (*3rd edition*)
Working with Animals (*5th edition*)
Working with Children and Young People (*3rd edition*)

Running Your Own Antiques Business, Noël Riley and Godfrey Golzen
Running Your Own Boarding Kennels, Sheila Zabawa
Running Your Own Building Business, Kim Ludman
Running Your Own Catering Business, Ursula Garner and Judy Ridgway
Running Your Own Estate Agency, Val Redding
Running Your Own Hairdressing Salon, Christine Harvey and Helen Steadman
Running Your Own Mail Order Business, Malcolm Breckman
Running Your Own Photographic Business (2nd edition), John Rose and Linda Hankin
Running Your Own Playgroup or Nursery, Jenny Willison
Running Your Own Pub, Elven Money
Running Your Own Restaurant, Diane Hughes and Godfrey Golzen
Running Your Own Shop (2nd edition), Roger Cox
Running Your Own Small Hotel (2nd edition), Joy Lennick
Running Your Own Smallholding, Richard and Pauline Bambrey